GRAHAM MASTERTON

DEAD MEN WHISTLING

HEAD
of ZEUS

First published in the UK in 2018 by Head of Zeus Ltd
This paperback edition published in 2018 by Head of Zeus Ltd

9 7 5 3 1 2 4 6 8

A catalogue record for this book is available from
the British Library.

ISBN (PB): 9781784976453
ISBN (E): 9781784976422

Typeset by Adrian McLaughlin

Printed and bound in Great Britain by
CPI Group (UK) Ltd, Croydon CR0 4YY

MIX
Paper from
responsible sources
FSC® C020471

Head of Zeus Ltd
First Floor East
5–8 Hardwick Street
London EC1R 4RG

WWW.HEADOFZEUS.COM

DEAD MEN WHISTLING

You can listen to a low-D tin whistle slip jig at
www.youtube.com/watch?v=hn4Qwr-xA4w
while you read

Níl a fhios ag aon duine cá bhfuil fód a bháis.
(Nobody knows where they will die)
Irish Proverb

One

The O'Regan family were in the middle of breakfast when their front doorbell started urgently ringing, again and again.

'Somebody's at the door, Daddy!' said three-year-old Grainne, with porridge all round her mouth.

Kieran looked across the kitchen at Moira, who was standing in front of the oven frying colcannon cakes. Her eyes widened, and she laid down her spatula as the bell began to ring continuously.

'Shall I go?' asked five-year-old Riordan, slipping down from his chair.

The ringing carried on, but then somebody started beating their fist against the door, too. Kieran laid his hand on Riordan's shoulder and said, 'No, no, I'll go. Whoever it is, it sounds like they're pure vexed about something.'

'Kieran,' said Moira, taking the skillet off the gas. It was eight o'clock and gloomy in the kitchen. The window was speckled with fat glistening raindrops.

'It's all right, it'll only be old Roddy, moaning about the kids playing long slogs down the street and denting his car again. Just because I'm a guard he thinks I should be keeping a twenty-four-hour watch on the whole neighbourhood.'

He stood up and went to the kitchen door, but as he did so Moira said '*Kieran*,' again, and she had to raise her voice because the ringing and the banging were so loud. Little Grainne covered her ears with her hands, still holding on to her drippy porridge spoon.

'Nothing to worry about, love,' said Kieran, by which he was reminding Moira that these days he kept a pistol in the pocket of the duffle coat hanging by the front door.

He had only just stepped out into the hallway, though, when there was a louder bang and a splintering, shuddering sound and the front door was kicked wide open. Three men came bursting in out of the rain, all wearing black balaclavas to hide their faces, black leather jackets and jeans. The leading man was toting a sawn-off shotgun.

Kieran took two stumbling steps back into the kitchen. He tried to slam the door shut but the leading intruder kicked it open again with his boot and lifted his shotgun so that it was pointing only thirty centimetres away from Kieran's face.

'Whatever it is you're thinking of doing, head, don't even fecking think about it,' the man told him, in a thick, rasping voice. 'Not unless you want your wains to be eating their daddy's brains along with their breakfast.'

Grainne dropped her spoon and let out one piercing scream after another, while Riordan began to sob and twist the front of his jumper in distress. Moira stepped forwards, ashen-faced, and said, 'Get out of our house! Just get out!'

'Will you get that fecking babby to hold her whisht or else I'll fecking shut her up myself,' the man retorted.

'Don't you dare to touch my children,' said Kieran. 'I don't know what it is you want but you're going to be in deeper shite than you could ever dream of. Now get out of here.'

'Oh, we're not going without what we came for,' said the man, still keeping his shotgun pointed at Kieran's face. 'And for Christ's sake shut that fecking wain up, will you?'

Grainne continued to scream. Her face was scarlet and tears were rolling down her cheeks. Moira came across the kitchen to pick her up but the man was quicker. He sidestepped around Kieran, transferred his shotgun to his left hand, and smacked Grainne hard around the side of the head, so that she tipped off her chair on to the floor, still screaming.

Kieran seized the man's arm and tried to twist the shotgun out of his hand, but the man kept his hold on it and fired it with a deafening blast into the ceiling. Plaster showered down all around them like a snowstorm, and even when it had settled acrid grey smoke was still sliding sideways across the kitchen. Kieran swung a punch at the man but only managed to hit him a glancing blow on his shoulder. Before he could punch him again, the two other intruders came bustling into the kitchen and seized his arms. Kieran was short but he was blocky and fit, yet these men were much heavier and stronger. He could smell the stale cigarettes and alcohol on their breath.

'Right, that's enough of this fecking scrapping,' said the man with the shotgun. 'You're coming along with us for a ride in the country, like, so that you and me can have a bit of a blather.'

Kieran struggled to free himself from the two men holding him, and kicked out like a galloping horse, but they were gripping him too fiercely, and they almost wrenched his right shoulder out of its socket. Panting, wincing with pain, he stared into the hazel-coloured eyes of the man holding the shotgun and said, 'I reck you. I'm sure I do. If you had the balls to take that mask off, I could put a name to you, I'm sure of it.'

The man grinned. 'Maybe you could, head. But this isn't about me, like. It's about you and the fecking hames you've made of everything. So why don't you come along nice and co-operative, like, do you know what I mean? And we can get a few matters cleared up.'

'Where are you taking him?' Moira challenged him, although her voice was shaking. She was holding Grainne in her arms now and rocking her to calm her down, while Riordan was clinging to her apron, his mouth turned down in misery. 'You're not going to hurt him, are you?'

'Don't you fret, girl,' the man told her. 'We just wanted to take your old man somewhere dead quiet so we could talk about this, that and the other without being disturbed. I'll tell you this, though, it wouldn't be at all advisable for you to be calling the cops, like. We'll know if you do, and the consequences for your old man here… well, they could be desperate.'

'Please don't hurt him,' said Moira, her eyes crowded with tears. 'He's a very good man. The very best. And you wouldn't be depriving these poor little wains of their father, would you?'

Kieran said, 'It's all right, Moira. These fellows obviously have a grievance but I'm sure we can come to some kind of a compromise. Just stay here and try to keep calm, okay? I'll be back as soon as we've sorted everything out. Do as he says, though. Don't call this in. In fact, don't call anybody. I love you. And I love you, too, Riordan, and you too, Grainne darling.'

'That's it with the fecking sentimental mush,' said the man with the shotgun. 'You'll have me fecking puking in a moment. Let's go.'

Kieran offered the men no resistance as they ushered him out of the broken-open front door and into the rain. From here, on St Christopher's Road on the north side of Cork city, he could see the ragged black clouds racing in from the hills on the far side of the River Lee. He thought that they looked like a tumultuous horde of flying witches, with their torn cloaks trailing behind them.

As the men led him up the street towards a silver Mercedes saloon his knees suddenly turned watery, and if they hadn't been holding his arms he would have collapsed. Whatever reassuring words he had given Moira, he had never been so terrified in his life, not even when he had been shot at during a botched bank robbery in Macroom, and the garda standing next to him had been killed. He had to clench his bladder to stop himself from wetting his jeans.

The men opened the rear door of the car and pushed Kieran inside. A driver was sitting waiting, smoking a cigarette. He too was masked in a black balaclava. The man with the shotgun climbed into the front passenger seat while the other two wedged themselves into the back, with Kieran in the middle.

The driver reached across to the glovebox and took out a pair of Garda-issue semi-rigid handcuffs. He gave them to the man with the shotgun, who passed them back to the man sitting on Kieran's left.

'These are for health and safety, like,' said the man with the shotgun. 'As in, *our* health and safety, not yours.'

The man sitting next to him clipped the handcuffs on to Kieran's wrists, and sniffed.

'All right, where are we headed?' asked Kieran, trying to sound brave, as the Mercedes pulled away from the kerb and turned right up Murmont Lawn towards Ballyvolane.

'Like I promised you, head, somewhere dead quiet,' said the man with the shotgun. It was now laid across his lap and Kieran had the grimmest feeling that he had come out this morning with every intention of using it.

'So what's this all about, then?' he persisted. They were driving north now on the Ballyhooly Road and the rain was lashing harder than ever, so that the windshield wiper was whacking from side to side at full speed.

He had guessed why these men had abducted him, and who they were, but he wasn't going to say that he knew. Let them come out with it, and admit that they were involved in it.

The man sitting on his left sneezed loudly and wiped his nose with the back of his hand. Without turning around, the man with the shotgun said, 'For the love of Jesus, Hoggy! Do you want us all to catch our death?'

The driver and the other man all chuckled at that and shook their heads. Kieran closed his eyes and thought: *If I concentrate hard enough, maybe this isn't happening, and I'm not really in this car at all, I'm back at home eating my colcannon cakes with Moira and Riordan and Grainne.* But when he opened them again, they were just passing Dunnes Stores at Ballyvolane and the windscreen wiper was still whacking and he was still jammed in this car with these four rank-smelling gurriers. Apart from them, only the Lord God had any idea where they were taking him, or what they intended to do to him when they got there.

'Did you see that fecking qualifier last night?' said the man on his right. 'Coen was shite. If he hadn't been interceptimicated for that free, Connolly would never have got that fecking equalizer.'

'Oh, that was a fecking blip, that's all,' said the man with the shotgun. 'The pace of the game at inter-county level these days, it's fecking mental. You wait and see. Coen's going to be a starlet when he gets himself up to speed.'

They're abducting me, thought Kieran. *They're abducting me and they're talking about football*. Somehow that filled him with even greater dread. The game that they had watched on television last night was more interesting to them than his life.

They drove through Upper Dublin Hill and then turned left at Kilcool into a narrow, hedge-lined road. They passed a few neat bungalows and then they arrived at a deserted car park beside a long grey stone wall. Over the top of the wall Kieran could see crosses and stone angels, and he knew where they had brought him. The man with the shotgun had described it perfectly, somewhere 'dead quiet'. It was St Catherine's Cemetery at Kilcully.

The driver reverse-parked close to the cemetery gates, and they all climbed out. Although a chilly wind was still blowing, the rain had suddenly eased, and breaks were appearing in the clouds.

'Come on, then, let's go and pay our holy respects,' said the man with the shotgun. There was nobody around, and so he was carrying the gun quite openly, tilted over his shoulder. Hoggy the sneezer opened the boot of the Mercedes and lifted out a large grey nylon bag, about the size of an airline carry-on case, but before Kieran could see clearly what it was, the other man had gripped his arm and was pushing him towards the cemetery's small side gate.

The black-and-gilded wrought-iron gate was locked, but the man with the shotgun gave it three hard kicks to break the latch and it swung open. He then led the way along the asphalt path between the gravestones and the statues. None of them spoke, and apart from the wind rustling in the trees, the cemetery was silent. Its shrubs and flower beds were all neatly tended, and in the distance Kieran could see the green hills of Ballynahina. The peacefulness only added to his fear, and he stumbled again.

'Didn't have a couple of cups of Paddy's for your breakfast, did you, head?' the man with the shotgun asked him.

They reached a secluded plot at the back of the cemetery surrounded by yew bushes. An angel stood at each corner of the plot, three of them with their heads bowed and the fourth looking up towards the hurrying clouds. Between two of the angels there was a metal bench, and the man with the shotgun said to Kieran, 'Here. This is the place. Let's sit down and have that blather, shall we?'

'I've nothing to say to you,' said Kieran. 'I think I know who you are, and if you are who I think you are, then I'm keeping my bake shut.'

'Fecking sit down, will you?' said the man with the shotgun.

'Do I have to repeat myself? I've nothing to say.'

The man with the shotgun nodded to the man who was holding Kieran's arm, and the man pushed him backwards towards the bench so that he was forced to sit down. The bench was still wet from the rain and he could feel it through his jeans.

'Do you know who's buried here?' asked the man with the shotgun. 'That grave right there, with that angel gazing up to heaven?'

Kieran said nothing, and made a point of looking in the opposite direction.

'That's Billy Ó Canainn,' the man continued. 'And you know full well yourself who was responsible for the premature demise of our Billy, now don't you?'

'What do you want me to tell you?' said Kieran. 'I'm not going to pretend that I didn't know your man, but I had nothing to do with him getting himself shot. The only person responsible for that was him.'

'Oh, you think so? But it was you who shopped him, like, didn't you, when all you had to do was make out that you hadn't seen him. If it hadn't been for you, head, our Billy would still be walking and talking and drinking at the Gerald Griffin.'

'He might have been walking and talking but he wouldn't have been drinking anywhere. He would've been banged up in his cell on Rathmore Road, which is where he should have been anyway.'

Hoggy was standing close behind Kieran and Kieran was aware that he had set his grey nylon bag down on the ground and was unzipping it. He half-turned his head but he still couldn't see what the bag contained.

'You've heard of live and let live, like, haven't you?' said the man with the shotgun. 'Why couldn't you have done that with our Billy? Like, what gave you the fecking right to think that you could be judge and jury and pass the death sentence on him? He had a wife and five kids to take care of. Now he's lying there under that angel and he can't take care of nobody. And it's all because of you.'

'I'm saying nothing,' said Kieran. 'I didn't bear Billy Ó Canainn any personal ill will whatsoever. I was only doing my job.'

'Well, you should have been a musician rather than a fecking cop,' said the man with the shotgun. He reached inside his leather jacket and drew out a shiny nickel low-D whistle, almost sixty centimetres long. He held it out to Kieran and said, 'There. That's your speciality, isn't it? Whistle-blowing. Why don't you give us a tune? How about "The Ships are Sailing", or some fancy slip jig like "Drops of Brandy"?'

Kieran looked at the whistle, and then up at the man's eyes. He said nothing. Not only did he have nothing to say, but his lips felt numb. Even if he had known how to play the whistle, he wouldn't have been able to. He could see that this was all leading up to some terrible dénouement and he could barely breathe.

'You don't want to give us a tune, then?' asked the man with the shotgun. 'Sure like, that's not very generous of you, is it? Is it something I've said? From what I hear, you've been blowing the whistle fit to bust your fecking lungs, especially to Chief Superintendent O'Malley.'

Kieran was almost certain now that he knew who the man was. He had to be a guard, or else it was highly unlikely that he would have known the name of the Garda's regional Protected Disclosures Manager. Despite this, Kieran was afraid to challenge him by name, in case he immediately decided to silence him with his shotgun.

'Well, if you won't give us a tune voluntarily, like, we'll have to see if we can get it out of you some other way,' the man told him. 'Patrick – why don't you hold our friend here steady while Hoggy does the honours?'

Patrick sat down on the bench on Kieran's right side. He wrapped his left arm around Kieran's shoulders and pulled him in tight. Kieran turned to look at him, but he was so close that he could hardly focus on him, and all he could see behind his balaclava was his bloodshot eyes and a grin with four front teeth missing.

'All right?' Patrick asked him, and winked. His breath was so foetid that Kieran had to turn his face away.

It was then that he heard Hoggy start up the chainsaw, right behind him. It didn't fire up the first time, so he had to tug the pull cord four or five times more. Once it was going, though, it sounded like a moped revving up, impatient for a traffic light to change.

Kieran heaved himself sideways and tried to stand up, but Patrick clenched him even tighter and grabbed hold of his short curly hair.

'*Get off me, you bastard!*' Kieran screamed at him, over the noise of the chainsaw. He attempted to shake his head from side to side but Patrick had his fingers so firmly in his hair that his fingernails were digging into his scalp.

The man with the shotgun stepped right up to him and made the sign of the cross, as if he were giving him benediction.

'Shoot me!' Kieran screamed. 'If you're going to fecking kill me then shoot me!'

'I would, but it's not even loaded,' the man retorted, holding up the shotgun and shaking it. 'And besides, I wouldn't give you the compassion.'

With that, he stood back and gave Hoggy the thumbs up.

Kieran screamed again, but this time his scream was wordless, more of a shrill roar, and it didn't stop until the teeth of the chainsaw bit into the back of his neck, ripping his denim shirt collar into tatters and then spraying a blizzard of blood and fragments of flesh all the way along the back of the bench. Next, the teeth bit into his vertebrae, and for a split second there was a sharp high-pitched *chip!* sound.

With one last sideways sweep, Hoggy cut through Kieran's larynx and then Patrick lifted off his head. Blood pumped out of Kieran's severed neck, gushing over his shoulders and down the front of his shirt.

'Look at the fecking state of me jacket!' said Patrick. 'I look like I've been working all day at Feoil O'Criostoir Teo!'

'They wouldn't employ you there, boy,' said the man with the shotgun. 'They want fellows who know how to kill cows and sheep, not feens.'

Patrick held up Kieran's dripping head so that it was staring directly at the man with the shotgun. Kieran's eyes were open and his mouth was gaping but his expression was one of bewilderment rather than pain. Patrick turned it around so that he could look at it himself, and then said, 'I'd say he looks kind of shook, myself. But he didn't take it too bad, wouldn't you say?'

Hoggy, meanwhile, had switched off the chainsaw and was stowing it back into its carrying bag.

'That was fierce easier than I thought it was going to be,' he said, wiping his nose with the back of his hand again. 'I don't know why them Isis fellows didn't use chainsaws instead of them knives. Much more efficienter, do you know what I mean, like?'

'Yeah, sure, but the trouble with that is, your man here hardly felt nothing at all. For what he did, I think he should have suffered. Still, his loved ones won't have all of him to bury, so they'll be suffering for him. You didn't forget the bag for his head?'

Hoggy pulled a Tesco plastic bag out of his jacket pocket. Patrick dropped Kieran's head into it and spun it around to tie up the top, as if he were serving potatoes in the greengrocer's.

'Right, let's be out the gap before any grieving relatives get here,' said the man with the shotgun. 'Hoggy, the cuffs. We don't want to be leaving any circumstantial, now do we?'

Hoggy removed the handcuffs and stuffed them into his pocket. The man with the shotgun laid it down on the bench beside Kieran's headless body and then carefully poked the low-D whistle into his windpipe, so that only about seventeen centimetres were sticking out.

'There, head,' he said. 'Now you can sit and whistle to your heart's content, and nobody's going to be raging about it.'

'You're going to love this one, ma'am,' said Detective Markey, as he opened the door of Katie's car for her.

'You really think I needed to see it first hand?' Katie asked him, zipping her dark green anorak and tugging up the black nylon fur collar. She had only just recovered from a bad cold and if Detective Markey hadn't been so insistent she would have preferred to have stayed in her office in the warm.

'Well, it's fierce unusual, like, the whole scene, and of course he's a bit of a celebrity, so I reckoned the media are going to be asking you a rake of questions about it. Like what the motive could have been and all that.'

Three patrol cars and two vans from the Technical Bureau were parked in the steep driveway of the house in Woodhill Park in Tivoli, as well as an ambulance. The lower end of the road had been cordoned off from Lover's Walk.

The house itself was huge, white-painted, with a grey tiled roof and art deco windows. It stood in at least half an acre of shrubs and decorative flower beds, with a wide patio at the side that overlooked the River Lee far below. A red Bentley Continental GT was parked in front of the double garage, measled with raindrops.

'Do you know how much one of *them* would set you back?' said Detective Markey, as they walked around the Bentley to reach the front porch. 'Quarter of a million yoyos, easy.'

'Oh, is that all, Nick?' said Katie. 'In that case I'll order two.'

Detective Sergeant Kyna Ni Nuallán was standing outside the

wide oak front door talking to Detective Patrick O'Donovan. Her short blonde hair was covered with a green knitted beanie and she was wearing a baggy purple raincoat and knee-length boots, which made her look more than ever like one of the *aos sí*, the fairy folk. Detective O'Donovan was unshaven and his hair was all messed up, as if he had been called here straight from his bed.

Kyna turned around as Katie approached and gave her a wide-eyed look that conveyed everything intimate that she wanted to tell her without her having to say it out loud. They hadn't seen each other for over two weeks because Kyna had been at Garda HQ in Dublin on an Evo-FIT training course. *How are you? I missed you.*

In return, Katie closed her eyes for a moment to acknowledge that she had received and understood what Kyna was trying to convey.

'So what's the story?' she asked. 'I would have thought that Jimmy Ó Faoláin would be the last person that anybody would want to send off to higher service.'

'I agree with you, ma'am,' said Kyna. 'He was minted and he was always throwing parties and he was everybody's best friend. A legend.'

'Maybe it's connected to the GAA,' suggested Detective O'Donovan. 'He was chairman of the Rachmasach Rovers, wasn't he – well, apart from being chairman of about a million other clubs and societies and charities and the Lord knows what.'

'What about it?' asked Katie.

'Have you not heard? There's been some rumours recently about the Rovers throwing games deliberate-like.'

'Why would they want to do that? I thought they were hoping to be top of the league this year.'

'I haven't a baldy. Myself, I wouldn't know one end of a hurley from the other.'

At that moment, Bill Phinner, the chief technical expert, came out of the house, tugging back the hood of his white Tyvek suit.

He looked even more miserable than usual. Katie knew that he had not only given up smoking but given up vaping as well, which had done nothing to relieve his permanent state of pessimism. Bill Phinner believed that if they were given half a chance almost everybody in Cork was capable of committing a serious misdemeanour, and whenever they did it was his dreary duty to find the evidence to convict them.

'How are you going on, Bill?' said Katie.

'You can come in now and take a sconce for yourself, ma'am,' Bill told her. 'So far the only evidence we've managed to retrieve is one ricocheted bullet. Apart from that we've found no circumstantial and no material evidence whatsoever, although we'll obviously have the rest of the bullets to examine once the pathologist has dug them out for us. There's no indication of forced entry. There's no footprints on the floors, even though the morning's been so wet. We're testing for dabs but I'm not very hopeful. There's no cartridge casings, neither, so the shooter must have picked them all up.'

'No sign of a struggle?'

Bill shook his head. 'You'll see why when you come in.'

Kyna said, 'We have Jimmy's iPhone. It's facial recognition so we won't have any problem getting into it. We'll also be taking his computers and his books and sending them up to the fraud squad.'

'Them books are going to take some going through, I'll tell you,' put in Detective O'Donovan. 'I reckon your man has twice as many books as the Vatican Library – except that *his* are all accounts, like, not the holy scriptures.'

'That doesn't surprise me,' said Katie. 'From what little I know of Jimmy Ó Faoláin, it was grade first and God second.'

'I met him once at a charity dinner in Dublin,' said Kyna. 'He had a silver tongue, I can tell you. If he hadn't been a financier, he could have been a hypnotist. I almost fell for him myself.'

Katie raised her eyebrows, but said nothing. Only she knew for certain that the possibility of Kyna ever falling for a man was beyond remote.

'Who reported him dead?' she asked.

'His latest girlfriend,' said Detective O'Donovan. 'She's a Ryanair stewardess, Viona Caffrey. Jimmy gave her a key because of the odd hours she gets in and he's often away at some conference or other. She came here directly from the airport at approximately ten forty-five and that's when she found him.'

'Where is she now?'

'Oh, still here. She's in the conservatory with Garda Malone. She said she doesn't want to leave here until he does.'

'I'll have a chat with her in a minute,' said Katie. 'Meanwhile, let's take a lamp at our unfortunate friend.'

She took two Tyvek shoe covers out of her anorak pocket and lifted up her feet to snap them on. She pulled on black forensic gloves, too, in case she needed to touch or handle anything. Then she followed Bill Phinner into the hallway.

Inside, the house was lavishly decorated. The floor in the hallway was chequered with beige and white marble, and a sweeping staircase came down on the left-hand side, its newel post surmounted by a brass statuette of a bare-breasted nymph. A huge crystal chandelier was suspended from the ceiling, softly tinkling in the draught from the open door, and the walls were lined with original oil paintings by Walter Osborne and James Jebusa Shannon, or at least very passable copies of them.

'You see that one,' said Detective Markey, jerking his thumb towards a portrait of a woman feeding a cat with a bowl of milk. 'I reckon that's worth at least eighty-five thousand, that one.'

'You should have been an auctioneer, Nicky,' said Detective O'Donovan.

'My old feller used to restore pictures at the Crawford Gallery,' said Detective Markey. 'Some of the paintings looked like the artist just gawked up his tripe and drisheen all over the canvas, that's what he used to tell me, but it made no odds. They'd never have any bother finding some pretentious flute who'd pay them thousands for it.'

They went through to the living room. Two French windows

looked out over the patio, and the floor was highly polished parquet. The sofas and armchairs were all mock-rococo, and the side tables were crowded with antique lamps and porcelain figurines and gilded vases. The far end of the room was dominated by a large marble fireplace, and above the fireplace hung an enormous landscape painting of the Old Head of Kinsale, with fishing smacks and rolling cumulus clouds.

Katie noticed that the grate was heaped with wood ash.

'The fire's not made up. Don't tell me your man doesn't have any hired help around the house.'

'Oh, he does of course,' said Kyna. 'He has a Polish woman who comes in every day to make up the fire and change the bed and clean the windows and whatever, and another local woman who comes in to cook whenever he needs her, and a gardener, too, who's also a bit of a handyman.'

'So where were they this morning?'

'The Polish woman had the morning off because she had to go to the dentist and the gardener only shows up twice a week.'

'So it's possible that whoever shot your man knew that the house was going to be empty, apart from him.'

'It's a fair bet, I'd say,' said Detective O'Donovan.

'See that Chinese vase with all them red bats on it?' said Detective Markey. 'You could get a couple of thousand for that, no problem.'

Bill Phinner took them into the corridor on the opposite side of the living room, which led through to the kitchen. Halfway along this corridor there was an open door, and four technical experts in white Tyvek suits were clustered around it like a gathering of snowmen, scanning the floor with a green OPS laser and taking flash photographs and powdering the paintwork for latent fingerprints.

'Hey there, fellers, give us a couple of moments, will you?' asked Bill Phinner, and the technicians shuffled back along the corridor.

Bill Phinner reached in for the door handle and closed the door.

A few centimetres above the central rail there were five bullet holes in a tight diamond pattern, with another two higher up. Attached to the centre post was a driftwood plaque with a carved wooden heart hanging from it, engraved with the word *Jacks*.

'Caught in his office, sending a fax to Poolbeg,' said Detective O'Donovan.

'He probably didn't even know who killed him,' said Kyna. 'Not unless they shouted out before they shot him to make sure that he was in there.'

'All right, let's take a sconce,' said Katie. She took out the Chanel-scented handkerchief she always carried in her pocket and held it up to her face, partly to mask the smell and partly because her nose had started to run.

Bill Phinner opened the door wide. Jimmy Ó Faoláin was still sitting on the toilet, although he was leaning sideways against the wall. He was a dark-haired, rather Italian-looking man with sharply defined cheekbones and a strong but narrow chin. His eyes were open but they had already darkened to a reddish-brown with *tache noire*. He was wearing a silky maroon pyjama jacket with patterns of lilies on it, and his trousers were gathered around his ankles.

One bullet had hit him five centimetres above his left eye, drilling a small, neat hole in his forehead, but it had exploded inside his skull so that the hair at the back of his head was sticking up in a wild coronet. Lumps of bloody brain tissue were splattered all the way up the white tiled wall behind him and were sticking to the pale blue blind. One large lump dropped off on to the floor even as Katie was watching it.

Bill Phinner went into the toilet and pointed to a triangular chip in one of the tiles.

'That was one of the two higher shots,' he said. 'The bullet ricocheted and like I say we've recovered it, so we should be able to identify the calibre pretty quick. If the seraphs are smiling on us we might be able to put a name to the type of weapon and even where it came from. And if the Lord God Himself is smiling on us it might have been used before, and we'll have it on our database.'

Delicately, as if he were opening the curtains of a toy theatre, he parted the front of Jimmy Ó Faoláin's pyjama jacket. Katie could see that the remaining five bullets had hit him in a cluster in the chest, around his heart. Runnels of blood had dried over the folds in his stomach and into his dark curly pubic hair.

'He's a grand healthy suntan, your man, doesn't he?' said Detective Markey. 'Always hopping off for holliers in the Caribbean from what I hear. Me – I can't even stretch to a long weekend in Santa Ponsa.'

Detective O'Donovan said, 'Pff! I'd rather be broke as a joke than minted and six feet under. Why do you think cemeteries don't have shops?'

Katie said, 'Approximate time of death, Bill?'

'Judging by his eyes and his body temperature, sometime around nine-thirty this morning, I'd say.'

'We're going house to house,' said Kyna. 'Not that there are many houses around here to go to, and there's no CCTV either end of Lover's Walk.'

'Okay,' said Katie. 'Let me talk to Jimmy's girlfriend and see if she knows why anybody might have wanted to see him dead.'

Viona Caffrey was sitting at one end of a white wickerwork sofa in the conservatory, clutching a damp handkerchief in her lap. Garda Malone stood close behind her, her arms folded, looking bored. Garda Malone was often put in charge of female suspects who might be a flight risk, because she had a soothing and sympathetic way of talking to them, but she was stocky and strong and a fast runner, too. Detective Ó Doibhilin called her 'Mount Knocknaskagh with legs', although not to her face.

The conservatory had underfloor heating and it was filled with giant ceramic plant pots, so that every breath was fragrant with sweet bay and stephanotis and begonias. As she walked across the tiled floor, Katie couldn't help thinking of the two dried-up violets on her own kitchen window sill.

'Viona,' she said. 'I'm Detective Superintendent Maguire. How are you coming along there?'

Viona looked up, her eyes red and swollen from crying. She was a handsome girl, with a long face and large violet eyes, although she had quite a prominent nose. Her ash-blonde hair was fastened in a French pleat, so that she looked like a typical hostess from an airline advertisement. She was still wearing her bright-blue Ryanair uniform, although she had taken off her rose-pink wrap overcoat and hung it over the back of the sofa, and Katie could see from the label that it was Sies Marjan. She had tried on one of those coats herself in Brown Thomas, but she hadn't bought it. Apart from being too long for her, its price tag had been €2,420.

Katie also recognized Viona's shoes – pink T-bar courts with square gold studs all around them – although she hadn't tried those on. They were Valentino Garavani and at least €700 a pair.

She knew roughly what the salary scale was for Ryanair's cabin crew, so she could only guess that Jimmy Ó Faoláin must have been lavishing a fair amount of money on her.

'We'll need to talk to you down at Anglesea Street,' she told Viona, sitting down beside her. 'For now, though, there's a couple of things I need to ask you, if that's okay.'

Viona nodded. 'I just can't believe that Jimmy's dead,' she said, miserably. 'I keep thinking he's going to come walking in the door any moment, laughing and saying that he was only spoofing, like, do you know what I mean?'

'When was the last time you saw him?'

Viona's lips puckered, and she gave a deep, heaving sob. 'Monday morning. We'd spent the weekend together. We didn't often get the chance to do that, because he was always so busy with this and that. We went down to Kinsale and had lunch at Finns' Table. That was Jimmy's favourite restaurant, Finns' Table. He loved the baked lobster.'

'So where have you been since Monday morning?'

'Malaga. I was called to step in because one of the other girls was sick.'

'Were you and Jimmy in contact while you were there? Any texts or emails between you?'

'We texted each other Monday night, and then I texted him again on Tuesday afternoon telling him when I was going to be back.'

'Did he reply to that?'

'Only with the thumbs-up emoji, like.'

'So you had no indication that he might be in trouble, or worried about something?'

Viona shook her head.

'Were you aware that he might have been having any bother with his business? Any arguments with anybody?'

'Jimmy never argued with nobody. He was always smiling. He used to say that he was born in the crock of gold at the end of the rainbow.'

'You never heard anybody threaten him?'

'Why would they?'

Katie looked up at Kyna and Detectives Markey and O'Donovan.

Kyna said, 'As far as we can make out, nothing's been taken. There's a safe behind a painting in the study, but it doesn't look as if there's been any attempt to open it. No paintings or statues or ornaments appear to be missing.'

'What about Jimmy's family?' Katie asked Viona. 'Did he get along okay with them?'

'Both of his parents are dead, but he has two sisters. One of them lives in Macroom and the other one I'm not sure, England somewhere I think. He never talked about them much. He was married before and his ex-wife married again and she lives in Carrigaline.'

'Any children?'

'A boy by that marriage. I only met him the once. He's only about twelve and he seemed happy out, so far as I could tell.'

'Did he ever mention Rachmasach Rovers to you?' asked Detective O'Donovan.

'The Rovers? They're playing on Saturday at Thurles. He was going to take me along.'

'But he didn't say anything about match-fixing, like?'

Viona shook her head again. 'He talked about his business all the time, and how much so-and-so was going to be paying him, and when, but nothing much else. Not about the Rovers, no.'

'How long had you and he been doing a line?' asked Kyna.

'Six months, more or less. We met on a flight back from Naples. He came straight out and asked me to have dinner with him. I was dating another feller but he was a right langdang so I said yes.'

'And how serious would you say your relationship was?'

Viona shrugged. 'With Jimmy you could never tell. Like, he was always smiling and laughing and paying me compliments, but his eyes were always roaming around, do you know what I mean?'

'Do you know who else had a key to the house apart from you?' Detective Markey asked her.

'Agata… she's his daily. And Maeve, his cook, too, she must have done, because sometimes he'd ring her and ask her to come in and have his dinner ready for him for when he came home.'

'Was your key always in your possession? Is there any chance that somebody might have borrowed it from you without your knowledge, even if it was for only a few seconds?'

Viona reached over and picked up her pink Mulberry satchel, which Katie estimated must have cost over €1,000. *Mother of God,* she thought, *I'm getting as bad as Markey, putting a price on everything*. But the coat and the shoes and the satchel spoke volumes about Jimmy's feelings for Viona. Maybe his gifts were a substitute for genuine affection. Maybe they also betrayed what Viona had come to expect him to give her.

She opened up the satchel and showed Detective Markey the key, on a silver St Brigid's cross keyring. 'There. It's always in my bag. I don't see how anybody else could have borrowed it.'

Kyna said, 'Did Jimmy ever give you gifts of money, or an allowance, even?'

'He'd pay for a taxi if I needed one to get home. And he bought me things. But he never gave me big handfuls of cash, if that's what you're talking about. I never asked him for any, neither.'

'Okay,' said Katie. 'I think that wraps things up for now. Like I say, we'll be asking you to come to Anglesea Street once the technical experts have completed their tests.'

'Can it be tomorrow morning? I'm supposed to be going to Lanzarote tomorrow afternoon, unless they give me compassionate leave, but the way they are at the moment, Ryanair, I'm not so sure.'

'All right,' Katie told her. 'We'll be talking to Agata and Maeve, too, and the gardener. Do you have his name?'

'Dermot,' said Viona. 'I only knew him as Dermot.' She paused, and then she said, 'What's going to happen to Jimmy?'

'We'll take his remains to CUH, and arrange for the deputy pathologist to examine him. After the post mortem he can be released to the undertaker, if the coroner okays it. I imagine it'll be quite some funeral, what with all the friends he had.'

'I don't know,' said Viona. 'He knew thousands of people, and they all liked him, but he didn't really have any friends. I tried to be his friend, but it was hard. Everything was always a laugh. I don't think I ever saw him serious, not once. We had some gallery, I tell you, but gallery's not the same as love, is it?'

'Now there's a question,' said Katie.

Three

She had only just taken off her anorak and sat down at her desk when Conor rang her.

'Conor? What's the story?' she said, leafing through the files that had been left on her blotter while she was out.

'You still sound coldy,' he said.

'I had to go out. But I'll be taking some more Lemsip in a minute. I don't feel too bad.'

'That's grand, and I've some news that's going to make you feel even better. The surgeon has just rung me from Gilabbey and said that Barney's brain operation was one hundred and ten per cent successful. Thankfully his skull wasn't fractured and they've relieved all of the intracranial pressure.'

Katie burst into tears. Her assistant, Moirin, heard her from her open office door and poked her plump Snow White face around to see what was wrong. Katie flapped her hand and smiled to tell her that everything was fine. Her Irish setter, Barney, had been dog-napped by Travellers and beaten so badly that when he was dumped on her doorstep she was sure that he was going to die.

Conor had driven him immediately to Gilabbey Veterinary Hospital in Togher, where he was friends with one of their leading surgeons, Dr Domnall O'Sullivan. At first the prognosis had been grim. Barney's legs and several ribs were fractured, and he had suffered several impact injuries to the head, most likely caused by being repeatedly hit with a brick.

'Oh, Jesus, I thought I was never going to see him again,' said Katie, tugging out a Kleenex and wiping her eyes. 'What about his broken bones?'

'It's going to be one thing at a time, darling,' said Conor. 'They're giving him thoracentesis at the moment to clear the fluid from his chest, and then they'll be carrying out a full radiographic scan to locate all of his fractures. But Domnall says he's amazing. He's never come across a dog as badly injured as Barney who's managed to survive. We'll have to give thanks to Saint Roch.'

'Conor, I don't know what to say to you. You're the one I should be thanking, not Saint Roch.'

Conor said, 'I have another surprise for you, too.'

'What is it?'

'It wouldn't be a surprise if I told you, now would it? What time will you be home?'

'Late. We've had a homicide, and I'll have to hold a media conference in time for the Six One News. Do you know Jimmy Ó Faoláin?'

'You're codding me! I've met him a few times, at dinner dances mostly. What did the *Echo* call him? The Carbon Credit King. Jesus. Who killed him?'

'If I knew that I wouldn't be staying late. He was shot in his own house, up in Tivoli. The perpetrator let himself in and fired seven bullets through his toilet door.'

'Holy Saint Michael. Do you have any idea what the motive was? I never heard anybody say a single bad word about him, ever.'

'That's why we're all flummoxed. But listen, I'll get home as soon as I can. What do you want to eat tonight? There's some of that corned beef casserole left over if you want to heat it up.'

'I don't know yet. Maybe I'll just ring Apache for a pizza.'

Katie took a breath, and then she said, 'Thank you again for taking care of Barney. If I didn't love you already, I'd fall in love with you just for that.'

'We're not out of the woods yet, Katie, but Domnall's pretty optimistic.'

'And you're still not going to tell me what your surprise is?'

'No. Definitely not. I'll see you later. I love you.'

Katie put down the phone, and as she did so, Chief Superintendent Denis MacCostagáin came shuffling into her office. He was wearing his usual shirt sleeves and red braces and baggy grey trousers, and his fine white hair was sticking up as if he had been rubbing a balloon on it and it was full of static. Up until now, Katie had always thought he looked seasoned and capable, but today his shoulders were stooped and his stomach was sagging and she thought he looked elderly.

'I gather you've been up to see the late lamented Jimmy Ó Faoláin,' he said, dragging out the chair on the opposite side of her desk and easing himself down.

'Yes, sir. And there's a mystery for you, if ever there was one. The second most popular man in Cork after Daithí Ó Sé. It doesn't look like a robbery that went wrong – not unless there was something specific in the house that his killer came to steal and there's no way to tell that it's gone. Unless I'm stroked, I'd say that it was a highly professional hit.'

'We're going to be under fierce pressure to get this one wrapped up quickly, Kathleen. Have you heard what came out about Garda Mulligan yesterday, at the Disclosures Tribunal? Holy Saint Joseph and all the carpenters! What with the district court throwing out our case against Joe Falsey last week, we're beginning to look like a right collection of culchies.'

'I'm aware of that, sir,' said Katie. 'But it's far too soon to speculate what the motive might have been. Jimmy Ó Faoláin was popular all right, but he had his finger in so many pies, it wouldn't be surprising if he'd put at least one person's nose out of joint, even if he hadn't done it malicious-like. But whoever shot him, they knew what they were up to, and unless we have DNA or a credible witness, they're not going to be easy to track down.'

Moirin came into the office with a cup of cappuccino and a plate of cranberry and almond biscuits.

'Would you care for a cup of tea in your hand, Chief Superintendent?' she asked him.

'No, I'm grand altogether,' said Chief Superintendent MacCostagáin, although he picked up a biscuit and took a bite out of it. He sat there chewing morosely for a few moments as if life were all too much for him, but then he said, 'What I really came to see you about was McManus.'

Katie felt a chill, because she could sense what was coming. In co-operation with Inspector Carroll from Tipperary Town, she had arrested Guzz Eye McManus for dog-fighting, and he was due to appear in court in two weeks' time. Guzz Eye McManus was a Traveller, although he was permanently based at the Ballyknock halting site on Palmer's Hill, and he made no secret of the fact that he organized all the major dog-fights in Tipperary.

He had also made no secret of the fact that he had arranged for Barney to be dog-napped, and that Barney had been beaten because Katie had refused to drop the case against him.

His nickname 'Guzz Eye' came from the alarming cast in his eyes, so that nobody was ever sure if he was looking at them or not.

Chief Superintendent MacCostagáin said, 'I've been instructed that we won't be pursuing the prosecution against McManus.'

'Instructed? Instructed by whom?'

'Frank Magorian. But before you throw a sevener, it wasn't really Frank's decision. The deputy commissioner was lobbied by Pavee Point to drop the case. They said that McManus was being discriminated against as a member of an ethnic minority.'

'I didn't arrest McManus because he was a buzzie. I arrested him because he was making a fortune out of having dogs ripped to pieces.'

Chief Superintendent MacCostagáin swallowed the rest of his biscuit and smacked his hands together. 'I know that, Kathleen, and *you* know that. But we have to be seen to be fair to the

Pavee community, and considering that McManus would only be fined, if that, going ahead with a prosecution wouldn't be worth the candle.'

'The Pavee community? What about the canine community? What about those poor dumb animals who are tortured all their lives to make them fight, and then have their guts torn out so that scum like McManus can make a fortune out of them? Don't *they* have any rights? Don't we have to be fair to them?'

'Unfortunately, the Pavee have lawyers, and the dogs don't.'

'Even more unfortunately, sir, the Pavee put the fear of God into people. I'm allergic to Frank Magorian, and I don't make any secret of it, but I thought he was braver than that. What – is he frightened that a bunch of buzzies are going to come bursting into his golf club and beat him with his own putters?'

Chief Superintendent MacCostagáin stood up. 'I'm sorry, Kathleen, but it's a politically correct world these days, and we've quite enough turmoil in the Garda to be going on with.'

'I'm angry,' said Katie. 'In fact, I'm raging. As you know, my own dog, Barney, was taken by McManus and almost killed. I've only just been told that he's probably going to pull through. I love that dog. You don't know how much he means to me. But I wasn't going to let McManus off the hook, even if it meant that I'd lose Barney for ever, because every day there are hundreds of dogs going through hell – hundreds – and that's what I'm determined to put a stop to.'

'Kathleen – we don't have the budget or the manpower to protect the human beings who need our help. We can't be fretting about dogs. Besides, these dog-fighting gangs... you wouldn't want to cross them unless you knew that you could lock them all up, and the law doesn't give us the power to do that. They make more grade out of one dog-fight than a major drug deal, and they're not going to pass that up and take up knitting.'

Katie said nothing. She liked and respected Chief Superintendent MacCostagáin, even though his first reaction to her promotion had been grudging, like many other senior male officers in the southern region. Now he accepted her, and defended her whenever she needed defending, although that was rarely necessary these days. Her success rate was well over sixty per cent and she had learned to hold her own against the golfers and misogynists and freemasons like Assistant Commissioner Frank Magorian, whose grip on the Garda was gradually weakening.

Chief Superintendent MacCostagáin looked down at her and she could sense his sadness. 'I'll see you later so,' he told her, and took another biscuit.

Mathew McElvey, the young press officer, came up to see her at about three o'clock so that he could run over what she was going to say to the media about Jimmy Ó Faoláin.

'Not very much, to be honest with you,' she told him. 'I'm going to appeal for witnesses, but that's about all. I'll say that his girlfriend found him shot dead at home, but I'm not going to say that he was found on the jacks and I'm not going to hazard any guesses about possible motives. I'm not going to say that everybody liked him, either. One person obviously didn't, and that one person was enough.'

'You don't have any suspects at all?' asked Mathew. 'What about his girlfriend?'

'I'm not ruling anybody out, but I can't see the lovely Viona wanting to do away with him. He was the goose that laid her golden eggs. Of course we tested her hands for gunshot residue, just to be sure, but the result was negative, and we didn't find any discarded gloves on the premises.'

'She didn't have a jealous ex, nothing like that?'

'We'll be checking that out, of course. But my feeling is that we may find some clues when the forensic auditors go through his books. Hell hath no fury like a man cheated out of a stock option.'

'Right,' said Mathew, looking at his watch. 'I've told the journos to come in at four, if that's okay with you.'

As he got up to leave, Detective Ó Doibhilin knocked at Katie's open door. He was unshaven and his hair was scruffed up and he was wearing a bronze puffa jacket and light grey skinny-fitting tracksuit pants, with beer stains on them.

'Michael,' she said. 'How's it going with the Twomeys?'

'Finally – *finally* – I think I have a result,' he told her.

'You look beat out. Come and sit down.'

'Not so much beat out,' said Detective Ó Doibhilin. 'More like bored right out of my skull. I never heard so much horrid craic in the whole of my life. All those gowls ever talk about is football and drugs and who's the next slag they're going to be getting off with, as if. I thought I was going lakes. Apart from having to dress up every day like a walking advertisement for Champion Sports.'

Katie couldn't stop herself from smiling. Detective Ó Doibhilin prided himself on being sharply dressed, but he had been under-cover with the Twomeys and the Quinns for the past two months, which had meant living in a rented bedsit in Fair Hill and strutting around like a disaffected young Norrie.

'They're bringing in a camper van through Rosslare next Tuesday on the sixteen twenty-five ferry from Fishguard. It's going to be stuffed with fentanyl.'

'Now that *is* a result,' said Katie. 'You've told DS Begley?'

'I will be, as soon as he's back from his lunch.'

'There, you see, I told you all those evenings at the Halfway Bar would pay off in the end.'

'Sure like, they have, but I think I'll have to send my liver to the Mercy for a detox and my brain along to the Dean Clinic for some serious unscrambling.'

'We'll have to plan this very carefully,' said Katie. 'We don't want the Revenue jumping on them as soon as they land, and when we follow them from Rosslare to Cork we don't want them to catch on that they're under surveillance. The small fry I don't care about. It's Seamus Twomey and Douglas Quinn I want, and that means we'll have to try to lift them *in flagrante fentanyl.*'

'There's a couple of places they use to store stuff,' said Detective Ó Doibhilin. 'The back of the Maxol garage on Watercourse Road and an empty house on the corner of Great William O'Brien Street. They've also mentioned guns and explosives but I don't know where they are. I didn't like to push them too hard to find out in case they sussed me.'

'You've done well, Michael. I know it wasn't easy.'

'I think the hardest part is fighting off Seamus Twomey's sister. She's forever inviting me back to her gaff for what she calls a scoop and a tickle. But you should see the size of her. Jesus. She's like a blue whale in a miniskirt.'

Once Detective Ó Doibhilin had gone, Katie finished her coffee and went through all the messages and reports that had been left on her desk that morning. Conor's news about Barney had made her feel much less harassed and unsettled, and if Detective Ó Doibhilin's tip-off led to Seamus Twomey and Douglas Quinn being successfully prosecuted for drug-smuggling, that would make her year. More and more people of all ages in Cork were becoming addicted to opioids, and there had been seventeen opioid-related deaths already since January. Patients would start off with prescription drugs for a minor ailment like a sore back, but then quickly become addicted and turn to the illicit market to feed their habit.

Fentanyl was one of the most devastating opioids, because it could be fifty times stronger than heroin. It was fentanyl that had killed the singer Prince. Katie's drugs team had been warning her that it was increasingly being offered for sale in several of the city's pubs and clubs, either as carfentanil, which had originally been formulated to tranquillize large animals like cattle and even elephants, or as OxyContin – or fake OxyContin, anyway.

Her neighbour's twenty-four-year-old daughter, Siobhan, had died of an overdose of fentanyl on the first day of June. She was the mother of a seven-month-old baby girl, and had been taking opioids to cope with chronic pain after a difficult birth. Katie had attended her funeral at St Colman's Cemetery under a granite grey sky but a rainbow had appeared as her coffin was being lowered into the ground. At that moment, Katie had doubled her determination to stamp out opioid smuggling completely.

She had never imagined that it was going to be easy. Most of the fentanyl dealers were IRA splinter groups, like the gang run by Seamus Twomey and Douglas Quinn. *Fola na hÉireann*, they called themselves, the Blood of Ireland, and they were by far the most violent gang in the city, if not the county. One of their favourite punishments was to force their victims to sit on an upright scaffolding pole, so that they would slowly be impaled by their own body weight.

Moirin put her head around the door again. 'Would you care for another coffee, ma'am?' she asked her.

'No, thanks, Moirin. If I have any more caffeine I'll be hopping around like a flea on a griddle.'

'It was a shock to hear about Jimmy Ó Faoláin all right,' said Moirin. 'He paid for my neighbour's little girl to go to America to have her cancer treated, and never asked for any credit for it. From what I hear he was awful *flaithiúlach* – one of the most generous men you could hope to meet.'

'That's what everybody tells me,' said Katie. 'But even saints have their enemies, don't they?'

She jotted down the bullet points for the statement that she was going to present to the media, then she got up from her desk and went into the small bathroom at the back of her office. She stared at herself intently in the mirror over the washbasin, and thought that she was looking fresher and prettier than she had for a long time. Conor's news about Barney had brightened her up, but last week she had gone to Solo Hair Design on Camden Wharf and been given a sharp new bob. Her hair had been coloured a darker shade of red, almost as dark as red cherries, and she loved the way it swung when she shook her head from side to side.

She had always felt that it shouldn't be necessary for her to use her appearance against those of her fellow officers who treated women gardaí as inferior, but there was no avoiding reality. She was always given much more respect when she was looking her most attractive.

Superintendent Pearse had even confessed to her once that he hadn't been listening to what she was saying about the systematic vandalism of water meters 'because I never noticed before what a powerful shade of green your eyes are'.

Four

The five of them were helped out of the minibus by the driver and two younger relatives. Their hair was either grey or white, although one of them was bald except for a long comb-over, which kept flying up in the wind like the wing of an injured seagull.

They shuffled close together through the gates of St Catherine's Cemetery, almost in lockstep. They were all dressed in black except for one of the women, who was wearing a dark green overcoat. The two younger relatives followed behind them carrying cellophane-wrapped bunches of red roses.

They made their way between the blind stone angels and the flower beds, until they reached a grave with a tall black marble headstone. It was shielded on three sides by a dark yew hedge, almost three metres high, and there was a long stone bench facing it, where the five of them all sat down, three brothers and two sisters. There was no mistaking that they were related: they all had the same broad face and pug-like nose. The two younger relatives laid all the roses on the grave and then they stood behind the bench, two young men in their early twenties looking dutiful but uncomfortable. One of them yawned.

After a minute of silent contemplation, the oldest man used his walking stick to lever himself to his feet. He cleared his throat, and then he said, 'So another year has rolled by since Brianna's passing. It's hard to believe that it's six years now since we last heard her voice and raised our glasses together to celebrate the

O'Leary family and all its achievements. Six years! And whatever people say about time being the great healer, I know that all of us miss her more than words can express.'

He paused, and then he went on, 'She was always singing it, wasn't she, "The Last Rose of Summer", and we sang it together at her wake. I'm no John McDermott so I'm not going to try to sing it, but don't the words still have the resonance that they did when she left us, well before her time.

'I'll not leave thee, thou lone one! / To pine on the stem; Since the lovely are sleeping, / Go, sleep thou with them. / Thus kindly I scatter / Thy leaves o'er the bed, / Where thy mates of the garden / Lie scentless and dead.'

He was less than halfway through his quotation when they heard a faint, eerie whistling. At first they thought it was nothing more than the sound of the afternoon breeze, blowing through the branches of the cemetery's trees. But it persisted, quavering and low, occasionally hesitating, but then starting up again. They all looked at each other, and at last one of the young men said out loud what all of them were thinking.

'Jesus, that's not Granny Brianna's ghost, is it?'

'Don't be such an eejit,' said the other young man. 'That's the wind, that's all.'

'There's no way that's the wind! Listen! If that's not a ghost playing the whistle, what is it, then?'

The oldest man lifted up his walking stick and said, 'Hold your whisht you two, will you? Don't be so disrespectful! We're here to honour your mam's mam and if her spirit chooses to join us in our remembrance then so be it!'

'Sure like,' said one of the young men. 'But I don't think Granny ever played the whistle.'

They sat listening for a few moments, and even though it was tuneless, breathy and intermittent, the whistling continued. It was like listening to a musician who couldn't decide what to play next. One of the women clasped her hands together and closed her eyes in prayer.

'Dear Brianna if you're here with us now then we love you and miss you from the bottom of our hearts.'

The whistling was suddenly interrupted by an angry outburst of crows cawing at each other, and they could hear wings furiously beating and a scrabbling sound.

'That's all coming from right over yonder, like,' said one of the young men. 'Stall the beans and I'll go and take a sconce.'

'I'll come with you, boy,' said the other young man. The two of them left the elderly memorial party sitting on their bench and crossed over the path to see where all the noise was coming from. The crows were still croaking and flustering as they came around the next hedge, but as soon as they appeared they all took off with a noise like somebody shaking out a wet umbrella.

The young men saw four life-size stone angels, one standing at each corner of a small gravelled square. They didn't notice that three of the angels were looking down in sorrow while the fourth was gazing up at the sky. Their attention was riveted on the man sitting on the metal bench in between two of the angels. He was wearing jeans and a denim shirt and his hands were lying in his lap. He could have been simply resting and meditating, but he had no head, and a tin whistle was sticking out of his windpipe.

'Holy Mother of Jesus,' whispered one of the young men. 'Do you think that's real, Sean? Come on, it must be one of them Halloween pranks, surely.'

Sean was standing stock still with his hand clasped over his mouth. The headless man's shoulders and the front of his shirt were drenched dark maroon with dried blood and there were spatters of blood on the legs of his jeans, too. The flesh around his severed neck was ragged, and the two young men could only guess that the crows had been tearing at it.

'There was this prank I seen on the interweb,' the young man went on, his voice increasingly shaky. 'There was this feller lying in front of a garage door like it had come down and chopped off his head, and there was blood all over the shop. They called the cops but it was only a joke, like, do you know what I mean?'

He was still speaking when the wind rose up, and dry leaves stirred on the cemetery path, and the whistle began to blow again. Soft and tuneless, but just as melancholy as 'The Last Rose of Summer'.

'When true hearts lie withered / And fond ones are flown, / Oh! who would inhabit / This bleak world alone?'

A single crow fluttered down and perched defiantly on the headless man's shoulder. It started to peck at his neck, glaring at the two young men one-eyed as if it were challenging them to chase it away.

The young man said, 'Sean... Jesus. It has to be a real feller. The crows wouldn't be eating it, would they, if it was only a dummy?'

Sean didn't answer, but spun around, leaned forwards, and vomited a half-digested fry-up all over the cemetery path, pale brown and garnished with tomato skins like dead red roses.

Five

Katie was on her way to the lift when she heard it *ping!* and Inspector O'Rourke stepped out of it and came hurrying towards her.

'Francis,' she said.

Inspector O'Rourke was short, barrel-chested and crimson-faced, with a belligerent chin, and Katie always thought that he looked as if he were ready to pick a scrap with anybody who contradicted him.

'I wanted to catch you before you spoke to the media, ma'am,' he told her, and then smacked his chest with the flat of his hand because he was out of breath.

'We don't have a suspect, do we?' Katie asked him.

'No, it's nothing to do with Jimmy Ó Faoláin. We had a 112 call less than a half-hour ago, from St Catherine's Cemetery up at Kilcully. I know – we all thought the same thing – "Don't tell me there's somebody in the cemetery who's dead." But there is. There's some feen sitting on a bench there and he's been decapitated.'

He held out his iPhone and showed her a photograph that had been sent by a garda from Kilcully. Katie studied it for a moment, horrified. It was hard to believe it was real.

'Where's his head?' she asked. 'I mean, do we know who he is?'

'There's no sign of it so far. But we haven't searched the whole cemetery yet.'

'And *that* – what's that stuck in his neck?'

'Would you believe it, that's a tin whistle.'

Katie looked at Inspector O'Rourke with her eyes widened. 'A tin whistle? Really?'

'There was a party of people there at the cemetery paying their respects at their granny's grave. They heard this whistling noise and that's what it was. The wind blowing down it.'

'This is too weird for words,' said Katie. 'Was there any ID on him?'

'Nothing at all. No wallet, no phone, no keys. And he's wearing only slippers. But the technical experts are on their way up there now.'

'Have we had any calls about missing persons?'

'Only three schoolgirls on the hop from Christ King Secondary and an old one with the dementia who's gone wandering off from Brookfield.'

'Well, this is all I need,' said Katie. 'A local celebrity murdered by person or persons unknown and a person unknown murdered by person or persons unknown.'

Inspector O'Rourke sniffed and nodded. 'That's a rake of unknown persons and no mistake about that, like.'

'All right,' said Katie. 'But keep me informed minute by minute, will you please, Francis, even if you have to text me during the media conference?'

'I will of course.'

'It's that tin whistle that bothers me. Why would anybody want to stick a tin whistle down his neck?'

'I don't know. Maybe he's a member of a folk group and some rival musician found out that he was playing around with his missus.'

'*Francis.*'

'No, stall on, there was a case like that in Wexford a couple of years ago when some guitarist was diddling the bass player's moth and the bass player garrotted him with his own guitar strings. Do you remember that?'

'Don't let's get too imaginative, Francis. Let's find out who the victim is first. That should answer most of our questions.'

'Oh, you know me, ma'am. Imagination is not what you'd call my strong point. Do you know, I gave herself a new steam iron as an anniversary present last week because she'd been cnaveshawling for so long about the old one. Mother of God! She almost flattened me with it.'

Katie had arranged to hold the media conference in the smaller lecture room because she was expecting only the usual hard core of reporters, but when she walked in she found that there were more than twenty journalists there, as well as TV and video cameras.

All of the usual Cork suspects were there – Fionnuala Sweeney from RTÉ was sitting up at the front, along with Dan Keane from the *Examiner*, Fergus O'Farrell from RedFM and Jean Mulligan from the *Evening Echo*. But as she sat down between Mathew McElvey and Superintendent Pearse, Katie could see Kieran Dennehy from the *Irish Times*, Dara Kerrigan from the *Mirror*, and Thomas O'Neill from the *Sun*. She also recognized three or four familiar freelancers and even reporters from *The Corkman* and *The Southern Star*, provincial papers that covered local life in north and west Cork, and rarely concerned themselves with Cork city stories.

The TV lights were switched on and Katie shielded her eyes with her hand. Mathew McElvey leaned towards her and said, 'I can't understand why there's such fierce interest in Jimmy Ó Faoláin.'

'He was a celebrity,' said Katie. 'Maybe not a Gerald Kean or a Brendan O'Connor, but a *minor* celebrity, anyhow.'

'Fair play, ma'am – and of course I notified all of the media that we were going to be making a statement about him, like I always do. But there's no way I expected all of *this* crowd to show up – not in person. What's Megan Daly from the *Southern Star* doing here? Usually she's writing stories about twenty-five-euro lottery winners from Skibbereen or farmers from Clon getting their feet run over by tractors.'

'Michael?' said Katie, turning to Superintendent Pearse. 'Any ideas?'

'There's something in the air all right,' said Superintendent Pearse. 'The whole room's been buzzing since I got here.'

Katie reached out for the mic in front of her, switched it on and tapped it to make sure that it was working. She looked around at all the reporters and nodded to acknowledge them, although she didn't smile. She was making a statement about a homicide, after all.

'Good afternoon, everybody,' she said. 'I'm here to confirm that gardaí were called to Woodhill Park in Tivoli this morning and there we discovered the body of Jimmy Ó Faoláin, the CEO of Leeside Investments. He had been shot several times and it was clear that his death had been instantaneous. His body has now been removed to the university hospital where the assistant deputy state pathologist will carry out a post mortem.

'Technical experts are examining the scene of the shooting, and forensic auditors will be looking through Mr Ó Faoláin's accounts to see if they can give us any indication as to motive. As far as we know at this time, no threats were made against his life, and there appears to be no obvious reason why anybody should have wanted to kill him.'

'Where exactly was he found?' asked Dan Keane.

'In his house, on the ground floor,' said Katie.

'In which room?'

'I'm not prepared to say until we've carried out further tests.'

'Well, what was he doing when he was shot?' asked Thomas O'Neill. 'Reading? Talking on the phone? Watching TV? Eating his breakfast?'

'I'm not prepared to say until we've carried out further tests.'

'How did his killer get into the house?'

'We don't know for certain yet. There was no obvious sign of forced entry.'

'So he might have known his killer, and let him in himself? Or *her*, of course.'

'It's possible.'

'Who found him?'

'His girlfriend, Viona Caffrey. She's a Ryanair stewardess. She arrived at the house after returning from Malaga and admitted herself with her own key. She called us immediately.'

'Is she a suspect?' asked Kieran Dennehy.

'She's being questioned, of course, but no. We have no reason to believe that she could have been involved in Jimmy Ó Faoláin's killing. For the time being we're keeping an open mind about who might have shot him, and why, but we're confident that in due course we'll find enough evidence to make an arrest.'

There was some coughing and shuffling of feet, but none of the other reporters raised their hand. Despite this, Katie had the strongest feeling that they were still expecting more answers from her. None of them were packing up and preparing to leave, even Fionnuala Sweeney, who had a tight deadline to meet.

'Is that all?' she asked. 'Has no one any more questions?'

It was then that Thomas O'Neill lifted his ball pen and said, 'What about the headless man?'

The lecture room fell silent. Katie looked at the expectant faces in front of her, and realized that they knew about the decapitated body that had been found in St Catherine's Cemetery – all of them, and that was why so many of them had showed up here. What she couldn't guess was how much they knew, or how they had found out.

She couldn't deny any knowledge of it, but at the same time she didn't want to make a statement until her detectives had managed to discover who the man was. Usually when a body turned up that they couldn't immediately identify, such as a floater in the River Lee, they would put out a public appeal for any information. There was something about this case, though, that made her feel deeply reticent about giving the media any details – not that she had many details to give them.

It was the tin whistle. It had been stuck down the man's

severed neck for a reason, and she had a growing suspicion what that reason may have been. That was why she didn't want to say anything about it, not yet. If her suspicion proved to be correct, or even half correct, she could only imagine what a catastrophe could follow. By comparison, the collapse of the walls of Jericho would be no more disastrous than a garden fence blowing over in a gale.

'Which headless man in particular are you talking about?' she replied.

'Oh come on, Detective Superintendent. There's only been the one headless man found today.'

'So what do *you* know about him, Thomas?'

'It's yourself who's supposed to be answering the questions here, ma'am, not me. But let's say that I know where he was found, and I know who he is. Or *was*, rather.'

'In that case you know more than I do,' said Katie. 'A man was found dead at St Catherine's Cemetery this afternoon at Kilcully, and yes, he had been decapitated. Up until the time I came into this room to make my statement about Jimmy Ó Faoláin, however, I had no idea of his identity.'

'So if I gave you a name, you wouldn't be able to confirm if it was true or false?'

'I wouldn't, no. You're correct. And it's really far too early for me to be able to make any statements about this specific case.'

'If I said that it was Garda Kieran O'Regan, would that surprise you?'

'Who suggested that?' Katie demanded.

She was beginning to lose her temper now. She always took considerable pains to make sure that her relationship with the media was friendly and constructive. There were bound to be times when she thought the press were being too critical, or too obtrusive. In spite of that, she had to rely on them to carry appeals for eyewitnesses to crimes and traffic accidents, and to warn the public about road safety and theft and drugs, and in return she gave them as many tip-offs and as many titbits of inside information as she reasonably could. But she wasn't going to be baited.

'I'm sorry, Detective Superintendent,' said Thomas O'Neill. 'I can't reveal my source. But it's a highly reliable source, I can assure you of that.'

Katie said, 'Thomas – I don't actually care if it was the Angel Gabriel himself, whispering to you in your sleep. I've no more comment to make, especially about unsubstantiated rumours. I've brought you up to date on the murder of Jimmy Ó Faoláin and that's all I'll be giving out this afternoon. This conference is closed.'

She switched off her microphone and stood up. Superintendent Pearse and Mathew McElvey stood up, too. Almost every journalist in the room shouted at them, and they were all shouting the same question. 'Ma'am – was it Garda O'Regan?' 'That headless man – was it Garda O'Regan?' 'Can you tell us for sure if it was Garda O'Regan?'

Katie stalked back to the lift with Superintendent Pearse hurrying to catch up with her. Mathew McElvey started to follow her, but then turned back to the lecture room to try to calm the journalists down, although while she waited for the lift Katie could hear them still shouting.

As they rose up to the second floor, Katie and Superintendent Pearse stared grimly at each other, and they said nothing as they walked along the corridor to Chief Superintendent MacCostagáin's office, and knocked.

Chief Superintendent MacCostagáin was standing by the window with a cup of tea. He turned around and smiled as they came in.

'Ah, Kathleen,' he said. 'Michael. What's the story?'

'That headless feen who was found sitting in St Catherine's Cemetery,' said Superintendent Pearse.

'Oh, yes?'

'We've just been making a statement to the press about Jimmy Ó Faoláin but all they wanted to know about was him.'

Chief Superintendent MacCostagáin looked across at Katie. 'I thought you were going to keep the lid on that until we knew who he was.'

'Well, somebody's told them,' said Katie. 'And not only that, somebody's told them that it's Kieran O'Regan.'

'Holy Saint Patrick. Do you think that it is?'

'I have no idea yet. The body had no head and there was nothing on him to identify him. I'll have O'Donovan contact his family to see if he's missing. Meanwhile I'll be asking Bill Phinner to get the giodar on with the fingerprinting and the DNA.'

Superintendent Pearse said, 'O'Regan's still on indefinite leave, like, so it's not as if we were missing him when he didn't turn up for his shift.'

'Did you ask the press why they think that it's him?' asked Chief Superintendent MacCostagáin, but before Katie could answer he said, 'Of course you did, and of course they wouldn't tell you.'

'No, they wouldn't,' said Katie. 'But it doesn't matter two hoots what their code of conduct says, they can't legally refuse to disclose who or where that information came from.'

'I hope you reminded them of that.'

'No, sir, I didn't push them today because I want to confirm the victim's identity first. Horses before carts. But I *will* be pushing them, believe me, especially if it turns out that it really *is* Garda O'Regan. They always forget that qualifying clause, don't they, those reporters. They can keep their sources anonymous except when there's vital public or individual interests at stake. If it is Garda O'Regan, then I'd say both of those interests are at stake, public *and* individual. And big time.'

'Jesus, what a pig's dinner,' said Chief Superintendent MacCostagáin. He sat down and stared at his cup of tea as if he had never seen it before and was wondering how it had magically appeared in his hand.

Katie said, 'Whoever tipped the media off about the headless body, they must have wanted it well-publicized because they contacted every newspaper, every radio station, and of course RTÉ. That makes me suspect that they were the perpetrators. If you think about it, they must have taken a fair amount of time to prepare a list of all the media they were going to get in touch with, so they probably had that list ready in advance, before the victim was killed.

'And of course the cruncher is, how did they know it was Garda O'Regan, unless it was them who killed him? I know his picture's been in the papers, and on the TV and all, but he had no head. If *we* couldn't identify him, how could anybody else recognize who it was?

'Then – on top of all that – there's that tin whistle that was stuck down his neck.'

Chief Superintendent MacCostagáin looked up at her when she said that, and his expression was one of huge weariness. There was no question that the same thought had occurred to him, too, and the implications could only be guessed at. It might even signal the end of the Garda in its present form, and the early termination of his career.

'Just one tin whistle,' he said. 'Who'd have thought it?'

Katie said, 'We don't know for sure, sir. It could mean something and it could mean nothing at all. But if it *was* meant as a message, I think we all have a fair suspicion what that message might be.'

'This is breaking my melt,' said Chief Superintendent MacCostagáin. 'As if it wasn't going to cause enough trouble when O'Regan stood up and gave his evidence. When was that scheduled for? I know it's supposed to be soon.'

'Next Thursday, so far as I know,' said Katie. 'It would have depended on Sergeant Duffy giving his evidence about the breathalyser tests, how long that went on for.'

'What a mess. It doesn't surprise me one iota that Nóirín O'Sullivan threw in the towel. I would have done the same if I'd been her. Not that I was ever asked to be Commissioner. I never had the golf.'

'Anyway,' said Katie, 'this is going to go nowhere at all until we find out if it's Garda O'Regan or not. If it *is*, we'll have a rake of suspects, no doubt about that. If it isn't, then God only knows.'

Katie found Detective O'Donovan in the squad room, tapping away two-fingered at his computer and eating a ham-and-tomato roll.

'Patrick – I'd normally send out a uniform to do this, but it could be iffy and I wouldn't want the neighbours seeing a squad car outside the house – or anybody else for that matter. You might want to take Padragain with you, too, in case there's a shoulder that needs to be cried on.'

'Well, let's hope that it isn't him,' said Detective O'Donovan. 'He's a decent enough fellow. Bit of a stickler, like, do you know what I mean? Even if he was attending a murder he wouldn't park on a yellow line.'

'I don't care where he parked. Right now I just want to know if he's alive or dead.'

Detective O'Donovan stood up, took one more bite out of his ham-and-tomato roll, and then went across to take his raincoat down from the peg.

'I've a fierce bad feeling about this,' he said, with his mouth full.

'You're not the only one, Patrick,' said Katie. 'But maybe this was a tragedy waiting to happen.'

Six

It had started drizzling again when Detective Michael Ó Doibhilin crossed Baker's Road to the Halfway Bar and Lounge. He stood in the entrance brushing the rain from his bronze puffa jacket before he went inside.

The Halfway Bar and Lounge was a one-room pub at the end of a run-down terrace of shops on the Northside, next to St Mary's Health Campus. The Drop Dead Donkeys were playing there tonight, and he could hear them shouting their way through 'You'll Never Beat the Irish', with guitars and bodhrán drum and bagpipes. Over that, there was the usual roar of conversation and laughter.

He would be heartily glad when this assignment was over. It had been exciting to start with: turning up at the pub with his cover story that he had been a drugs mule for the Cavey gang in Dublin. He had claimed that things had got too hot for him there, what with the Brogans trying to muscle in on the Cavey's drug racket, and the Garda intensifying their campaign against drug-dealers. That was why he had returned to his native Hollyhill, although he had told the Halfway regulars that he was still looking for gainful employment, especially ill-gotten-gainful employment.

After nearly two months of pretending to be Tommy Ó Frighil, though, he was bored and exhausted by having to turn up to the pub almost every night, drinking and talking about football and hurling, and returning to his flat in the small hours of the morning, stinking of alcohol and cigarettes. He had given up smoking five years ago, and smoking wasn't allowed inside the pub, but unless he had joined Seamus Twomey and Douglas Quinn whenever they went outside in the street for a cigarette, he would have missed half of the information that he had gleaned from them about their fentanyl and spice smuggling.

He had developed a persistent cough, and his girlfriend, Eithne, had told him that if he didn't give up smoking she would dump him. Whenever she stayed over, she complained that he came staggering in every night smelling like Stink McCrink. For the sake of security, he couldn't explain to her where he had been, and what he had been doing, and why.

The pub door opened abruptly and one of the regulars came out, accompanied by a wave of loud music. It was Dermot O'Leary, a plumpish fellow with grey hair and glasses and a grey zip-up sweater, with a Johnny Blue already dangling between his lips.

'Oh, there you are, boy,' he said, so that his cigarette waggled. 'I was thinking that maybe we wouldn't be seeing you in tonight.'

'I was doing the messages for my Auntie Branna. She's just had this replaceable hip, like, so she can't get up to the shops.'

'So you're a bit of a saint on the quiet, are you, Tommy? And there's you, giving out like you're some tough aish.'

'Don't tell me you ever forget your mam's birthday,' said Michael.

'I wouldn't, no, if I knew who the feck me mam ever was. I was brung up at St Vincent's.'

'Oh. Sorry. No offence.'

Dermot jerked his head towards the pub door. 'Seamus was asking after you before. Said he had a bone to pick.'

'Oh, yes? What about?'

'You'd best ask him, like. Either that, or take tackie. You know what Seamus is like when he gets thick about something.'

'I've done nothing to upset him,' said Michael. 'Not that I can think of, anyhow.'

Dermot shrugged, took out his lighter and lit his cigarette. 'Up to you, boy. All I can say is, g'luck.'

Michael hesitated. He had seen Seamus Twomey when he was angry, and it was enough to make anybody shake in their trainers. Most of the time, he was louder than anybody else in the pub, with a laugh like a hysterical donkey. When he was raging, though, he became utterly silent, and his face turned expressionless. He would only have to give the slightest nod of his head and whoever had offended him would be lifted out of his sight by two or three of his gang and given a fearsome going-over. They could count themselves lucky if they suffered no more than black eyes and a broken nose and a couple of fractured ribs.

So what's this bone that Seamus Twomey wants to pick? Does he suspect that I'm an undercover cop? If he does, and I can't convince him beyond reasonable doubt that I'm not, I could easy be found tomorrow morning floating downriver in the Lee, after God knows what agonizing torture.

As apprehensive as he was, Michael knew that if he failed to show up, he could well be putting the whole drug-smuggling operation at risk. Dermot O'Leary would tell Seamus Twomey that he had walked away, and that would only serve to confirm Twomey's suspicions about him.

He started coughing, mostly out of nervousness. He looked around and Dermot O'Leary was standing under the awning at the front of the pub, smoking and watching him to see what he was going to do next. The rain was pattering on the awning with a sound like rats running across an attic floor.

Michael pushed open the door and stepped inside the bar. The Drop Dead Donkeys had just come to the end of 'You'll Never Beat the Irish' and were taking a break for a couple of bojonters. Despite that, the small L-shaped room was still so noisy that everybody had to shout to make themselves heard. It had a low ceiling and the walls were crowded with photographs of local hurling teams and framed red T-shirts and wooden plaques, which always made Michael feel claustrophobic.

He could see Seamus Twomey and Douglas Quinn sitting at their usual circular table on the right-hand side of the bar. On either side of them sat two of their henchmen, as well as an anorexic-looking young blonde girl with two silver rings through her lower lip and tattoos all the way down to her elbows, and Seamus Twomey's sister Gwenith.

Michael gave them a salute as he made his way to the bar, which none of them returned. The owner's wife, Maureen, grinned at him and said, 'Your usual, Tommy, is it? You're late in this evening, aren't you?'

Maureen wore a curly black wig and a low-cut blue satin dress. She had a prominent black mole on her upper lip and Michael always concentrated on that while he was talking to her so that she wouldn't catch him staring into the crinkled abyss of her cleavage, where a tiny Jesus dangled perilously on a golden chain.

'I was fetching the messages for my aunt,' he said. 'She's immobile, like, at the moment. Fell off the 202 bus and had to have a new hip.'

'Well good man yourself,' said Maureen, as she poured him a pint of Murphy's. 'These days it seems like you can't catch nobody doing nothing at all for nobody.'

She passed him over the pint, and nodded towards Seamus Twomey's table. 'Are you going to be sitting with them? I think Seamus wants a word in your wiggie.'

At that moment, Seamus Twomey was giving out one of his loud, braying laughs. 'That's fecking mental, that is! Jesus! It's a wonder it didn't give you a dose of the scutters!'

However, he stopped laughing as soon as he saw Michael walking across to his table. Douglas Quinn and the two henchmen and the tattooed girl and Gwenith all shifted around to look at him as he approached.

Seamus Twomey wasn't a big man, maybe 5 foot 4 inches, with sloping shoulders, but he had a disproportionately large head. He was not only bald but alopecia had taken away his eyebrows, too, which made his features even more expressionless.

His eyes were the palest citrine and his skin was an unnatural shade of pink, as if his head had been reproduced in plastic in a 3-D printer.

In contrast, Douglas Quinn was tall and bony with long black hair that was beginning to turn grey, and a black and grey beard. He had a sharply pointed nose and eyes that glittered underneath his tangled eyebrows like a wolf watching the world from inside a cave, ready to pounce at anything edible that might come innocently wandering past. Even his friends called him *An Duine Dorcha*, the Dark Fellow.

The two henchmen could have been twins. Both had prickly ginger hair that had been shaved down to grade one, and both had faces that resembled large knobbly potatoes. They even wore matching black T-shirts, with Irish flags on them and the motto *Unrepentant Fenian Bastard*. They had no necks, and they bulged with muscles, as if their T-shirts were crammed to bursting with even more potatoes.

Michael glanced at Gwenith and gave her a quick, uneasy grin. He guessed that Gwenith must have weighed at least 90 kilos. She had frayed bleached-blonde hair with brown roots beginning to grow out, and a round moon-like face resting on a half-moon double chin. Her nose was short and snub, and her bow-shaped scarlet lips were so small that it was a wonder she could eat as much as she did. This evening she was wearing a purple cardigan with buttons that were straining like a chain of mountain rescuers to contain her enormous breasts, and a black leather miniskirt, with laddered black tights.

'Tommy! C'mere till I tell you a question,' said Seamus Twomey, tapping his finger on the table. Michael dragged over a chair and sat down next to the blonde girl with the tattooed arms. He noticed that she had a series of diagonal scars on her left wrist, which could have been caused by self-harm.

'What's the craic, Seamus?' Michael asked him, taking a sip from his Murphy's so that he wouldn't appear to be anything but calm and unconcerned. At the same time, he was calculating if he could make it to the door before the two potato-faced henchmen could grab hold of him.

'Our Gwenith,' said Seamus Twomey. 'Have you taken against her for some reason, or what?'

Michael turned to Gwenith, who had a triumphant gleam in her eyes, and then turned back to Seamus Twomey. Douglas Quinn was looking deeply amused, and stroking his beard in anticipation of how Michael was going to answer.

'Of course not, Seamus,' said Michael. 'What makes you think that, like?'

'She's been giving you the eye ever since you started joining us for drinks, and don't tell me you're too fecking blind to have noticed.'

'For sure I've noticed, how couldn't I? But you know, she's your sister, and I didn't like to take the piss, like, do you know what I mean? For all I know, she's doing a line already with some other feen.'

'If she was doing a line already, why would she be giving you the eye? You're not a sausage jockey, are you?'

'Go'way with you, Seamus. Do I look like a fecking twink?'

'I don't know, boy. You tell me. All I know is, our Gwenith's been flirting with you like crazy, and you haven't even asked her if she'd fancy the flicks or a hod in the fields.'

Michael grinned at him and tried hard not to let it look as if the very idea of taking Gwenith to the cinema or out for a walk in the country made him feel queasy. Apart from anything else, it would be far too risky. He could just imagine coming out of the Gate Multiplex with Gwenith and one of his old school friends clapping him on the back and chirping, 'Michael! Haven't seen you in donkey's years! What are you at, horse? Holy Mary, who's yer oul' doll? She's built for comfort, I'd say.'

For his school friend, it would mean an incredulous laugh. For Michael, it would mean a severe beating or even death, since Gwenith would be bound to tell her brother that 'Tommy' wasn't Tommy after all.

'To be honest with you, Seamus, I've been up the walls these past couple of days,' he told him. 'I've fixed myself up with this temporary job painting and decorating them new houses in Coolroe Court, in Ballincollig.'

'You'll not be painting and decorating tonight, though, will you, boy?' said Seamus Twomey.

'Well, no. I thought I'd just be coming out for a few scoops, like. I'm flah'd out.'

'Don't tell me you're too tired for a jag with our Gwenith.'

Gwenith had been sucking a bright green apple poitini through a straw. She wiped her lips with the back of her podgy wrist and said, 'We can go back to my place, Tommy. I have the box set of *Can't Cope, Won't Cope*, and a rake of drink, and a whole giant-sized bag of them Tex-Mex Taytos.'

'There,' said Seamus Twomey. 'Who could resist an offer like that?'

Michael looked across at Douglas Quinn. He could tell by the way Quinn's eyes were shining and his lips were pursed that he was trying desperately hard not to laugh. The two henchmen remained impassive, as if they hadn't heard what Gwenith had been offering, or didn't understand English.

Gwenith reached out and took hold of Michael's hand. Her fingers were cold and damp, probably because of poor circulation. Her fingernails were painted with sparkly nail varnish, although most of them were chipped.

'How about it, then, Tommy?' she coaxed him.

'Yes, well, grand,' said Michael. 'Do you live far from here?'

'Only a couple of streets away. The flats down the bottom of Sprigg's Road. Farry will drive us there anyhow, won't you, Farry?'

One of the henchmen gave her a barely perceptible nod.

'I've time to finish my drink, though?' Michael asked.

'Sure like,' said Seamus Twomey. 'In fact, I'll treat you to another, and then maybe one for the frog. It's not every day of the week a feller makes my sister so happy out.'

Gwenith told Michael to shift his chair towards her so that they could sit close together and she could squash her thigh against his. She smelled strongly of Estée Lauder Beautiful. He knew what perfume it was because his previous girlfriend, Clodagh, had worn it and it had permeated the passenger seat of his car so deeply that it had outlasted their relationship by over two months. Underneath the Estée Lauder, though, he could faintly detect chopped onions and cooking fat.

'The minute you walked in I thought what a fine thing you were,' said Gwenith, snuggling in to him even closer. 'And when you opened your mouth, well, I was totally won over. The last boyfriend I had, what a weapon he was, and he talked like a fecking padjo.'

'The feeling was mutual, Gwenith, when I first saw you,' said Michael, aware that Seamus Twomey was listening to everything they were saying. 'It was like I told Seamus, though. I wasn't sure if you were available. I didn't want to be treading on anybody's toes.'

'Oh, you can tread on my toes any time you like, Tommy,' said Gwenith, squeezing his upper arm and letting out a strange high-pitched squeak.

It was half past ten now and the Halfway was starting to empty, although a few of the customers would stay drinking until two or three, with the doors locked. Gwenith noisily sucked the last of her apple poitini, picked up her bag from the floor and said, 'Right then, Farry, we're out the gap now. Sup up.'

The henchman named Farry swallowed what was left of his Guinness and let out a long, complicated burp, punching his chest as he did so. He had drunk four pints since Michael had arrived, and could well have drunk two or three more. If Michael hadn't been undercover, he would have demanded that Farry hand over his car keys, and if he had refused and attempted to drive his car he would have arrested him.

Gwenith and Michael stood up, and Seamus Twomey raised his glass to them and said, 'Have a great ride, you two. I'll see you tomorrow and you can tell me all about it. *Sláinte!*'

They left the pub and walked up the road to the Centra store where Farry's silver Toyota was parked, sparkling with raindrops. Gwenith climbed into the back, bouncing herself over to the other side of the car and patting the seat to indicate that Michael should come in and sit next to her. Farry lit a cigarette and then eased himself in behind the wheel. He started the engine and simultaneously burped out a cloud of smoke.

As they backed out into Baker's Road and headed for Cathedral Road, Gwenith pulled Michael towards her and said, 'How about a lend of a shift, Tommy? I promise I'll give it back.'

Michael puckered up his lips, closed his eyes and kissed her. Her tongue instantly slid into his mouth, slithering around his teeth like a stranded porpoise. Her lips were plump and sticky with cheap lipstick and her saliva tasted of the apple poitini that she had been drinking, sweet and slightly medicated, as if somebody had mixed a cocktail out of Aunty Nellie's Apple Drops, rectified spirit and nappy rash cream.

He opened his eyes momentarily, and he could see Farry's eyes in the rear-view mirror, watching them. He knew that if he showed the slightest indication that he didn't find Gwenith at all attractive and that her kisses disgusted him, it could prove to be fatal. He kissed her back, hard, and licked her tongue, and then he grasped her left breast and fondled it, even though her support bra was so hard that it was like fondling a football.

'Oh, Tommy,' Gwenith breathed in his ear. She took hold of his wrist and guided his hand away from her breast, underneath her leather miniskirt and deep between her thighs.

'Can you feel me?' she said, pressing his fingers up against her knickers. 'I'm as wet as an otter's pocket.'

Michael glanced again at the reflection of Farry's eyes, and tried to think about anything except for the damp nylon of Gwenith's underwear. He thought of all the training he had been given at the Garda College at Templemore. He had been taught how to deal with a terrorist wearing a suicide belt but he had never been taught how to handle a horny fat woman whose brother was an unconvicted killer.

'Gwenny, Jesus, you're amazing,' he told her, rubbing the tip of his middle finger up and down the cleft in her slippery knickers. 'I never met any beour who got turned on so quick as you.'

Farry burped again, and Michael thought, after what I've just said, I don't blame you, sham. I really don't blame you. I'm surprised you didn't gawk, to be honest with you.

They reached the top of St Enda's Road and turned into Sprigg's Road, where terraces of flats overlooked a wide grassy slope. Farry drove down to the end of the road and heaved himself out of the driver's seat so that he could open the back door for Gwenith to climb out. It was still raining, but much more softly. Before he got back into the Toyota, Farry came up to Michael and said, 'You'll be treating her good, won't you, Tommy? Like a princess, okay? No messing, no acting the maggot.'

'Is that what Seamus told you to tell me?' said Michael.

'Seamus is no moggy dan, Tommy. He knows how fecking fat she is, and why she can hardly ever get a feller to have a jag with her. Christ, the tide wouldn't take her out. But you're doing him a favour, like, do you know what I mean, and he won't forget you for this.'

'Come on ta fuck, will you?' Gwenith called out. She was waiting for Michael on the steps outside her front door. 'I'm getting wet outside now as well as in!'

Michael said nothing to Farry, but nodded to show that he had understood him, and then jogged across the road to join Gwenith.

Seven

Katie closed the report she had been working on, switched off her computer and decided it was time to go home. It was ten twenty-seven and she was surprised that she hadn't yet heard from Detective O'Donovan. She thought of ringing him but he was always totally reliable and if he hadn't yet contacted her she knew that there had to be a good reason for it.

She took her coat down from the coat-stand and was buttoning it up when Bill Phinner knocked at her door.

'You're working late, Bill,' she said. 'Haven't had a row with the missus, have you?'

'To tell you the truth, we've been working on the bullet we found at Jimmy Ó Faoláin's house and I didn't realize how late it was.'

He held up the bullet in a transparent plastic evidence bag. It looked like a tiny silver daisy, with its petals bent back.

'So, what's the story? Have you identified it?'

'We believe so, yes. We went back to the house and took a few measurements, and then we built ourselves a simulated jacks. Not the whole thing, mind. Just a door and a wall with the same type of tiles. We fired a whole selection of bullets through the door so that they ricocheted off of the tiles, and then we compared them.'

'And?'

'We'll wait until we receive the other six bullets from Dr Kelley before we make a final decision, because they won't be so distorted.

Myself, I don't think there's any doubt at all that it was a .357 Sig hollow point. The .40 Smith & Wesson hollow point came close, but the .357 had almost exactly the same characteristics. We tried several different guns, too. From the lands and the grooves in the bullet and the rifling twist, we're ninety-nine and a half per cent sure it was fired by a Sig Sauer P226.'

'Which is only one of the most popular handguns in the world,' said Katie. 'Even our Regional Support Units have them.'

'Sure like. But at least we know what type of weapon we're looking for, and we can put out an appeal for anybody to contact us if they've seen somebody with a gun that looks like a Sig. If we can find the weapon, we'll have no trouble at all in matching the bullets to it.'

'All right, Bill, thanks. I'm kind of reminded of haystacks and needles, but it's a start. You haven't found any more forensic evidence at the house, have you?'

Bill shook his head. 'Nothing whatsoever, which is pure unusual. Everybody leaves some trace of theirselves, no matter where they go. Even if it's nothing more than half of a footprint, or a few flakes of dandruff, or a fine spray of phlegm on a wall from having a sneeze.'

He swung the evidence bag from side to side, and then he said, 'All the same, I'm sending Jones and O'Keefe up to Woodhill Park again tomorrow morning, and I'll be giving them a brief to go over every square centimetre with the Coherent TracER, all over again. You never know. We might have missed something on the first sweep. A red hair lying on a red carpet. It happens.'

'Well, good luck with that,' said Katie. 'I'd better get off home now. I'm starving. I could eat the lamb of Jesus through the rungs of a chair.'

She was driving along the N25 in the rain and as she was passing Slatty Water her phone played *Siúil A Rún*.

'O'Donovan here, ma'am. Sorry to ring you so late but

Scanlan and me we've been chasing around all over the shop like blue-arsed flies.'

'What's the story, Patrick? Have you talked to Mrs O'Regan?'

'Would you believe we've not been able to locate her. We went around to St Christopher's Road but there was nobody home. One of the neighbours said that she'd seen Moira O'Regan leaving with her two kids in the family car about half past one, but she's not been back since.'

'I assume you've tried ringing her.'

'We have of course, repeatedly. We've texted her too. But we've had no response whatsoever. So first we went around to Kieran O'Regan's parents' house in Mayfield. They hadn't heard from Kieran for at least a week, and they'd not seen hide nor hair of Moira O'Regan or the kids for longer than that. But at least they gave us the address and the phone number of Moira's mam, who lives in Togher.'

'But she hadn't seen Moira either?'

'She'd a fierce funny phone call from her about the middle of the morning. She was sure that Moira was crying, but when she asked her why she was so musha she wouldn't tell her. She kept saying "I can't, I can't, I don't know what they'll do to him".'

'What did you make of that?' asked Katie, as she turned off the N25 and headed south on the Cork Road towards Cobh.

'Hard to tell for sure, like,' said Detective O'Donovan. 'But if that feller with the no head really *is* Kieran O'Regan, my guess is that he was being held hostage by somebody who'd threatened him, and that his old lady knew about it.'

'That's what I'd guess, too. We need to find her, Patrick, and fast. Even if she has only an inkling of who it was killed him, she's in serious jeopardy, too.'

'Her mam gave us a list of all Moira's brothers and sisters, and all the friends that she could think of, and that's what we've been doing, either ringing them or going around to see them. We're on our way back from Mallow right now. We've just seen the last of them, Moira's best friend from Scoil Mhuire.'

'Sergeant Mulvaney's on duty tonight, isn't he? Have you brought him up to date?'

'We have, yeah. We've already given him a recent picture of Moira and the kids and the registration of the family car. Dark blue Honda Civic, three years old.'

'Okay, Patrick, thanks. I'll be coming in early tomorrow morning, so I'll catch up with you then.'

She had reached Carrig View now. The lights of Monkstown on the opposite side of the River Lee were winking and sparkling in the water. That was where her father lived, only a five-minute ferry crossing away, and she felt a momentary twinge of guilt that she hadn't been to visit him for nearly a month. She turned into her driveway, where Conor's black Audi Q7 was already parked, turned off her windscreen wipers and switched off her engine, and sat in meditation, trying to think of nothing at all.

The rain dripped from the yew hedge beside her window. *Peace*, she thought. *Silence*. But she had been sitting there for only half a minute before her iPhone played *Siúil A Rún*.

'Conor,' she said.

'Are you coming indoors or what? I've been waiting here all evening to give you your surprise.'

'I'm sorry. I'm coming. I was just having a third *bhūmi* moment, trying to attain *kṣānti*.'

'The *what*? Oh. The *kṣānti*. I should have known. Any luck with it, whatever it is?'

'It seems to be working. *Kṣānti* means ultimate patience, and I'm not shouting at you, am I?'

She climbed out of her car and hurried to the porch, just as Conor opened the front door for her. He hustled her inside and helped her to take off her coat.

'Welcome home,' he said, hanging up her coat and then holding out his arms. 'From the sound of it, you've had one hell of a day.'

She hugged him tightly and pressed her face against his chest. He always made her feel so protected, not only because he was tall and muscular, but his straight nose and his dark brown beard made him look like one of those mythical knights. Seán Ruadh, maybe, the thirteenth son of one of the kings of Erin, who had cut a ravenous sea serpent in half to rescue a princess, not to mention the heads of twenty men who had falsely claimed to have saved her.

She loved the smell of him, too. Chanel Bleu, and just him.

'Made any progress?' he asked her, at last.

'With Jimmy Ó Faoláin? Nothing to speak about.'

'What about your headless friend from Kilcully Cemetery?'

'Again, we're nowhere yet, although we should have some DNA results tomorrow. Poor Patrick and Padragain have spent the whole afternoon scampering around the city trying to find out if it really is Kieran O'Regan. The whole day's been pure cat.'

'What if it wasn't pure cat? What if it was pure dog?'

Katie brightened up. 'You've some news about Barney?'

'More than that. Come into the living room and I'll show you.'

For the first time, Katie noticed that the living-room door was closed, although it usually stayed open, except in the middle of winter when a north-west wind blew and the hallway was draughty.

'What are you up to, Conor?' she asked him.

He opened the door. Inside, a wood fire was crackling in the grate, and on the coffee table stood a silver ice bucket with a bottle of champagne resting in it, and two champagne flutes. But Katie barely noticed these, because as they walked into the room, a red-and-white Irish setter stood up from where it had been lying in front of the fire, and came padding towards them, bright-eyed and with its tail swishing from side to side.

'Oh dear God,' said Katie, and immediately burst into tears. 'Oh dear God, Conor, she's beautiful! She *is* a she, isn't she?'

'She's a she, all right. No question about that. And more than that, she's yours.'

Katie sank down on to her knees on the carpet and the setter came up to her and sniffed her and licked her hand. She stroked the setter's head and gently tugged at her ears and the setter snuffled and did a little step-dance with her front feet.

Katie had seen very few red-and-white setters because they had almost become extinct until the 1980s, when a concerted effort had been made by the Irish Kennel Club to revive them. They were gun dogs, obedient and affectionate, and this bitch was almost a perfect example of her breed. Her coat was long and silky and pearly white, with a saddle of chestnut colouring on her back. Her cheeks were chestnut, too, and so were both of her ears. She had the characteristic feathering on her throat and chest, and on her outer ear flaps, and a feathery tail.

'I don't know what to say, Con,' said Katie. She stood up and pulled out a crumpled tissue to wipe her eyes. 'Where did you *find* her? She's gorgeous.'

The setter stayed close to her, looking up at her as if she were concerned that she was so emotional. Katie couldn't resist stroking her head again, and lifting up her long feathery ears.

'I'm all right, sweetheart,' she assured her. 'It's just that your Uncle Conor said he was going to give me a surprise, but I never guessed in a million years that the surprise was going to be you.'

'I got her from a vet I know in Limerick, Niall Mac Seáin. He owes me one from years ago. Three really valuable salukis got stolen from his surgery, and I tracked them down for him. She's a beauty now, isn't she? She's three years old, and she's been vaccinated and chipped – oh, yes, and wormed, too. Her owner has to go overseas for his job, so he was looking for somebody to adopt her. Niall told me she's been well trained and very well cared-for.'

'What's Barney going to think about her, when he comes home?' said Katie. She paused and then she said, 'He *will* be coming home, won't he?'

'I don't have any doubt about it, darling,' Conor told her. 'And Barney in fact is the whole reason I bought her – so that the poor lad has a girlfriend to keep him company while he's convalescing. You can't be there during the day for him, but he's going to need a lot of support and affection, and this young lady can make him happy while you're at work chasing the scumbags.'

'She'll need a fierce amount of exercise, though,' said Katie. 'I saw a red-and-white on the beach at Dingle once, and he went off like a bullet, and kept on going, until he was only a red-and-white speck in the distance. I mean, Barney could run all right, but this dog made Barney look like a shellakybooky on four legs.'

'Don't you worry about that. I've had a chat with Jenny Tierney next door and she said she'll be delighted to take her out whenever I'm not here. Between you and me, I think there's some old fellow she meets when she's out dog-walking, down by the end of Rinacollig.'

Katie kneeled down again and wrapped her arms around the setter's neck. 'I love her already. What's her name?'

'Foltchain, which means "beautiful hair". Niall said that was the nickname given to Fliodhais the goddess who was the lover of Fergus mac Róich. Any night that Fergus couldn't have Fliodhais, it would take seven other women to satisfy him.'

'Mother of God, I hope Barney's going to be up to it.'

Katie changed into her pink fluffy dressing gown while Conor opened the bottle of champagne. He had made a plateful of smoked salmon sandwiches, too, because he knew that she wouldn't have much of an appetite this late in the evening.

'You spoil me,' she said, tucking up her bare feet on the couch.

Conor kissed her. 'You deserve to be spoiled, everything you do for everybody else. Apart from being the most tempting woman I ever met, ever.'

Foltchain was lying contentedly on the mat in front of the fire, although every now and then she rolled up her eyes to look at Katie and Conor as if she were checking that they were still there, and weren't magically going to disappear and leave her alone.

After a long peaceful silence, Katie said, 'We won't be prosecuting Guzz Eye McManus.'

'You're codding me.'

'No. Denis told me this afternoon. He said we haven't the finance to worry about dogs. Besides, he'd only get a slap on the wrist and what good would that do? He makes a fortune out of those dog-fights, him and all those other sadistic gowls.'

Conor shook his head. 'I can't believe it. Your man organizes the ripping apart of living dogs, not to mention all the suffering they go through when they're being trained, and he doesn't even have to pay a fine? He should be hung, drawn, quartered and castrated and sentenced to everlasting doom.'

'I told Denis I was fuming, darling, but it didn't make a difference. If there's no money there's no money, and you can bet that McManus would be hiring the most expensive lawyers you could find.'

'What did Inspector Carroll have to say?'

'I haven't had the time to talk to him yet, but it's an awful land. He'll be gutted.'

Conor sipped his champagne and reached over for a sandwich. 'Somebody needs to do something about McManus, I tell you. Niall was telling me that he's arranging a huge dog-fight in about two weeks' time, and guess what it's for? To celebrate his daughter's matrimonials. Talk about your big fat blood-soaked gypsy wedding.'

'I don't know what we can do, except to keep on breaking up the fights whenever we get tipped off about them.'

Conor said nothing, but ate his sandwich in quick, angry bites. Katie shifted herself over and rested her head on his shoulder.

'Don't get too stooky,' she said, stroking the back of his hand. 'If this job's taught me nothing else, it's that we don't have the resources to put right everything that needs to be put right, and even if we did, we may not have the legal power to do it. That's what *kṣānti*'s all about. Acceptance. Patience.'

'Like, if you wait by the banks of the river for long enough, you'll see the bodies of your enemies float past?'

'Something like that.'

'But while I wait for Guzz Eye McManus to float past, how many dogs are going to die in agony?'

Katie kissed his cheek. 'I can't answer that, Conor. But we'll get him one day, you wait and see.'

That night, as Conor breathed deep and slow, Katie sat up in bed and listened to the rain. Earlier she had heard Foltchain padding around in the kitchen, her claws clicking on the tiles, but now she seemed to have settled down.

Despite what she had said to Conor about patience and acceptance, Katie had a stomach-tightening feeling of apprehension that she hadn't experienced in a long time. She couldn't stop thinking about the murder of Jimmy Ó Faoláin, and the more she thought about it, the more it unsettled her. Outwardly, he had been so well-liked that she couldn't help thinking there had to be some seriously rotten secret behind his killing. There had been a similar murder five years ago when a popular Cork TD had been shot. Only after his death had the Garda discovered that he had been taking bribes amounting to tens of thousands of euros to approve planning permission and other political favours.

Katie called it her 'Easter chicken' feeling. She had bought a free-range chicken years ago when she was married to Paul. It had looked plump and healthy on the outside, but when she had cut open the twine that bound its legs she had found that, inside, it was a writhing mass of maggots.

She was equally worried about the headless body that might or might not be Garda Kieran O'Regan. Since his wife and children had disappeared, she was almost sure that it must be him, and if it were, God alone knew what repercussions that could have.

On his day off seven months ago, Garda O'Regan had been driving to Kinsale. He had stopped for a drink at the Babbling Brook pub in Riverstick and in the bar he had recognized a notorious Cork city drug-dealer named Jer Brogan. He had got into conversation with him, making out that he was something of a shady character himself, because Brogan was supposed to be in Rathmore Road prison serving a three-year sentence. He had sold crystal meth to a young woman in a nightclub and the young woman had died later that evening from a cardiac arrest.

Drunk and boastful, Brogan had confided in Garda O'Regan that a combination of money and threats had persuaded the prison service escorts who were supposed to be driving him to prison not to take him there at all. Not only that, one of the senior prison officers had falsified records to show that because of his violence he had been transferred from Rathmore Road to the controlled behavioural unit in Mountjoy Prison in Dublin. In reality he was living back at home in Blackpool, and wouldn't be spending a minute behind bars. He also admitted that he was far from being the only convicted drug-dealer in Cork who had never served his sentence.

After he had talked to Brogan, Garda O'Regan had carried out his own private investigation into who was behind the threats and the bribery that were making sure that certain convicted criminals never went to jail. When he believed that he had amassed sufficient evidence, he had reported what Brogan had told him to Chief Superintendent Joseph O'Malley, his Protected Disclosures Manager.

Garda O'Regan had been due to give his evidence to the ongoing Disclosures Tribunal at Dublin Castle, under the chairmanship of His Honour Mr Justice Peter McGuigan. Although very few details of his investigation had yet leaked out, it was rumoured that what he had discovered could be 'devastating'.

What worried Katie more than anything was who might have killed him. The tin whistle stuck into his neck strongly suggested what the motive might have been. But had he been murdered by members of a drug-dealing gang, who didn't want it known who was paying off the prison staff, or had it been prison officers themselves, or had it been gardaí? The worst scenario of all was that it might have been a combination of all three of them.

Katie laid her head down on the pillow again. The rain

continued to gurgle in the downpipe outside the window, and she felt as if it were raining inside her brain.

She laid her hand on Conor's bare shoulder, and he stirred, and said, '*Mmmph – you wait.*'

Eight

Gwenith unlocked the door of her second-floor flat and let Michael in. The narrow entrance corridor was made even narrower with all the coats that were hanging up, one on top of the other, and the floor was littered with worn-out boots and shoes, as well as letters that Gwenith hadn't bothered to pick up.

'You fancy a scoop, Tommy?' asked Gwenith, struggling out of her coat. She tried to hang it up but it fell to the floor and she left it there. Michael took off his puffa jacket and dropped it on top of it.

'There – go through, boy,' said Gwenith. 'Make yourself at home.'

Michael went into the living room and Gwenith switched on the lamps. This room was even untidier than the entrance corridor, and it smelled of stale cannabis and cooking fat. It was dominated at one end by a huge flat-screen Sony TV, while the rest of the room was furnished with a cream-coloured vinyl couch and two mismatched armchairs, one with wooden arms and the other with its seat cushion split open and its hairy brown stuffing hanging out. Michael couldn't stop himself from thinking of the slang phrase 'burst sofa' to describe a fat woman in crotchless panties.

The couch and the chairs were heaped with discarded sweaters and tights and dog-eared copies of *VIP* magazine and empty pizza boxes. In the centre of an oval coffee table there was a large glass ashtray crowded with bent cigarette ends, and the ashtray was surrounded by crumpled cigarette papers and lottery scratch cards and Tayto cheese-and-onion chocolate bar wrappers, as well as a hairbrush thick with blonde hairs.

Up at the windows, the lime-green loose-weave curtains were sagging because several of the nylon hooks had snapped. In the blackness outside, Michael could see the lights of the city centre winking at him, and he wished he were anywhere but here in this flat, with this woman.

'Here, park your arse,' said Gwenith, picking up an armful of clothes and magazines and dumping them behind the couch. 'I have Murphy's if you want it. I've noticed you always drink Murphy's.'

'Thanks a million,' said Michael, sitting down. 'Murphy's would be grand, thanks.'

'You're pure polite for a Hollyhill boy, I'd say,' Gwenith told him. 'And no studs in your ears, neither, and no tattoos, and a twenty-euro bazzer at least. That was why I fell for you the second I saw you. "That feen has class," I told myself. "Not like the usual wankers I go out with."'

'Well, I learned that you can get away with almost anything at all if you look smart and you speak proper,' said Michael.

Gwenith went to fetch the drinks, while Michael sat up straight on the couch and looked around him. He didn't like to lean back because the vinyl was so sticky and, when he did, half-hidden under a magazine he could see a large white bra, its withered wings stained yellow with sweat.

On the wall facing him hung a 3-D picture of Jesus, who gazed back at him in sorrow, one hand uplifted, as if he were saying *What are you doing here, my son, with this overweight bowsie?*

Gwenith came back and handed Michael a chilled bottle of Murphy's. In her other hand she was carrying a pint mug still half-filled with brownish foam.

'What you got there?' Michael asked her.

She cleared away more of the rubbish on the couch and sat down next to him, her thigh pressed hard against his. 'Johnny

Jump-up,' she said, meaning half-Guinness and half-cider. 'You wouldn't have a smoke on you, would you? I'm gasping.'

Michael reached into his jacket pocket for his packet of Carroll's cigarettes and took out two. He put both of them into his mouth, lit them, and then handed one to Gwenith. She took a deep drag and stared at him lustfully, smoke leaking out of her nostrils.

'You doing a line with anyone, Tommy?' she asked him, more smoke puffing out with every word. 'Come on, be honest with me. A good-looking ride like you.'

'I was seeing a girl in Dublin, like, but I haven't hooked up with anyone since I've been back here in Cork.'

She swallowed some of her drink and wiped her mouth on her sleeve. 'So there's nothing holding you back, then?'

No, nothing at all girl, except that you look like a hippopotamus in a miniskirt and you smell like the Halfway after closing time.

'Do you know the first person I ever had it with?' said Gwenith. 'Father Kennedy after catechism. I'd been acting the goat in class and he took me into his study and locked the door and said that I'd had the Devil in me that day and there was only one way to drive the Devil out. Because he was a holy man, with the Holy Spirit in him, he could inject the Holy Spirit into me, and that would get rid of the Devil and make me pure. Kind of like vaccination, do you know what I mean?'

'How old were you?' asked Michael, although he was immediately aware that he sounded more like a detective than a gurrier from Hollyhill, and so he quickly added, 'Them fecking pervy priests, they ought to cut their nuts off and feed them to the fecking nuns.'

'I was eleven,' said Gwenith. 'Father Kennedy told me that I mustn't breathe a word about it to anyone, even my dad and my mam and my brothers, otherwise it wouldn't work, and the Devil would jump back inside of me before you could say Christ on a bicycle.'

'Is he still alive, this priest?' asked Michael. 'If he is, I'll go round and beat the shite out of him for you.'

'Oh, I'd say he died years ago. In any case, like, what's the point of grieving over the past? Your virginity's like something you wish you'd never said. Once it's gone there's no way you can get it back.'

They sat and drank in silence for a while. They could hear a couple arguing in the next flat, and a loud bang like a chair being kicked over.

'The Dolans,' said Gwenith. 'Always scrapping them two. I don't know why she stays with him, he's such a gowl. Maybe we can drown them out with the bed springs.'

Michael was just finishing the last of his bottle of Murphy's, and he had been trying to think of a way to make his excuses and leave, or at least put off the inevitable. He raised his empty bottle and said, 'I could use a refill, if it's no trouble.'

She stood up, took the bottle from him and set it down on the coffee table. 'After,' she said. 'Let's work up a thirst first, shall we?'

She seized his hands and heaved him on to his feet, so that her breasts were pressing hard against his chest. Then she hooked her left arm around his head and pulled him down so that she could kiss him, and this kiss was deeper and longer and squelchier than the kiss they had shared in the back of Farry's car. Michael held on to her hips because he felt as if he were drowning and needed to cling on to something to stop himself from going under. When at last her tongue had finished squirming around in his mouth, and she gave him a final wet smacker, he gave her a helpless smile.

'Jesus, that was a shift and a half,' he said, trying to get his breath back.

'You just wait, boy. I haven't even started. By the time I'm finished with you, you'll feel like you've been slurped all over by the merrows.'

Yes, Gwenith, and if you're anything like them merrows, I'll probably have the benjy of herring off me, too.

She gripped his hand tightly and dragged him out of the living

71

room and into the bedroom, catching his foot on the curled-up carpet. The bed was unmade, with crumpled pillows and twisted sheets and a stained pink satin quilt lying on the floor at the foot of it. On either side of the bed there were small chests of drawers with lamps on, and each of them was cluttered with empty teacups and beer glasses, as well as overflowing ashtrays, more chocolate wrappers and, on one of them, two blue plastic tampon applicators.

A multi-coloured venetian blind was drawn down over the window, although some of its slats were bent or missing. On the wall over the curved wooden bedhead hung another 3-D religious picture in a plastic frame, the Last Supper, with a tattered poster for the Black Dog Saloon & Mezcaleria tucked underneath it.

Gwenith let go of Michael's hand and started to unbutton her purple cardigan. She tossed it across the bedroom and then she came up close to Michael and unfastened the buckle of his belt. She gripped him through his jeans and gave him a squeeze that made him wince, and then cough.

'What's the matter, Tommy?' she smiled, nuzzling his cheeks and tugging open his fly-buttons. 'You're not pining for a cold, are you? Come on, I'll soon warm you up, boy. I'll sweat it out of you in no time at all.'

His jeans dropped down to his knees, and Gwenith started to fondle him through his red-and-white striped boxer shorts.

'Glad to see you support the blood and bandages,' she said, meaning the red-and-white colours worn by the hurlers and footballers of the Cork GAA. 'Seamus used to be savage with a hurley, wouldn't you know, when he was at school. These days he only uses it to smash in people's heads.'

Despite the underlying threat in what Gwenith was saying, and her huge black Valkyrie-size bra pushing against him, Michael's penis began to stiffen, and as it did, Gwenith tugged at it even harder. She pulled down his boxer shorts and gripped his shaft tightly, rubbing it furiously up and down and digging her fingernails into his skin. With her left hand she played with his testicles as if they were billiard balls in a cotton bag.

'Come on, Tommy, aren't you going to take off my bra for me?' she breathed, right into his ear. 'I do expect a bit of reciprimocation, do you know what I mean?'

Michael blinked and winced again as she juggled his testicles with even more enthusiasm, as if that would encourage him.

'For sure, like,' he told her, and he reached around her pillowy shoulders until he found the three hooks-and-eyes at the back. He had always prided himself that he was good at deftly unfastening a woman's bra, but Gwenith's straps were straining against each other like the hawsers of a suspension bridge and it was impossible for him to use his usual sliding technique.

'Mother of God, Tommy,' she said, impatiently. She let go of his penis, batted his hands away, and reached around behind her with a deep grunt. Her bra dropped off, and her huge breasts tumbled out, soft and heavy and pendulous, with stiff purplish nipples and areolas as wide as beermats. Michael cupped them in the palms of his hands and couldn't help wondering how much they weighed.

'Oh, Tommy, you're a pure turn-on, you are, boy,' she breathed, and pushed him back on to the bed. After she had levered off his trainers, she wrestled his jeans and his boxer shorts down to his ankles, yanking them violently three or four times to pull them over his feet. She didn't bother to take off his beige cotton sweater or his shirt. She unzipped her black leather miniskirt and tugged down her laddered black tights. Under her bulging stomach, her vulva was waxed bare, but decorated with a sparkling array of red and green vajazzles. She climbed on top of Michael and the mattress bounced up and down like a trampoline.

'Here, don't you go all soft on me,' said Gwenith. Michael's penis was beginning to subside, so she rubbed it again and sucked it hard, leaving a crimson lipstick ring around it.

Once he had stiffened sufficiently, she took hold of him and guided him up inside her, tucking him into her slippery vagina with a frown of concentration on her face. As soon as she had inserted him, she leaned forwards and started to jolt up and down, her breasts swinging from side to side and brushing against his sweater. Every now and then she slobbered a wet kiss on his lips, and thrust her tongue into his mouth, but it wasn't long before she was panting, and drops of perspiration fell on to Michael's face as if it were starting to rain.

'Oh God oh Jesus you're amazing,' she gasped, and jolted harder and harder. She was so heavy that Michael's pelvis felt as if it were going to crack apart, and with every jolt her thighs let out a loud farting noise. All Michael could do was close his eyes and pray for this to be over.

'Oh God I'm coming. Holy Mary I'm almost there.'

To Michael's own surprise, he ejaculated, and only a few seconds afterwards Gwenith began to convulse, pressing her weight down even more oppressively with every convulsion, and snorting like a mare.

She collapsed on top of him, crushing all the breath out of him, but then she rolled sideways and lay next to him, wheezing and sweating and still trembling with the aftershocks of her orgasm.

'Oh I needed that,' she said at last, kissing his cheek. 'You don't know how long it's been since I've had a good flah.'

'Well I have to tell you that you're fantastic,' said Michael. He lay there for a while, stroking her shoulder, trying to work out how he felt. Should he be disgusted with himself, for being a coward and giving in to Seamus and Gwenith? Technically, he had cheated on Eithne, which made him feel even worse, although his climax had felt no more involving than masturbation. What worried him more was what might happen when it came to arresting Seamus for drug-smuggling and taking him to court. Would his lawyers try to suggest that Michael had deliberately seduced Gwenith in order to gain incriminating evidence?

Gwenith reached across and started to play with his penis again, digging her thumbnail under his foreskin.

'How about an action replay?' she said, and kissed him noisily on the ear.

'Well, it's tempting, like, but I really need to be out the gap.'

'What? I thought you were parching for another scoop. Go on, have another scoop and then we can have another rattle. You know you want to.'

'Yeah well, maybe. Okay.'

Gwenith heaved herself up from the bed and padded off naked to the kitchen to fetch some more drinks. Michael sat up, partly because the sheet smelled so sour, as if Gwenith hadn't changed the bed in weeks. He had thought about another possible consequence of having sex with her, apart from the legal complications. He hadn't worn a condom, and how could he be sure that she was on the pill? What if she fell pregnant? The thought of being the father of Gwenith's child was the stuff of nightmares. What if she were infected with some STD, and he accidentally passed it on to Eithne?

Gwenith came back carrying a cold bottle of Murphy's and a pint glass of Johnny Jump-up. She kissed him on the lips, and it tasted as if she had taken a quick swig of Guinness while she was mixing her drink.

'Could you fancy some Taytos to go with that?' she asked him, as she sat down close to him. Her thigh was still sweaty, but the sweat had chilled now. 'I have some Jonnie Onion Rings, too, but they've been open awhile and I think they've gone a bit soft. Like you, Tommy. How would you like a gobble? That would get you going again I'd say.'

Michael attempted to laugh, although it sounded as if he were choking. Gwenith lifted her glass and said, '*Dea-ádh leat cara daor!* Good luck to you, dear friend! May the crows never pick your haystack and may your donkey always be up the duff!' She took a swallow of her drink, wiped her mouth with her hand, sniffed, and then bent over and took his flaccid penis into her mouth.

After nearly five minutes of sucking, though, she sat up again.

'No, Tommy, it's no use, boy,' she told him. 'I can't get you chubbed up for love nor money. What you need is to sup up your drink and get yourself a combat nap. We can try again when you have your strength back.'

Michael didn't know what to say. There seemed to be no escaping this. He calculated that the best way he could avoid having to have sex with Gwenith again would be to feign sleep until she fell asleep, and then try to collect his shoes and his jeans and his puffa jacket and creep out of the flat without waking her. He could give her some excuse tomorrow about why it had been necessary for him to leave. He could say that he had eaten a burger at lunchtime that hadn't been cooked through, and it had given him a bad dose of the scutters.

He finished his bottle of Murphy's, while Gwenith sat beside him smoking a half burned-out joint that she had found in her ashtray. He didn't have to say much to her: she talked almost incessantly about herself and how she was training to be a masseuse and the holliers she had spent on Gran Canaria and how her boyfriend had left her feeling angry and humiliated because he had told her that he had only had sex with her for a bet with his friends, to see if he could 'pull the piggy'. 'Seamus went round to the garage where he worked and threw him through a window. Your man was lucky that he didn't shove the air hose up his jacksy and blow him up like a fecking balloon.'

'Right,' said Michael. 'I'll just catch myself some zees. See you in an hour or so.'

He turned over with his back to her and closed his eyes. Gwenith leaned over with her breast squashed against his shoulder and switched off his bedside lamp. Then she lay down herself, continuing to smoke what was left of her joint.

Half an hour passed, and Michael fell asleep for real. He dreamed that he was trying to dress himself to go out, but he had forgotten how to tie shoelaces. He could hear somebody in the next room calling to him to hurry up, but he didn't want to call out and admit that he wasn't ready, and why.

He was still trying to work out what he was going to do when the overhead light in the bedroom was switched on. He woke up instantly, and turned over, blinking.

Gwenith was standing in the doorway, wrapped in a shiny turquoise dressing gown. In her right hand she was holding up a Samsung phone. *His* phone, which had been zipped up in the pocket of his puffa jacket.

'No wonder I thought you was too smart for a Hollyhill boy,' she said, and her voice was shaking with anger. 'I'll bet you've never even been to fecking Hollyhill.'

'Gwenith… I can explain. That isn't even my phone.'

'Aye right, Tommy. Well, you're not Tommy, are you, and you flah'd me out of false pretences. You're Michael, that's your real name, and you're a fecking cop. That's going to look good, don't you think, in the *Echo*? "Cop pretends he's not a cop, so he can shag poor unsuspecting girl." Except the story won't be that at all. It'll be "Cop found floating in the Lee with a scaffolding pole up his arse".'

Michael rolled off the bed and picked up his boxer shorts and his jeans. 'Right,' he said. 'I'm out of here.'

He quickly dressed himself and put on his trainers, although he didn't tie the laces. Then he held out his hand and said, 'Give me the phone, Gwenith.'

'As if.'

'I said, give me the phone. Otherwise you're going to be in all kinds of shite.'

He approached her with his hand held out, but she stepped back into the corridor. As she did so, Michael heard a car pulling up outside the flats, and three car doors slamming, one after the other.

'It's not me who's going to be in all kinds of shite, boy,' said Gwenith. 'I rang Seamus as soon as I found your phone, and that's him now.'

'Give me the phone, or I'll take it from you by force if I have to.'

'There's no way, Tommy or Michael or whatever your name is. That would be assault, wouldn't it? And besides, I can't have you calling for your cop friends to come and save you, can I?'

There was a knock at the flat's front door, and Seamus called out, 'Gwenny? It's me. Is that bastard still there?'

Gwenith stared at Michael and called back, 'He's here all right, Seamus! And he can't wait to see you!'

Nine

Katie had set her alarm for six but when she opened her eyes she saw that it was seven-thirteen.

Foltchain was standing beside the bed with her chin resting on the patchwork bedcover, her feathery ears spread out on either side like Falkor the lucky dragon from *The NeverEnding Story*. Her eyes were wide and she was looking at Katie as if she expected to be invited into the bed with her.

Conor was standing behind her in his bathrobe with a mug of coffee, smiling.

Katie stroked Foltchain's head and fondled her ears. 'You're beautiful,' she said. 'But you're very bold. I needed to get into the station early this morning. I have a rake of work to get through.'

'Your health and your well-being come before work,' said Conor. 'And what difference will an hour make? You need as much sleep as you can get.'

'So who's going to be taking the lovely Foltchain for her walk this morning?' asked Katie.

'That'll be me today so,' said Conor. 'I had a call yesterday afternoon to find a missing spaniel in Carrigaline but his owner's sent me a text to say that he's found his way back home on his own. If every dog was that cute I'd be out of business.'

Katie sat up and Conor plumped up one of the pillows and put it behind her back. 'What would you like for your breakfast? I could make you some scrambled eggs if you'd like.'

'Just a couple of slices of toast with that Folláin gooseberry jam, that'll do me,' Katie told him.

'Your wish is my command,' said Conor. He set the coffee mug down on the bedside table and kissed her. 'I just want you to keep your strength up.'

'Do you have any plans for today, after you've taken this little darling for her walk?'

'I'll be going up to Tipp this morning to meet with that ISPCA inspector, Alice Cushley. I first met her when she was at Waterford, and she's dead set on putting an end to dog-fighting. I shouldn't be back too late.'

'Don't try to be challenging McManus directly, Conor. It's bad enough those poor dogs getting torn to pieces. I don't want anything like that to happen to you.'

'Come on, Katie. I've been in the pet detective business long enough to know how to take care of myself. I've been threatened by worse scummers than Guzz Eye.'

'I didn't know there *were* any – worse scummers than Guzz Eye, I mean.'

'You should meet some of the dog-breeders, in that case.'

'The breeders?'

'Oh sure, like. Not all of them. But there's a few who deliberately breed dogs with deformities to make them look appealing, and they make a mint out of them, I can tell you. They breed German shepherds with sloping backs and we call them "half-frog dogs". Then there's bulldogs and Pekineses and pugs with their noses so squashed they can barely breathe – or Basset hounds with legs so short and bellies so droopy they can't even run through a field to chase a rabbit. If you ask me, the bastards who breed those poor creatures should be locked up in the same boxes they use to give their dogs short-spine syndrome.'

Katie said, 'I sometimes wonder about human beings. I think to myself, "What have all the poor innocent animals who live on this planet ever done to deserve us?"'

'Just don't ask that question of a Limerick dog-breeder. You'll be lucky to escape with a clatter.'

'Well, be doggy wide with McManus, that's all I can say. Have I told you lately that I love you?'

Conor kissed her again, on the forehead. 'I'll make your toast for you.'

Foltchain looked up at him, licked her lips, and did her little step-dance.

'No toast for you, sweetheart,' Conor told her. 'Not to bother – I've bought you a packet of those Molly & Murphy dog biscuits. They're the peanut butter and bacon flavour, and they smell so good I could eat them myself.'

When Katie arrived at Anglesea Street, Moirin came in to tell her that Chief Superintendent MacCostagáin had been looking for her.

She was wearing her grey trouser suit today, with a black roll-neck sweater, and she wished now that she had chosen something more colourful, because the day was grey, too, and so gloomy that she had to switch on her desk lamp. Far from refreshing her, the extra hour's sleep that Conor had allowed her had made her feel even more weary than usual, and she would have done anything to drive straight back home, climb into bed and sleep until suppertime.

'Coffee?' asked Moirin.

'Yes, please, Moirin. And black. I'm not fit to wag this morning, for some reason.'

'Those criminals, they never let up, do they?' said Moirin. 'You'd think they'd give us a few days' peace.'

When she took her coffee along to Chief Superintendent Mac-Costagáin's office, she found him sitting under the window talking to Assistant Commissioner Frank Magorian. They were both looking serious, as if they were discussing funeral arrangements.

Frank Magorian was tall, several inches over six feet, with a long handsome face like George Clooney and black, slicked-back hair that was greying at the edges. At the age of fifty-three, he was one of the most qualified officers in the Garda with a formidable list of degrees in both criminology and business management, including the executive leadership programme for chiefs of police worldwide that was run by the FBI.

Katie liked her men to be well-groomed, like Conor, but she had always found Frank Magorian to be far too smooth, and not only smooth, but patronizing. He always spoke to her indulgently, as if to remind her that her appointment to detective superintendent had been part of a special drive by the Garda to promote women to more senior positions – lending them at least an outward appearance of sexual equality.

'Ah, DS Maguire,' said Frank Magorian. Denis MacCostagáin stood up, but he didn't. He looked at his watch and said, 'We were expecting you somewhat earlier, to be fair.'

'Traffic was a nightmare,' said Katie. 'Cement lorry turned over on the Dunkettle roundabout.' She didn't say anything about oversleeping.

'Well, now that you're here, do you want to hear the bad news or the worse news?'

Katie sat down opposite him and placed her cup of coffee on the window sill. A hooded crow landed on the ledge outside, rapped aggressively at the glass with its beak and then flew away. Katie had always considered the *caróg liath* to be omens of bad luck. When she was little, her grandmother had told her to throw a stone, a bone and a clump of turf at them. Depending on which way they flew off, that would tell her who she was going to marry, or if she was going to get married at all.

'The bad news is that Moira O'Regan, the wife of Garda Kieran O'Regan, was seriously injured in a car accident late last night. She had her two children with her, a boy and a girl, and the little girl was killed.'

'Mother of God,' said Katie. 'Where was this?'

'It was on the N30 at Ballyrue Cross in County Wexford.

The road is straight enough there, but it appears that she drifted across to the wrong side of the carriageway and collided head-on with a truck coming the other way. It's conceivable that she fell asleep at the wheel.'

'Which way was she heading?'

'East.'

'Were any ferry tickets found in the car? She could have been making her way to Rosslare.'

'Not as far as I know. But you can book online these days.'

'Where is she?'

'Wexford General. She's in a coma, apparently, with severe head and chest injuries.'

'What about her son?'

'Broken ribs and concussion, but otherwise okay. The little girl smashed right into the back of her mother's seat. In spite of her car seat, her neck was broken. She was only three years old.'

'This is just terrible. What's Mrs O'Regan going to go through when she wakes up and finds that her little girl's dead? That's *if* she wakes up, please God.'

Katie paused, looked at Denis MacCostagáin, and then back to Frank Magorian. 'All right, that's the bad news. What's the worse news?'

'The fellow who was decapitated at the Kilcully Cemetery, it *was* Garda O'Regan. The Technical Bureau took DNA from his toothbrush and his comb in his locker, as well as fingerprints.'

'I was fair certain it had to be him,' said Katie. 'What with that tin whistle stuck down his neck.'

'It seems fairly obvious that somebody didn't want him to give his evidence at the Disclosures Tribunal,' said Frank Magorian. 'The million-euro jackpot question is *who*. We haven't yet had the chance to see the full results of his investigation, but whoever killed him, this is going to put an H-bomb under the whole Garda establishment, not to mention the prison service. This could mean the end of the Garda as we know it.'

Katie said, 'I'll arrange for a warrant to search the O'Regan home as soon as I can. Garda O'Regan must have logged his evidence on his computer, or on paper somewhere. Who was going to represent him at the tribunal?'

'Well, clearly it was going to be his lawyer, but I don't know who that is.'

'I'll have DS Ni Nuallán contact Mr Justice McGuigan's office. Somebody there must know. And don't tell me his lawyer hasn't already had sight of all of his evidence.'

Frank Magorian stood up and buttoned up his jacket. 'I can't emphasize strongly enough that if and when you get access to Garda O'Regan's findings, whatever they are, you have to keep them strictly confidential. No leaks to the media, no gossip here at Anglesea, nothing. I don't want anybody setting eyes on them except for those involved in downloading the details of his investigation from his computer, or copying them from any documents he may have filed.'

'That may not be so easy, sir,' said Katie. 'Garda O'Regan's evidence may call for some immediate arrests, or at least some people hauled in for questioning under caution. After all, this is so much more than a potential scandal now, sir. This is a homicide enquiry, with huge political and criminal ramifications that I can only guess at. As you say, it could mean the end of the Garda as we know it.'

Frank Magorian came across and loomed over her, so close that Katie couldn't stand up. 'Whatever evidence Garda O'Regan claimed to have found, I insist that you send it to me first, and that you refrain from making any arrests or bringing anybody in for questioning until I've given you the green light. Is that absolutely clear?'

'I believe I have both the duty and the authority to arrest or question anybody I suspect of a major crime, sir, without having to seek your approval first.'

'Not in this case you don't, Kathleen, and believe me I can make life very awkward for you if you don't comply. One head has already rolled in Kilcully Cemetery. It could be that there are more to come. Don't let one of them be yours.'

With that, he stalked out of the office and left Katie and Denis MacCostagáin looking at each other with a variety of complicated expressions – annoyance, bewilderment, contempt, but maybe some *kṣānti*, too.

'Let's hope that Frank Magorian doesn't know more about this than he's letting on,' said Katie.

'Oh Mother of sweet divine perpetual divinity,' said Denis MacCostagáin, walking back to his desk and slumping down in his chair. 'I don't know who's worser – the criminals or us.'

Shortly after half past eleven, Detective O'Donovan came in, with Detective Scanlan. They both looked as tired as Katie felt, although Detective Scanlan was much more smartly dressed than usual in a pale blue chunky knit sweater and a short navy skirt, and her blonde hair was clipped back with a pale blue hairslide.

They had just driven back from Wexford, where they had been to see Moira O'Regan at the general hospital, and to talk to her doctors.

'She's still in a coma,' said Detective Scanlan. 'She had bleeding on the brain, but they've managed to drain it. They can't be sure yet if it's caused any neurological damage.'

'How's her little boy?'

'Riordan, his name is. Very poorly, but he's conscious and his ribs have been strapped up. He doesn't yet know that his sister has died.'

'How old is he?'

'Five.'

'Mother of God,' said Katie. 'Let's hope for his sake that his mother survives.'

'What's the plan now?' asked Detective O'Donovan.

'Well, now we know for sure that it *was* Garda O'Regan who

was murdered, we need to carry out a thorough search of his house, top to bottom. In particular we're looking for your man's computer, as well as any USBs or notebooks or phone records – but anything else unusual that you can find.'

'Right. I'll hop on across to the District Court and fix up a warrant.'

They were still talking when Kyna knocked at Katie's door. She came in and handed Katie the ripped-off page from a notepad.

'I've just come off the phone to His Honour's secretary,' she said. 'If I told you that she was unhelpful, that would be an understatement. But that's the barrister who was going to be representing Garda O'Regan at the tribunal – John Deneen. His office is on South Mall, which is no surprise at all.'

'Yes, I know John Deneen,' said Katie. 'I met him when was defending Brendan Daly. You remember Brendan Daly – he was the fellow who put in all those fraudulent tenders for the Lower Lee tidal barrier. What a cute hoor he was. Deneen got him off, though, which left me totally gobsmacked. If you can have a persuasive word with him, Kyna. He's bound to be holding a copy of O'Regan's evidence, and maybe he'll send us a PDF.'

'I'll do my best, ma'am. He might quote client confidentiality at me.'

'Oh, come on. O'Regan was about to give his evidence in public, so I don't think that holds much water. Besides, John Deneen's a senior counsel, and he doesn't want to be seen to be obstructing justice. If he gives you any bother, mind, tell him we'll apply for a warrant.'

'Yes, ma'am.'

Moirin came in. 'Sorry to interrupt you, ma'am, but Detective Markey says that Viona Caffrey's arrived, and he's ready in the interview room when you are.'

'Thanks, Moirin. Patrick – let me know as soon as you have a search warrant. Padragain – ring Dr Kelley would you, at CUH, and ask her what progress she's making with Jimmy Ó Faoláin and Garda O'Regan. In Jimmy Ó Faoláin's case we have no obvious motive and in Garda O'Regan's case we have more motives than you could shake a stick at. I really want to get both of these investigations moving forwards and we badly need some material evidence.'

Once Detectives O'Donovan and Scanlan had left, Katie tidied up her desk and then went to tell Moirin that she could take an early lunch if she wanted to.

As she went down in the lift to the interview room, she looked at herself in the mirror and she could see that look of certainty in her eyes that came from eleven years of trying to solve murders. Jimmy Ó Faoláin's killing appeared to have no motive at all, while Garda O'Regan's had far too many. But the possibility that either of them had been been killed by terrorists or disturbed housebreakers or jealous husbands was remote. One way or another, what had led to both of their deaths was money, and somebody's fear of losing it, or anger that they had lost it already.

Ten

When she entered the interview room, she found Detective Markey chatting to Viona Caffrey as if they were old friends who had met in a café.

Detective Markey stood up and pulled out a chair for Katie to sit down. Viona was looking far less tragic than she had yesterday, and she was wearing false lashes and eyeshadow, an indication that she wasn't expecting to cry. Katie couldn't help noticing that she was wearing a different coat this morning – camel-coloured, double-breasted and belted, and if Katie's guess was right, it was by Max Mara and easily cost as much as her pink coat, if not more.

'How are you going on, Viona?' Katie asked her.

'I still can't get it into my head that I'll never see Jimmy again,' said Viona. 'I was lying in bed last night and I could swear that I heard him laughing in the other room.'

'I asked you this yesterday, Viona, and I hope you don't mind if I repeat myself, but apart from the various gifts and clothes that he bought you, did Jimmy ever give you any cash?'

'I'm not a brasser.'

'I didn't mean that. I was simply wondering if he gave you any kind of allowance. Some wealthy men do, especially in a long-term relationship. Maybe not cash, but a credit card; or maybe he took out insurance in your favour, in case anything happened to him.'

'What are you trying to say?' Viona demanded, with an

aggressive twitch of her head. 'I had him murdered for some insurance payout? Is that it?'

'Of course not, Viona. But we're looking for a reason why anybody should have wanted to kill Jimmy, and because he had so many business dealings we have to consider that the motive might have been financial.'

'Well, you can think what you like, but Jimmy never paid me cash and he didn't take out insurance for me. All he ever did whenever one of his clients gave him any money was to take me out for a fabulous meal or a weekend away and buy me anything I wanted.'

'I expect you'll miss that, as well as missing him.'

'Last week he was going to buy me a rose gold and diamond bracelet that I'd seen in Keanes. I said I wanted something that would remind me of him for the rest of my life. Kind of like an eternity ring, do you know what I mean, except a bracelet. He said I'd have to wait a few days, though, because the auld wan who was supposed to be paying him hadn't coughed up yet.'

Katie said, 'Oh. Do you happen to know who this "auld wan" was?'

Viona shook her head. 'They was *all* auld wans, his clients. Well, most of them, anyway. They all had these pension pots, that's what he told me, and he invested their money for them so that it wasn't just lying idle in Our Lady Crowned Credit Union, making hardly no interest, or under their mattress.'

'So you'll never get the bracelet now, to remember him by?'

'No,' said Viona, and twitched her head again, and sniffed, as if to show Katie how grief-stricken she was. 'And it was so-o-o beautiful. All diamonds, set in rose gold, with more twinchy little diamonds set around them. Pavee they call that, although I don't know what it has to do with the knackers.'

'*Pavé*,' Katie corrected her. 'It has nothing to do with Travellers. It means small diamonds set close together, so that they look like a pavement.'

'Oh. But it was so beautiful. Now I can only go and look at it in Keanes' window, for as long as it's still there. But I reckon it's going to be there for a fair while, do you know, and I was thinking that maybe I could take a selfie with it. I tried it on before and maybe they'd let me try it on again, just for the picture.'

'You don't think that it's going to be snapped up tomorrow?' asked Katie, trying to sound nonchalant. 'How much are Keanes asking for it?'

'I wouldn't know for sure. It wasn't cheap. Jimmy said it cost a mammy sow, but he was still going to buy it for me.'

'All right,' said Katie. 'Let's go back to his business connections, and Rachmasach Rovers in particular. You told me yesterday that he never had trouble with any of his business partners – not that you knew of, anyway. Have you thought any more about that? Maybe there was some argument with somebody that you'd forgotten about.'

'No, not at all. Like I told you, Jimmy got along with everybody. I'll grant you, he could be like thorny wire when he couldn't get his own way, but it was all over and done with in an instant. He was never one to bear grudges, and I can't think of anybody who bore a grudge against him.'

'And there was nobody who gave him grief about the Rovers throwing matches? Well – *allegedly* throwing matches?'

'No, because I don't think they did. They lost Connie Cadogan, right, when he had that stupid car accident and broke his leg, and he was their best left centre forward, easy. Jimmy was as sore about that as anybody. You can't win games without a cracking good *lántosaí clé*, that's what he always said.'

Detective Markey said, 'You told me that when you arrived at Jimmy's house you saw nothing unusual at all – nobody making a bust to leave, like?'

'There was nobody. You never see a soul up at Woodhill Park anyway, do you know? You'd think that everybody who lived up there was dead.'

★

As Katie was zipping up her anorak, Bill Phinner came into her office, and this time he was holding up an evidence bag with six bullets in it.

'Dr Kelley sent these over first thing this morning,' he said. He sounded so miserable that Katie could almost have imagined that the pathologist had sent him notice that he was dying of emphysema. 'She dug them out of Jimmy Ó Faoláin last night.'

'And?' Katie asked him.

'And we were spot on, of course. These are all .357 Sig hollow points. All fired from the same weapon, more than likely a Sig Sauer P226. None of the bullet wounds caused fatal injury in itself, or even collectively, not in Dr Kelley's opinion. She knows it's controversial, but she reckons it was the hydrostatic shock that killed him.'

'Has she come up with anything else on him?'

'There's traces of cocaine in his system, and the indications from his lungs are that he usually smoked it. She also found benzoylecgonine in the little urine that he had left in his bladder, which would confirm that he's a user. But apart from being dead, he was fit as a butcher's dog.'

'How about the crime scene itself? Anything new?'

'Nothing at all. Whoever shot him either knew exactly what they're doing or else they didn't but somehow managed not to leave a trace. It might have been a ghost who shot him, I swear it.'

'Well, I've interviewed his girlfriend, Viona Caffrey,' said Katie. 'It seems to me that she had every reason for wanting him to stay alive, and not only because she had any feelings for him.'

'It couldn't have been a jealous ex?'

'We thought of that, of course, but Scanlan checked up on her former boyfriend and he wasn't even in the country at the time. He's a heating engineer and he's over in the UK working for some building company. His brother said that he was glad to see the back of Viona, and he would have wanted to buy Jimmy a drink, not shoot him. No... I think we're looking for somebody he was doing business with. Hopefully the fraud squad can sniff it out, but it could take weeks.'

They had found seventy-three books of accounts in Jimmy Ó Faoláin's office. All of them had been sent to the Garda National Economic Crime Bureau in Harcourt Square in Dublin, where forensic accountants would be combing through them for any signs of fraud. They would also be checking to see if he had been laundering money or financing any criminal or terrorist organizations. Even though she was convinced that the motive for his murder was financial, Katie wasn't optimistic that they would find anything incriminating. Jimmy Ó Faoláin had been an archetypal 'cute Cork hoor' and no matter what he was involved with, it was doubtful that he would have left any written evidence of it.

She left the station and walked across Parnell Bridge. The sky was a strange orangey-grey, with the sun just visible behind the clouds, and the south channel of the river was the same colour. The lighting was so unusual that she felt as if she were walking through the city in a surrealistic dream.

She went to Merchants Quay shopping centre first, and bought herself some new black tights in Marks & Spencer, as well as two ready meals, chicken supremes and smoked pork shoulder, for those nights when Conor had been out chasing missing pets all day and she was too tired to cook. Then she went upstairs to O'Briens sandwich bar and sat at a table on her own with a bowl of chickpea and chorizo soup with autumn kale. The shopping centre was busy, and there was a long line at O'Briens' counter, but despite the noise and the music she somehow felt isolated. She wondered if she had spent too much of her life judging other people, and picking on them simply for being human, and making stupid mistakes, like humans do.

On her way back to the station she walked along Oliver Plunkett Street and stopped at Keanes, the jewellers. She looked in the window but she couldn't see the diamond bracelet that Viona had been talking about, so she went inside.

A smart young salesman who looked like a young Dustin Hoffman came gliding up to her with his head tilted on one side and a welcoming smile. 'How can I help you today, madam?' he asked her.

'You were after displaying a diamond bracelet in the window – rose gold, with large diamonds all the way around it, and smaller *pavé* diamonds set all around them.'

'Oh, yes,' said the salesman. 'A customer wanted to take a look at it this morning, so I still have it here under the counter.'

He went around behind the brightly lit glass showcases and produced the bracelet, setting it down on a small green velvet cushion. 'It's a wonderful piece. Handmade locally here in Cork city. Is it for yourself?'

'I wish,' said Katie. She picked up the bracelet and examined it closely. 'This is the only one you have like it?'

'It's the only one there is,' the salesman nodded. 'Not only that, it's unique.'

Katie produced her ID. 'Detective Superintendent Maguire from Anglesea Street Garda station,' she told him.

The salesman stared at her, horrified. 'Oh my Lord! This isn't stolen, this bracelet, I can vouch for that! We had it direct from Aoife Tubridy. She has her workshop on Rutland Street. She's a wonderful, wonderful jeweller. You can go and ask her about it if you like.'

'Don't worry,' said Katie. 'I know it isn't stolen. I'm just interested to know if Mr Ó Faoláin had been in to see it. You know Mr Jimmy Ó Faoláin, don't you?'

'Of *course*, who doesn't? And I heard about him being murdered. That was devastating. He was a regular customer, one of our best. He'd be in here maybe two or three times a month looking for something – earrings, necklaces, bracelets.'

'But did he come to look at *this* bracelet?'

'He did, yes. His girlfriend fetched him in. She'd looked at it before and she wanted to show it to him.'

'And what did he say?'

'He asked how much it cost, and when I told him, he said that, sure, she could have it, but she'd have to wait a while. She looked fierce disappointed, I have to tell you, and I saw them outside in the street after, having one hell of a row. She was really giving out.'

'So how much does it cost?'

'Thirty thousand euros, on account of the diamonds being such good quality. But I said I might go down to twenty-eight, him being such a good customer.'

Katie slipped the bracelet on to her wrist and turned it this way and that, so that it sparkled. She loved it, but she couldn't see Conor's earnings as a pet detective stretching to €28,000, just for a bracelet, no matter how much he swore that he loved her.

She walked back to Anglesea Street. A thin bearded man in a floppy beret was sitting cross-legged on the pavement playing a tin whistle and she dropped €5 into his mug. What interested her now was that Jimmy Ó Faoláin had offered to buy Viona the bracelet after he had been paid by some 'auld wan'. Surely the 'auld wan' would have been giving him the money so that he could invest it for her. That was Jimmy's principal business, after all. She certainly wouldn't have been giving it to him so that he could treat his air-stewardess girlfriend to a piece of expensive jewellery.

The question was: how many more pensioners had Jimmy Ó Faoláin been fiddling out of their money to keep up his lavish lifestyle, and was he ever expecting to pay them back, along with the interest they should have been earning? And even more to the point: had any of them found out what he was up to?

Eleven

Alice Cushley was waiting for Conor by the small brick fireplace when Conor came through the door of the Kickham House pub on Tipperary's main street. It was early, so the bar was almost empty, and the smoke from lighting the fire hadn't yet cleared, which gave the interior a hazy look, like a 1950s colour photograph.

'Alice, sorry I'm late,' said Conor. 'Ridiculous roadworks at Ballyporeen. What can I get you to drink?'

'A coffee would be grand, thanks. With milk.'

Alice was a large woman, almost as tall as Conor, with a round face and slightly bulging eyes, and her brunette hair was pinned up in a messy fishtail bun. She was wearing a black ISPCA anorak and baggy black boots. She looked as if she would stand no nonsense from anyone, and she didn't. Conor had liked her since the day he had first met her because she was unrelentingly brave in the face of farmers who had been mistreating their heifers, or pet shop owners who had been keeping their animals cramped in tiny cages. Even more than that, she was as dedicated as he was to seeing dog-fighting brought to an end.

Conor came back from the bar with a glass of whiskey and water and sat down opposite her.

'A little early for that, isn't it?' Alice smiled.

'I don't think so. Not if I'm going to be facing up to Guzz Eye McManus.'

'I honestly don't know what you think you can achieve, Conor.

The number of times we've threatened him with prosecution, but he doesn't give a tinker's.'

'Listen – the charges against him for that dog-fight at Cappamurra were dropped, but I want him to be aware that we're not going to forget him. I also want to tell him straight to his fat ugly face that I intend to bring a private prosecution.'

'I'm sorry, Conor, but I think he'll just laugh. That's if he doesn't get a couple of his thugs to beat the dust off you.'

The barman brought over Alice's coffee, and Conor watched her as she stirred milk into it, and dropped in two brown sugar cubes. Then he said, 'We have a rake of evidence still from Cappamurra – videos and witness statements. If I can take some more videos today, that will prove to the court that Guzz Eye is still at it – still mistreating and torturing dogs and making illegal money out of it, and that he isn't repentant in the slightest.'

Alice pulled a face. 'If you're prepared to take the risk, then fair play to you, Conor, but I'd advise against it myself. Guzz Eye knows where you live, and what he had done to Barney he could easily have done to you.'

'No, Alice, I'm not scared of him and I'm going to do this. You said he's holding some practice fights all day today.'

'That's right. A guard I know overheard one of his gang blowing about it yesterday in Billy Foley's bar in Cashel. From what he could hear, it's in a back field of Keegan's farm just north of Ballynonty.'

'I'm not even sure where that is, to be truthful with you.'

'Head east up Palmer's Hill past the Ballyknock halting site and keep going. You'll cross over the M8 and after that it's about fifteen kilometres to Ballynonty. Take a left when you reach the crossroads and Keegan's farm is about two kilometres up the road there.'

'Okay. I have you. Thanks, Alice.'

Alice reached over and laid her hand on his. 'Be wide, Conor. I'm serious. I don't want to be sitting in church next week listening to your eulogy.'

'A life is a life, Alice, and as far as I'm concerned a dog's life is just as important as a human's life. You don't kill what God created for amusement or money.'

He finished his whiskey. After that he stood up, leaned over and kissed Alice on the cheek. When he stepped out into the chilly air on Main Street, he could smell burning logs on his coat.

Conor drove east on Palmer's Hill but he went no further than the Ballyknock halting site, where Guzz Eye McManus had his mobile home. He parked his Audi in front of a rusty farm gate next to the entrance to the halting site, and then climbed out, lifting a dark green rucksack out of the boot.

He knew that if there were any Travellers around this could turn out to be nothing more than a reconnaissance mission, but as he climbed the steeply sloping curve that led into the site, he could hear nothing but the swishing of traffic on the M8 and the breeze blowing across the surrounding fields, soft and persistent, like a man trying to blow a reluctant fire alight. No children playing, no women laughing.

He reached the row of white-painted mobile homes, shielded from the road by high concrete fencing and bushes. Two SUVs were parked at the end of the site, a Range Rover and a Toyota Land Cruiser, and two sway-backed horses were steadily munching the grass beside them, but there was nobody in sight. He guessed that the children were still in school and that the adults had all gone off to watch the dog-fighting at Ballynonty.

He walked up to Guzz Eye McManus's huge white mobile home, the second one in line, and climbed the concrete steps to the door. The window next to the door was partially open, but the blinds were all drawn and there was no sound from inside. Just to make sure there was nobody home, though, he knocked and waited to see if there was any response.

He looked around. The grey clouds were moving slowly over-head and apart from the two sway-backed horses and five crows sitting on the telephone line, he could have been the only living creature on the planet. For once in his life, he could believe that God was on his side.

He set down his rucksack and lifted out a two-litre Tanora bottle. Taking a last precautionary look around, he unscrewed the cap, eased open the window a few centimetres further, and carefully poured the contents inside. He could hear the liquid splashing on the floor inside.

When the bottle was empty, he took out a book of matches, tore one off and struck it. When it flared up, he used it to light all the rest of the matches and quickly dropped the whole book through the gap in the window.

He waited for a few seconds, in case the matches had fizzled out, but then acrid brown smoke began to leak out of the sides of the door, and he could see a flickering orange light behind the blinds. He picked up his rucksack, went back down the steps, and walked quickly down the slope to his Audi, trying not to look as if he were trying to get away from the halting site as fast as possible. He couldn't see any witnesses, but he knew from some of Katie's cases that you could never be sure.

He climbed back into the driver's seat and started the engine. He hesitated for a few seconds to see if any smoke was rising from behind the fences, but when he saw none, he released the handbrake and sped away. He drove as fast as the narrow roads would allow, taking a sharp left northwards, and then joining the M8 motorway at the next junction.

As he approached Cloghabreeda he saw a Garda patrol car up ahead, and he slowed down to a legal 120 kph. The last thing he wanted was to be caught speeding southwards from Ballyknock only ten minutes after Guzz Eye McManus's mobile home had been set ablaze, especially since his hands still smelled of petrol.

He was trembling with adrenaline, and he slapped the steering wheel with malicious delight at the thought of Guzz Eye returning from his day of dog-fighting to find that everything he owned was burned to ashes. With any luck, all his cash had been stashed in his mobile home, too.

After a while, though, Conor began to calm down. By the time he reached the junction with the N25 and turned towards Cobh, he felt deeply serene – almost saintly. St Conor of the Martyred Canines. All of the dogs that Guzz Eye McManus had so brutally killed had at last been given their revenge, and he could imagine that they were howling their appreciation in Heaven.

Twelve

Katie was climbing the station steps when her iPhone pinged and she saw that she had a text message from Detective Sergeant Begley. *Urgent I speak 2U.*

He was waiting for her when she walked through her office door, standing by the window with a tight expression on his face. He had lost weight lately, although his blue shirt still bulged over his waistband and his red braces hung down behind him like a toddler's reins.

'What's the form, Sean?' Katie asked him, hanging up her coat.

'You won't believe this. I've just had a phone call from Seamus Twomey.'

'Stop the lights! Seamus Twomey? Serious?'

'He didn't try to disguise who he was or why he was ringing. Somehow he's sussed out that Michael Ó Doibhilin was working undercover. He says he's holding him hostage. Well – "protective custody", that was the way he put it.'

Katie said, 'Mother of God. He hasn't hurt him, has he?'

'He said that he's persuaded Michael to tell him how much he's found out, and he wasn't backwards in telling me what it was, either. That fentanyl coming in through Rosslare and all the spice and crack and biscuits that his dealers are out peddling for him in discos every night. "Persuaded" – sweet lamb of Jesus! Knowing Michael, I'd say that Twomey probably had to mangalate him to get that out of him.'

Katie sat down at her desk. 'Have we managed to trace the call yet?'

'We're working on that now, but Twomey must have known that we could pinpoint where he was ringing from, and that we'd be audio logging whatever he said. Clearly he didn't care. This wasn't your anonymous threat by any means.'

'So what is he demanding, as if I couldn't guess?'

'We turn a blind eye to any drugs that he's bringing in and we don't harass his dealers in the nightclubs. Provided we leave him in peace, Michael will stay safe and well. Those were his exact words.'

'Did he give you any idea of how long he's going to hold him?'

Detective Sergeant Begley shook his head. 'I asked him that but he didn't answer. But think about it. He'll only hold him until he's of no further use to him, won't he? And then there's not a chance that he'll let him go free. He'll have too much incriminating evidence.'

'God protect him,' said Katie. 'He's only twenty-six.'

'What's the plan, then?' asked Detective Sergeant Begley. 'This is going to take fierce careful handling, this is. They could be holding Michael anywhere at all, like, even up north, and we'd only have to stop one of Twomey's shipments or haul in one of his dealers, even if we did it accidental, and that could mean a bullet in the back of his head. I don't want to be attending Michael's wake, ma'am, let me tell you that for nothing.'

'Have you told anybody else about this?' asked Katie.

'Only the officer tracing the call, and I doubt if he'll realize what Twomey's on about. If you didn't know that Michael was undercover, and what Twomey was up to, not much of what he said makes a whole lot of sense.'

'For the time being, then, Sean, don't say a word to anybody. And I mean *anybody*. I'll tell Superintendent Pearse to hold off on all arrests of suspected drug-dealers – not only Twomey's – and I'll personally make sure that the customs officers at Rosslare don't confiscate any of Twomey's shipments of opioids.'

'They'll be after knowing why, surely?'

'Don't worry, I'll think of some story. I have to work out a way of finding out where they're keeping Michael without Twomey picking up even a sniff of what we're doing.'

Katie didn't add that Anglesea Street Garda station was leakier these days than an old Kinsale fishing boat. Again and again, the media were being tipped off about supposedly secret operations long before they could be put into action, and once the media knew the criminals knew, too. Only last month a raid that she had organized on brothels in Grafton Street had to be cancelled because reporters from the *Examiner* and the *Echo* and Cork 96FM were all waiting on the corner of South Mall when the gardaí patrol cars arrived.

She was convinced that two or three uniformed gardaí had been passing out confidential information, in order to make themselves a little extra grade. But even though she had only scant evidence to back it up, she also suspected that several higher-ranking officers might have a vested interest in thwarting some of the stings that she had set up.

She had sensed a palpable tension in Anglesea Street ever since the Disclosures Tribunal had opened and she was sure that corruption was one of the reasons – or at least the granting of dubious favours. And the whistle-blowing was far from over. Among several other informants, a Cork sergeant called John Lacey was due to give evidence to the tribunal on Monday morning, and he was going to testify that twenty-seven prosecutions for car theft had all been quietly dropped, supposedly for 'insufficient evidence'.

Sergeant Lacey was on indefinite leave for the time being, as Garda O'Regan had been, mostly because of the abuse he had been given by his fellow officers. One of them had even tied a dead rat to the door handle of his house. But even Superintendent Pearse had called him a 'bit of a sneaky snake'.

Detective Sergeant Begley snapped his braces back up over his rounded shoulders, although one of them immediately slipped off again. 'Okay, ma'am – however you want to play it,' he said. 'But don't hesitate to let me know if you need any backup. There's a couple of uniforms I know to be sound.'

'Thanks, Sean,' said Katie. It was obvious that he understood why she wanted Detective Ó Doibhilin's abduction kept under wraps, at least for now.

Detective Sergeant Begley was about to leave when one of the gardaí from the communications centre knocked at the door, a young bespectacled officer with his ginger hair shaved up at the sides and his bright scarlet ears sticking out.

'Sorry to interrupt you, ma'am. DS Begley – I have that location you wanted, sir. Seamus Twomey's call was made from the Halfway Bar and Lounge on Baker's Road in Gurra, right by St Mary's Health Campus. I have the number, too, and Twomey's billing address, on St Rita's Avenue.'

'The Halfway Bar and Lounge?' said Katie. 'That was where Michael went every night to meet up with Twomey and Quinn.'

'I know it,' said Detective Sergeant Begley. 'After the Flying Bottle they reckoned it was the second roughest pub in Cork, and now that the Flying Bottle's shut down, it must be the first roughest.'

'Still, that gives me the germ of an idea,' said Katie. 'Where there's a bar there's drink, and where there's drink there's drunken men, and what do drunken men like most?'

'A kebab?'

'Oh, come on, Sean. They like pretty, slutty girls. And craic.'

'I think I'm beginning to see where you're going with this,' said Detective Sergeant Begley.

Katie said, 'Let me give this some thought. Meanwhile, let's say a prayer for Michael, that the Lord keeps him safe from harm.'

'Amen to that,' said Detective Sergeant Begley, and crossed himself.

*

Kyna said, 'Isn't there anybody else who can look like a slut?'

Katie couldn't help smiling. 'There is, sure. There's Padragain Scanlan, and Aíbhilin Sheónín. But you make the best slut by far. Come on, Kyna, when you played barmaid up at the Templemore Tavern, you were a slut in a million.'

'Oh, yes. And nearly got myself killed.'

'I'm not pretending this isn't going to be dangerous, Kyna. Seamus Twomey is a header. But I can't think of any other way in which we're going to be able to find out where Michael's being held.'

'Can't we tail the members of Twomey's gang when they leave the bar at closing time, and see where they go?'

'There's two problems with that. A – we don't know all the members of *Fola na hÉireann* by sight, and – B – we'd have to arrange it with Superintendent Pearse, and that would mean that every uniform in the station would get to know what we're up to. It would only take one of them to tip off Twomey and we might just as well sign Michael's death certificate.'

'We're tracking his phone, though?'

'The phone that he used to ring Sean, of course – but all we've picked up so far is a call to his garage about his car being serviced and another to his ma about taking her out to Blarney for Sunday lunch. He obviously doesn't use that phone for any of his drugs business, or anything to do with his political activities, such as they are.'

'He's some bottle, though, hasn't he?'

'That's what worries me, do you know? He's kidnapped a Garda detective and made it clear that he'll do him some harm if we don't let him carry on with his drug-dealing. But what really gets me is that he seems to be convinced that he's immune. So why is he so confident that we can't touch him? That's why I want to keep a tight lid on this, at least for now.'

Her iPhone played *Siúil A Rún* and it was Conor.

'Katie? Oh, glad I caught you. I've just had a call from Domnall at Gilabbey.'

'How's Barney? Oh, God. Don't tell me he's worse.'

'Totally the opposite, darling – totally the opposite. He's making fantastic progress and we should be able to fetch him home in a couple of days. He won't be running along the beach for a while, or jumping over any fences, but Domnall thinks he'll be making a full recovery in a month or so.'

'Oh, that's wonderful news, Con. Thanks. How did it go with Guzz Eye?'

'Not the way I'd hoped, to be honest with you. He had so many heavies around him that I couldn't get anywhere near him. But I'll tell you all about it later. I have some more good news, though.'

'That's great. But why don't you save it till this evening? I'm tied up with Kyna at the moment.'

'You're tied up with Kyna? That sounds interesting. Maybe I should come and join you.'

'Be whisht, will you? I'm going to see the father on my way home but I shouldn't be too late.'

'Give the old fellow my regards, won't you?'

Katie put down her phone and said to Kyna, 'That was Conor. Barney's much better and I should be able to have him home soon.'

'Oh, that's grand. I'm happy for you. And I'm happy for Barney, too, the poor dote.'

'By the way, any progress with John Deneen?' asked Katie.

'I heard from his secretary about an hour ago. He says that if we can give him written assurance that the body has been positively identified as Garda O'Regan he's prepared to send over a copy of the evidence that he was going to present to the Disclosures Tribunal. I've already arranged that with Bill Phinner.'

'Frank Magorian has told me that he wants to see the evidence first.'

'Oh, does he? Well, how will he know if you've taken a sneaky peek? Eyes don't leave tracks, do they?'

Katie couldn't help smiling. Whatever he had said, there was nothing that Assistant Commissioner Magorian could do to stop her reading the evidence before she handed it over to him, and of course he knew that, but he had been giving her a warning that she shouldn't act on it without his say-so, regardless of what it contained.

Kyna said, 'Listen – if you want me to start at the Halfway Bar this evening I'll go back to my flat right now and get myself changed into my slut's uniform. I'll come back after so that you can have a quick sconce and make sure I look slaggy enough.'

'I can't wait.'

Kyna looked around to make sure that Moirin's door was closed, then she came up to Katie, touched her cheek gently with her fingertips and kissed her on the lips. They stood close together for a moment, looking into each other's eyes.

'I'm so pleased about Barney,' said Kyna. 'I know what he means to you. You know – more than just being your dog.'

Katie smiled and gave her a quick peck, and then said, 'Okay. I'd better get on. I have to go over to CUH now with Patrick and Padragain to see Dr Kelley. I should be back here around three.'

'You're going to see Garda O'Regan? Don't eat anything first.'

Being surrounded by cadavers hadn't put Dr Kelley off eating. She came out of her office at the far end of the morgue with her mouth full, brushing hand-pie crumbs from the front of her pale green gown.

She was a short, tubby woman with a round face and round glasses and a double chin and bushy, mannish eyebrows. The hair that curled out from underneath her surgeon's cap was brown and frizzy, like horsehair. Despite that, Katie had often thought that with her eyebrows plucked and some bright red lipstick she could look reasonably pretty, like an old-fashioned china doll.

'Sorry,' she said, still chewing. 'I had no breakfast and I was starved.'

Katie gave her the faintest of smiles. The smell in the mortuary always made her feel nauseous. She knew that the bodies were embalmed with deodorizing cavity fluid, which stiffened the tissues and killed the *clostridium perfringens* bacteria, but she was still sure that she could detect the foetid odour of human decomposition. She wondered sometimes if her nose had a memory, and what she was smelling was all the dead bodies that she had come across during her career in the Garda.

Outside, the clouds had cleared and the day had become unexpectedly bright, so that shafts of sunlight were shining down from the mortuary's clerestory windows, giving it the appearance of a chapel rather than a morgue.

Dr Kelley called out to her assistant, 'Masks, please, Pratima!' and a young Indian woman came over and handed surgical masks to Katie and Detectives O'Donovan and Scanlan. Then Dr Kelley led them across to the trolley where Garda O'Regan was lying, covered by a green sheet.

'No sign of his head yet?' she asked, as she lifted the sheet and folded it down to Garda O'Regan's waist. His skin was now a waxy yellow, like tallow, and covered in purplish bruises. Although Dr Kelley had made incisions to release the gases in his abdomen, his stomach was still swollen.

Katie said, 'His head? No. It's probably buried in a bog somewhere, or floating down the Lee. Who knows?'

'If you come around and take a look at his neck, you'll see that I've restored it more or less to its original shape,' said Dr Kelley.

They all gathered around the top of the trolley so that they could peer into the gristly red mess of Garda O'Regan's severed neck. Dr Kelley had inserted a thin adjustable ring of transparent celluloid just inside it, so that the flat platysma muscles at the front of the neck didn't droop downwards.

'That looks like one of them plastic rings they put in a new shirt collar,' said Detective O'Donovan.

'Very observant of you,' said Dr Kelley. 'That's exactly what it is, and it was ideal for the purpose. Once your man's neck was approximately back to the configuration that it was when he still had his head on him, I was able to photograph it and print out a 3-D model and examine the edges of the wound and his severed vertebra.'

Katie leaned over so that she could see the back of Garda O'Regan's neck. Immediately below the point where his head had been taken off, there were three parallel cuts, one above the other. They were ragged and shallow, each about seven centimetres wide.

'What are those?' she asked. 'Hesitation marks?'

'Not so much hesitation as kickback,' said Dr Kelley. 'I've seen multiple wounds like this dozens of times, but mostly you find them on the front left thigh, or the back of the left hand, legs, or the left side of the face. They're entirely consistent with a chainsaw injury. With a leg injury, that's when somebody's lost their grip on their chainsaw, or cut through a branch quicker than they expected. With a facial injury, that's when the chainsaw's jerked upward and back, and it's usually lucky if the user doesn't take his own eye out, as well as chopping off half of his forehead.'

'And in this case?'

'In this case, we know that your man was sitting upright when he was beheaded, and I'd say without any doubt that his assailant was standing behind him with a chainsaw. He would have had to be holding it horizontal, which in any event would have made it fierce awkward to keep steady. When he started to cut into your man's neck the saw kicked back before he was able to get a firm grip on it and cut in deep. I could tell from the 3-D model that the chainsaw teeth were worn and blunt, and that the rakers had been filed too low. A sharp chainsaw with its rakers set to the right depth will almost *slide* itself into a log – or in this instance, into the victim's neck. But if your teeth are worn and your rakers are set too low they'll be after setting up excessive vibration and then you'll have the risk of a kickback or three. I'm sure that's what happened here.'

'You've informed Bill Phinner of this?'

'Oh, yes. I've sent him all my data and his technical experts should be printing out a model for themselves.'

Katie stood for a few moments by Garda O'Regan's headless body, and then she said, 'All right. Are you finished with him now? When can we release him to his family?'

'As soon as you like now. I've no more tests to run on him. He was clear for drugs and alcohol. His cholesterol level was a little high, but his heart and his liver and his kidneys were all in good shape. I just need to find out from his family which funeral directors to send him to.'

Dr Kelley draped the green sheet back over the body. Katie looked across at Detectives O'Donovan and Scanlan, and she didn't have to say out loud that funeral arrangements for Garda O'Regan might prove to be problematic, considering that he was about to appear before the Disclosures Tribunal with evidence about Garda corruption. A state funeral with full honours might be out of the question. Apart from anything else, they had not yet announced publicly that the headless body had been identified.

'How about Jimmy Ó Faoláin?' Katie asked Dr Kelley. 'Are you all finished with him?'

'I am, yes. We'll be packing him off to Jerh O'Connor's this afternoon.'

'Oh, well. At least *he* should be having a lavish send-off.'

As they drove back to Anglesea Street, Katie said, 'I'll bet you money that we find the motive for Garda O'Regan's killing buried somewhere in his tribunal evidence.'

'I don't like to think about the implications of that,' said Detective O'Donovan. He blew his horn impatiently at the car in front of him, which hadn't yet moved even though the traffic lights had turned to green. 'What's he doing, the gowl, saying a novena?'

'No, I don't like to think about what it means, either,' said Katie. 'If we can't trust ourselves, who can we trust?'

★

Bill Phinner texted her to tell her that he had an update for her, so before she returned to her office, Katie went down to the Technical Bureau laboratory. Bill was standing next to the water tank with ear mufflers and plastic goggles on, supervising the shooting of bullets from a Sig Sauer pistol that had been found in a skip earlier that morning by Horgan's Quay. As Katie walked in, there was a muffled bang, followed by the bubbling sound of a bullet being slowed by the water in the tank.

Bill Phinner took off his ear mufflers and his goggles and led Katie back to his office.

'That's not the same model of gun that shot Jimmy Ó Faoláin, is it?' Katie asked him.

'No, ma'am. That's a 9mm P238 with a double action Kellerman trigger. I'm thinking that it might be the weapon used in that shooting in Mayfield last month, although I can't imagine why anybody should chuck it away in a skip.'

'I've just been to the mortuary to see Garda O'Regan's remains,' said Katie. 'Dr Kelley seems to be sure that he was beheaded with a chainsaw.'

'No question about that,' Bill Phinner told her. 'You saw the kickback wounds on the back of his neck, I expect. The way the skin and the muscle and the vertebrae were cut through, you only see that pattern with a chainsaw. It was what they call a full complement chain, with a pitch of 8mm and a gauge of 1.5mm. That's fairly standard but you never know your luck. You might catch somebody red-handed, with Garda O'Regan's DNA still stuck in their chainsaw teeth.'

'The chances of which are just about nil. As you know, we're still holding back on announcing whose body it was, so we can't even appeal for witnesses.'

'Well, I might have some slightly more encouraging news for you,' said Bill Phinner. He reached across his desk and picked up a transparent evidence bag with the tin whistle in it that had been removed from Garda O'Regan's severed neck. 'Whoever inserted this whistle left no fingerprints, but would you believe that they couldn't resist having a quick tootle on it before they pushed it into his trachea.'

'Mother of God. I wonder what they played.'

'Well, we can't tell that, but we found traces of dried saliva on the mouthpiece and we sent the DNA sample up to Dr O'Donnell at the FSI this morning for a rapid analysis.'

'Any luck?'

'No... she couldn't find any existing match on the database, I'm sad to say. But if and when you do haul in a suspect, at least we'll have the DNA profile all ready for you.'

'That's something, thanks,' said Katie. 'To be honest with you, though, I don't know when that's going to be. Right now we seem to be coming up against nothing but brick walls.'

'Every brick wall has a way around it, DS Maguire, or a ladder to climb over it. And there's something else about this whistle, too, which is the main reason I wanted to see you. You remember I was telling you about that old fellow I took on last month to help out with the fibre analysis—'

'The one who came out of retirement?'

'That's him. Brendan Mulvihill. He used to play the hammered dulcimer in a céili band and when he saw that tin whistle this morning he reckoned he had a fair idea where it might have come from. It's nickel alloy with a wooden head and he said it was definitely handmade. He could think of only two or three shops in Cork where you could buy one, and most likely it came from the Music Market on the Old Blackrock Road.'

'Now that *is* a useful piece of information. Thank you, Bill. I'll have Padragain Scanlan go around there right away.'

'I love puggalizing cases like this,' said Bill Phinner, as another dull pistol shot echoed around the laboratory. 'They're so much more satisfying when you finally crack them, don't you think?'

Katie didn't know what to say to that. She would have preferred a world in which nothing was stolen and no humans or animals ever got hurt – a world in which there were no crimes to solve, no matter how easy.

Kyna was waiting for her when she returned to her office. She was perched on the edge of Katie's desk, wearing a short, strawberry-coloured wig, a sparkly gold sleeveless top, and crimson yoga pants. She had sprayed herself with so much Estée Lauder SpellBound that Katie had only breathed it in twice before she sneezed violently.

'Slutty enough?' asked Kyna.

'Jesus, Kyna. If there was a national award for Irish Slut of the Year, you'd win it hands down.'

Kyna slid off the desk and turned around, showing how tightly the yoga pants clung to her bottom. 'We should take a selfie,' she said.

'I don't think so. Somebody would be bound to hack it and then it would probably go viral. But listen to me, Kyna. I know you're wide about Twomey and Quinn, but please, please be careful. If they find out who you are, I could be losing the both of you – you and Michael.'

Kyna laid her hands on Katie's shoulders. 'I'm not going to kiss you,' she said. 'This lip gloss is way too sticky. But I will when this job is over, and that's a promise.'

Thirteen

On her way home Katie drove down to Monkstown to see her father. His house was visible across the river from her own front gate and she felt guilty that she hadn't been visiting him often enough. The trouble was that she always felt so exhausted at the end of the day. She had been overwhelmed with new cases lately, and more cuts in her budget had left her seriously short of experienced detectives.

At least her father had Blaithin taking care of him these days, the cook from the Roaring Donkey pub on Orilia Terrace, in Cobh. Apart from feeding him well, she ironed his shirts and hoovered his carpets and one of her sons came by now and then with his yappy mongrel to make sure that his garden was tidy.

When Katie parked in front of his large, green-painted Victorian house, she found that there was another car parked there already, a white Toyota Prius. The front door opened as she climbed the steps to the porch, and there was her younger sister Clodagh, smiling, with her arms spread wide.

'Clo! What a nice surprise! How's it going on?'

Clodagh gave her a hug and a kiss. She could have been Katie's twin, although she was slightly taller and had inherited their father's sharp, distinctive nose. She was wearing a thick beige cardigan with a floppy shawl collar and a necklace of huge ceramic beads and Katie guessed she had made both the cardigan and the necklace herself. She ran a gift shop in Henry Street in Kenmare, along with her partner, Fanchea.

'I'm grand altogether,' said Clodagh. 'And how are you? I keep seeing you on the TV. You ought to make a career of it, you know? I can just imagine you in *Fair City*.'

'Who is it?' called their father, from the living room.

'It's the only daughter who followed in your footsteps, Da!' Clodagh called back.

Their father appeared. His hair was fraying and grey, but his green eyes were bright and his cheeks were ruddy. Blaithin's cooking had led to him putting on weight, but this evening he looked even bulkier than usual in a dark green fisherman's sweater.

'Katie! So good to see you, darling! What's the craic?'

Katie kissed him. He had been smoking, but at least he smelled clean, unlike the months after Katie's mother had died, when he had neglected both himself and his house.

'Blaithin not here?' asked Katie, as they went through into the living room. A log fire was crackling in the grate and a cut-glass vase filled with orange roses was standing on a side table.

'She came in to cook my breakfast for me all right, but this is her day off and she's gone to see her cousin in Fermoy. What do you think of my sweater? Clo knitted it herself, by hand.'

'I'm so sorry I haven't been to see you for so long, Da,' said Katie. 'We're up the walls at the moment, what with Jimmy Ó Faoláin getting himself shot and the fellow up at the cemetery in Kilcully with no head. Plus the drug-dealing and the people-smuggling and the prostitution and the shoplifting. And the usual station politics.'

'It's not a bother, Katie. Don't get upset about it. I know how busy you can be.'

'Come here, we caught some cheeky feen walking out of Penneys only yesterday toting a shop-window dummy complete with all its clothes on. He said he'd mistook it for his friend and he thought that his friend had suffered an epileptic fit and gone all rigid-like, so he was helping to carry him home.'

Katie's father shook his head. 'Unbelievable. Some of the

excuses that suspects used to come up with, you didn't know whether to laugh or burst into tears. One fellow told me he'd taken a ladder so that he could look in through his bedroom window and see if his wife was having an affair with the next-door neighbour. He couldn't explain why he'd also lifted an electric drill and a sander.'

Clodagh said, 'Would you care for a cup of tea in your hand, Katie? Da?'

'I'd rather have a vodka if you have one,' said Katie. 'It's been one of those days. To be truthful, every day is one of those days these days.'

'How's it going with Jimmy Ó Faoláin?' asked her father, opening up the silver cigarette case with the Garda crest engraved on it. It had been given to him when he resigned from An Garda Síochána, but his resignation had been forced on him because of a trumped-up charge of corruption, and for years afterwards he had refused to use it. Katie didn't remark on it, but assumed that maybe the years had mellowed him.

'Jimmy Ó Faoláin?' she said. 'Very little progress so far. In fact, almost none. We're ninety per cent sure we know what kind of weapon was used, but the lack of evidence at the scene was remarkable. Like, there was nothing at all. No footprints, no fingerprints, no stray hairs, no fibres, no sign of forced entry, and nothing was taken.'

'Sounds like a professional hit to me,' said Katie's father. 'Any idea of a motive?'

'The forensic accountants up in Dublin are combing through his accounts books for us now, but who knows how long that's going to take. I'm guessing it was probably financial, because everybody in the world appeared to love him.'

'And the headless fellow? Have you found out who he is? Or *was*, I should say.'

Katie was torn. This was her father, and she knew that she could trust him absolutely. On the other hand, she knew that he still met up with some of his old colleagues from the Garda from time to time, especially those who had supported and sympathized with him when he had reported bribery among his fellow officers. It might be tempting for him to confide in them that it was Garda O'Regan who had been murdered, only days before he was due to give evidence at the Disclosures Tribunal, or he might simply slip up and tell them without thinking. He wasn't suffering from dementia but he could be forgetful.

'We're working on it, Da,' Katie told him. 'We do know that his head was taken off with a chainsaw, but that's about it.'

'Holy Saint Joseph. At least it must have been quick.'

Clodagh came back in with two cups of tea and a cut-glass tumbler of vodka and tonic for Katie.

Their father lit a cigarette and blew out smoke for a while, and then he said, 'I'm glad you're both of you here this evening. I'm hoping to see all of you girls in the next week or two. The thing of it is, I'm thinking of selling the house.'

'That's a shock, Da!' said Clodagh. 'You *love* this house. You always said you were going to live here for the rest of your life.'

'Where will you go?' asked Katie.

'I have Lisney's scouting around for a bungalow for me somewhere,' said their father. 'Somewhere not too far from here, maybe Castlefarm or Strawberry Hill. The point is, I don't need a rambling great house like this any more, and I can't see myself ever getting married again. Your Ma's gone, and after your Ma there was Ailish , of course, and I thought I might stay here then, once we were married. But Ailish was taken away from me, too, and I couldn't find another woman to replace either of them – not Ailish and not your Ma.'

Katie looked at him narrowly. She could tell by the way he wasn't looking at them directly that there was something he wasn't telling them. He sipped his tea and puffed at his cigarette, and when he glanced at Katie and saw the expression on her face, he quickly looked away again.

'It's not really anything to do with getting married, is it, Da?' she asked him.

He shrugged, but he still didn't look at her. 'You're too good a cop, Katie, that's your trouble.'

'So what's the real reason you're selling up?'

'Money, if you must know. I'm broke as a joke. But this house is worth eight hundred and fifty thousand easy, and that will get me straight again.'

'But what about all your savings? And your pension?'

'Let's just say that I made some unwise investments. You know they're always warning you that your investments can go down as well as up. All of mine went down like a goat down a well.'

'For the love of God, what did you invest in?' asked Clodagh.

Their father blew out more smoke. 'It doesn't matter now. I've talked to my solicitor and a friend of mine who used to be a broker, and there's nothing I can do to get the money back. A risk is a risk. All I can do is cut my losses and make sure that I never invest in anything like that again.'

'How much was it?' said Katie.

'Nearly two hundred and seventy-five thousand. I know. Enough to make your eyes water. Well – enough to make you cry.'

'Are you sure there's nothing we can do to help you out?' said Katie.

'No, you're grand. Don't worry about it. Like I say, this house is far too big for me anyway, and maybe it'll do my head good to get away from the memories of your Ma. Sometimes I still think that she's upstairs, in bed, and I have to go up just to make sure that she's not.' He paused, and then he said, almost inaudibly, 'She never is.'

'Well, let me know if you need me to take you around to view any properties,' said Katie. 'I'm so sorry to hear that you've lost so much money. It's heartbreaking.'

'It makes no odds in the long run, Katie. You can't spend money when you're lying in your grave.'

They talked for another hour. Katie tried to persuade her father to tell her the details of how he had lost his investment, but he wouldn't be drawn. She could understand why. He must be feeling foolish and deeply embarrassed that almost all his life's savings had vanished, and that he was having to give up his house. Katie knew what he meant about feeling that her mother was still here. She felt that herself. In the summer she had looked out of the kitchen window and almost expected to see her mother in her vegetable garden, weeding.

Eventually the long-case clock in the hallway struck eight, and she stood up. 'I have to go, Da. Conor says he has some good news for me, although I haven't the faintest notion what it is. I'll tell you what – I'll bring Foltchain over with me on Sunday, so that you can meet her, and we can take a walk along the river.'

'I'll look forwards to it, Katie. And I'm so pleased that Barney's getting better.'

'Take care, Da.'

Katie looked around the living room. Behind the curtains was the window seat where she used to hide on winter evenings when she was little, and play with her dolls. She looked back at her father, staring into the fire, and she was filled with sadness at how life passes by.

Fourteen

Kyna parked her white Mini Countryman around the corner from the Halfway Bar and Lounge, in Mount Saint Joseph's Heights. As she climbed out of her car and locked it, an elderly woman who was putting out her rubbish stared at her as if she were an alien who had just arrived in a flying saucer. Kyna gave her a quick smile as if to reassure her that she didn't always look this slutty, and then made her way along the pavement to Baker's Road, wobbling on her six-inch stiletto heels.

Three men were standing outside the pub smoking as she approached, and they too stared at her as she pushed open the door and went inside. She heard one of them say, 'Jeez, I'd beat the beard off her, boy!'

The bar was crowded and noisy with music and raucous laughter. A guitarist and a violinist and a tin-whistle player and a bodhrán drummer were sitting at a table clustered with Guinness glasses. They were playing 'Blue Tattoo', and when they came to the chorus, all the drinkers around them were stamping their feet and singing along.

'In a blue tattoo! In a blue tattoo! I've got your name written here in a blue tattoo!'

Kyna made her way across to the bar, aware that heads were turning and all eyes were now on her. The music continued, but when it came to the next chorus, only two or three voices joined in.

'How are ye, girl?' asked Maureen the barmaid. 'Good to see a new face. Have you moved in local?'

'No – I'm only down from Dublin for a week or two to help my sister out,' said Kyna. 'She's just had baby twins and she doesn't know if she's coming or going. I've been changing nappies and feeding them and rocking them to sleep all day and I'm parching for a scoop, I tell you.'

'What can I get you?'

'One of them WKD Vodka Blues if you have one.'

While Maureen was fetching Kyna's drink, Gwenith came up to the bar carrying three empty pint glasses. She was wearing a tight red GAA T-shirt and her black leather miniskirt.

'You on your own, like?' Gwenith asked her.

'I am, yeah. Like I was telling the barmaid here, I've been helping my sister look after her newborn twins all day, and I'm gasping.'

'Why don't you come over and join us? You don't want to be standing here all on your ownsome, do you?'

Kyna looked across at Seamus Twomey and Douglas Quinn. Only one of their shaven-headed henchmen was sitting between them, and he had his head tilted back and his eyes closed and his mouth hanging open, as if he had already had far too much to drink.

'Come on, that's my brother Seamus and his friend Dougie and they're both good craic. They like pretty girls and you're a dead feek and no mistake. When you walked in the door just now, the eyes were falling out all over the shop.'

'Okay, then,' said Kyna, with a shrug, as if she were quite used to being openly told that she was sexy and had nothing better to do.

'Don't bother about paying for your drink,' said Gwenith. 'Maureen – put that WKD on Seamus's tab, would you, and give us two more pints of Murphy's, and an apple poitini for me.'

'I'll fetch them over,' said Maureen.

Kyna walked across from the bar to the corner table and sat down next to Seamus Twomey. Douglas Quinn looked at her and gave her a wink.

'What's your name, then, sweetheart?' said Seamus. 'I never saw you in here before.'

'I live in Dublin, that's why,' said Kyna. 'And you can call me Sparkle if you like. That's what all my friends call me.'

'Sparkle! All right, Sparkle. So what do you do to make ends meet? If you don't mind my putting it that way, like.'

'A bit of this and a bit of that. Some modelling, like, do you know what I mean? I had my picture in *The Gloss* a couple of months ago.'

'That doesn't surprise me,' said Gwenith, and she reached across and laid her podgy little hand on Kyna's knee. 'You know there's some people who are *so* sexy it doesn't matter if they're a boy or a girl. And you're one of them.'

'Chill the gills, Gwenny,' said Douglas. 'You go diving straight in there, don't you, and never give me and Seamus a look-in. You're worse than you were with that Tommy. Not that I was ever interested in Tommy, like, don't get me wrong. I'm not a cigire.'

Seamus laughed and banged the table. 'He's right you know, Gwenny! Here's me and him trying to be all flirtatious, like, and you're in like Flynn. But you're not a rug-muncher, are you, Sparkle? It's us good-looking bucks that tickle your fancy.'

He laughed again, loud and harsh, and so did Douglas. Kyna smiled but kept her eyes on Gwenith. It was obvious from the way that Gwenith was repeatedly stroking her knee that she found her attractive, and perhaps Gwenith had that sexual sixth sense that had already picked up that Kyna was more interested in women than she was in men.

'So who's this Tommy?' asked Kyna, looking around the bar to give the impression that she wasn't particularly interested in knowing the answer.

'Just a fellow,' said Gwenith. 'One of them me-feiners who only makes out that he fancies you so he can get something out of you, you know that kind of a way?'

'Oh. So you dumped him?'

'You could put it like that, yeah,' said Gwenith, and glanced across at Seamus. This time he let out a short, abrupt laugh that had no humour in it at all.

They carried on talking for well over two hours. Seamus told a long joke about a man who had been caught drinking and driving so many times that he called his family together and told them he had given up driving. Douglas tried to tell a joke about a man who took his three-legged dog for a walk on the beach and found a genie in a bottle, but he forgot the punchline.

All the time they were talking, Gwenith continued to stroke Kyna's leg, and her hand crept its way further and further up the inside of her thigh. Whenever Kyna looked at her, she licked her lips suggestively and then smiled her cupid's-bow smile, as if to say *You know what I'd relish doing to you, girl, don't you?* Kyna thought she was so moon-faced and repulsive that it took all of her self-control not to slap her hand away and tell her that she was ugly as mutton and a flabag. But Gwenith had implied that something had happened between her and Tommy, and of course Kyna knew that Tommy was the name that Detective Ó Doibhilin had been using while he was undercover.

At about ten-thirty, Seamus's phone rang. He picked it up from the puddle of Murphy's on the table and wiped it on his sleeve before he answered it.

'Yes? Oh – it's you, Davo. What the feck do you want now? Oh, don't tell me. Okay. Not that fecking eejit of an under-manager again, was it? Listen – don't get your knickers in a twist, boy. I'll come down there myself right now and sort him out. Okay.'

He stood up and said, 'Sorry, one and all. I have a spot of bother down in the town I have to be dealing with.'

He shook the shoulder of his slumbering henchman and shouted in his ear. 'Farry! Wake up, will you, you lazy bollocks? We've some business to attend to!'

The henchman opened his eyes and sat blinking, as if he had no idea where he was.

'Do you want me to come with you?' asked Douglas.

'No, you're all right, boy. It's just the usual shite. That under-manager at Nightowls has been giving Davo a hard time. Followed him into the jacks and tried to pat him down and everything.'

'Who does he think he is? The fecking drug squad? I'll come with you anyway. I have to see Kevan about fixing me up with a car tomorrow.'

Seamus and Douglas and Farry all drained what was left of their drinks, banged down their empty glasses and walked out of the pub. Kyna noticed that nobody called out goodnight to them, not even Maureen the barmaid.

'I'd better be going too,' she said, but Gwenith gave her thigh a hard squeeze.

'Why don't you come back to mine for a nightcap?' said Gwenith. 'We can have a bit of a girly chat, like. Seamus and Dougie, they're all right, like, but I get fed up listening to all of their stupid jokes and all their talk about football and hurling and cars.'

'I don't know,' said Kyna. 'I should be getting back to rescue my sister. She has fierce trouble getting those twins off to sleep.'

'Oh, come on. Only for an hour or so. You can tell me all about your being a model. I always wanted to be a model. I heard that they're looking for the larger-sized girls these days.'

Yes, they are, thought Kyna. *But we're talking about size 14, not size 22 with a face like a bag of spanners.*

'Maybe the one,' she said. 'I haven't had an evening off in weeks. I don't just do the modelling, like, because it's not steady work.'

Kyna decided to leave her car parked where it was. Who knew what might go wrong this evening, and she didn't want any of the gang to be able to recognize her when she was driving around town sometime in the future.

'I don't live too far,' said Gwenith, as they left the pub and started to walk along Cathedral Road. It was chilly outside, and the stars were hidden by the clouds. 'Seamus or Dermot usually give me a lift home but I think the walk is good for me, do you know? I think my only problem is that I can't say no to chips. Chips are my downfall, you know that kind of way.'

'I can't even look at a chip,' said Kyna. 'When I'm not modelling I'm serving behind the counter at the Chicken Express on Fairview. Well – you have to make a living, like, don't you?'

Gwenith took hold of Kyna's hand. 'I think you and me, we're going to be the best of friends. Even bester than that.'

Gwenith opened the front door of her flat and let Kyna in.

'There you are, Sparkle. You can hang your coat up here. There – go through to the lounge and I'll fetch you a drink and some nibbles. I don't have any WKD but I have some Little Island Cider if you fancy it.'

'Yes, whatever,' said Kyna. The side lamps in the living room were already lit, so that she could see the heap of sweaters and damp towels and crumpled magazines on the couch, as well as the empty pizza boxes on the coffee table and the grubby discarded slippers on the floor. The room smelled sour and airless as if Gwenith never opened the windows, or even drew back the curtains.

'You'll have to forgive all the mess,' Gwenith called out, from the kitchen. 'I never seem to find the time to tidy up, like.'

'Oh, don't worry, I'm the same,' Kyna called back, thinking of her immaculate flat with its pink Chinese rug and its framed reproduction of a nude by Sarah Purser. She sat down on the couch, perfectly still with her hands clasped together to put herself into a totally professional frame of mind. No matter what she had to tolerate with Gwenith, she was here to find out what had happened to Detective Ó Doibhilin, and that was all.

It was almost five minutes before Gwenith reappeared. She had a lighted cigarette dangling from her lips and she was carrying a bottle of cider in one hand and a pint glass of Johnny Jump-up in the other. She had taken off her red GAA T-shirt and her bra and her miniskirt and her tights, and she was now swathed in her shiny turquoise dressing gown with a pattern of tear-shaped stains down the front, which could have been dried blood but which Kyna guessed were much more likely to be YR brown sauce.

'There you are, girl,' she said, sitting down next to Kyna and handing her the bottle of cider. She blew smoke out of the side of her mouth and flapped it away with her hand. 'How about a shift, like?'

Without waiting for Kyna to answer, she leaned over and kissed her on the cheek, and then on the lips. She stuck out the tip of her tongue but Kyna kept her lips closed. Gwenith's breath reeked of cigarettes and Guinness.

Gwenith sat back, undeterred that Kyna hadn't opened her mouth for her. She took a deep drag at her cigarette and then she said, 'You like it both ways, don't you, I can tell. You're just like me, you are. I don't care if it's a feek or a feen, so long as they're a ride and they're raring to go.'

'It sounds like that Tommy fellow put you off, though,' said Kyna.

'Oh to feck with Tommy! He was a lying toerag, he was. Making out that he was a local lad and all sweet and friendly and all.'

Kyna took a swig of her cider. 'Did he – you know?'

'What? Give me a go? He did, yeah, before I found out who he really was. He wasn't too bad, like, better than throwing a banana up Pana, but he wasn't exactly lashing into me, you know that kind of way?'

'So what was he lying about?'

'I shouldn't tell you. Seamus will get fair bull thick with me if I do. But his name wasn't even Tommy.'

Kyna laid her hand on Gwenith's plump shoulder and stroked it through her slippery dressing gown. 'I swear to God, girl, I won't tell a living soul.'

'Why don't you make yourself comfortable first, Sparkle? You know, maybe take off those pants. You must be fierce warm in them, like. And I'll show you what *I've* got that sparkles.'

'No, you're all right,' said Kyna. 'I'm thinking about my sister now. She's going to be wondering where in the name of Jesus I've got to.'

'Aw, come on, ten minutes won't make no difference, will it? Here, look. What do you think of these, then? All genuine Swarovski.'

With that, Gwenith stood up and peeled off her dressing gown. Out tumbled a landslide of huge swaying breasts and drooping belly and cellulite-rippled thighs, with her vajazzle glittering deep beneath the folds of fat.

Gwenith lifted her stomach with her left hand so that Kyna could see the crystals around the swollen lips of her vulva more clearly.

'It's amazing, isn't it? I love it so much! Makes me feel like a pole dancer, you know that kind of a way, except I don't have a pole. Well, only that fellow Marek who works down at Kearys Motors! Do you get it? He's a Pole. Do you get it?'

Kyna smirked but she was too stressed now by the sight of Gwenith's bulging nudity to manage a laugh. She started to lift herself off the couch, but before she could manage to sit up straight, Gwenith dropped down to her pillowy knees right in front of her, grasped the waistband of her yoga pants and started to tug them down.

At first Kyna snatched at the waistband and tried to pull her pants back up again, but Gwenith only grinned at her and said, 'Come on, Sparkle, you don't have to be shy! We're just two girls together, aren't we?'

She dragged Kyna's pants over her feet and tossed them across the living-room floor. Then she leaned forwards, parting Kyna's knees with her shoulders, opening her thighs wide with her fingers, and dipping her head down.

Kyna glanced down only once, to see Gwenith's dry bleached-blonde hair bobbing up and down between her legs as if she were swimming a length at the Churchfield public baths. Then she leaned her head back against the leatherette couch and tried to remember her favourite poem from school.

'She thinks, part woman, three parts a child,
That nobody looks; her feet
Practise a tinker shuffle
Picked up on a street.'

Gwenith kept on licking and licking and in spite of her revulsion the nerve endings in Kyna's clitoris couldn't help responding to the persistent stimulation of her tongue-tip. All the same, she knew that she wasn't going to reach an orgasm. She was too rigid with disgust and anxiety and she simply didn't want to. She had once had a friend who encouraged her Labrador to lick her, but this was worse, because the dog hadn't understood what it was doing, while Gwenith had sensed that Kyna wanted something from her, even if she hadn't fully realized what it was, and she was taking every sexual advantage of it.

'*Like a long-legged fly upon the stream
Her mind moves upon silence.*'

Gwenith licked faster and faster, and now she had wedged her hand down between her own thighs and was gasping and panting and letting out extraordinary snorkelling noises. She suddenly reached a quaking climax, and Kyna took that as her cue to simulate an orgasm, too. She bounced up and down on the couch and breathed, '*Yes! Yes! Yes!*' and gripped Gwenith by both of her shoulders.

After a while Gwenith sat up and wiped her face with the back of her hand. 'Oh, Sparkle, you little dancer!' she said. 'Jesus, you're some sexy biscuit you are!'

She heaved herself up and sat close to Kyna, turning her head around with both hands and kissing her full on the lips. 'I think it's my turn for a lickout now, don't you?'

Kyna had kept her mouth tightly closed while Gwenith was kissing her and she shook her head. 'I can't, Gwenith. I'm sorry. I have these fecking horrible mouth ulcers. That's why I haven't been able to shift you proper, and I wouldn't be wanting to give you an infection down there, like.'

Gwenith sat back, clearly disappointed, but then she leaned forwards again and gave Kyna one quick kiss on the cheek. 'You're all right, girl. That's pure considerate of you. I'll tell you what, we can meet up again when your bake's better. My gran always used to swear by orange juice for the mouth ulcers – the fresh stuff, mind. Not your Tanora.'

She picked up her dressing gown and tied it around herself tightly, and then she went over and picked up Kyna's yoga pants for her.

'I'll fetch us another couple of drinks,' she said. 'I don't know why the taste of flange always makes me so thirsty. You'd think it would do the opposite, you know that kind of a way.'

She was walking across the living room when her phone warbled. She picked it up and said, 'Yeah? Yeah, of course it's Gwenny, who the feck did you think it was? No, I haven't, no. No, I didn't get none of that neither. Listen, Seamus, I haven't had the time to get down to Tesco but I will in the morning, all right?'

She listened for a while, nodding impatiently, and then she said, 'All right. Stall it, will you, for the love of God. I'll go down and get all the messages first thing tomorrow. Who's going to take it all down to Crosser, because I can't? Farry? All right, so long as he's not still feeling like a shite in a swing swong.'

Eventually she put the phone down. 'That Seamus!' she complained, with a chicken-like cluck. 'Always expecting me to run around after him like I'm his fecking moth or something! As if I haven't got enough on my plate!'

Kyna, pulling on her yoga pants, gave her a weak but sympathetic smile.

'So what's he expecting you to do now?' she called out, as Gwenith went into the kitchen to open another bottle of cider and pour herself another pint of Johnny Jump-up.

The second that Gwenith was out of sight, she danced quickly across the room, picked up Gwenith's phone and checked the number that had just called her. It was an o87 mobile number and she quickly memorized it by remembering the number of her first flat in Drumcondra, to which she added her mother's birthday and the last two digits of her own phone number. By the time Gwenith came back with the drinks, she was sitting on the couch again.

'Oh, I have to buy all this stuff like bog roll and tea and tinned pies, although what we're doing feeding him and giving him paper to wipe his arse with, I can't fecking imagine. He would have had all of us in jail if we'd given him half a chance.'

'You're talking about this Tommy character?'

'Spot on,' said Gwenith. She swallowed a mouthful of Guinness and cider and then let out a long, rasping and complicated belch. 'Don't tell Seamus I told you this, but it turned out that he's a cop in real life. He's been hanging around the Halfway for weeks now, with his ears flapping. If I hadn't flah'd him, we'd never have never found out what he was.'

'But why do you have to buy him food and all?'

'Because he's an unpaying guest of ours at the moment, girl. Just to teach him a lesson, that's what Seamus says. We'll probably let him go if the guards agree to stop mithering us.'

'And what's going to happen to him if they don't?'

'Well, just like the feller said when he showed up at the fancy-dress ball with a rubber johnny on his beezer and the doorman asked him what he'd come as – "fuck nose".'

Gwenith burst out laughing at her own joke and sprayed Kyna's face with her drink.

Fifteen

As Katie walked towards her front porch the door opened and there was Conor standing in the lighted hallway with Foltchain standing beside him. He always dressed well, but this evening he was looking even smarter than usual in a grey tweed blazer and a pale grey shirt and he was even wearing a tie.

She kissed him and said, 'Look at you la! Are you planning on heading out somewhere?'

'I am, as a matter of fact. I'm planning on taking you for dinner, if you're not too beat out. I have a table booked for us at Gilbert's.'

'Wow! So what's this all about? Did that fellow from Killarney pay you at last for fetching those schnauzers back?'

'He did actually. But that's not the reason. Like I told you on the phone, I have some good news.'

'Fair play. Just give me ten minutes to change.'

Katie went through to the bedroom, undressed and took a shower. Foltchain came into the bedroom to watch her as she dried her hair in front of her dressing table. Katie blew the hairdryer at her so that her feathery ears flapped up, and Foltchain closed her eyes as if she were standing in a warm breeze by the sea.

'Can I fix you a drink?' called Conor.

'No, thanks. I'll wait till we get to the restaurant. And one of us is going to have to stay sober.'

She put on one of her favourite dresses, a simple black long-sleeved button-through, and shiny black patent shoes. When she came out of the bedroom Conor was waiting with her coat.

'You have a mysterious look on your face, Con,' she told him. 'I'm dying to find out what this is all about.'

They drove in Conor's Audi along to Pearse Square in Cobh, which overlooked the waterfront. The sea was black, so that only the reflected lights from the promenade gave away the presence of the second-deepest harbour in the world. This had been the *Titanic*'s last port of call before she sailed out over the Atlantic and never came back.

Conor had booked them a table in the corner at the back of the restaurant. It was crowded this evening, and noisy, with its shiny white floor and its plain wooden chairs and tables. Before Katie could decide what she wanted to drink, Conor beckoned to the waitress and asked her to bring over the bottle of champagne that he had already arranged to have on ice.

'Don't keep me in suspense any longer,' said Katie, as Conor opened the bottle with the softest of pops and poured her a fizzy glassful. 'I've spent my whole day trying to solve puzzles. I don't need any more.'

'*Sláinte*,' said Conor, lifting his glass. 'May trouble neglect you, the angels respect you and heaven accept you.'

'Conor—!'

'Very well,' he said, smiling. 'I heard from my solicitor today that the business with the house is all settled, and that the Nuisance and I have been living apart for long enough over the past five years to be eligible to apply for a divorce.'

'That *is* good news, although you shouldn't call her that. She probably calls you something much worse. What's the deal with the house?'

'She gets to keep it but I don't have to pay the mortgage any longer. I know, I'll lose all of my equity, but it's a relief to get it all over at last. That's not really why I brought you here, though.'

The waitress came over and handed them a menu each. 'We have seafood chowder and smoked salmon and the catch of the day today is grilled whiting.'

Conor looked up at her and said, 'No, that's where you're wrong. *This* is the catch of the day.'

He took a small blue box out of his jacket pocket, opened it up and showed Katie the diamond ring that was sparkling inside it.

'I love you with all of my heart, Kathleen Maguire,' he told her. 'Will you do me the rare honour of becoming my wife?'

Katie stared at him numbly. She had such a *tocht* in her throat she could barely speak, and it was all she could do to stop herself from bursting into tears. As it was, she had to pick up her napkin and dab at her eyes, so that most of her mascara came off.

The waitress grinned, half in delight and half in embarrassment. 'Do you want me to come back later?' she asked.

'No, sweetheart, I want you to stay and be a witness, whatever she says,' said Conor. 'I'm only a poor dog-catcher, but I'm fit and healthy and solvent and I know all the words to "The Rising of the Moon".'

He picked the ring out of the box and held it out. Katie's hand was lying flat on the table but she didn't lift her finger so that he could slip it on. She was surprised, and flattered. From the moment she had first seen Conor walk into the station she had been attracted to his neat beard and his Viking cheekbones and his confident manner. But did she really want to get married again? Her late husband, Paul, had been attractive too, but he had turned out to be an unreliable finagler, as well as unfaithful. And then there had been John. She had really loved John, but she had always felt that she had jinxed him, and that bad luck had started to follow him from the moment they had first got together, as close behind him as a dark shadow.

She looked into Conor's eyes and she could see that he was pleading with her. *Marry me, Katie, please. I'll be on top of the world.*

She felt as if time in the bistro had slowed down, and all the music and talking and laughter that surrounded them had decelerated into a deep, groaning blur.

'Con,' she said at last, laying her hand on top of his wrist. 'I don't want to hurt your feelings but you'll have to let me think this over.'

'Katie, I *love* you! I want you to be my wife.'

'I hear you, darling, and I think you're a wonderful man, believe me. You couldn't have paid me any more of a compliment. But my life is in such a tangle right now, I can't think straight. And marriage... that's for the rest of our lives.'

The waitress pressed her fist against her front teeth as if she were trying to stop herself from blurting out, '*Go on, say yes.*' Conor turned to her and said, 'Sorry, sweetheart. Why don't you come back in a couple of minutes? I don't think we're quite ready to give you our orders just yet.'

He hesitated for a moment, and then he tucked the ring back into the box, snapped it shut, and returned it to his pocket.

'I didn't mean to distress you,' he said. 'It seems like I misjudged my moment, doesn't it?'

Katie swallowed, and stroked the back of his wrist. 'You know how I feel about you, Con. But up until now my relationships have been such a mess. It's not that I can't trust you, darling. I can't trust myself. There's such confusion at work it seems like the whole world is falling apart, and I don't want to say "yes" to you this evening simply because I'm stressed.'

'It's no bother, Katie,' said Conor. 'I have you. I totally understand what you're saying.' He topped up their champagne glasses and then sat back, sipping at his drink as if it didn't taste quite right. Then he lifted his glass and said, 'Why are we drinking champagne? I don't know what we're supposed to be celebrating.'

'Con—' said Katie, 'I didn't say no. I'm only asking for some time, that's all. It's a mega decision, not just emotionally. I have a job that takes up all of my days and most of my nights and needs my constant attention, seven days a week. I'm thinking of *you*, darling, as well as me. It was my job that wrecked my marriage to Paul and it was my job that killed poor John, in the end.

I'm deeply, deeply fond of you and I don't want the same thing to happen to you.'

'Oh,' said Conor. 'You're "deeply, deeply fond" of me.'

The waitress came up again with her notepad. 'Have you made any choices yet? The whiting's delicious. I had some myself earlier, for my lunch.'

Katie looked at the menu and then at Conor. 'I'm sorry. I don't think I'm very hungry any more.'

'No,' said Conor. 'We'll leave it, shall we? I'll just pay for the champagne.'

Katie said nothing as he took out his credit card and paid. She didn't know what to say to make him feel any better. They left the bistro in silence and walked across the square. The breeze smelled of sea and diesel fumes, and the smell brought some words that Katie had read at school into her mind, a description of leaving port. 'Out to the open we go, to windy freedom and trackless ways. Light after light goes down, the old prides and the old devotions glide abeam, astern, sink down upon the horizon, pass – pass.'

By the time Conor opened the car door for her, she was in tears.

As they drove back to Carrig View, Katie said, 'You didn't get a chance to speak to McManus, then?'

'No. Like I say, he was ringed around by even more scumbags than usual. They don't scare me, those gurriers, but I didn't want to propose to you tonight with my nose broke. Not that it would have made any difference.'

'Con, I only asked you for some time to think it over, that's all. I'm not very good with surprises, like, do you know what I mean? When you came out with that ring you almost put my heart crossways.'

'I should know you better.'

'You *will*, I hope. Look – it's still not too late. Let's take

Foltchain for a walk and we can have a chat. I don't want you to go to bed tonight feeling rejected, because you're not.'

Conor parked in the driveway and Katie went to fetch Foltchain. Somehow Foltchain sensed that this was special, and her tail wouldn't stop flapping eagerly from side to side.

'I wonder what she's going to think of Barney,' said Katie, as they walked along by the river. In the harbour behind them, a ship let out a long, mournful hoot, like a mother whale calling for her lost baby.

'I think they'll get along fine. She's pure amenable, Foltchain. And Barney – he's soft as a googey, isn't he – except when somebody threatens his mistress.'

Katie took hold of Conor's hand and gripped it tight. 'We don't have to hurry this relationship, Con. We have all the time that God gives us. You and me, we were both put into this world to do more than most – like saving innocent people from being killed and injured and innocent dogs from being tortured for the fun of it.'

'I hope we're allowed to think of our own pleasures now and again, though,' said Conor.

'Now and again,' smiled Katie, and gave a little skip so that she could reach up to kiss his cheek. 'Not during rush hours, that's all – the same as the parking restrictions on MacCurtain Street.'

They walked all the way to the ferry terminal. The last cross-river ferry of the evening was coming in, and they stood and watched its lights as it moored. Foltchain stood beside them, looking up at them from time to time. Katie felt she was still a little anxious that she might unexpectedly find herself on her own, with no home to go to.

They were about to start walking back when Katie's phone played *Siúil A Rún*.

'Hallo?' she said. She didn't recognize the number.

'DS Maguire? Oh – glad I caught you. This is Inspector Carroll from Tipp. I thought you'd be interested to know that there's been a serious fire up at the Ballyknock halting site. I've just had a call from the Fire Investigation Association. They've sent two investigators up there now, because the assistant fire chief reckoned it looked like a clear case of arson.'

'Really? Was anybody hurt?'

'Two fatalities. A young Pavee woman, Rosella Rooney, and guess who? Guzz Eye McManus.'

'Serious? McManus? When did this happen?'

'Midday or thereabouts, but they only recovered the bodies about half an hour ago.'

'Midday?'

'That's right. Apparently there was nobody else on the site when the fire was started – only McManus and this young Rooney woman. Everybody else had gone off to watch some dog-fight that was being held on a farm near Ballynonty.'

'Why wasn't McManus there?' asked Katie. 'At the dog-fight, I mean.'

She turned around to see if Conor was listening to her, but he had already started walking back down the road with Foltchain, and he was out of earshot.

'From what we were told, McManus suffered a severe attack of gout, and by ten-thirty or thereabouts he was in so much pain that he decided to call it a day and go back to the halting site. We're not exactly sure what his relationship with this Rosella Rooney might have been, but she drove him there anyway. They were both in McManus's mobile home when the fire started. They might have been sleeping or watching TV, there's no way of telling. But there was no way out of there once the fire had taken hold. All of the windows were locked except one and that wouldn't have opened wide enough for McManus to squeeze his fat carcass out of it.'

'And it definitely looks like arson?'

'It has all the signs of it. An accelerant poured in through that one open window, more than likely.'

'Who raised the alarm?'

'A local farmer was passing on his tractor and he saw smoke and flames coming from behind the halting site wall. We can't say exactly when the fire was started because it had taken a real hold by then, but the farmer called 112 at twelve oh-seven.'

'Where are they sending the bodies? The morgue at Limerick Regional, I imagine.'

'That's right. But from what the assistant fire chief told me, they won't be requiring much more in the way of cremation.'

'Thanks for ringing anyway,' said Katie. 'Keep me in touch, will you?'

She walked quickly to catch up with Conor. Her mind was whirling inside like a child's windmill. She felt like bursting out and asking him how he could possibly have seen Guzz Eye McManus at a dog-fight in Ballynonty, surrounded by his heavies or not, when he had been back in his mobile home suffering from gout. But even in the few seconds that it took her to reach him, her Garda-trained mind had already asked her, *If Conor wasn't at Ballynonty, where was he? And who started the fire that killed him?*

'Who was that?' asked Conor, linking arms with her.

'Oh, just routine.'

'They don't leave you alone, do they?'

'They won't, ever, until I retire, or people stop committing crimes, whichever comes sooner.'

She was silent for the rest of the way home. When Foltchain had curled herself up in her basket in the kitchen, she went through into the living room and switched on the lamps. Conor was already in the bedroom, getting undressed.

'Aren't you coming to bed?' he called her.

'I'm not tired yet. I thought I'd have a drink and read my book.'

She went over to the side table and poured herself a small glass of Smirnoff. Then she sat down on the couch, tucked up her feet, and picked up her copy of *The Girls in Green*.

Conor appeared in the doorway in his blue pyjama trousers, tugging down his T-shirt over his dark hairy chest. He watched her turning over the pages of her book for a while, and then he said, 'You're angry about something.'

'No, I'm not.'

'But you have something on your mind, haven't you? Is it because I proposed to you? I'm sorry again if I read our relationship all wrong. I probably understand dogs better than women.'

Katie sipped her drink and pretended to read another page, but then she put down her book and said, 'You *did* go to Tipp, didn't you?'

'Of course I did. Why would you think that I didn't? You can ask Alice Cushley. You don't think I'm having a clandestine affair, do you?'

'Did you really go to Ballynonty and see Guzz Eye McManus?'

'What's this about, Katie? Just because I didn't manage to confront him face to face, like I wanted to, that doesn't mean I didn't get to see him. I'll catch him some other time.'

'No, you won't.'

Conor came into the living room and sat down beside her on the couch. 'I've sworn to stamp out dog-fighting, Katie, one way or another, and I will. McManus can't get away with brutalizing dogs for ever.'

'Well, he has, Conor. He's dead.'

Conor stared at her intently, searching her eyes to see if she was testing him, or teasing him. 'You're not serious. He's *dead*? How did he die?'

'His mobile home was burned out, most likely by an arsonist. He was inside it at the time, along with some young Pavee woman. She died too.'

Conor opened his mouth but then he closed it again without saying anything.

'He went to the dog-fight all right,' said Katie, trying to keep her voice steady. 'He wasn't well, though – gout, apparently – so he called it a day. By the time you'd got to Tipp and met up with Alice Cushley, he was back at Ballyknock.'

There was a long silence between them. Conor kept staring at Katie but it was plain that he couldn't think what to tell her.

At last Katie said, 'That's why I asked you if you really went to Ballynonty, and if you genuinely saw him. Because you didn't, did you?'

Conor stood up. He walked around the room, smacking his fist into the palm of his hand, and then he sat down again.

'I had no idea there was anybody in there,' he said, so quietly that Katie could hardly hear him.

'*What?*'

'I said, I had no idea there was anybody in there. I knocked, but nobody answered.'

Katie put down her drink and lowered her book.

'Oh, Conor,' she said, but this time she didn't cry.

Sixteen

About an hour before dawn, it began to rain. It clattered on the hood of John Lacey's yellow waterproof jacket and the light from his torch picked out thousands of silver circles on the surface of the river.

John shouted back to Aidan, 'I think it's time we called it a night, son! This looks like it's going to get worse before it gets better!'

Aidan stuck his head out of the tent, his face illuminated by the game he was playing on his iPhone. 'Okay, then! Do you want me to start packing everything up?'

John thought, *You don't have to sound quite so happy about it.* He had thought that an all-night fishing expedition on the banks of the Lee would be a good way to bring him and Aidan closer together again. He had brought him here to Innisleena, on the narrow track that led beside the river to the ruins of St Senan's Abbey, where he had fished when he was a boy himself. He had packed a new two-man tent and fishing rods and hamburgers and six bottles of Satzenbrau in a cooler, even though Aidan was only thirteen.

It was almost silent here, except for the gurgling of the river and the rustling of the trees and the sporadic quacking of ducks. But Aidan had been silent, too, spending hour after hour playing *Dragon Hills 2* and *Oxenfree*, and responding to John's attempts at jokey conversation with nothing but grunts or one-syllable answers or simply by rolling his eyes up.

Shortly before midnight they had caught three bream and a rudd, but when John had told Aidan that their fishing licences required them to throw them back, he had lost interest in catching any more.

'I mean, what's the point, like?'

John had felt like asking him what the point of his video games was, but he had simply shrugged and said, 'It's the challenge, Aidan, that's all. Man against fish.'

'Oh yeah.'

John wound in his line. He collected up their rods and their khaki tackle bag and collapsed the two stools that neither of them had sat on. By the time he had walked back to the tent, Aidan had already folded it up and was rolling up the groundsheet.

'Let's just stow this lot in the car,' John told him. 'We can come back for the rest of it.'

Aidan walked ahead of him up the track to where he had left his Volvo estate car. It was hard for him to believe that this sulky teenager with his close-shaved bazzer was the same small boy who used to sit in his lap and suck his thumb and listen to stories. He knew that it was mostly his own fault that he had lost contact with him. It hadn't helped his marriage to Riona, either. But once he had discovered that senior Garda officers were taking bribes, he hadn't been able to ignore it. It was against his training as a guard, and against his religion, too. His grandfather and his late father had both been gardai, and they would have been angrily pounding on the lids of their coffins if they could have heard about the backhanders that were routinely being taken so that some of the most serious criminals in Cork could avoid prosecution.

John's principal target was the city's biggest organized gang of car thieves, who had been able to carry on their racket year after year without any fear of arrest. He had been spending almost every waking hour ferreting out witnesses and evidence, and as consequence of that his marriage and his three young children had become secondary, as if they were nothing more than a television serial playing at low volume in another room.

The gang was composed of two Cork crime families, the Coakleys and the Lynches, both of them based in Mayfield. John hadn't found it difficult to collect evidence against the gang members themselves. There was plenty on file already – forged car registrations and false index marks and paint-spray jobs, as well as CCTV videos of new cars being driven away from dealers' forecourts, and dozens of witness statements. What John had been tracking down was the huge sums of money that the Coakley-Lynch gang had been regularly handing over to senior Garda officers in exchange for immunity, and still were. It was mostly in cash or through offshore funds.

His estate car was parked on the grass by the side of the track. He unlocked the rear door and he and Aidan stowed away the tent and all the fishing gear. The rain was coming down hard now, so that it sounded as if the trees were on fire.

'You get in,' he told Aidan. 'No point in both of us getting skited.'

Aidan didn't need telling twice. He climbed into the passenger seat and started playing another game on his phone. John walked back down the track to fetch the camping stove and the beer cooler and the plastic shopping bag filled with leftover burger buns. He didn't mind the rain. It suited his feeling of failure.

He was just picking up the stove when he heard Aidan shouting out.

'Get off me! What are you doing? Let go of me, will you!'

He turned around to see that the passenger door of his estate car was hanging wide open and that Aidan was being frogmarched down the track towards him by three men in black leather jackets and jeans, their faces masked by black balaclavas. As they came closer, he could see that one of the men holding Aidan's arms had a sawn-off shotgun tilted over his shoulder, while the man who was walking behind them was swinging an orange chainsaw.

John dropped the camping stove into the grass and stood up straight. The three men pushed Aidan up in front of him and then stopped.

'How's it going, head?' said the man with the shotgun, lowering his weapon and pointing it down at the ground. 'Jesus, it's a blessing your old girl knew where you were. We never would have found you, else.'

'What?' said John. He was suddenly feeling chilled, and breathless, and his heart was beating painfully hard. 'You haven't been round to my house, have you? You haven't been threatening my wife? You haven't hurt her, have you?'

The man with the shotgun wiped his nose against his black leather glove. 'What kind of scummers do you think we are? Of course we haven't hurt her. She was very obliging as it goes. We only had to tell her that we'd blow your daughter into doonchie little bits if she didn't tell us where you were.'

'Who the hell are you?' John demanded, and he was so breathless now that his voice sounded as if he were suffering an asthma attack.

'Who are we? Who the feck do you think we are? Have a guess, head. We're the friends of those fellows you've been bothering so much lately, sticking your caincin in where it's not welcome. We've come out to have a bit of a chat with ye, that's all.'

'I have nothing to say to you,' said John. 'I imagine you know that I'm a garda sergeant so I'm telling you now to clear off out of here, or else you'll be in deeper shite than you can ever imagine.'

'You're having a laugh, aren't you? There's three of us and there's only two of you and one of you's nothing but a spotty maneen. On top of which, I happen to have this shotgun, which is loaded, but which I'm more than happy to unload into your lad's left ear to see if his brains can reach the other side of the river.'

John said, 'Don't you dare to touch him. Don't you even fecking dare. Let him go now and I'll have a talk with you, all right?'

'There you are. I knew we could sort this all out amicable-like,' grinned the man with the shotgun. Turning to Aidan he said, 'Give my pal here your phone, son.'

Aidan clutched his iPhone tightly against his chest and looked at John in desperation.

'I said, give my pal your fecking *phone*, son,' the man with the shotgun repeated, and this time there was a much harder edge to his voice.

John nodded and said, 'Go on, Aidan. It's only a phone. They don't want you calling anybody, that's all. I'll buy you another one.'

'See what a *flaithiúlach* dad you have there,' said the man with the shotgun. 'I'll bet generosity is his middle name. Pity he isn't more *flaithiúlach* when it comes to his colleagues, do you know what I mean?'

Aidan reluctantly handed his iPhone to the man beside him. The man took two steps back, swung his arm, and threw the phone high across the grass and into the rain-spotted river. It plopped into the water close to a duck, which flapped away in alarm.

'Come on, then, let's go and find ourselves some consecrated ground, shall we?' said the man with the shotgun.

'I thought you were going to let my boy go,' said John.

'Oh, we will, as soon as you and us've finished our bit of blather. But we can't have him running off just yet. You never know who he might bump into. Even farmers have phones these days. Besides which, I think he'll find this all highly edumacational, especially if he decides that *he* wants to be a cop when he grows up. Loyalty, that's what it'll teach him. Blood is thicker than water, do you know what I mean, but money can soak the both of them up, the blood and the water, and it can wipe up a lot of the shite too.'

The man with the shotgun started to walk further along the track, and the other two men indicated with sideways jerks of their heads that John and Aidan should follow him.

'I'm not going!' shouted Aidan, backing away. 'You can't make me! And my dad's a guard so you can't make him, either!'

One of the men reached out to seize Aidan's arm, but Aidan spun around and kicked him in the shin. The man turned around to look at his two companions, as if to say, *Lamp this chisler, would you, he's a neck like a jockey's bollocks.* Then, without any hesitation, he slapped Aidan across the side of his head, so hard that Aidan tumbled backwards into the bushes.

John shouted out, 'Hi!' and started to step forwards, but the man with the shotgun dodged in front of him and raised the gun so that it was pointing directly at John's face.

'I wouldn't think about it if I was you, head,' he warned him. 'Not if you want St Peter to recognize you when you roll up at the pearly gates.'

John's voice was shaking with anger. 'I've said I'll talk to you, whatever you want to talk about. But leave my boy out of this.'

To Aidan, he called out, 'Just keep calm, Aidan, okay? They've something they want to discuss with me, that's all, and once we've come to some kind of agreement we'll be able to go.'

Aidan disentangled himself from the bushes, brushing burrs from his sleeves. He climbed back on to his feet and followed them along to St Senan's Abbey, scowling, one hand still cupping his ear. None of them spoke as they approached the low limestone wall that surrounded the graveyard, and the rain continued to dredge down across the river like a procession of ghostly mourners. The abbey had been abandoned in the early nineteenth century and although its tall square tower remained, it was a hollow shell and its windows were empty. All the graves were overgrown with weeds and most of the headstones were tilting and covered in lichen.

The man with the shotgun trod his way between the graves, looking left and right as if he were searching for one grave in particular. Around the side of the abbey ruins he stopped and said, 'Here – this'll do,' and he pointed with his gun to a low rectangular memorial slab with a headless statuette of an angel standing at one end of it. 'In fact that's most fecking appropriate, wouldn't you say?'

'So what do you want to talk about?' asked John. 'Or do you just want a tip for tomorrow's race at Punchestown?'

'Oh, you're a gasman, you are!' grinned the man with the

shotgun, but at that moment Aidan shrilled out, '*Dad!*' as one of the other men quickly stepped up close behind John, reached around him and snatched his left wrist. He twisted his arm behind his back and locked a handcuff on him and then reached around for his right wrist and locked that too.

'What in the name of God is this all about?' John protested. 'You have a gun, don't you? You don't need to fecking cuff me to keep me here!'

'Well, maybe,' said the man with the shotgun. 'It's just that we've a little more than banter in mind, do you know what I mean, and so we need to make sure that you stay good and steady. We wouldn't want to hurt you more than necessary.'

The man who had handcuffed John now pushed him roughly towards the memorial, until his feet were touching its kerb. Then he forced him to lie face downwards on the rough granite slab, wrenching back the hood of his waterproof jacket to expose the back of his neck.

As he lay there with his cheek against the wet stone, John heard the distinctive sound of the chainsaw cord being tugged. It took five or six attempts before it started up, but then he heard it being revved up like a motorcycle on the starting grid.

Oh dear Mary Mother of God what are they going to do to me? If they're going to kill me, please let them kill me outright. Please don't let them mutilate me. He had a vivid flashback to a suicidal man who had thrown himself in front of an Iarnród train at Kent Station. He had been lying by the side of the track with his legs severed just below his pelvis, staring up at John with an expression that had given him nightmares for weeks afterwards – an expression that said, *I thought I was going to die. I thought it would all be over in an instant. Instead I'm still awake and it's still Thursday morning and I've been maimed beyond salvation.*

The man with the shotgun came close to the memorial and leaned over so that John could hear him over the noise of the chainsaw.

'Thought you were cute as the red-arsed bees, didn't you, Sergeant Lacey? Thought you could sneak on your friends and your fellows and all you'd get was a pat on the back. Well, now you know that life doesn't work that way. In the Garda, your friends and your fellows come first, no matter what tricks they've been up to. They might have been doing a babs but it's not up to you to pass judgement. It's all for one and one for the other.'

The man carrying the chainsaw was standing right next to him now, and he kept giving it little revs as if to emphasize what the man with the shotgun was saying.

'You've just time for a prayer,' said the man with the shotgun. 'If I was you, I'd be begging the Lord Jesus to forgive me for being such a grass.'

'I have children,' said John, his voice reedy with fear.

'Well, this'll teach your wains a pure unforgettable lesson, won't it?'

At that moment, Aidan suddenly made a run for it. He hurdled over the nearest memorial stone and pelted towards the graveyard gate. The man with the shotgun snapped, '*Patrick!*' and the man who had handcuffed John started to run after him.

For a big, heavily built man, Patrick was surprisingly fast. Aidan was running wildly, all arms and legs, but Patrick's legs were pumping mechanically, like the legs of a man who works out on a treadmill every morning, and Aidan hadn't even reached John's estate car before he caught up with him. He grabbed the sleeve of Aidan's jacket and dragged him back along the track to the abbey. Aidan deliberately let himself drop to the ground, but Patrick kept on dragging him, and at last he dragged him back into the graveyard and threw him down in front of the man with the shotgun.

'And where the feck did you think that *you* were heading off to, kid?' the man with the shotgun shouted at him, over the rasping of the chainsaw.

Aidan started to sob, his mouth turned down in terror and despair. 'You can't – *don't!* – don't hurt my dad—!'

'Do you know what you are?' the man with the shotgun bellowed at him, close to his ear. 'You're a fecking pain in the arse, that's what you are! You're a fecking flight risk!'

He turned to the man holding the chainsaw and shouted, 'Deal with him, will you, Hoggy, before he tries to leg it again!'

'Wha'?' said Hoggy, holding the chainsaw to one side so that he could hear better.

'I said, *deal* with him! Like, the feet, boy! Anything to stop him running off!'

Aidan was sitting on the ground now, in between two kerbstones. He kicked his heels into the shingle and tried to back away, but Patrick was standing right behind him and caught hold of his shoulders. He threw himself from side to side trying to break free but Patrick was far too strong for him.

'*Let me go!*' he screamed. '*Let me go! I won't run off again, I swear it, cross my heart!*'

But Hoggy approached him with his chainsaw raised and roaring at full speed. He lowered it towards Aidan's feet and Aidan jumped and hopped and galloped, trying to avoid it. There was no escaping it, though. Hoggy swept it from side to side and the teeth ripped into the heel of Aidan's left trainer so that blood and shreds of canvas flew all the way across the nearby memorial. Then Hoggy caught his right ankle, tearing through his jeans and cutting through skin and bone with a high-pitched screech. Aidan's foot dropped off and Hoggy kicked it aside as if he were a tree surgeon kicking a fallen branch out of the way.

John shouted, '*Stop! Stop! For the love of Jesus, stop, will you!*'

He tried to lift himself up off the memorial slab but he was like a beached seal, and when he raised his head the man with the shotgun casually turned his shotgun around and struck him behind the ear with the butt – not hard enough to knock him out, but hard enough to make him drop his head down again.

Aidan had stopped screaming now. His face was deathly white and he was convulsing in shock. Hoggy revved up the chainsaw again and this time he started to cut him just below the left knee, except that the chainsaw skidded all the way down the front of his shin, shredding his jeans and the skin underneath them. Hoggy lifted the chainsaw and tried again, and this time he managed to sever his lower leg almost completely, although it still dangled from a twist of muscle. The shingle between the kerbstones was glistening with blood, although the rain quickly began to wash it away.

'That's enough, sham!' called the man with the shotgun. 'Let's get down to what we came for! Patrick, come and hold this scummer's legs, would you, while Hoggy does the business?'

Patrick dropped Aidan on to the ground, and Aidan lay back shivering and twitching with the rain falling directly into his face. Hoggy walked around the memorial slab on which John was lying, while Patrick kneeled down beside it, almost as if he were praying in church, and gripped John's legs to stop him from kicking.

'Any last words, Sergeant Lacey?' shouted the man with the shotgun.

'What have you done to Aidan?' John shouted back at him. 'What have you done to my son, you gowl?'

'Is that it? Is them's your last words?'

'You'll burn in hell for this!' John yelled at him. 'The Lord will judge you and you'll burn in hell!'

The man with the shotgun stepped back and nodded to Hoggy, and Hoggy revved the chainsaw up to full speed.

Meanwhile the rain continued to make thousands of circles on the surface of the river, and in the distance, over towards Kilcrea Hill, there was a deep grumbling of thunder, as if God had been woken up by the feeling that something in the world was badly wrong.

Seventeen

Even though it was ten past five in the morning, they were still in the living room, talking. Katie felt exhausted and befuddled but she knew that even if she went to bed she wouldn't be able to sleep. Conor was sitting on the couch with her but he was so agitated that he kept getting up and circling around the room and then sitting down again.

Foltchain had heard that they were awake and had scratched at the kitchen door, so Katie had let her into the living room so that she could lie by the warm ashes of the fire. Perhaps she had been worried that they had been discussing how to get rid of her. Katie leaned over now and again and ruffled her ears to reassure her that she was wanted, and safe.

'All I can say is that it seemed like the best way to put McManus out of business,' said Conor. 'In fact, it was the only way that I could think of. You decided not to prosecute him, the ISPCA decided not to prosecute him, and even if you'd got a court injunction preventing him from keeping dogs, he would have ignored it. Besides which he never actually kept any dogs himself.'

'Con – what you did was *insane*! Even if McManus and his woman friend hadn't been inside it, you had no justification at all for setting fire to his mobile home. Sometimes we have to accept that we don't have the power to right what's wrong. If we start taking the law into our own hands, we'll be lowering ourselves down to the same level as the criminals.'

'You can't tell me you're sorry that McManus is dead. When you think of all the hundreds of dogs who suffered unbelievable pain because of him – I mean, Jesus.'

'I'm not sorry that he's dead, Con. I just wish that it hadn't been you who killed him. Can't you see what position this puts me in now? You've admitted to me what you've done and as a police officer I'm duty bound to arrest you. But can you imagine what the repercussions are going to be? Denis MacCostagáin will probably have to suspend me – at least while we're preparing the book of evidence against you. And what a meal the media are going to make of it! "Detective superintendent's lover kills dog-fight supremo in arson attack." Mother of God, Con, I could lose my job because of this.'

Conor sat down and covered his face with his hands. Foltchain looked up at Katie as if she were asking why he was so upset.

'I knocked,' said Conor, at last. 'I knocked but there was no answer.'

'Guzz Eye and his woman friend were probably both langered, even at that time of the day. But even if you knocked, that doesn't mitigate what you did. Honest to God, Con, I don't know what I'm going to do now.'

Conor lowered his hands and looked at her directly. 'We're not lovers any more.'

'What?'

'We broke up a couple of days ago. We had a fierce argument about Guzz Eye and I threw a sevener and stormed off and you haven't seen me since.'

'Con, that's simply not true.'

'Who's to say it isn't? Nobody's seen us together in the past day or two. It was dark when we took Foltchain for a walk and only a couple of cars went past.'

Katie stared at him, not knowing what to say. He had obviously been lying to her when he had claimed that he had seen McManus at Ballynonty, but even though he had confessed to her that he was the arsonist who had set fire to McManus's mobile home, she would have no way of proving it if he subsequently decided to deny it. It was possible that the technical experts up at Tipperary might find forensic evidence that it was him, footprints or fingerprints or tyre tracks, but she didn't think it very likely.

'Katie,' said Conor, taking hold of her hands, 'I'm thinking of you and you alone. Maybe what I did was pure mental, but I can't regret it. All I want to do now is make sure that this doesn't cause you any grief. You didn't know I was planning on doing it. You had no involvement whatsoever, so there's no reason for you to suffer.'

'But if we pretend that you didn't tell me, what are you going to do?'

'I have a cousin in Sligo. I can always say that I didn't see McManus at Ballynonty so I decided to go up and pay him a visit instead. I can go and stay with him and I know he'll back me up.'

'Con... I love you. I think I love you. Holy Mary, I *thought* I loved you. How could you have done this?'

'I suppose I was sure that I could get away with it.'

Katie turned away from him. It had been a long time since she had felt angry with anyone. She found Frank Magorian misogynistic and arrogant, and sometimes Detective Sergeant Begley annoyed her with his bull-headedness, but neither of them were supposed to love her and care for her, not like Conor. Although she had desperately wanted to see Guzz Eye McManus prosecuted for his wanton cruelty to dogs, she couldn't help thinking that Conor had been more concerned about the dogs' welfare than hers.

Yes, she could say that she and Conor had argued and broken up, and that she had never had any inkling that he was going up to Ballynonty to confront McManus. But as damaging as it would be for her if she arrested Conor for arson and manslaughter, it would be even more damaging if she didn't, and if she was caught out lying to save her own skin, as well as his.

She also knew from her own investigations that it was quite

possible that somebody *had* seen them together, or at least seen Conor's Audi parked in her driveway after his return from Tipperary.

She tugged her hands away from his. 'You're breaking my melt, Con. I don't know what I'm going to do now. Mother of God, talk about a rock and a hard place.'

'I'm sorry, Katie. I'm really so sorry. I've made a right hames of everything, haven't I?'

Katie was almost tempted to pour herself another large vodka, but she was too tired and she didn't fancy the taste of it, not at this time of the morning. She picked up a cushion from the couch and threw it across the room, but that seemed to be such a feeble protest against Conor's recklessness. Her late husband, Paul, had jeopardized her career by trading in stolen building materials, and he had been unfaithful to her more than once, but at least he had never killed anybody.

'Maybe I should go,' said Conor.

'Yes,' said Katie. 'Maybe you should. And maybe you shouldn't even tell me where you're going, or when I might hear from you again, if ever.'

Just as Conor stood up, Katie's phone played *Siúil A Rún*. She picked it up and saw that Kyna was ringing her.

'Kyna? What's the story? What time is it?'

'Five thirty-two, ma'am. I'm sorry to wake you.'

'You didn't, as it happens. I haven't been to bed yet.'

'I've only just managed to escape from Seamus Twomey's ten-ton sister, Gwenith. I'm craw sick to say that she took a fancy to me.'

'You're codding me.'

'I wish. I managed to keep the intimacy down to the minimum, thank God. But it was her who found out that Michael Ó Doibhilin was undercover. It seems like she dragged him back to her flat and insisted on taking a rasher off him. I don't quite know how she discovered he was a cop, but she must have called Twomey and then he had no chance. While I was there, though,

Twomey rang, and from what I overheard they're holding Michael in Crosshaven somewhere. Twomey wanted Gwenith to go to Tesco and buy food and toilet paper for him, and then hand it all over to some gurrier called Farry to take it down there.'

'That's brilliant work, Kyna. I'll ring Buckley and O'Brien and get them to tail her, and then this Farry character. Where does she live?'

'Last block of flats on Sprigg's Road, just off Sunvalley Drive. In the messiest pigsty I've ever seen.'

'And you don't think she decked that you were a cop, too?'

'Not a chance. She even wants to see me again for some more ping ping. Urgh! Thank the saints I don't have to! You ought to see her. I'll tell you, ma'am, you wouldn't ride her into battle.'

'I'll ring you back directly,' said Katie, ending the call and prodding out Detective Buckley's number.

As she did so, she heard the front door close, and when she turned around she saw that Conor had gone.

Immediately, she ran out of the living room and flung the front door wide open. She was dazzled by the headlights of Conor's Audi as he reversed out of her driveway and on to Carrig View. It was raining hard.

'Conor!' she called out, running out after him in her stockinged feet. 'Conor, stop! *Conor!*'

Either he couldn't hear her or else he didn't want to. He sped off northwards, leaving her standing on the wet pavement. She blinked against the raindrops as his red tail lights disappeared into the distance.

She heard a small voice say, '*Hallo? Hallo? Is that you, ma'am? Hallo?*'

She lifted up her phone and said, 'Yes, Kieron, this is me. Sorry to call you at this godforsaken hour.'

She walked back towards the house. Foltchain was standing in the hallway waiting for her, and almost tripped her up.

'Don't you worry, girl,' said Katie. 'I'm not going to leave you. Not for anything.'

Eighteen

Detective Scanlan was waiting in her Volkswagen Polo outside the Music Market when the owner came around the corner, carrying a cardboard cup of coffee in one hand and a saxophone in the other. He hung the saxophone on the door handle so that he could unlock the front door, and then he went inside. Detective Scanlan climbed out of her car to follow him.

The Music Market was a small single-storey building opposite the rear entrance to the South Infirmary Victoria University Hospital. It was painted a dull red colour and its windows were hung with rows of acoustic guitars. As Detective Scanlan approached, the owner reappeared. He was lugging a large plywood sign in the shape of a double bass, with the lettering *The Music Market, Discount Guitars* painted on it, which he planted on the pavement.

'How's it going, sir?' said Detective Scanlan, taking out her ID and holding it up in front of him. 'I'm Detective Padragain Scanlan, from Anglesea Street Garda station.'

'Oh, yeah?' said the owner, suspiciously. He was short and bald with owlish glasses and a droopy grey moustache. He was wearing a lime-green shirt and a purple waistcoat and baggy brown corduroy trousers.

'Are you William Ó hUiginn?' Detective Scanlan asked him.

'What if I am?'

'Well, I need to speak to the owner of this store and the registered owner of this store is William Ó hUiginn.'

'I'm the owner so that would be me.'

'That's cleared that up, then. Is it okay if we go inside so that I can ask you a couple of questions?'

'Sure like. Come on in.'

William Ó hUiginn led Detective Scanlan into the store. The shop was small and low-ceilinged and cramped, and it was filled with so many musical instruments that they could barely squeeze their way to the counter. There was a strong smell of stale pipe smoke mingled with the piney aroma of violin rosin.

'So, what can I do you for?' asked William Ó hUiginn, prising the lid off his coffee and taking a quick slurp at it.

'I was wondering if you'd sold any low-D tin whistles lately.'

'Low-D tin whistles? Why would you want to know that?'

'It's just part of an enquiry, that's all.'

'You know that they were stolen, then? How in the name of God did you find out about that? I never reported it. I mean, why would I bother to report it? It wouldn't be any use, would it, because I wouldn't be able to sell them again even if I got them back. Health and fecking safety, like.'

Detective Scanlan said, 'You should have reported it, really. Even if you never got them back, it could have helped us to catch some petty thieves. When were they stolen, these whistles?'

'Two Thursday mornings ago. About half past ten in the morning.'

'And do you have any idea who took them?'

'I do, yeah. But I'd be hard put to give you much of a description. He was a big feller with a shaved head, like, wearing a black leathery kind of a jacket, do you know what I mean? But that was all I saw of him because one of your lot was here when he came in, talking to me about thieving, would you believe?'

'You mean a guard?'

'That's right. He came in to tell me about a gang that's been going around the city hobbling from shops and burgling from houses. He said they come down from Dublin for the day, rob as many shops and houses as they can, and then they whizz back up to Dublin before you can say pikey.'

'Well, that's true,' said Detective Scanlan, because Cork had been plagued recently by a spate of thefts and break-ins by visiting gangs from up north. As far as she knew, though, Superintendent Pearse hadn't specifically been sending gardaí around to give local shopkeepers warnings about them. He wouldn't have been able to spare them, and there had been plenty of news reports about them on the TV and the radio, and in the *Echo*. She didn't mention this to William Ó hUiginn. The guard could have been an imposter, deliberately distracting him while an accomplice stole the tin whistles, and she didn't want to start speculating and complicate what might have been a perfectly straightforward case of shoplifting.

'I mean, that was pure ironical, like,' said William Ó hUiginn. 'There was this feller stroking my whistles while a guard was right there standing in the shop. But it wasn't until later in the day that I saw that the whistles were gone, so I couldn't be totally sure that it was your man who took them. I can't think who else it might have been, though. The rest of the customers I had that day were all musicians I know, plus a couple of kids who wanted to buy a harmonica but didn't have the grade for it.'

'You say "whistles" in the plural,' said Detective Scanlan. 'How many are missing altogether?'

'Five,' said William Ó hUiginn. He slurped his coffee again and his glasses steamed up, so he took them off and wiped them on his shirt sleeve. 'Yeah, *five*, and I've been asking myself, who in the name of Judas Iscariot would want *five* low-D tin whistles? Like, what the feck for? You don't have tin-whistle bands, and even if you did you wouldn't have them all playing at the same pitch, would you?'

'Do you have any left, so I could see exactly what they look like?'

'I do, yes. I had seven altogether and the feller left two behind. I thought that was quare, too, you know. He could just as easy have stroked them all, like, which I would have done myself if I was planning on selling them on.

'Look,' he said, and went across the shop to a circular wooden bin with two tin whistles sticking out of it. He took one out and gave it two-handed to Detective Scanlan as reverently as if he were handing her a holy relic. 'These here whistles are all hand-crafted by Feadóga Lámhdhéanta in Kerry. I sell them for two hundred and twenty-five euros and that's a bargain price I can tell you. I've seen them advertised for three hundred.'

'Do you mind if I borrow this?' asked Detective Scanlan. 'I'll give you a receipt for it and return it as soon as I can.'

William Ó hUiginn frowned at her. 'Yeah, okay then. But... it's not only my stolen whistles you're interested in, is it? There's something else going on here, isn't there?'

'You should have been a detective, Mr Ó hUiginn,' said Detective Scanlan. 'I'm afraid I can't tell you any more right now, but let me put it this way: you've been more help than you know.'

She took out her notebook and a pen and started to write out, *Borrowed from the Music Market, one low-D tin whistle*—

As she was writing, she said, 'This guard who came in to warn you about the robberies – is there anything you can remember about him? His name? His badge number? What he looked like?'

William Ó hUiginn stuck out his bottom lip and slowly shook his head. 'They all look the same to me, guards – except for the banghardaí, of course. Tall feller he was, chunky – but then they all look chunky in them yellow jackets, don't they? I'll tell you something, though, I reckon he originally came from Waterford or thereabouts, the way he kept calling me "head" and there was a couple of other Waterfordy things he said which I forget now.'

Detective Scanlan tore off the receipt she had written. 'I may have to come back with a few more questions, Mr Ó hUiginn, but meanwhile, thanks for your co-operation.'

William Ó hUiginn dropped the tin whistle into a shiny green paper bag and gave it to her. 'Don't be tempted to be playing it, mind,' he told her. 'It's the health and safety. You never know what some folks have in their spit.'

Nineteen

Katie didn't reach the station until nine forty-five. She had showered at about six o'clock but after that she had flopped herself back on her bed in her fluffy dressing gown for a moment's relaxation and the next thing she knew she had been dead to the world for two and a half hours.

Moirin brought her in a cup of black coffee and a glass of water. She always seemed to know when Katie needed a caffeine jolt and some serious rehydration.

'Anything else I can fetch you?' she asked. 'I bought a couple of those raspberry tarts from Heaven's Cakes this morning if you'd like one. You've had a rake of calls and Padragain Scanlan was asking after you.'

'Yes, she texted me. And, no, I don't want anything else just yet, thank you, Moirin. I have a tongue like Gandhi's flip-flop.'

Before Katie started to answer all her phone calls and sort through her messages, she wanted to ring her father. She had been thinking about him as she drove into the city, and if she hadn't been running so late, she would have crossed the river to see him. She wanted to talk to him further about the money that he had lost, and whether it might be possible to get all or at least some of it back. She was friends with Peter Doody, a first-class commercial solicitor on South Mall. Apart from being smooth and dark-haired and handsome and owning a yacht down at Kinsale, Peter Doody had often given her legal advice on cases of fraud and money laundering.

After she had dialled her father's number, it rang and rang, but at last Blaithin answered.

'Blaithin? This is Kathleen. Is my dad there?'

'Oh, hello, Kathleen. How are you? Your dad's not at home, I'm afraid. Did he not tell you? He's away off at a funeral at St Oliver's, in Ballincollig.'

'No, he didn't mention it. Whose funeral?'

'His old friend Brian Cooney. One of the last friends he had left, wasn't he? He always used to say that if it wasn't for Brian, he would have nobody to call when any of his old acquaintances passed away. But now Brian's gone too.'

'That's sad. I can't believe he didn't tell me when I was round there yesterday. Brian wasn't that old, was he? Only in his mid-seventies, I'd have guessed. Had he been ill?'

'Seventy-four, he was. But, no, he wasn't ill. He took his own life, poor creature. Swallowed about a hundred ibuprofen, your dad was telling me.'

'Mother of God, that's desperate.'

'He'd lost all of his money, that's what it was. Gone bankrupt. One day he had a comfortable pension and he was going off on cruises and all that. The next he didn't have two yo-yos to rub together.'

Katie didn't say anything to Blaithin about her father losing so much money, because she wasn't sure if he had told her about it. Instead, she said, 'Would you tell him I rang, please, Blaithin, when he gets back? And tell him I can probably call around to see him again this evening.'

'I will of course.'

Once she had put down the phone, Katie stood up and went across to the window. The clouds were tearing apart like grey dishrags and a watery sun was beginning to shine. The news about Brian Cooney was not only tragic, it was disturbing, too. She wondered if Brian and her father had both lost their money in the same investment, and if any other pensioners had been bankrupted by the same scheme. There had been scores of online scams lately, all offering older people the chance to increase their savings, but the victims were often too proud or too embarrassed to report that they had been swindled.

Next, her thoughts turned again to Conor. He hadn't made any attempt to contact her since he had disappeared last night, and although she had been tempted to send him a text, she had decided in the end to wait for him to get in touch first. She knew that she ought to tell Denis MacCostagáin that Conor had confessed to setting fire to Guzz Eye McManus's mobile home, but she was also aware that as soon as the words were out of her mouth, her whole life could collapse all around her, not only her relationship with Conor but her career.

Perhaps Conor had been right, and she should lie, and deny all knowledge of what he had done.

She sat down at her desk again, and as she did so Detective Scanlan knocked at her door. She came in, holding up the tin whistle in the green paper bag.

'It matches,' she said. 'I took it down to Bill Phinner and it's identical to the whistle that was stuck in Garda O'Regan's neck.'

She told Katie about her visit to the Music Market, and what William Ó hUiginn had said about the guard, and the five tin whistles that had been stolen.

'He thought it was pure strange that only five were taken, when the thief could have hobbled all seven of them.'

Katie took the tin whistle out of the bag and turned it over and over. 'Maybe five was all he wanted. If the whistle that was stuck in Garda O'Regan's neck was one of them, then maybe he wasn't intending to sell them at all. How many officers are scheduled to be giving evidence at the Disclosures Tribunal?'

'I don't know for sure, but I could ring Mr Justice McGuigan's office and find out for you. You're not suggesting what I think you're suggesting?'

'I hope not, Padragain. God, I hope not. Would you ring His Honour now as a matter of urgency, and get a list of all the whistle-blowers' names and addresses. Can you also check what each of them is expected to be testifying about. I know for sure that one of them is going to be giving evidence about racism.'

'I heard that one witness has a whole heap of inside information about financial irregularities at the Garda College, too,' said Detective Scanlan. 'Money being spent on luxury trips abroad, and lavish dinners, and even prostitutes. Some heads are going to roll, no doubt about it.'

Katie said, '*Padragain*—'

'Oh… I wasn't talking about Garda O'Regan. Not his head. I was meaning that there's some quite high-up officers are going to be facing the sack when all this comes out.'

'Yes, I know. But let's pray it doesn't happen literally.'

Half an hour later, Detective Sergeant Begley came up to tell Katie that Detectives Buckley and O'Brien were still waiting outside Gwenith Twomey's flat on Sprigg's Road. Gwenith had been down to Tesco in Paul Street and had returned home at nine fifty-five, but so far there was no sign of Farry.

'All right, thanks, Sean,' said Katie. 'Just tell them to be patient. From what Kyna told me, this Farry is likely to have a monster hangover, so who knows what time he's going to be rolling out of bed.'

'At least if those scumbags are buying food for him, young Michael must still be alive and reasonably well,' said Detective Sergeant Begley.

'Let's hope so. But we'll have to be double wide, the way we play this. They'll only have to pick up a hint that we're tailing this Farry fellow and it could be disastrous.'

'I've alerted the RSU. As soon as we have some indication of where Michael's being held, they can send along an armed unit to back us up.'

'Okay. Grand. Keep me up to the minute, won't you?'

Katie followed Detective Sergeant Begley out of her office and went along the corridor to see Chief Superintendent

MacCostagáin. She found him sitting morosely at his desk, talking to Assistant Commissioner Frank Magorian.

Frank Magorian looked as if he were dressed for the golf course. He was wearing a yellow cable-knit sweater and loud blue chequered trousers. He also smelled strongly of Issey Miyake aftershave.

'Ah, Kathleen,' said Denis MacCostagáin. 'I was just about to call you. Frank has been asking me what progress we've been making with Garda O'Regan.'

'Some, but not as much as I would have liked,' Katie told him. 'We have some encouraging forensics, but our only potential witness so far is Mrs O'Regan and of course she's still in Wexford General and she hasn't yet regained consciousness.'

'But you've still no idea of a motive?'

'I don't want to get ahead of myself, sir, because I'm still waiting for Garda O'Regan's solicitor to send me over a copy of his evidence, but I'd lay money that he was killed to prevent him from testifying at the Disclosures Tribunal. And that could mean that all the other whistle-blowers may be in jeopardy, too.'

'What – just because he had a tin whistle sticking out of his neck?' asked Frank Magorian.

'I admit that's not conclusive, sir. But if his killer wasn't trying to make some kind of a statement about whistle-blowing, you have to ask yourself why he would have done that.'

'There could have been any number of reasons. If he was mad enough to cut off the poor fellow's head, he was mad enough to do anything, I'd say.'

'Maybe. But the way that his killers immediately tipped off the media, even before we could do it ourselves – that was surely a warning to any other whistle-blowers. I know that if *I* was due to give evidence to the Disclosures Tribunal in the next few weeks, and I heard that one of the witnesses had had his head cut off, I'd at least be having second thoughts about it – wouldn't you?'

'Probably I would, Kathleen. Probably I would. But these whistle-blowers, I don't think they're easy frightened. If they were easy frightened, they wouldn't have blown their whistles in the first place, would they? They've all seen what Sergeant Maurice McCabe had to go through. All those false accusations of incompetence and sex abuse that were levelled against him, not to mention the death threats. But McCabe was never put off, was he? No... I'm pretty much convinced that you're looking for a lone header, Detective Superintendent. That's the feeling I have in my water.'

'Header,' repeated Denis MacCostagáin, with a grunt. 'That's pure appropriate.'

'Even if it *was* a header, sir, it must have been more than one. I can't see how a single individual could have forced Garda O'Regan out to the cemetery and then made him sit still while he cut his head off. At least two offenders were involved in this, and possibly more than two.'

'Fair play, Kathleen,' said Frank Magorian. 'But we've had plenty of cases where psychos have committed murders in pairs. The Scissor Sisters in Dublin, for instance. They cut that fellow's head off, didn't they – not to mention his mickey.'

'Whatever you say, sir,' said Katie. She had decided several months ago that she wasn't going to argue with Frank Magorian, no matter how much he tried to undermine her. He was the Assistant Commissioner, after all, and although the Garda was undergoing radical changes, he still had supreme authority over the Southern Region and he still had a network of powerful connections both in Dublin and Cork. Now that she had the thorny problem of Conor to deal with, this was not the time to be putting his back up.

She turned to Denis MacCostagáin and said, 'Actually, sir, I only came to tell you that we've had a sound tip-off and we may be close to finding Detective Ó Doibhilin.'

She explained that Detectives Buckley and O'Brien were waiting to follow Farry down to Crosshaven, or wherever it was that Michael Ó Doibhilin was being held, although she didn't say how Kyna had acquired the information. Kyna's sexuality was her own business, and Katie felt bad enough that she had exploited it, even if it did mean that it had given them the chance of saving Michael Ó Doibhilin's life.

'Fingers crossed, then, Kathleen,' said Frank Magorian. 'But it's still going to be hard to haul in Seamus Twomey, even if we do manage to get Ó Doibhilin free. Twomey wouldn't have personally abducted him, would he? And Ó Doibhilin's cover being blown, that's put a right spanner in your drug-running case against Twomey and Quinn. They won't be smuggling all that fentanyl in through Rosslare now, will they? Who knows where they'll be bringing it in, and you can bet they'll be keeping sketch for the slightest sign of us lot, undercover or not.'

'We'll have to see about that, sir,' said Katie. 'There's more than one way to skin a canary.'

Twenty

The twenty-one boys from Dripsey National School were shout-ing and laughing and tussling with each other as they climbed out of the school bus and scrambled into the clubhouse to change.

They had two teachers with them – their sports master, Tadhg Daley, and his assistant, Cliona Brennan. Tadhg was tall and lean and fit with a wave of gingery-blond hair like somebody waving a duster out of an upstairs window, while Cliona was tubby with a round pink face like a doll.

'Come on, get your groove on, lads!' Tadhg shouted, and blew his whistle by way of emphasis. 'I want you all changed and out here in three minutes flat! Every second you're pulling your nix on is a second wasted on the pitch!'

As he waited with Cliona for the boys to struggle into their football kit, he hopped up and down on the spot and chafed his hands together. 'I have the strongest feeling we're going to win the Sciath Na Scol again this year! I don't think Rylane have a snowball's chance in hell! Not that I'm demeaning them, mind! They're a great team but ours is greater.'

Cliona had torn the wrapper off a muesli bar and was solemnly chewing it. She was just about to take a second bite when she looked up, and frowned, and turned around and around in circles. '*Hush!*' she said.

'What is it?' asked Tadhg. He was still hopping up and down, and now he was punching the air like a boxing kangaroo.

'Would you please be still and whisht awhile, Tadhg?' she told him. 'I'm sure I can hear someone bawling.'

'They'll all of them be bawling if they don't come out of that changing room by the time I count down to nothing.'

But now Cliona stood absolutely still, and held up her hand, and Tadhg stopped hopping, and after a moment's silence they both heard a faint, eerie howling coming from somewhere close by.

Tadhg looked around O'Brien's Field. It was deserted, soggy and flat. To the east, there was only a tall row of floodlights and the misty green woods of Inniscarra beyond. To the south, the pitch was bordered by the low stone walls of St Senan's Abbey, but its ruined tower and its graveyard were mostly screened from sight behind cypress trees.

'It sounds like a dog to me, or a fox more likely. Maybe it's snagged itself in a fence or it's broken its leg or something.'

They listened for another few seconds. There was another long silence, but then the howling started up again, thin and plaintive at first, but gradually rising higher and louder, and even more distressed. Cliona said, 'I'm sure I heard it say "help me".'

'Oh, come on, Cliona. The foxes round here are cute all right, but I never heard none of them talk.'

'No. I'm sure it said "help me",' Cliona insisted. She began to jog towards the abbey, just as the boys from the football team came clattering out of the clubhouse, all wearing their maroon-and-white Dripsey NS shirts.

'Cliona!' Tadhg called her. 'Cliona, we're ready for the kick-off!'

Cliona ignored him, swinging open the metal five-bar gate and disappearing behind the cypress trees into the graveyard. Tadhg swore under his breath, picked up the football and threw it towards the team's goalkeeper, so hard that it almost knocked the boy over.

'There, have a bit of a kickabout will you, to warm yourselves up. I won't be long.'

He stalked after Cliona, his fists clenched and his nostrils flaring. He had always been short-tempered and it made him furious if things didn't go the way he had planned them. It made him a good sports master but unbearable to live with, which was why his wife had walked out on him two years ago, taking their children with her.

'Cliona!' he shouted. 'We can't be bothering ourselves with dogs or foxes or whatever! We have a football game to supervise, for God's sake!'

He had crunched only halfway along the shingle path before Cliona suddenly appeared from behind one of the limestone memorials. She came stumbling towards him, jabbing frantically at her phone.

'I can't get a signal!' she panted. 'I have to get a signal!'

'Cliona, what in the name of Jesus is going on?'

'Call for an ambulance, Tadhg! And call the guards, too! There's a young fellow desperately hurt back there, and another fellow dead with no head on him!'

'*What?*' said Tadhg, in total disbelief. 'What do you mean, dead with no head on him?' But then there was another howl, and it was so agonized and so unearthly that he could only stare at Cliona in horror. Now that he was nearer, he could tell that it was a human being, and not an animal.

'Tadhg! See if you can get a signal!'

Tadhg took his phone out of his tracksuit pocket and dialled 112. The emergency operator answered almost instantly. '*Emergency – which service?*'

'Here – you talk to them,' said Tadhg, and handed the phone to Cliona. He left her to tell the operator what she had discovered while he carried on walking stiff-legged between the gravestones to see for himself who was howling in such pain.

He found Aidan lying on his back between two memorials, gripping their granite kerbstones as if he were trying to lift himself out of a bath.

His face was ghastly, more like a white Halloween mask than a young boy's face, and his hair was sticking up. His jacket was sodden with rainwater and his jeans were sodden with blood. Both of his feet had been cut off and were lying on their sides on the shingle – one at the ankle and the other below the knee. Tadhg could see his bare white tibia protruding from the shredded left leg of his jeans, and a tangle of gristle where his right ankle should have been. It was a miracle that he was still alive, and hadn't bled to death, or died of shock.

Tadhg kneeled down beside him and cradled his head in his hand. Aidan stopped howling and opened his eyes and stared up at him.

'Please, no more,' he blurted out. 'Please. I won't try to run away again, I swear it.'

'I'm not going to hurt you, boy,' said Tadhg. 'I've called for an ambulance for you. What's your name?'

'Aidan. Aidan Lacey. Is my dad all right?'

Aidan tried to sit up, but then he howled again in agony, and his head fell back into Tadhg's open hand.

'Who did this to you?' Tadhg asked him.

'I don't know. I don't know who they were. Three fellers all with masks on. Is my dad all right? They haven't hurt my dad, have they?'

Cliona appeared around the memorial, still holding Tadhg's phone to her ear.

'They're on their way now,' she told Tadhg. 'The ambulance and the guards, both of them. How is he?'

Aidan had closed his eyes, although he kept twitching and muttering as if he were asleep and trying to talk to somebody in a nightmare. Tadhg pressed two fingertips to his neck to feel his pulse.

'Hundred and forty. It's a little high but at least his heart's still beating. He was asking after his father.'

'Over there,' said Cliona, pointing over her shoulder without turning around. 'I don't want to look at him again. I'll never unsee him as it is.'

Tadhg leaned sideways so that he could see past Cliona to the gravestones behind her. Two rows away stood a lichen-encrusted cross, tilted slightly at an angle. A man in a yellow waterproof jacket was tied to the cross with his arms outspread. There were runnels of blood all the way down the front of his jacket and his collar had been pulled down to expose his neck. His neck, though, was nothing more than a bloody stump, and he had no head. Tadhg could see something stick-like and shiny sticking out of his windpipe, but he was too far away to see exactly what it was.

'Holy Mary,' he said, and he looked down at Aidan, whose eyes were still closed, although he could see that they were moving frantically from side to side underneath his eyelids. 'That must be his dad. Who the hell could have done a thing like this to them?'

'Yes, I'm still here,' said Cliona, on the phone. 'The boy's horrid shook but we've taken his pulse and he's still with us.'

'Cliona, go back to the field, would you, and tell the boys that the practice is off, and could they change back out of their nix. Tell them to stay in the clubhouse and play games on their phones until we're ready to take them back to school. Just say that there's been a bit of an accident.'

Cliona went off, leaving Tadhg alone in the graveyard with Aidan and the headless man. Three hooded crows came fluttering down, and settled on a memorial nearby. They were obviously attracted by the sight of human carrion, but too cautious to start pecking away at the dead man's neck while Tadhg was so close.

Tadhg didn't want to look at the dead man again, but he couldn't help himself from glancing over from time to time. He wished that he hadn't wolfed down his breakfast so quickly, because he could feel the half-chewed sausages rebelling inside his stomach, and his mouth was suddenly flooded with bile.

Aidan opened his eyes again, and stared up at the sky, and let out an ear-piercing scream. The three hooded crows rose, startled, from their perch, but didn't fly far. They circled around the cypress trees and then settled again, a little further away, but still within sight of the headless man with the shiny stick-like object protruding from his neck. Soon they were joined by seven or eight others, and they clustered around the graveyard, croaking.

Fifteen minutes later, though, a Garda patrol car drew up outside the abbey, followed by an ambulance and then a second patrol car, all with their blue lights flashing. Doors slammed and feet came running along the shingle path. Sulking, the hooded crows rose from their gravestones and flew off westwards, over the river, their wings beating like black paper fans.

Twenty-One

'I'll tell you, boy, I'm starving,' said Detective O'Brien. 'If this scummer doesn't show up soon I'm going to start eating my fecking notebook, page by page.'

It was eleven-thirty now, and Detectives Buckley and O'Brien had been waiting in their unmarked blue Toyota outside Gwenith Twomey's block of flats for three and a half hours, since the first damp light of dawn.

They had seen a taxi arrive to take Gwenith off to Tesco, and another Hailo bring her back an hour and ten minutes later, with five bulging carrier bags. Since then, nobody else had arrived at the flats and only three people had left, and they had clearly been residents on their way to work.

Detective O'Brien was twenty-nine years old, and whippet-thin, with sandy hair and almost invisible eyelashes. Detective Buckley was thirty-six, with a thick neck and black hair that was already turning grey. Despite the difference in their age and experience, they were comfortable in each other's company, like an older brother and a younger brother, which was why Katie often teamed them together.

'There's that Sun Valley stores down the arse end of Fair Hill,' said Detective O'Brien. 'Do you reckon I'd have time to run down there for a hang sangwidge, like, and a packet of Taytos?'

'Oh, you would yeah,' said Detective Buckley, meaning no. 'And what would happen if your man showed up in the mean-time and we lost him because you'd gone off for a nosebag? She might look like some beour but have you ever seen DS Maguire when she's bulling? I mean, like, keep your hand on your mebs, boy, because she'll bite them off for you and spit them out the window.'

Detective O'Brien sniffed and looked out of the window. 'I'm still fecking wallfalling. I could eat a scabby baby through a tennis racket.'

Only three minutes later, though, a silver Mercedes saloon turned into Sprigg's Road from St Mary's Avenue. It parked at an obstructive angle outside Gwenith's block of flats and a meaty-shouldered man with a shaved head climbed out. He was wearing a grey suit that looked two sizes too tight for him, with a black T-shirt underneath. A silver earring glinted in his left earlobe.

'If that's not our Farry then I'm a Kerryman,' said Detective Buckley.

'Hey – I've run into that gurrier before,' said Detective O'Brien. 'In fact I'm sure of it. It was years ago, when I was in uniform. He used to be a bouncer down at the Night-Night Club on Carey's Lane. I hauled him in for beating seven shades of shite out of one of his customers. If it *is* him, they gave him three months in Rathmore Road for it.'

They waited another five minutes and then the grey-suited man reappeared, awkwardly carrying the shopping bags that Gwenith had brought back from Tesco. After he had stowed them into the boot of his car, he reversed with a loud screech of tyres and sped off. Detective Buckley waited until he had turned back down St Mary's Drive before he started the Toyota's engine and went after him.

'If he's heading for Crosser he's going the right way,' said Detective O'Brien, as they followed the Mercedes down towards the Lee. When they reached Camden Quay, though, they were stopped by a red traffic light, and they could only watch help-lessly as Farry crossed the Christy Ring Bridge and turned east along Lavitt's Quay on the opposite side of the river.

'Please Virgin Mary don't let us lose him,' prayed Detective Buckley. But now they could see that the Mercedes had been halted by the next set of lights at Patrick's Bridge, so that when the lights changed to green they were able to speed across the river and catch up with it. They kept just two cars behind it as it drove along Merchant's Quay and then turned south and out of the city centre. Soon they were out past Douglas and driving between farms and woods and misty fields of grazing cows, with Farry keeping up a constant 110 kph – 10 kph faster than the speed limit.

'If we weren't tailing him I'd have the greatest pleasure in pulling him over and giving him a fixed charge notice,' said Detective Buckley. 'I mean – *Jesus!* – did you see the way he overtook that fecking artic? He's going to be killing himself and then I won't have to pull him over.'

They sped for nearly twenty minutes down the N28, until they had almost reached Carrigaline.

'Maybe he'll stop for a scoop and a bite to eat somewhere,' said Detective O'Brien, hopefully.

'Don't bet on it,' said Detective Buckley, and he was right. Instead of driving into the centre of town, the Mercedes turned left along the bypass that ran along the south side of the Owenabue River and directly into the village of Crosshaven. The sun came out as they passed Drake's Pool, and glittered between the yachts that were bobbing at anchor.

'Twomey and Quinn must be pure minted if they can afford a place here,' said Detective O'Brien, craning his neck so that he could see the prosperous houses that overlooked the estuary. 'You and me are in the wrong job, Steve. Maybe we ought to jack in this detective lark and take up drug-smuggling. That'd be a fair handy number, now wouldn't it, with our inside knowledge? You and me, we could easy sneak half a million euros' worth of opioids in through Ringaskiddy without the Revenue even getting a sniff of them.'

'Forget it,' said Detective Buckley. 'It would be just our luck to be lifted by two detectives as cute as we are, and I don't fancy spending the next ten years of my life sharing a cell with you in Portlaoise, thank you very much, smelling your farts and listening to you droning on about Lorcán McLoughlin's chances in the senior hurling.'

Traffic was sparse along the last stretches of the road that led into the village, so they stayed at least a hundred and fifty metres behind the Mercedes in case Farry caught on that they were following him. When he reached the harbour car park he made an unexpected swerve to the right and disappeared up a steep winding hill. Because he had given no signal the two detectives overshot the entrance, slithered to a halt and had to reverse. A van driver behind them leaned on his horn and shouted obscenities.

'I hope to God Farry hasn't copped on that we're tailing him,' said Detective Buckley, as he spun the steering wheel and turned up the hill. The irate van driver blasted his horn again, so Detective O'Brien put down his window and shouted, 'Away to feck, would you, you big baluba!'

They drove up to the top of the hill and found out that it joined up with Middle Road, by the white-painted Anchor Bar. Farry had parked almost directly opposite the front of the pub at the top of Daly's Lane, a narrow pedestrian dogleg that led back down to Lower Road, and the harbour. There was no space for another car to park there, and in any case Farry would have seen them if they had pulled in right behind him, so Detectives Buckley and O'Brien had to drive straight past.

'Shite,' said Detective Buckley, under his breath. He drove all the way back down to Lower Road, took a sharp right, and parked at the bottom end of Daly's Lane.

The two detectives were just in time to see Farry teetering bow-legged down the steeply sloping lane, trying to keep his balance as he carried all five Tesco bags in both hands. He stopped at a small grey-painted cottage halfway down the lane and kicked at its brown front door. He waited, and when he got no response, he kicked it again, harder. Eventually somebody opened it, although from where they were sitting in their car, Detectives Buckley and O'Brien were unable to see who it was.

Once Farry had disappeared inside and the door had closed behind him, Detective Buckley said, 'Right – I'll call DS Maguire and give her the latest SP. It looks like there's a kind of a yard at the back of that cottage. Why don't you hop over the wall there and see if you can take a sconce inside?'

'Got you,' said Detective O'Brien, and climbed out of the car. As soon as he had done so, he knocked on the roof and pointed across the road, to a small square building beside the harbour wall. There were large letters on the side of it, *Chish & Fips*, and he ostentatiously rubbed his stomach. Detective Buckley put down the passenger-side window and said, 'Maybe after, you fecking gannet. Just feck off up there and see if you can get a visual of Michael, will you?'

He called Katie. Of course she already knew exactly where they were and what they were looking at, because they had been tracked from the communications room upstairs at Anglesea Street from the moment they had started to follow Farry's Mercedes, and their car was fitted with a 1080p dashcam.

'O'Brien's checking to see if Michael Ó Doibhilin's actually inside there,' Detective Buckley told her. 'Myself, I reckon that it's ninety-nine per cent certain that this is where they're holding him. Why else would Farry have fetched half of Tesco down here?'

'Fair point – but why did they have to do that?' asked Katie. 'They have shops in Crosshaven, don't they?'

'Sure, like. I can see a big Centra from where I'm sitting here, right across the other side of the car park.'

Katie thought for a few moments. Then she said, 'Even if Michael's tied up, maybe Twomey and Quinn can spare only one of their gang to guard him. If that's the case, your man wouldn't have wanted to risk leaving him on his own, would he, while he went to the shops?'

'That's a thought, like,' said Detective Buckley. 'And if there's only Farry and one other feen for us to take care of, that definitely stacks the odds in our favour. The trouble is we have no way of knowing if they're armed, like. We have to assume that at least one of them will have a weapon.'

'I've alerted Sergeant Clery at Crosshaven Garda station,' Katie told him. 'There's only him and one other guard on duty just at the moment, but in any case I've told him to stay put until we need them. We don't want Farry to realize that we've found out where Ó Doibhilin's being held. Always presuming that he *is* being held there.'

'So what's the plan?'

'I've already dispatched DS Begley and an RSU team to meet up with you and they should be with you within the next twenty minutes at the outside. They'll have a hostage negotiator from the HNU with them too.'

'What if Farry leaves before they arrive?'

'Then let him go. Don't alert him. We'll be tracking him, although we won't be stopping him. But whatever you do, don't go knocking on the door or confronting him until you're totally sure that Ó Doibhilin's inside there. If they're holding him somewhere else, they could decide to hurt him or even kill him if Twomey thinks that we're not playing ball.'

'Okay, ma'am. I'll let you know just as soon as I can.'

Detective Buckley sat back in his seat and waited. He had been called out to an increasing number of hostage situations and threatened suicides in the past few years, especially since the economic crash in 2014. None of them had ended happily, and some had ended tragically, but several innocent lives had been saved.

For some reason, though, he was filled with a chillier sense of foreboding than he had felt in a long time. Usually, there was hope that a drugged-up killer could be persuaded to put down his knife and give himself up, or some hysterical girl could be talked down from the top of Paul Street multi-storey car park. But Detective Buckley couldn't help feeling that in this case it was all too late. He had known Seamus Twomey and Douglas

Quinn for years, and how violent they could be. If Detective Ó Doibhilin wasn't dead already, then there was a serious risk that he very soon would be, and that there would be other deaths, too, before it grew dark.

Detective O'Brien made his way up the narrow passageway at the back of the cottages. The whitewashed concrete walls were less than one and a half metres high, so he had to keep ducking his head down in case he was noticed from any of the rear windows.

He had reached only the third cottage up the lane when a dog started furiously barking and leaping up at the back-yard gate. He stayed absolutely still but the dog kept on barking until he heard a door open and a woman's voice snap, 'Madra! Will you shut your bake, you eejit! What's the matter with you? Come along in!'

He waited until the door had closed and then he continued up to the next back yard, which was behind the cottage where Farry had taken the shopping. Cautiously, he peered over the top of the wall. The back yard was crammed with junk – an old gas stove, a rusty bicycle with no front wheel, a sodden single mattress with a dark stain in the middle of it, and a heap of piled-up beige carpet. The paint on the back door was peeling, and the net curtains at the back window were sagging and amber with nicotine. The window itself was so filthy it was difficult for Detective O'Brien to see inside, especially now that the sun was brighter, and reflecting from the concrete wall. Detective O'Brien could even see the reflection of the top of his own head in it.

He could hear a man's voice, though, and after a few seconds he saw the pale grey shape of Farry, walking backwards and forwards inside the window like a shark seen in shallow water. It sounded as if he were talking on a mobile phone. Then he heard another man's voice, sharper, although he couldn't make out what he was saying.

He took out his radio and cupped his hand over his mouth.

'I'm outside the back of the cottage now,' he told Detective Buckley. 'I can't see Michael yet but I'm going to try to get close to the window so that I can take a lamp inside.'

'Just be wide,' Detective Buckley warned him. 'You know what these bastards are like.'

'I have you.'

Detective O'Brien lifted the latch on the back gate, but when he pushed against it, he found that it was bolted. He waited for a moment, and then he peered over the top of the wall again. There was no sign of anybody inside the window, although he could still hear voices.

He ducked along to the back gate of the next yard up the passageway, and tried that. It opened easily, and inside the yard was freshly swept, with green boxes planted with dwarf junipers and winter cabbage. The wooden shutters over the window were closed, so he presumed that there was nobody home. On the left-hand side there was a lean-to coal bunker, and he reckoned that if he could climb on top of that, he would be able to see at an acute angle into the room where Farry was talking.

He unbuttoned his dark green pea coat and the tweed jacket that he was wearing underneath it, and loosened the Sig Sauer automatic in the holster that he wore on his hip. If Detective Ó Doibhilin was in there, he wanted to be prepared for anything, even though he knew that they should wait for the Regional Support Unit to arrive. One of his friends had been shot during a post office robbery in Macroom while he was still fumbling to tug out his gun, and even though his injury hadn't been life-threatening, it had effectively ended his career in the Garda.

He let himself into the back yard and quietly closed the gate behind him. Then he dragged over one of the plant boxes and placed it up against the coal bunker so that he could use it as a step. He heaved himself up on to its sloping lid, balancing himself on his knees and gripping the top of the wall with both hands to stop himself from sliding back down. Now he could clearly see through the next-door window.

The room in which Farry was still pacing backwards and forwards was a dark, cramped kitchen with a pine dresser and an old-fashioned sink with upright brass taps, although Detective O'Brien also noticed the gleam of a shiny new electric cooker. The kitchen door was wide open, so that he could see right through to the living room at the front of the cottage, but he could only make out the back of a red-upholstered armchair with a man's black hair sticking up. It could have been Detective Ó Doibhilin or the man who was guarding him, or neither.

There was nothing more that Detective O'Brien could do. If he couldn't confirm that Detective Ó Doibhilin was being held here, the RSU wouldn't be able to negotiate with Farry to release him unharmed. They would have to smash their way in with a battering-ram and stun grenades. If he was here, they couldn't allow Farry even a few seconds to harm him or hold a gun to his head and use him as hostage. But even if he wasn't, they would still have to stop him from picking up his phone and warning Seamus Twomey that the Garda hadn't kept their side of the bargain – which could mean that, wherever he was, Detective Ó Doibhilin was in real danger of being instantly shot.

Detective O'Brien carefully released his grip on the top of the wall and slid down the lid of the coal bunker. As he dropped to the ground he knocked over the plant box and spilled peat across the freshly swept bricks. He picked the box up and carried it back to where it had been before, but as he did so he heard the back door of the cottage being unlocked. The door was flung open, and a white-haired man in a long black overcoat appeared, brandishing a long copper fire-poker in one hand and staring at Detective O'Brien like an outraged heron.

'What in the name of Jesus are you doing in my garden, you tinker? Thought I was out, did you? Thought you'd rob me? Well, I was out but now I'm back and I'm calling the guards. You just wait there, you no-good knacker!'

'Stall it, will you?' said Detective O'Brien. 'I'm not here to rob you. I'm a guard myself. Look, I can show my ID.'

'Oh, that's the oldest fecking trick in the book, that is!' the old man spat at him. 'You can get them IDs on the interweb these days, everybody knows that! You think because I have a few white hairs that I'm some kind of gom? You just wait there!'

'Listen, I'm sorry I knocked over your plants there but you'll just have to take my word for it that I wasn't here to rob you and now I have to go. So, goodbye.'

As Detective O'Brien opened the back gate the old man came hobbling out and struck the gate hard with his fire-poker. 'You stay right there! I'm calling the guards! I might have caught you before you robbed me but it'll be one of my neighbours you'll be robbing next, as sure as eggs is eggs!'

Detective O'Brien held his warrant card close up in front of the old man's face, although he wasn't sure that he was able to focus on it. 'There,' he said, trying to stay patient. 'An Garda Síochána. Detective Garda Kenneth O'Brien. Now get yourself back inside before I haul you in for threatening behaviour.'

He swung the gate around to force the old man back and then he stepped out into the passageway. As he did so, though, the next-door gate opened and Farry appeared.

'What's the feckin' bang here, fellers?' he asked. 'All this feckin' shoutin', like. What the feck's goin' on?'

'This tinker here was only trying to climb into my upstairs window,' the old man protested. 'When I caught him, he had the nerve to tell me he was a guard.'

Farry stared at Detective O'Brien, and as he did so his piggy eyes widened in recognition and his mouth slowly opened, as if he were letting out a long silent shout.

He didn't say anything but in slow motion Detective O'Brien saw his right hand plunging into his jacket. His bright red tie was tangled for a second around the butt of an automatic pistol.

Detective O'Brien flapped back his pea coat and went for his own pistol. The two of them pulled out their guns almost simultaneously and stood less than three metres away from each other, both of them crouching, both of them holding their weapons double-handed. The old man looked from one to the other and uttered a low croaking sound.

'I'm a guard,' said Detective O'Brien. 'Drop it.'

The old man dropped the fire-poker with a clang and as he did so Farry fired. The narrow concrete passageway echoed with a deafening bang as Detective O'Brien was hit in the chest and pitched backwards on to the ground. He lifted his head and tried to curl his gun-hand around, so that he could fire back at Farry, but then his head fell back and the gun clattered on to the bricks.

Farry went up to him and leaned over.

'It's fecking him all right. Gobshite. Got my own back at last.'

'Holy Mary we should call for an ambulance,' the old man told him.

'What for, boy? He's stone fecking dead. A wheelbarrow, that'll do it.'

'But he said he was a guard.'

'What feckin' difference does that make? He was trying to rob you, wasn't he? And he whipped out a gun, didn't he? What was you supposed to do? Let him shoot you first, and then rob you? That was self-defence, like, no question about it. Primey fashey.'

Another man appeared from the junk-filled back yard. He had greasy swept-back hair and a sharply pointed nose and a jumble of bad teeth. He was carrying a large Colt automatic, and he had it cocked.

'Christ on a bicycle, Farry. What have you been and done now?'

'Self-defence,' said Farry. He was beginning to pant now, as if he were suffering the beginnings of an asthma attack. 'He pulled his gun on me, Vincent. Didn't give me no feckin' warning at all. What else was I supposed to do? Hey, you – you'll back me up, won't you, old feller?'

'Oh sure, like. I'll back you up all right,' said the old man, although he kept glancing nervously down at Detective O'Brien lying on the ground. Rivulets of dark red blood were creeping along the pattern of the bricks.

'So what in the name of God are we going to do with him now?' asked Vincent. 'We can't just fecking leave him here. The cats'll be after him.'

'I should ring the emergency,' said the old man, picking up his fire-poker.

'No, no, you don't want to be after doing that,' said Farry. 'We have friends who can handle this, without any of the bother. Vincent, give Seamus a bell, would you, boy.'

'Why me? You fecking shot him, Farry, not me.'

They were still standing in the passageway wondering what to do when they heard a shout, *'Freeze! Armed garda! Drop those weapons and put up your hands!'*

They turned around and saw Detective Buckley stalking up the passageway towards them, with his pistol raised.

'Oh Christ!' said Farry, with a breathless wheeze. 'Come on, Vincent, sketch!'

'Hey!' said the old man, but Farry and Vincent bundled back into their back gate, slammed it shut, bolted it, and then locked the back door, too.

Detective Buckley reached the gate and hammered on it with his fist. Then he looked down at Detective O'Brien.

'Self-defence,' said the old man.

Detective O'Brien's pale green eyes were open and he was staring blindly at the sky.

'What?' said Detective Buckley. He was too shocked to understand what the old man meant. But then he looked over the back-yard wall into the kitchen window, and he could see Farry and Vincent open the front door of the cottage. He could see another man, too, and they seemed to be pushing or dragging him out.

'Call 112!' he told the old man. 'Tell them what's happened, and where – there's a garda been shot. Do it now!'

With that, he pelted back down the passageway to Lower Road, so fast that he nearly stumbled over. He climbed into his car, started up the engine and U-turned in the middle of the road, his tyres slithering on the tarmac. His guess was that Farry would be returning to his car opposite the Anchor Bar and speeding off down Middle Road, which joined Lower Road down by the harbour wall.

He felt numb, and everything around him was a jumble of disjointed images – the russet-painted houses and the stone wall flashing past him, the yachts in the harbour, a man and his dog skipping to cross the road in front of him. All he could hear was the blood thumping in his ears.

Farry's Mercedes came hurtling out of Middle Road, just past the Oar Bar pub. It collided with the side of Detective Buckley's car with a smash that sent the Toyota rolling sideways over the retaining wall in the middle of the road and into the path of an oncoming van. There was another loud crash and pieces of van and Toyota were scattered across the carriageway. Detective Buckley's car ended up on the pavement, on its roof.

Farry didn't stop. Although his Mercedes had lost a hubcap and its offside headlight was hanging down like a gouged-out eyeball, he put his foot down and headed off towards Carrigaline and Cork.

On Lower Road, by the harbour, the only sound was the keening of seagulls. Three yachtsmen hurried over to Detective Buckley's car and tried to prise open the driver's door. Several customers from the Oar Bar climbed over the wall to help them, and one of them brought a tyre-iron.

Detective Buckley was upside-down, hunched against the Toyota's roof. His head was resting at an acute angle against his right shoulder, and even somebody with no medical training could see that his neck was broken.

Twenty-Two

Katie was trying to decide if she wanted a chicken-and-stuffing sandwich when Chief Superintendent MacCostagáin called her.

'Kathleen – would you come along and see me right this minute, please. It's urgent.'

'Have you made up your mind what you want for your lunch?' asked Moirin, as she passed her door.

'Oh, I don't know. Some sandwich or biscuit or other, you choose. So long as it's not tongue.'

When she reached Denis MacCostagáin's office she found, unusually, that the door was closed. She knocked and when she went in, she saw that Superintendent Pearse was there, too, and Inspector O'Rourke, and Sergeant Nolan. She could tell by their expressions that something serious had happened.

Denis MacCostagáin stood up from behind his desk and said, 'We've had a call from a schoolmaster in Dripsey. He was taking his boys for a practice match at the Dripsey GAA grounds by St Senan's Abbey. He and his assistant heard somebody crying out, so it seems, and when they went to investigate they found a young fellow in the graveyard there badly injured. Both of his feet were severed.'

'My God, how? Was it an accident?'

'Very far from being an accident, Kathleen. The young fellow's name is Aidan Lacey, and he's the son of Sergeant John Lacey. I'm sorry to say they found Sergeant Lacey, too, tied upright to a gravestone. He's been beheaded, just like Garda O'Regan, and a tin whistle has been stuck down his throat. There's no sign of his head. The only way we know it was him was because Aidan told this schoolmaster fellow that it was his da.'

Katie sat down. 'That's terrible,' she said. 'Jesus, that's beyond terrible. That's tragic. He was pure sound, Sergeant Lacey.'

'Well, yes, our paths didn't cross very often, but from what I recall he was a most effective officer. A bit holier-than-thou maybe.'

'As far as I know, sir, he was only asking why we were failing to go ahead with so many prosecutions when we had more than enough evidence to get a conviction. I wouldn't call that "holier-than-thou".'

'All right, maybe not. But he was what you might call a maverick. Sometimes a little too individual for his own good. You'd only have to show him a line and he'd go out of his way not to toe it.'

'His murder proves one thing, though, doesn't it?' said Katie. 'Frank Magorian was totally off beam with his theory about a lone header being responsible for killing Garda O'Regan. There can't be any question at all now. Somebody was out to prevent both O'Regan and Lacey from saying their piece at the Disclosures Tribunal – and to make a show of them, too, I'd say, to warn off any others who are supposed to be giving evidence.'

'Has Justice McGuigan sent you the full list of whistle-blowers yet?' asked Superintendent Pearse.

'I'm expecting it any minute. It might even have arrived already.'

'Well, this may sound like shutting the stable door, but as soon as you know who they are, I'll be making immediate arrangements to have them all protected.'

'Protected how?' Katie asked him.

'Depending on their own preference, we can either instal them in a safe house somewhere until they've given their evidence, or else we can give them a twenty-four-hour armed guard from the RSU.'

'That's all very well. But we have to consider who might have murdered Garda O'Regan – and now Sergeant Lacey, and what their motive was. Are they going to be safe, even in a safe house, or under guard?'

'What are you suggesting?' asked Denis MacCostagáin.

'I'm not suggesting anything. I'm simply asking the same question that I always ask when a crime's committed – who stands most to benefit? In the case of these two whistle-blowers, it could be a garda who's been bending the rules, and might be found guilty by the tribunal.'

'You're seriously saying that O'Regan and Lacey could have been murdered by a serving Garda officer?'

'Or *officers*, yes, plural. It's a possibility we have to consider. In fact, with those tin whistles pushed down their throats, it's more than just a possibility. Who else would think of doing that, but somebody who was resentful about whistle-blowers, and didn't want their evidence to come out?'

'Well, you never know,' said Inspector O'Rourke. 'It could have been done deliberately to put us off the scent, to make us suspect that it was gardaí who killed them. There's more than one criminal gang in Cork that is happy with the status quo.'

'I hope you're not saying that *we* should be happy with the status quo, too?'

'There has to be some level of live-and-let-live when it comes to policing, ma'am, you know that as well as I do. We don't have the budget or the manpower to follow up every single minor transgression.'

'There's a difference between live-and-let-live and outright bribery, Francis.'

'It depends what degree of bribery you're talking about. If a guard has a burger in the CoqBull and asks them if they take warrant card, does that really constitute corruption? It's more like friendly community relations if you ask me. Come on, ma'am – all of us have been approached at one time or another and offered a favour to turn a blind eye. I was approached myself by the Authentic IRA, you'll remember, when Bobby Quilty was running it, and I believe that even Frank Magorian has had hundred-euro notes waved under his nose from time to time.'

Katie was too impatient to argue about potential perpetrators any longer. 'Sergeant Lacey – have the Technical Bureau been notified?'

'They have, yes,' said Superintendent Pearse. 'Bill Phinner's putting a specialist team together right now.'

'Well, I'm going to Dripsey to see this for myself,' Katie told him. 'The media don't know about it yet, do they?'

'No, we're keeping a lid on it, just like we tried to do with Garda O'Regan, although that will probably do us a fat lot of good. Mathew McElvey down in the press office says there's no indication that the media have been tipped off about it yet, but it won't surprise me if they will be very soon.'

'I think I'll come with you,' said Denis MacCostagáin.

'Really?' asked Katie.

'To pay my respects, so to speak. I knew Sergeant Lacey's father. And it's been a while since I saw a real live dead body. Perhaps I need to remind myself of the reality of this job. It's not all paperwork and policy meetings and masonic dinners.'

When they arrived at the ruins of St Senan's Abbey, they found that the graveyard was cordoned off and crowded with uniformed gardaí from Ballincollig as well as forensic technicians and photographers. A coroner's ambulance was parked across the entrance to the GAA pitch.

Although the sun was shining, the surface of the lane and the bushes all around it were still wet with this morning's rainwater, so that they sparkled, and a thin mist was rising between the gravestones so that it looked like a scene out of a ghost story.

Katie had driven here with Detective Inspector Mulliken and Detective O'Donovan, while Chief Superintendent MacCostagáin had followed them in another car with Inspector O'Rourke.

Before she had left, Moirin had brought Katie a turkey sandwich and a packet of Keogh's crisps but Katie had asked her to keep them for later. She had once said to Conor that witnessing death was the most effective diet ever.

She had been thinking about Conor as Detective O'Donovan drove them out to Inniscarra on the Cork ring road. She had still had no word from him, and he could be anywhere. He might even have left the country. The death of Guzz Eye McManus and his female companion in the fire at Ballyknock had appeared on the TV news, and in the papers, but Inspector Carroll had been quoted as saying, 'We've no leads so far as to who might have started the blaze, and so we're appealing to anybody who might have any information at all to come forwards.'

She knew that included her, and she knew that with every second she hesitated to report Conor's confession, she was giving him a better chance to escape justice. She loved him. She thought she loved him, anyway, but her feelings were so mixed now. He was guilty of a major crime, no matter how passionately he had hated Guzz Eye McManus for the cruelty that he had inflicted on so many hundreds of dogs, and despite the fact that he hadn't deliberately set out to kill him.

But was it love that was holding her back from reporting him, or cowardice? Was she frightened that her involvement with him would damage her career, or even wreck it altogether? Her attempt to prosecute McManus had been stymied, and McManus's thugs had severely injured and almost killed Barney, although she had no way of proving that he had been behind it. Who wouldn't suspect that she might have wanted her revenge, and that she had encouraged Conor to take the law into his own hands, as well as a bottle of petrol?

She was still thinking about Conor when they all climbed out of their cars and walked into the graveyard. He was like a nagging headache that refused to go away. But as she crunched along the shingle path and saw the sunlight shining through the empty windows of the abbey tower, she knew that she had to turn her mind now to other things, and she also knew that she was close to making a decision.

Bill Phinner had arrived only a few minutes before them, and he was standing between the memorials where Aidan Lacey had been found, talking to one of his technical experts, who was taking blood samples from the stonework, and to a freckly-faced sergeant from Ballincollig.

'How's it going, ma'am?' he greeted her. 'This is Sergeant McPolin. He was one of the first on the scene. I'm afraid we have another execution on our hands.'

'Never saw nothing like it in all my career,' said Sergeant McPolin, shaking his head so hard that Katie could almost imagine his freckles flying off.

'Same m.o., Bill?' she asked him.

Denis MacCostagáin was coming up behind Katie and so before he answered her Bill Phinner said, 'How's it coming on, sir?'

'I wanted to see this for myself,' said Denis MacCostagáin. 'When you injure one garda, you injure all of us. This kind of thing – it shakes us right down to our very foundations.'

Katie turned to look at him. He had been sounding very pessimistic recently, and tired, but she had rarely heard him speak as if they were only a few days away from the end of the world.

Bill Phinner said, 'Come and see the poor unfortunate fellow for yourselves. We have all the outward appearances of the same m.o. His head was taken off his neck with a chainsaw, no question about that, although we'll have to check in the lab if it was the same chainsaw that was used on Garda O'Regan. There are some differences, though.'

'Such as?'

'Mainly that Garda O'Regan was sitting upright when he was beheaded and the marks on his wrists showed that his hands had been cuffed in front of him. But when Sergeant Lacey's head was taken off, he was lying face-down on that memorial with his hands cuffed behind his back. Look at this granite slab. Look at the blood all over it and also these fresh-cut grooves in the stone.

The teeth of the chainsaw bit into it, after it had ripped through his neck.'

'You can tell that he was lying face-down?'

Bill Phinner nodded. 'You'll be able to see for yourself. It's the way the teeth cut through the neck and the spinal column. It would have been over in a matter of seconds. It's not the way I'd want to go. Me – I just want to go to bed one night and wake up the next the morning to find that I've died. But Sergeant Lacey wouldn't have felt much.'

He led Katie to the stone cross where Sergeant Lacey's body was tied up, with his arms outspread. The blood had dried on his waterproof jacket like dribbles of red wax, and what with his stump of a neck and the tin whistle sticking out like a wick, he looked like some grotesque giant candle.

Katie crossed herself and whispered, '*Requiem aeternam dona ei, Domine, et lux perpetua luceat ei.*'

Denis MacCostagáin stepped forwards and stood staring at the headless body in silence for almost fifteen seconds. Then he said, 'What a sacrifice to make. And in the end, what good will it do? Did he really believe that he could change anything? And will his name be remembered in a hundred years' time?'

'Maybe not,' said Katie. 'But there might be improvements in the way that we run the Garda that are all to his credit – him and all the other whistle-blowers.'

'What about the whistle?' asked Detective O'Donovan. 'Does it match the whistles that were stolen from the Music Market?'

'I can't tell you for certain, of course,' said Bill Phinner. 'Not until we've finished taking all of our scene-of-crime pictures and examined it back in the lab. But it matches in every superficial respect. It's a low-D whistle made of nickel alloy and it has the hand symbol on it for Feadóga Lámhdhéanta in Kerry – Hand-made Whistles.'

'We've never released any information about the whistle, so it would be a huge coincidence if a copycat killer used the identical one,' said Katie. 'I'll wait for your report, Bill, but I think it's reasonable to assume that Sergeant Lacey was murdered by the same scummers that did for Garda O'Regan. Was his son in any fit state to describe who attacked them?'

'By the time we got here he was unconscious,' said Sergeant McPolin. 'But he spoke to the two teachers who found him, and according to them he said that it was three fellows altogether, all wearing masks. He'd lost so much blood that it's pure amazing he was still alive and talking. The paramedics took him to CUH, along with his feet. I don't know if they can sew them back on again, like, but they can work miracles these days with the surgery, can't they?'

Katie took a last look at Sergeant Lacey's crucified body and then at all her fellow officers and then started to walk back towards her car. Denis MacCostagáin caught up with her and walked close beside her.

'I don't see the point in keeping this embargoed any longer,' said Katie. 'We need to appeal for as many witnesses as we possibly can. I think it might be worth offering a reward for information, too, if Frank Magorian will agree to it.'

'I'm not so sure,' said Denis MacCostagáin. 'The public trust in the Garda is at an all-time low as it is. Don't you think it might be better if we dealt with this one as quietly as possible?'

'So you do believe that gardaí could be involved?'

'That's not what I meant. But – just as you were saying earlier – we have to consider *why* these two whistle-blowers were silenced, and that means we have to explore every possibility. Unfortunately, that includes the possibility that there may be certain Garda officers who are keen not to have certain evidence divulged in front of the tribunal, and who may go to some lengths to make sure that it doesn't come out.'

'I'm sorry, sir, but that sounds as if you're agreeing with me.'

Denis MacCostagáin reached his car and opened the passenger door. He looked around at St Senan's Abbey, and then back at Katie.

'We give so much to this job, Kathleen. We give everything.

We risk our lives, we risk our reputations, we endure the endless odium of so many people in our community, and all for the kind of pay that an Iarnród driver would spit at. Yet every single day we're expected to be paragons of virtue, upholders of the law, and to live our lives by a moral code that even priests struggle to abide by.'

He paused, and then he said, 'That's why I wanted to come here today to see Sergeant Lacey. I wanted to remind myself what it costs to be a member of An Garda Síochána.'

Katie was about to answer him when her phone rang.

'Sean Begley, ma'am. Everything's gone crazy down here at Crosser.'

He was silent for a few seconds, and Katie thought that he might have been cut off.

'Sean? Hallo? Are you still there, Sean?'

'I am, yes. Sorry. But O'Brien's been shot and Buckley's been involved in a car crash. They're both of them dead.'

'Oh, God. Oh God, Sean.'

'What's wrong?' asked Denis MacCostagáin. 'What's happened, Kathleen?'

Katie lifted her hand to him to indicate that she would tell him in a moment. 'What about Michael Ó Doibhilin?' she asked.

'We have him, safe and well, but in a fierce state of shock.'

'Thank God for one mercy. Who was the shooter, do you know?'

'Farry Logan. The same fellow that Buckley and O'Brien were following. He was trying to get away but we caught him just as he was steaming out of Crosser at about twice the speed limit with the front of his car all bashed in.'

In fits and starts, with an audible catch in his throat, Detective Sergeant Begley told Katie how Farry had shot Detective O'Brien, and how Detective Buckley had collided with his Mercedes when he had chased after him.

'Farry's insisting that he had no idea that O'Brien was a cop. He says he was sure that he was a knacker who was trying to rob the house next door, and when he pulled out his gun he feared for his life and shot him in self-defence.'

'Mother of God. I don't suppose he has any corroborating witnesses.'

'He does, as it goes. Some senile old fellow who lives next door.'

'It gets better, then. Jesus, Sean, it never rains but it lashes. I'm here in Inniscarra. Sergeant John Lacey has been found in the graveyard here with his head cut off, just like Garda O'Regan.'

'You're joking. Well, no, I know you're not joking really. It's like the doors of Hell have opened up this morning and all the demons have come dancing out to make trouble.'

'Listen, I'm going directly back to the station,' said Katie. 'I'll send DI Mulliken down to Crosser to take over there, but you'll be able to cope in the meantime, won't you? Where's Farry Logan right now?'

'He's in the Garda station here, along with another scumbag called Vincent Mulroney.'

'I'll have them collected and brought back to Anglesea Street. You've arrested them and read them their rights and everything? Good. And what about Michael Ó Doibhilin? Where is he?'

'He's in the Garda station, too, having a cup of strong tea.'

When Katie had finished talking to Detective Sergeant Begley, she put her hands deep into her coat pockets and looked at Denis MacCostagáin with an expression of infinite sadness on her face.

'Detectives Buckley and O'Brien are both dead,' she told him. 'You were right, weren't you, when you said that we give so much to this job? Those two have given everything.'

Denis MacCostagáin looked back at her for a long time without saying a word. It was almost as if he wasn't interested in finding out how they had died, or if it was more than he could bear.

A hooded crow fluttered down and perched on the graveyard gate. It rustled its feathers and then it let out a harsh, provocative croak, as if to say, *See? You humans think you're going to live for ever, but you never do.*

Twenty-Three

'Maybe it was Farry Logan who was actually holding the gun,' Katie told the five detectives who were sitting serious-faced on the couches in her office. 'It was Seamus Twomey, though, who pulled the trigger.'

As soon as she returned to Anglesea Street, she had started to put together a team to investigate the deaths of Detectives Buckley and O'Brien. Once they had been briefed and headed off to Crosshaven, she intended to set up another team specifically to investigate the murders of the two whistle-blowers, Garda O'Regan and Sergeant Lacey, but that would be a very different operation altogether.

She had chosen Detective Inspector Mulliken to lead the team that would be looking into the killing of the two detectives. This was because of his long experience in dealing with IRA splinter groups in Cork, and whatever the immediate circumstances that had led to the deaths of Buckley and O'Brien, they had died as a consequence of Seamus Twomey's abduction of Michael Ó Doibhilin.

She had also picked Kyna, because she trusted her implicitly, and she had an incomparable talent for wheedling information out of reluctant witnesses. Almost every witness who had ever had incriminating information about Seamus Twomey had been reluctant, and with very good reason.

'It was Seamus Twomey who abducted Detective Ó Doibhilin and threatened his life so that we wouldn't interfere with his opioid-smuggling business,' she continued. 'The ultimate guilt for Detective O'Brien's murder and for the accident that killed Detective Buckley is his. All we have to do is prove it.'

She held up her hand and ticked off on her fingers the charges she wanted them to prove against Seamus Twomey. 'I want him convicted as an accessory to murder, for hostage-taking as defined under the Terrorist Offences Act of 2005, for false imprisonment, for the threat to kill or cause serious harm, and for drug-running under the Misuse of Drugs Act.

'Now we have Detective Ó Doibhilin safely back with us, Twomey no longer has that leverage against us. It's just an appalling tragedy that his freedom was won at such a cost.'

'It's not only Twomey we need to be going after,' said Kyna. 'Douglas Quinn and Twomey's sister, Gwenith, are equally involved in *Fola na hÉireann*. In fact, I'd say that Gwenith has a heap more influence over their activities than you'd think. *Heap* – in her case – being a most appropriate word. Ugh! It makes me fair shudder to think of her!'

'Let's take this step by step, though,' said Katie. 'These are wily and influential and violent people, even if they might give the impression that they're nothing more than a gang of Fair Hill gurriers. I want Twomey to believe that we're swallowing Farry Logan's story about self-defence, right up until the moment when we have enough evidence to arrest him with a reasonable chance of conviction.'

When Katie had finished briefing them, the team trooped out of her office, collected their coats, and set off to Crosshaven. Bill Phinner's deputy, Fergus Kenny, had already left with three technical experts to photograph Detective O'Brien's body and Detective Buckley's overturned Toyota.

Katie was preparing her notes for a meeting about the whistle-blowers when Moirin came in.

'You had a call during your briefing. Dr O'Sullivan from Gilabbey Veterinary Hospital in Togher. He said he was sorry to disturb you but he's had difficulty getting in touch with Conor.'

'That's all right, Moirin. Thanks a million.'

'Would you care for your sandwich now?'

Katie stopped in the middle of prodding at her phone and shook her head.

'You should, you know, ma'am. Just when you don't feel like eating, that's the time you need to keep up your strength.'

'Well, okay, Moirin. Fetch it in and I'll look at it. Maybe I can absorb some nutrition through my eyes.'

Dr O'Sullivan answered his phone almost immediately, as if he had been waiting to pounce on it.

'Dr O'Sullivan, it's Katie Maguire. Have you news of Barney?'

'Oh, hallo, Katie! How are you going on there? Yes, I do, and it's good news, too! I tried to ring Conor but for some reason he wasn't picking up.'

'Conor's been tied up lately as it happens. Some investigation he's involved with.'

'It's grand work that Conor does for dogs, no question about it. Did you hear about that dog-fighting fellow, McManus? Got himself cremated when his mobile home burned down. Conor was always gnashing his teeth and deleting expletives about McManus, so I bet he won't be shedding any tears.'

'Yes – yes, I did hear about that,' said Katie. 'So – please tell me, how's Barney?'

'Barney's making the kind of recovery you could only pray for, Katie. He still has the body brace around the ribs, and the splint on his left hind leg, but he's able to hobble around. His respiration is fine and his appetite is back to what it should be. If you'd like to come over and pick him up, he's ready for you at any time.'

Katie, quite unexpectedly, found that her eyes were filled with tears. She reached over for a tissue and wiped them, just as Moirin came in with her sandwich and her packet of crisps.

'Is everything all right?' Moirin asked her, anxiously.

Katie nodded. 'Better than expected, Moirin. I can fetch Barney home. I'm wondering what he's going to make of Foltchain.'

'Don't you worry, ma'am. It'll be love at first sight.'

Katie sat and thought for a while, and then she rang Dr O'Sullivan again.

'Could you do me a favour, Dr O'Sullivan, and send Conor a text? I'm having some trouble getting in touch with him, too, and I'm up the walls for the rest of the day. Could you tell him that Barney's ready to be fetched home, and can he come to Togher and collect him – say at six-thirty this evening?'

'If you want me to, sure. But—'

Katie could tell that he was wondering why *she* couldn't text him.

'It's just that he'll think I'm missing Barney so much that I want him home before he's ready. It'll sound more professional coming from you.'

'All right, Katie. No problem at all. I'll do it now.'

Katie sat back and looked at her sandwich. She had made up her mind about Conor when she had seen the sunlight shining through the empty windows of St Senan's Abbey, but now she had put her decision into train, and she knew that there was no going back on it. Maybe she was being over-optimistic about Conor's feelings for her, and about his concern for Barney's welfare. Maybe he was too far away to reach Togher by half past six. Maybe – as she had thought before – he wasn't even in the country.

She finished preparing her notes on the whistle-blowers and she couldn't help being aware of how quiet the station was. There was none of the usual laughter or the slamming of doors. They had lost more officers in this one week than they had in the past three years.

Superintendent Pearse had sent two of his officers out about an hour ago to inform Detective Buckley's wife and Detective O'Brien's parents that they had been killed in the line of duty. She would visit them herself tomorrow morning.

Inside her head, she could still hear Detective O'Brien's cacophonous singing. He had always maintained that, because he was ginger, he could sing as well as Ed Sheeran.

'It's in the genes,' he had always insisted. 'When you have Tanora pubes, that's the only way you're ever going to get a girl – serenade her.'

She tried to smile at the memory of that, but she couldn't. She picked up her plate and dropped her sandwich into her waste-paper bin.

At four o'clock she went along to Denis MacCostagáin's office to set up her investigation to track down the killers of Garda O'Regan and Sergeant Lacey. All of her team were already gathered there, talking in subdued voices.

'I'm calling this Operation Butterfly,' she announced, as she sat down. 'It's after that traditional tin-whistle tune, "The Butterfly". I'm told it's one of the easiest tunes to pick up, so let's hope the murderers of Garda O'Regan and Sergeant Lacey are the same.'

'Well, we have at least two eyewitnesses,' said Detective Inspector Robert Fitzpatrick. 'The only trouble is that Mrs O'Regan's in a coma still and the lad's in no fit state to be interviewed yet.'

Detective Inspector Fitzpatrick would be heading up the operation, with Detectives Scanlan and O'Mara. Katie had also brought in two newer recruits, both of whom had only been posted to Anglesea Street at the end of August – Detectives Bedelia Murrish and Cairbre O'Crean. She had wanted them as part of the team because they were young and bright and had both shown themselves to have a natural talent for undercover work. She had also chosen them because they were so new to Cork, and were less likely to have picked up any bad habits from longer-serving detectives, or been influenced yet by any of the city's gangsters, either financially or by threats of violence. Detective Murrish came originally from Mayo and Detective O'Crean from Sligo.

She hadn't mentioned her reasons for selecting them to Denis MacCostagáin or Detective Inspector Fitzpatrick, and she felt a twinge of guilt that she was being so suspicious about her fellow officers. All the same, she believed that a healthy dose of suspicion might be the only way to make sure that no more whistle-blowers lost their heads.

'Bill Phinner says that he has a heap of forensic evidence,' said Detective Inspector Fitzpatrick. 'He has footprints, tyre tracks, and he has a cigarette butt too that may have been dropped by one of the offenders. There's no question that when we haul them in, we'll be able to prove beyond any doubt that they were the guilty parties. Always supposing we *do* haul them in.'

Detective Inspector Fitzpatrick was a handsome, athletically built man of fifty-two, with close-cropped grey hair and the face of a rugby player – strong forehead, strong jaw, and a short Roman nose with a bump in the middle. It was only his eyes that put Katie off. They were so pale and colourless that they could have been soaked in bleach all night, and it was almost impossible to tell what he was thinking. He had surprised her once by stopping her in the corridor to admire a Max Mara blazer that she had been wearing, even though his voice had been flat and his eyes had been equally expressionless.

She had gone home that night and told her previous lover, John, that she felt as if she had been complimented by a cod.

His colourless eyes and his flat voice weren't important, though. What counted was his huge experience in dealing with cases of bribery and fraud. It had taken him over two years, but he had eventually found damning evidence that several Cork county councillors had been paid hundreds of thousands of euros to approve housing developments in and around Clonakilty.

Detective Murrish was skinny, with straw-coloured hair that was usually plaited into a coronet. Her eyes were misty blue, and slightly hooded, and she had a tendency to sit with her mouth open when she was listening to anybody talking to her, which gave her the appearance of being dim. However, she had passed all of her tests at Templemore with outstanding grades, and she had applied to join the National Surveillance Unit, the most secretive arm of An Garda Síochána, with only about a hundred officers, all of whom remained undercover both on and off duty.

To look at, Detective O'Crean could have been any one of the young men crowded around the bar at Havana Browns nightclub every evening, with his hair shaved up at the sides and a bland, pudgy, innocent face. Like Detective Murrish, though, he had scored high marks in his training exams, and he was a fourth-grade kick-boxer.

'For beginners, we'll be combing through all of the evidence that Garda O'Regan and Sergeant Lacey were intending to present to the Disclosures Tribunal,' said Katie. 'They'll have named the names of Garda officers who they suspected of favouritism or corruption or incompetence or taking bribes. As far as possible we'll be checking on the whereabouts of those officers at the time that the murders were committed.

'We'll be showing deference to nobody in this investigation. It doesn't matter if the officers accused of malfeasance are traffic cops or chief superintendents. We need to assess if the accusations against them were likely to have cost them their careers, or possible demotion, if they were proved to be true. To that extent we'll be prejudging the conclusions that His Honour Mr Justice Peter McGuigan will eventually be coming to.

'Don't get me wrong. I'm not saying necessarily that it was gardaí who murdered our two whistle-blowers. Garda O'Regan was about to give evidence that criminals who were supposed to be locked up in prison were walking about free, while Sergeant Lacey apparently had information that the prosecutions for a rake of car thefts were quietly being dropped before they could be taken to court. So we'll also have to be looking into the movements and motives of prison officers at Rathmore Road, as well as prosecution solicitors in the DPP.

'What concerns me more than anything is that Garda O'Regan and Sergeant Lacey were preparing to give evidence about two totally different areas of corruption. If they were murdered by criminal gangs, it doesn't seem logical that it was the same criminal gang. The criminals who were let out of prison were drug-dealers, the others were car thieves. Yet both victims were murdered in exactly the same way. Both were beheaded and both had tin whistles stuck into their necks. So what's the connection?'

'How many more whistle-blowers are scheduled to be giving evidence?' asked Detective Murrish. 'And what are they giving evidence about?'

'There are three more, as far as I know,' said Katie. 'We've asked the justice's office for their names and the names of their lawyers so that we can find out exactly what testimony they're intending to present to the tribunal. Not only that – and this is urgent – we're also going to give them protection. I've already discussed that with Superintendent Pearse and I'll be discussing it again with him after this briefing.'

Denis MacCostagáin cleared his throat. 'I don't have to tell you that this investigation has to be kept strictly confidential at every level,' he told them. 'These days, with the social media, the Twitter and all that, you're guilty as soon as somebody accuses you. The whole reputation of An Garda Síochána is at stake here, and we don't want to see it sullied.'

They all looked at each other. They all realized that the evidence they uncovered could be devastating for the force's reputation. Katie had never known a case so critical to so many careers, including her own.

Her phone rang. It was Detective Sergeant Begley.

'How's it going on, ma'am? Sorry if I'm interrupting anything, but I've just managed to have a bit of a chat with Michael Ó Doibhilin.'

'Oh, yes, good. How is he?'

'He's still in shock, to tell you the truth, and I can't get too much sense out of him. I'm suggesting that I send him home for the night to recover, like. He can come in to the station in the morning and tell you the full story then. I'm sure he'll make much more sense tomorrow than he does now.'

'All right, Sean,' said Katie. 'That sounds sensible. You don't think he needs to see a doctor, do you?'

'I wouldn't say so. They didn't physically assault him at all. I think they just scared the shite out of him, like, do you know what I mean?'

'Yes,' said Katie. 'I know what you mean all right.'

Twenty-Four

Katie was getting ready to leave when Superintendent Pearse appeared in her office doorway. He looked deeply tired.

'What a day,' he said, and sat down on one of the couches under the window. 'It's been one of those days when you wish you could wind back the clock to breakfast time and start it all over again.'

Katie stood close beside him. She felt like putting her arms around him and giving him a consoling hug. 'I'll be visiting the Buckleys and the O'Briens myself tomorrow morning. It'll be full state funerals for the both of them. I'm going to miss them so much.'

'I thought you'd like to know that Farry Logan and Vincent Mulroney have just been brought in from Crosser. We're processing them now.'

'Do we know if they're going to be asking for legal aid?'

'No, they won't at all. That's almost the first thing that Logan said. He said he wasn't going to answer any questions but to ring for his solicitor – Nicholas Bourke, from Sweeney and Bourke, no less.'

'Nicholas Bourke? That slimeball? Fair play, he's a brilliant slimeball, as slimeballs go. He got Bobby Quilty off that sexual assault charge, didn't he, and I shall never know how he managed to do that. But he's not cheap, is he? I'll lay money that Seamus Twomey will be picking up the bill.'

Superintendent Pearse hauled himself up on to his feet again.

'I'll arrange for a preliminary interview tomorrow afternoon, if that's okay with you. We can do some further questioning when DI Mulliken and the technical boys and girls get back with whatever they've found.'

'I'll be coming downstairs in just a minute,' said Katie. 'I want to take a sconce at those two before I leave. I want to have their faces firmly fixed in my mind's eye, do you know what I mean, because I'm not going to rest until I see them on the front page of the *Echo*, convicted of murder and sent down for life.'

She was buttoning up her coat when Moirin told her that she had a call from a forensic accountant named James Gallagher, from the Garda National Economic Crime Bureau in Dublin.

'Me and my colleagues have almost finished going through Jimmy Ó Faoláin's books,' he told her. 'They've made pure entertaining reading, I have to tell you. Like, eat your heart out, Dan Brown, these are really great works of fiction. We'll have dotted the i's and crossed the t's tomorrow but I believe we've already pinned down what you're looking for. Perhaps I can come down to Cork the day after tomorrow and I can go through them with you.'

'That sounds perfect,' said Katie. 'Can you give me a clue what you've found?'

'It's somewhat complicated, to say the least, but basically Jimmy Ó Faoláin was running a pump and dump scheme with overvalued shares that was almost as hard to detect as Enron. At the same time he was operating a Ponzi game with carbon futures that didn't actually exist – not in the future, nor at any other time.'

'Was there any single investor or group of investors who lost out more than the others?'

'We believe there was one demographic group who were harder hit, yes, although it's not entirely clear from the code names that were used. You'll see for yourself, though, when I bring all our audits down to show you. It's fascinating stuff.'

By the time Katie came downstairs, Farry Logan and Vincent

Mulroney had been processed and photographed and locked in their cells. Superintendent Pearse came down to join her, and the duty officer led them to the cells so that she could see them.

He unlocked the door of Farry's cell and Katie stepped inside. Farry was sitting on the end of his bed with his arms folded. He didn't look up or acknowledge her in any way at all.

'He's had his phone call,' said the duty officer. 'He's also asked for a Ventolin inhaler because he suffers from the asthma. The doctor's seen him and says it's okay, and they're after sending one over from Phelans Pharmacy right now.'

Katie stood for a few moments and stared at Farry, until at last he glanced up at her. As soon as he had done that, she turned around without saying a word and walked out.

Vincent Mulroney was lying on his bed when they opened his cell, but he immediately rolled off it and stood up, snorting in one nostril and clenching his fists.

'Come here, I've done nothing at all,' he protested. 'I'm an innocent bystander. I never shot nobody and I never crashed no car.'

'You can tell the judge that, Vincent,' said Superintendent Pearse.

'I asked for a cup of tea and a cheeseburger too and nobody's fetched me nothing.'

'This is Anglesea Street Garda station, Vincent, not McDonald's. You'll be fed in due course.'

'Oh, will I? Thanks a million for nothing.'

Katie and Superintendent Pearse walked back to the reception area, with its domed glass roof and its tall black columns and its frondy palms. Two young women were sitting there, their hands tightly clasped together, red-eyed from crying. Whatever their story was, they were telling it to a sympathetic-looking female garda.

'Why is it always the best ones who die young, and the scum who live to a ripe old age?' asked Superintendent Pearse.

Katie said nothing, but squeezed his elbow, and gave him the saddest of smiles.

It took her less than ten minutes to drive to the Gilabbey Veterinary Hospital on Vicars Road in Togher, and she arrived at twenty
past six. The hospital was a grey, two-storey building in a long
road of discount bedding warehouses and car servicing garages.

As soon as she had made herself known to the receptionist, Dr
O'Sullivan came down to greet her. He was short, almost as short
as she was, with curly brown hair and huge black-rimmed glasses.
He was wearing the dark blue Gilabbey jacket with the hospital's
symbol of a stethoscope with a paw-print on the end of it.

'Katie, so glad to meet you!' he bustled. 'I'm so pleased that
you could come too! I got through to Conor at last and he should
be here momentarily!'

'Oh, that's grand,' said Katie. 'We've had a fierce difficult day,
I'm sorry to say. I don't know if you've heard it on the news, but
we lost two officers today. I wasn't sure that I'd be able to get
away, to be honest with you.'

'I heard, yes. And very sorry to hear it, too. They were part of
your team, were they? Sometimes I think that us ordinary people
fail to realize what danger you gardaí have to face every single
day, as a matter of routine. Mind you, that dog-detecting that
Conor does, that can be very risky, too.'

'You're not wrong there,' said Katie.

'Listen – if you wait here, I'll go fetch Barney for you. I can't
tell you how thrilled we are at his recovery. There's some dogs
who kind of give up the ghost when they're badly injured, but
your Barney, he's a fighter all right. Give him a few more weeks
and he'll be bounding around like his old self, I promise you.'

Dr O'Sullivan left Katie by the reception desk. The receptionist
smiled at her, but she was too tense to feel like talking. The
prospect of seeing Barney again was emotional enough, but at
any minute she could be seeing Conor again, too.

She sat down on a hard Formica chair and picked up a copy of
Show Dogs Ireland magazine, flicking through it without really

looking at it. She wished now that she had eaten something – not because she was hungry, but because she was starting to feel sick.

The door from the surgical wing and the front door of the hospital opened simultaneously. Dr O'Sullivan came in, with Barney limping beside him, and Conor came in, too, wearing his long brown overcoat with the collar turned up.

As soon as he saw Katie, Barney let out a sharp bark of delight and came hobbling towards her, his left hind leg still in a splint, and his chest thickly bandaged. He thrust his nose into her lap, licking and nuzzling at her hands, while she stroked his head and tugged at his ears. His eyes were bright and his dark red coat was glossy and he was furiously wagging his tail.

'Look at you, you brave fellow!' she said. 'They hurt you so bad, those monsters, didn't they, but look at you now!'

Conor came up to her and stood beside her for a few moments in silence, his hands deep in his coat pockets.

'I didn't expect you to be here,' he said, at last.

She didn't look up at him but carried on fondling Barney's ears.

'I thought I'd collect him and bring him home to you in Cobh,' Conor continued. 'I thought if I did that, maybe you might forgive me for disappearing.'

'Where did you go?' Katie asked him, still without looking up.

'I didn't go to Sligo as it happens. I have a friend in Mallow who runs a hotel. I didn't tell him what I'd done. I just said that I felt like a few days' break from pet-detecting.'

'What are you going to do now?'

'I was hoping that we could talk. But I heard on the news about those two detectives being killed at Crosshaven. I met one of them, didn't I, Buckley, at the station? Really sound fellow. My condolences. If you don't feel like talking this evening, I'll understand perfectly.'

The receptionist came out from behind her desk, holding up an envelope.

'I'm sorry to interrupt you, sir, madam. There's the matter of the bill.'

Conor reached out and took it. 'No bother at all. I'll settle it.'

'You don't have to, Conor,' said Katie, looking up at him for the first time. 'He's my dog, and he was hurt because of me.'

'Let's just call it an act of atonement. Or a penance. Or an early Christmas present.'

Katie gave Barney's ears one more tug and then she stood up. 'All right, then,' she said. 'Why don't you follow me home and we can talk.'

She had been worried how Barney would react to Foltchain. He had always been possessive about Katie, and when Conor had first come to live with her, it had taken Barney weeks before he had stopped following her around the house, pushing his way in between their legs in the kitchen and sitting between them on the sofa. Even when she had shut him in the kitchen at night, she had heard him standing close behind the door, inhaling deeply, as if he wanted to sniff what she and Conor were doing in bed.

She needn't have been concerned. When she opened the front door and brought Barney into the hallway, Foltchain greeted him as if he were an old friend of hers, and Barney appeared to be reassured that Katie had been looked after by another Irish setter. They snuffled at each other, of course, and Foltchain seemed to be particularly interested in the smell of Barney's body bandages, but then Katie shooed them into the living room and they both went over to the fireplace and stood there side by side, looking up at her with their tongues hanging out.

Conor came in and said, 'Will you look at those two? They could be boyfriend and girlfriend.' For a split second Katie thought that he was going to add, 'Like me and you,' but he didn't.

'I'll give them a drink and something to eat,' said Katie. 'Take off your coat, why don't you? Would you care for a drink yourself? Perhaps you wouldn't mind lighting the fire.'

'Thanks, I'll have a Satz if you've some in the fridge.'

Once she had seen to the dogs, opened a bottle of Saztenbrau and poured herself a Smirnoff, Katie prised off her shoes and sat with her feet tucked up on the sofa. Conor was kneeling in front of the fire, blowing on the kindling to make it flare up.

'It's been the worst day ever,' she said. 'At least it's ended with a little brightness, with Barney coming home.'

'I'm sorry,' said Conor. 'I haven't made it any better for you, have I?'

'You heard about Buckley and O'Brien being killed. But another officer was murdered, Sergeant John Lacey. He was one of the whistle-blowers who was due to give evidence to Justice McGuigan. He was found in a graveyard in Inniscarra with his head cut off and a tin whistle pushed down his throat. His young son was with him when he was killed, and the murderers cut the poor lad's feet off to stop him from running away.'

Conor turned and stared at her. 'Serious? Dear God in Heaven.'

'We haven't released any details about Sergeant Lacey yet. It could have so many ramifications, I hardly dare to think about them.'

'Listen, Katie, if this is such a bad night for you, I'll leave. I can always meet you tomorrow some time.'

Katie shook her head. 'No, stay. We really need to talk. I've been thinking about you ever since you left, even when I was down in Inniscarra.'

The kindling was crackling now, and Conor came over and sat on the sofa next to her. He lifted his hand as if he were about to lay it on hers, but then he dropped it again. In his mahogany-brown eyes she could see nothing but hurt.

'Let me say this first,' he told her. 'I love you, Katie Maguire. I love you more than I've ever loved any woman, ever.'

Katie said nothing, but waited for him to continue. Her chest felt so constricted that she could hardly breathe, and she was keeping her lips tightly pursed so she wouldn't start crying. She had shed enough tears for one day.

'What I did was pure cracked, I know that. Even if McManus hadn't been at home, it would have been cracked. But, Katie

– I was ripping that you weren't going to take him to court for organizing that dog-fight, and all the other dog-fights that he's ever set up. Are we saying that dogs can't feel pain, and that dogs don't have emotions, and that dogs don't have souls? And McManus was responsible for torturing and killing hundreds of them – hundreds!'

Katie reached over and held his hand, and squeezed it. 'Con, I love you, too,' she began, although she had to clear her throat before she carried on. 'We have to sort this out, though, or else it's going to be a disaster for both of us. You've admitted to me what you did, and I can't unhear it. Because you started that fire, you killed two people, even if that wasn't your intention. I'm a Garda officer, and when I became a Garda officer, I made a solemn declaration before God to uphold the law, impartially. "Impartially" includes the people I love, as well as the people I hate.'

'I understand that, Katie. I have you completely. I hope you don't think I'm a coward for shooting off the way I did, but I needed time to think it over. I was totally shocked when I found out that McManus and that young woman had been burned to death – just as shocked as you were. If only I could turn back the clock.'

'You're the second person who's said that to me today,' said Katie. 'If I had a time machine, I swear to God I'd be making a fortune.'

Conor gave her a wry smile, and shrugged. 'I've decided what to do anyway. If I don't hand myself in, I can't honestly expect you to stay quiet about what I did. Even if you *did* stay quiet, one of your forensic fellows is bound to find out sooner or later that it was me who torched that mobile home, and then you'd be in even deeper shite for trying to cover for me.'

At that moment, Barney came limping in, followed closely by Foltchain. The two of them went over to the fire and sat down beside it, both of them looking up at Conor as if they had come in specifically to hear what he was going to say.

'I'm going to go up to Tipp and surrender to Inspector Carroll. I'm going to make it crystal clear that you had no idea what I was intending to do, which of course you didn't, and that I never told you that it was me.'

'That would be a lie. You *did* tell me.'

'I know. But it could seriously mess up your career and it wouldn't help *me* in any way at all, would it? I was a lunatic, Katie. I went astray and I have to be punished for it, but there's no reason for you to suffer for it, too.'

'So you're really going to hand yourself in?'

'I'll go tonight. I'll go now.'

'Well, they're open twenty-four seven at Tipperary Town, but Inspector Carroll won't be there. Anyway, you're tired now, and you've had a drink. You'd be better off going in the morning.'

She paused, still squeezing his hand. At that moment she felt like two completely different people – the strict detective superintendent and the melting lover. She looked down and saw that Barney was resting his head flat on the rug in front of the fire and that Foltchain was resting her head on top of his.

'Stay,' she said.

They had another drink and Katie joined Conor in the kitchen while he made them two ham-and-mushroom omelettes, his speciality. They sat on the sofa and ate them while they watched Claire Byrne's current affairs programme. She was talking, ironically, about the growing problem of opioid addiction in Ireland, which was beginning to become as serious as alcohol.

Katie felt relieved that Conor had found the courage to face up to what he had done, but bitterly sad, too. It was so normal and comforting to be sitting here eating supper and watching television with Barney and Foltchain sprawled on the rug in front of the fire. But tomorrow Conor would go to Tipperary and they would never spend an evening like this again.

She didn't mention Guzz Eye McManus again, or ask Conor

to tell her any more about how he had set fire to his mobile home. She tried not to think about Detectives Buckley and O'Brien, either, or the grisly sight of Sergeant Lacey with the tin whistle protruding from his neck. All she wanted to think about was the food, and the firelight, and sitting here with Conor.

After they had eaten, they took Barney and Foltchain for a short walk along Carrig View, as far as the railings that overlooked the river. Tonight the tide was in, and the river glittered.

'I think poor Barney's beat out,' said Conor. 'Maybe I should carry him back.'

Barney managed to hobble home, though, with Foltchain running circles around him, but always coming back to him and giving him a nuzzle. Katie and Conor held hands.

When they returned home, Katie shut the dogs in the kitchen and went into her bedroom. Conor stood in the doorway while she switched on the bedside lamps.

'I can sleep in the spare room,' he said.

She went up to him and placed her hands on his shoulders.

'Just because you've done something mad that doesn't mean I've stopped loving you.'

'I've destroyed everything, haven't I? You and me, what we could have been. I've wrecked it all for ever. Wrecked it. Burned it down to the ground like McManus's mobile home.'

'We still have one night left, Con. Let's make it last.'

She kissed him, and he kissed her back. She loved the soft thick feel of his beard, and the smell of him. The tip of his tongue explored her teeth as if he were gently running his fingertips across a keyboard, trying to pick out a quiet, romantic tune.

He lifted off her dark grey boat neck sweater, and then he reached behind her and unclasped her bra. Her breasts were full and heavy, and he cupped them in his hands and rolled her nipples between his fingertips until they stiffened and knurled. Then he unzipped her skirt, so that it dropped to the floor. He picked her up in his arms and laid her on the patchwork counterpane, kissing her again and again.

'Katie,' he breathed. 'Oh God almighty, Katie, what have I done?'

'Shh,' she said, pressing her finger against his lips. 'You haven't done anything until tomorrow. Tonight, it's just us.'

He pulled down her thick black tights and then her thong. She lay back on the bed with her thighs wide open while he lapped at her, his beard brushing against her smooth waxed lips. She began to feel a tingling sensation rising up between her legs and so she buried her fingers in his wavy hair and lifted up his head.

'Come on, Viking,' she said. 'Let me see you naked.'

Kneeling up on the bed, Conor dragged off his sweater and unbuttoned his shirt. Then he rolled over on to his back so that he was lying beside her, unfastening his belt and kicking off his dark brown corduroy trousers, and then his socks. Katie dipped her hand into the waistband of his tight white shorts and felt how hard he was.

He lay beside her and made love to her slowly and almost dreamily, as if they were rowing up some peaceful stream. He slid right up inside her until she could feel his pubic hair against her, and then he slid completely out again, so that every time he entered her it was like being entered for the first time.

He kissed her dreamily, too, and fondled her breasts as if he could hardly believe that they were real. He had always been a considerate lover, even at his most demanding, but tonight she discovered a different Conor altogether – a Conor who realized what a strong and sensual woman he was going to be losing.

She came close to having an orgasm, but it kept sinking away, like the tide going out. Conor climaxed, and shuddered, but it was a very muted climax, and afterwards he simply lay beside her holding her in his arms while he gradually shrank.

'I've lost you, haven't I?' he said, and she could feel his beard and his breath against her bare shoulder.

She kissed him on the forehead. 'Not until morning,' she whispered.

Twenty-Five

They both woke early, while it was still dark. Outside the bedroom window, it was raining hard. Conor held Katie tightly in his arms and kissed her, and then he said, 'This is it, then. This is the day of reckoning.'

'I'll help you all I can, Con. I know a very good solicitor, Garret Delaney.'

'I'm guilty of manslaughter, Katie. The only thing you can do for me is visit me in prison now and again.'

They had mugs of coffee together in the kitchen, and Katie ate half a slice of toast and marmalade, although Conor had no appetite at all. At seven-thirty there was a ring at the doorbell, and it was Katie's neighbour, Jenny Tierney, in a hooded raincoat, looking like the good witch Biddy Early from the fairy stories. She had come to take Foltchain for her morning walk, and she was overjoyed to see Barney.

'You can't take him too far, I'm afraid,' said Katie, 'and he'll have to wear his waterproof to keep his bandages dry. But he's in good spirits, and he and Foltchain have been getting along like a house on fire.'

She suddenly realized what she had said, and turned to Conor and mouthed 'Sorry'.

After Jenny had taken the dogs out into the rain, Katie and Conor stood in the hallway and held each other for almost a minute without saying anything. Then Conor kissed Katie on her forehead and said, '*Slán mo ghrá*. Goodbye, my love.'

She had only just hung up her raincoat when Detective Scanlan came into her office.

'Good morning, ma'am. Holy Saint Joseph, it's spilling out, isn't it? You can hardly put your nose out the door. But I've just received the names now from Justice McGuigan's office, along with what they'll be giving evidence about. His secretary apologized for the delay but she said they had to clear it with the whistle-blowers' lawyers.'

Katie sat down at her desk and Detective Scanlan handed her a sheet of notepaper with three names on it, as well as their addresses and their phone numbers.

Sergeant Dolan MacAuley, scheduled to present evidence about penalty points removed from licences in exchange for bribes.

Garda Yasir Wassan, scheduled to present evidence about persistent bullying and racism at his local Garda station, which led to him taking indefinite sick leave.

Garda Eamon Ó Grádaigh, scheduled to present evidence about fellow officers accepting bribes not to arrest 1P-LSD pedlars in Cork nightclubs.

'Thanks, Padragain,' she said, and stood up again. She told Moirin to wait before she brought her cappuccino, and she went downstairs to see Superintendent Pearse. She found him standing in front of his mirror, the tip of his tongue between his teeth, carefully combing what was left of his hair.

She handed him the list and he read it while he was still combing. 'MacAuley and Ó Grádaigh I know well,' he said. 'Wassan – well, I heard about all his complaints, but I don't know if anything was ever done about them. None of them live more than a stone's throw from the city centre, so they won't be too hard to protect, like, even if they stay at home.'

'We'll have to be wide about who we assign to protect them, though,' said Katie. 'And if we do relocate any of them, we'll have to be double wide who knows where they are.'

'I can give you the names of officers I totally trust. Don't get me wrong – I trust *all* my officers, although there's always one or two gimps.'

Katie pointed to the list and said, 'Two and three make five, Michael. Five whistle-blowers were called to give evidence to Justice McGuigan's tribunal before the end of this year and five tin whistles were stolen from the Music Market. I find it hard to believe that's only a coincidence, and I don't want to see three more officers with their heads cut off.'

'I'll do everything I can to make sure that doesn't happen, that's all I can say.'

'Okay, thanks a million. Give me some time to think it over, can you? I think I might talk to each of these whistle-blowers in person before I make up my mind how to protect them.'

'You're sure? I can rustle up a team in half an hour. Ó Grádaigh's supposed to be giving his evidence first thing tomorrow morning so I think we need to make a bust.'

'Don't worry, Michael, I'll be back to you directly as soon as I've spoken to the three of them.'

Katie went back to her office. As soon as she had sat down, Moirin came in with a frothy cappuccino and a plate of fruit biscuits. 'Detective Ó Doibhilin's just arrived, ma'am. He's downstairs in the squad room whenever you want to talk to him.'

Katie looked at the clock on her desk. 'It's going to be one of those days, Moirin, I tell you. I'll be going out at eleven to give my condolences to Buckley's wife and O'Brien's parents. Can you nip out to Best of Buds and buy me two bouquets of white roses? I should be back by one. I'm expecting to interview the two scummers who killed them.'

'I don't know how you keep so calm sometimes,' said Moirin. 'I wouldn't be able to stop myself from spitting in their faces.'

'A judge and a jury will give them what they deserve,' said Katie. 'It's my job to catch them, that's all, and prepare the book of evidence, and if that leads to them being convicted and spending most of the rest of their lives behind bars, then I don't need to spit at them.'

In between sipping her cappuccino and eating her biscuits, she phoned each of the three whistle-blowers. They knew, of course, that Garda O'Regan had been murdered, and how, but so far they had heard nothing about Sergeant Lacey. Katie felt sure that his killers would soon be tipping off the media about his death, but for some reason they seemed to be biding their time.

Sergeant Lacey's wife had been informed immediately that he had been murdered and that their son Aidan had been brutally injured, and now she was waiting by his bedside at the Mercy. A support officer was with her, and Katie planned to visit her this evening before she went home.

Garda Ó Grádaigh was the first whistle-blower she rang. He was shopping with his wife in Dunnes stores in Ballyvolane.

'I'm sorry if I've caught you at a bad moment,' she told him.

'It's not a bother, ma'am. We're just doing some last-minute messages before I go above to Dublin this evening.'

As simply and as baldly as she could, she told him that Sergeant Lacey had been beheaded in the same way as Garda O'Regan, and that a tin whistle had been inserted into his severed neck.

When she had finished, Garda Ó Grádaigh said nothing, and she could hear the in-store music and the sound of shoppers talking in the background.

'Garda Ó Grádaigh?' she said. 'Eamon? Are you still there?'

'I'm still here, ma'am. Shocked, that's all. I think I'd best go outside to talk to you and leave the moth to finish the messages.'

Once he was out in the car park, Katie said, 'Myself I'm in no doubt at all that whoever killed O'Regan and Lacey, they're out to silence all five of you, one way or another. So far we have no idea who the offenders are, or why they should want to stop you from giving your evidence, considering that you all have such different stories to tell. But you need to be double wide, Eamon, and both you and your family are going to need protection.'

'But – ma'am – if any or all of the killers are gardaí, or related to gardaí, how can you guarantee that they're not going to easy find out where we are, and come looking for us? By the Lord lamb of Jesus.'

'Let me suggest something to you,' said Katie, and told him what she had in mind.

He listened, and then he said, 'Okay. That makes good sense. At least I'll know that none of them have any axes to grind.'

Katie rang Sergeant Dolan MacAuley and repeated exactly what she had said to Garda Ó Grádaigh. He listened in sombre silence, and then he said, 'I'll go along with that one hundred and ten per cent, ma'am. I've had a rake of death threats already. This morning some charmer sent me a tweet telling me that he was going to cut off my mebs and stuff them down my throat so that I wouldn't be able to testify. You'll have to excuse me for telling you that, but it's typical of all of the trolling I've been getting.'

It took a long time for Garda Wassan to answer the phone, and when he did he sounded extremely cautious.

'I don't know what to say to you, DS Maguire,' he told her. 'I have been frightened for my safety ever since I first complained about racism. I could have lodged many more complaints, because I have been a victim of bullying and harassment and racist insults from the first day I joined the force.'

'You're on sick leave now, though, aren't you?'

'The last incident was the breaking of me, ma'am. I brought a takeaway supper into the station and while I was signing in, another officer knocked it off the desk on to the floor and stamped on it, and said that he didn't want the station polluted with the smell of curry. That wasn't the worst incident. They used to call me "Paki rat" and say that I was a terrorist, but I always tried to take that as a joke. After that officer stamped on my supper, though, I fell to pieces and I just couldn't take any more.'

'Yasir – I totally understand,' said Katie. 'I get my fair share of bullying just for being a woman and a senior Garda officer. Do you have any family? Wife and children?'

'Only my sister and she lives in England, in Birmingham. She is married so she has a different name so I think she will be safe.'

'Well, here's what I'm going to suggest.'

When she had told him what she intended to arrange, Garda Wassan simply said, 'Yes. I will agree to that. I was afraid for my life already, before you told me about Garda O'Regan and Sergeant Lacey. Now I am sure that they will try to kill me. Please, DS Maguire, accept my gratitude. You are the first person in a long time who has spoken to me as if I am a human being whose life is worth more than nothing at all.'

Superintendent Pearse was sceptical when Katie told him that she was going to hire a private security firm to protect the three whistle-blowers and their families.

'How do you know that you can trust *them*?' he demanded. 'And do you honestly think they're up to it? They're all right those fellows for hauling in shoplifters and patrolling factories at night and answering burglar alarms that have gone off by mistake, but what are they going to do if they're faced with a gang of homicidal headers with guns and a chainsaw? They'll skirt, won't they? You won't see them for dust.'

'Don't you worry about it,' said Katie. 'I know a company whose guards are all highly experienced. They're more than capable of dealing with any threat like that.'

'Well, who are they? Do I know them?'

'It's possible, but you'll forgive me if I don't tell you who they are. They're fully licensed by the PSA, I can assure you of that.'

Superintendent Pearse stared at her in disbelief. He opened and closed his mouth twice before he said, 'You're not going to tell *me* who they are?'

'There's no need for you to know, Michael, and the fewer people who know who their security guards are, and where they've taken them, the safer our whistle-blowers are going to be.'

'Kathleen, I'm totally puggalized.'

'Michael – it's not that I don't trust you. Of course I do. But this is the first time we've ever had to protect our own people from ourselves.'

'We don't know that for sure.'

'No, of course not. But it's a possibility, and if it's a possibility, then we have to take all the necessary precautions.'

Superintendent Pearse blew out his cheeks. 'Oh, well, fair play to you, I suppose. But supposing something happens to you, God forbid, and none of the rest of us know who these security characters are, or where to find them, or where they've hidden these whistle-blowers for that matter. I mean, supposing you get run over by a bus and the whistle-blowers don't show up for the hearing? Then what?'

'You're not much of a pessimist, are you?' Katie smiled. 'If it makes you feel better, I'll tell Denis MacCostagáin, but nobody else. And I'll look both ways before I cross Pana.'

She found Kyna in the canteen, having a breakfast of fruit salad and lemon tea.

'What's the story with Buckley and O'Brien?' she asked her, sitting down opposite her. Kyna had pinned her hair up, and she was wearing Carmin Statement lipstick, so that she looked even more fairy-like than usual.

She lifted her teapot and said, 'Like some?'

There was an empty cup on the table so Katie pushed it over and said, 'Go on, then. Throw me a skite in. I'm parched. I feel like I haven't stopped talking ever since I got in this morning.'

'I interviewed the auld boy who witnessed Farry Logan shooting Detective O'Brien,' said Kyna. 'Lemon? No? In fact, I made a point of interviewing him twice... once when we first arrived in Crosshaven and once again before we left, with about two hours in between. It's amazing, isn't it, how witnesses change their stories the second time they have to tell them, especially when they're lying – or even when they're not.'

'And you think this auld boy was lying?'

'No question at all. First time he said that O'Brien pulled his weapon out first. Then he said that they pulled them out together. First time he said that O'Brien said nothing at all, and that Logan must have thought that he was a Traveller who was out on the rob, but then he admitted that O'Brien had told Logan to drop his weapon and put up his hands.'

Katie sipped her tea. 'The real question is... do you think he'll stand up in court and say that?'

'At the moment, I doubt it. It was obvious that he was freaked. I don't know what Logan had said to him but so long as Seamus Twomey and Douglas Quinn are still on the loose, I don't believe that he'll have the nerve to come out and say what really happened.'

'All right. And what about Buckley?'

'Dangerous driving by Logan. He came speeding out of the Middle Road without giving way, which he should have done, and collided head-on with Buckley's car. So we can certainly get him for that, if nothing else. Well – we'll still get him for illegal possession of a firearm, and for hostage-taking of course, and false imprisonment. Michael Ó Doibhilin will give us all the evidence we need for that.'

'Yes,' said Katie. 'I'm going to talk to him now... which was actually the reason I was looking for you.'

Kyna prodded the last two grapes in her fruit salad with her fork. 'I'm ready. If I can see Seamus Twomey locked up in Portlaoise and that porky sister of his in the Dóchas Centre, I don't care if I never catch any more offenders ever again, ever.'

Twenty-Six

Michael Ó Doibhilin knocked very softly at the door of Katie's office. Katie and Kyna were sitting close together by the window. Garda O'Regan's barrister, John Deneen, had just sent Katie a copy of the evidence that he had been intending to present to the Disclosures Tribunal, and they were carefully reading through it.

Michael looked pale and distracted and strangely childish. He was wearing a grey roll-neck sweater and baggy black tracksuit trousers and his hair was all scruffed up.

'Michael, come in, sit down,' said Katie. 'How are you coming on?'

'Oh, I'm grand altogether,' said Michael, sitting down on the very end of the couch. 'They didn't hurt me, anyway.'

'So – when did they grab you?'

'When I was round at Gwenith Twomey's place. Gwenith riffled through my jacket and found my phone, and that's how she found out I wasn't some gurrier called Tommy. Before you could say *Éire go Deo* they'd bundled me into the back of a car and driven me off to Crosser.'

'Was Seamus Twomey present when you were taken?'

Michael shook his head. 'It was only that Farry fellow and two other fellows whose names I didn't catch.'

'But you could identify these other fellows if we hauled them in?'

'I'm not so sure, ma'am. I'd only that moment woken up and it all happened so quick, do you know?'

'Was there anything at all distinctive about them? Their clothes or their faces or their accents?'

'Not really. Sweaters and jeans. Shaved heads. One had a silver earring. They didn't say much, but they all sounded Cork.'

'Did they tell you that Twomey had sent them?'

'No. They never mentioned Twomey at all.'

Katie looked across at Kyna. Droplets of rain were running down the window in fits and starts, and Michael was sitting with his hands clasped together between his knees, staring down at the carpet. If she hadn't known better, Katie would have thought that he was drugged.

'You had sex with Gwenith,' said Kyna.

'I did, yes.'

'Don't tell me you did it for choicer. She's a mountain, to put it politely.'

Michael shrugged one shoulder.

'Why did you have sex with her? Was it because your cover would have been blown if you hadn't?'

'She invited me back to her place, that's all. One thing kind of led to another, like.'

'Don't tell me you fancied her.'

'Like I said, one thing kind of led to another.'

'Did Twomey threaten to give you a hard time if you didn't?'

'No.'

'What happened when they took you down to Crosshaven? Were you physically restrained?'

'No.'

'You were handcuffed in the back of Farry's car, when DS Begley stopped it. But not in the cottage?'

'No.'

'So didn't you attempt to get out of there?' asked Katie. 'If you weren't tied up or cuffed and you only had Vincent Mulroney guarding you, what was to stop you from escaping? You have a purple belt in karate, haven't you?'

'Yes, ma'am, but I agreed not to give them any trouble.'

'You agreed not to give them any trouble? Why in the name of Jesus did you agree not to give them any trouble?'

'I knew that you'd come looking for me before too long, and we could all reach some kind of friendly agreement. That way, nobody would get hurt, do you know what I mean?'

'Some kind of friendly agreement? Are you serious? With Seamus Twomey? He rang DS Begley and said that he'd murder you if we went on messing up his drug-smuggling. Or words to that effect, anyway.'

'They never said nothing like that to me.'

'As for nobody getting hurt... both Detective Buckley and Detective O'Brien lost their lives trying to rescue you.'

'I know that, ma'am, and I'm in bits about it. I can't even believe that they're gone.'

Katie said, 'So neither Farry nor Vincent actually beat you – but did they *threaten* to beat you?'

'No. They barely spoke a word, except to talk about the racing at Mallow.'

Kyna got up and sat close to him. She stared at him for a long time without saying anything, and once or twice he glanced at her sideways, but otherwise he kept his eyes fixed on the carpet.

'They *did* threaten you, didn't they?' she said, very gently, and she rested her hand on his knee.

'No. No, they never did.'

'No – *no*, you're right,' said Kyna, snapping her fingers. 'It wasn't *you* they threatened, was it? You have a girlfriend, don't you? You brought her into the station about a month ago. A very pretty girl, too. What's her name now? Eithne. That's it.'

Detective Ó Doibhilin's eyes widened and then he closed them, and kept them closed, as if he wanted to shut out the world altogether.

'They've threatened Eithne, haven't they?' said Kyna. 'Holy Mary Mother of God I can understand why you don't want to tell us what happened. I wouldn't either, if a girlfriend of mine was threatened.'

Katie said, 'Michael, you're not alone. We know how frightened you are that Twomey's going to hurt Eithne if you testify against him, but we can protect her. We need your evidence, Michael. We need you to point the finger at Twomey so that we can put him inside for good and all. It's going to be well-nigh impossible to prosecute him successfully for false imprisonment if you claim that you weren't physically restrained, and that they never threatened to kill you or harm you in any way. The judge is going to ask, why didn't you just get up and leave?'

Detective Ó Doibhilin remained silent.

'At least tell us where Eithne lives, so that we can arrange to have her protected. We can have an armed officer guarding her all around the clock.'

Still Detective Ó Doibhilin said nothing, and the rain continued to sprinkle against the window.

'Very well,' said Katie. 'I'll give you some time to think it over. But you have to realize that if you insist on withholding vital evidence, whatever the reason, it could well be a dismissible offence. I can guarantee Eithne's safety, Michael, but if you still won't testify against Seamus Twomey or any of his gang, I can't guarantee that you'll be able to keep your job.'

'Yes, ma'am,' said Detective Ó Doibhilin. He stood up and left Katie's office without another word.

When he had gone, Katie said to Kyna, 'How did you know about his girlfriend?'

'A bit of a wild guess, to be honest with you. Michael's something of a hard chaw usually, even though he doesn't look it. I saw him go for two guys who were fighting in the Voodoo Rooms once and he hauled in the both of them, by himself. He'd only be scared if somebody he cared about was threatened.'

'Fair play. But more to the point, how did Twomey know who she was? How did he know that he even had a girlfriend?'

'Let's hope it wasn't somebody here in the station who tipped him off.'

'Well, however he found out about her, it's shaken Michael

down to the core, hasn't it? We need to find her, and fast. Even if he won't agree to give evidence against Twomey, she needs to be aware that she's been threatened. If I know Twomey, he'll only have to *suspect* that Michael has given us incriminating evidence against him, and he'll be sending his scummers out after her.'

'I believe Nicholas Markey knows her,' said Kyna. 'I'll go down and ask him now.'

Katie picked up the folder of Garda O'Regan's testimony. 'I'll carry on going through this. Mother of God, we're only on page three and it's making my hair stand on end already.'

Katie already knew what had started Garda O'Regan on his whistle-blowing crusade – his chance meeting with the drug-dealer Jer Brogan at the Babbling Brook pub in Riverstick.

Brogan had boasted that he was supposed to be serving three years in Mountjoy Prison in Dublin, although in reality he had never spent a single day behind bars. According to the evidence he had prepared for the Disclosures Tribunal, Garda O'Regan had coaxed it out of him that he had been set free by an unholy alliance of corrupt gardaí, prison service escorts and prison officers – all of them bribed by one of the city's most notorious crime gangs.

When Garda O'Regan had investigated further, he had discovered that Brogan was only one of at least nine convicted criminals who had never seen the back of a cell door.

On the lower level, it hadn't been too difficult for him to find out who was being bribed to do what. There was very little love lost between the gardaí and the prison escorts, and even less between the prison officers and the criminals, and like Jer Brogan, most of them were fond of a drink or two. He had loosened their tongues for the price of thirty or forty rounds of Murphy's, with Paddy's chasers, and he had gradually built up a complex picture of bribery and forgery and threats of extreme violence.

As soon as the offenders had been convicted at the District

Court, the prison service escorts who were supposed to be taking them to prison would contact certain senior prison officers at Rathmore Road. The prison officers would draw up papers for their immediate transfer to another prison, such as Mountjoy or Cloverhill or Castlerea, ostensibly for behavioural training or for security reasons or because Cork was temporarily overcrowded. The offenders would then simply be driven home, or down to Kerry to spend a few months in a bed-and-breakfast in Killarney if their case had attracted too much publicity and they were likely to be recognized in the street or squealed on by a nosy neighbour.

Garda O'Regan had found it comparatively easy to discover which prison service escorts and which prison officers were being bribed. Thousands of euros were changing hands and the officers who were excluded from the scam were bitterly envious.

He had been able to discover that it was the Coakley drug gang who were paying some of the bribes, but he had come to a dead end when he had tried to find out where the rest of the money was coming from and who it was being paid to. One of the prison service escorts had told him that after he had driven convicted offenders back home or down to Kerry, his €500 bribe would be handed to him in cash by a man he knew to be a garda. When he had asked him where the money had come from, the man had said 'The Head Honcho' but that was all he would tell him.

Garda O'Regan had made several educated guesses at who 'The Head Honcho' might be, and at the end of his evidence he had named a senior director of the Prison Service Escort Corps, as well as two Garda superintendents. He had even drawn a question mark next to the name of Assistant Commissioner Frank Magorian, since Frank Magorian owned a six-bedroom country house overlooking the harbour at Castletownshend, as well as a holiday cottage in Spain, and his lifestyle appeared unduly lavish for a man on his salary.

Although she disliked him, Katie thought it was highly unlikely to be Frank Magorian. He was arrogant, yes, but he was inordinately proud of his reputation as a breaker of criminal gangs, and he would have thought that taking dirty money from a drug-dealer or a pimp or a people-smuggler was beneath him.

All the same, she wondered why Garda O'Regan had included him, and she made a note to see if his finances could be discreetly looked into. Maybe she would have a word with James Gallagher, the forensic accountant, when he came down to Cork tomorrow.

Moirin came in with two bouquets of white roses and two sympathy cards. Kyna came back right behind her. She picked up one of the bouquets and smelled the roses and then she looked at Katie with an expression of infinite sorrow.

'O'Brien... he was so young. He had his whole life in front of him.'

'You've had a word with Markey?'

'Yes. Eithne's a third-year student in creative media studies at the Crawford. Nicholas doesn't know where she lives but she works in the evenings at Scoozi's. I've sent him round there now to find out her address.'

Katie handed her the folder with Garda O'Regan's evidence. 'Read the rest of this. It'll make your blood run cold. Apparently it was the Coakleys who were paying out some of the bribes, but O'Regan wasn't sure who was taking them. It could have been somebody in the PSEC or a Garda officer. Whoever it was, they were paying him tens of thousands of euros. Or *her*, of course. When are we going to get a copy of Sergeant Lacey's evidence? Maybe that will give us a clearer idea. All we know so far is that he was called "The Head Honcho".'

'"If you can keep your head when all about you are losing theirs –"' Kyna quoted.

'Don't even joke about it,' Katie told her.

Fergus Kenny from the Technical Bureau came in to Katie's office just as she was about to go and visit Detective Buckley's wife and Detective O'Brien's parents. He looked at the two bouquets but said nothing. He knew what they were for.

'I have all the photographs here of the crime scene down at Crosshaven,' he told her. 'Dr Kelley extracted the bullet from Detective O'Brien's body and sent it up to us. It's a 9mm slug and it was fired from the Colt Combat Commander pistol that was taken from Farry Logan when he was arrested. There were no other fingerprints or DNA on the pistol apart from Logan's, and when Logan was brought in and processed there was evidence of GSR on his right hand and on his jacket.'

'Good. So we can conclusively prove that it was Logan who fired the fatal shot, even though he's claiming that it was in self-defence. What about the handcuffs that were taken from Detective Ó Doibhilin?'

'Heavy duty hinge handcuffs of the same type issued to gardaí. But anybody can buy them online for twenty euros or even less. The only fingerprints we found on them were Vincent Mulroney's and one other partial, which we haven't been able to identify.'

'Thank you, Fergus. Anything else?'

'We're taking Logan's car to pieces. He says that his brakes failed, and that's why he collided with Detective Buckley. I think we'll be able to show that he's lying. We may also be able to find evidence in the car that will link him to a fair number of other crimes. We've already found traces of cocaine on the seats and on the carpets, and there's some dried blood down the back of the rear seats.'

'Whatever you can pin on him, Fergus. Good job. Keep me up to date.'

Twenty-Seven

Katie parked outside Detective Buckley's semi-detached house on St Anne's Drive. It was a neat house, painted salmon-pink, with a diamond-shaped flower bed in the front garden. The curtains in the front room were drawn, and somebody had left a wreath in the porch.

It was always hard talking to the widows of officers who had been killed on duty. No matter how sympathetic she was, she could tell that they blamed her personally for their deaths, even though they never said so outright. It made no difference that she was grieving herself at losing them. They had died while they were trying to carry out her orders.

She sat in her car for a while, until the windscreen was beaded with raindrops. She was just about to get out when her phone played *Siúil A Rún*.

'Katie? It's Conor. I've just finished talking on the phone to your man Garret Delaney. He's coming up to Tipp tomorrow to see me. Meanwhile he's advised me to keep my mouth tight shut except when they feed me.'

'Oh, Con. Have they charged you?'

'Not formally. I've been arrested on suspicion of involuntary manslaughter. They won't be charging me until I've given them a statement.'

'I don't know what to say. I'm sitting here in the rain outside Detective Buckley's house. I only wish I could be there with you to give you some support. Or that you could be here, to give *me* some support.'

'Have you seen his wife yet?'

'No. But I'm about to. I'm dreading it.'

'Come on, Katie. If there's one thing I've learned from you, it's how to face up to life, no matter how much of a disaster it turns out to be.'

'Holy Mother of God, Con, it couldn't be worse. I feel like my whole world is crashing down around me like the walls of Jericho. I can't even go home tonight and have you hug me to make me feel better.'

'You'll have Barney, and Foltchain. They'll take care of you while I'm gone.'

'You could be in prison for years. You know that, don't you? *Years!*'

'Anger always has its consequences, Katie, even when it's righteous anger. I should have learned that a long time ago.'

It was nearly half past two by the time Katie arrived back at Anglesea Street. She felt drained. She had seen both Detective Buckley's widow, Anne, and Detective O'Brien's father and mother and his grandmother, too.

She had drunk tea with them and attempted to eat biscuits while they sat staring at her, their eyes glistening with tears. She had listened to herself telling them that the deaths of a dearly beloved husband and a precious son at the hands of a violent scumbag had not been in vain. They had each selflessly given their lives so that the whole community of Cork could feel safer, and more secure.

She had joined them in a prayer. 'Into your hands, O Lord, we humbly entrust our brothers. The old order has passed away: welcome them into paradise, where there will be no sorrow, no weeping or pain, but fullness of peace and joy for ever. Amen.'

Whatever she had said, though, she knew their deaths had been utterly pointless – a stupid and grievous waste of two good men.

It hurt even more that she had been responsible for organizing the undercover investigation that had led directly to them being killed.

When she returned to her office she sat at her desk with her head down and she could almost have opened her laptop and typed out her resignation.

Moirin came in and said, 'How are you feeling, ma'am? It's fierce distressing, isn't it, giving the condolences?'

Katie looked up and tried to smile. 'Yes. Because there's one question the bereaved always want to ask you but they never do, and even if they did ask it you couldn't answer it, because there *is* no answer, and there never will be. They want to know "why?".'

Kyna rang her. 'You're back,' she said. She didn't add, 'How did it go?'

'I've had a call from the slimy Nicholas Bourke,' Kyna told her. 'He's been held up in court but he'll be slithering around here about three to represent Logan and Mulroney.'

'What did I tell you?' said Katie. 'This is the day that just keeps on giving.'

She riffled through the papers that had been left on her desk. There was a lengthy report from the city council about illegal dumping at the Travellers' halting site at Spring Lane in Ballyvolane, and how council workers had been attacked by axe-wielding residents when they tried to carry out improvement work.

She was still reading when Moirin came in to say, 'Mr MacQuaid is here to see you. Would you be wanting another cup of coffee in your hand?'

'Oh, show him in, please, Moirin. And, no, I won't have another coffee. I have the jitters enough already. But Mr MacQuaid might like one.'

Stephen MacQuaid came into her office with a broad smile and his arms wide open. Katie had known him ever since they had trained at Templemore Garda College together, and she had always felt that if he hadn't had a steady girlfriend at the time, and she hadn't been dating her husband-to-be, Paul, they might have got together and made a perfect couple.

He was fair-haired and lean, with a sharply sculpted face and hazel-coloured eyes and a way of looking around that gave the impression that he was up to mischief. He was wearing a dark brown tweed jacket and a rusty-coloured shirt.

'I came as quick as I could,' he told her, giving her a kiss on both cheeks. 'How long is it now since I last saw you? We should have lunch together and catch up. Have you tried the Spitjack yet? Great food if you don't mind getting barbecue sauce plastered all over you.'

'How are you going on, Stephen? Your little girl must be walking and talking by now.'

'Walking and talking? She started bunscoil this September, and we have another little girl now, would you believe? I'm out-numbered now, three to one.'

They sat down together by the window and Katie looked at him and wondered for a few fleeting seconds what life would have been like if she had married him, instead of Paul. It was her father who had said to her, when she was first thinking of joining the Garda, 'Most people don't realize that you only get the one shot at life, Katie, and that you're old before you know it. So think deep before you decide.'

'I won't beat around the bush, Stephen,' said Katie. 'We've a serious security problem and I need some of your people for personal protection.'

'MacQuaid Security at your service,' said Stephen. 'We're a little short of staff right now, but I'm sure I can rearrange some rotas to help you out.'

Katie explained why she needed private security guards to protect the three remaining whistle-blowers. Stephen listened gravely, and then nodded.

'I have nine guys who are all trained and experienced in per-sonal protection. Three of them are ex-gardaí and one of them was picked for Queen Elizabeth's security team when she came to visit Dublin.'

'I've spoken to all three of the whistle-blowers and they've all agreed to have protection,' said Katie. 'It's vital, though, that nobody here at Anglesea Street knows how to find them. Apart from me, of course, and I'll have to notify Chief Superintendent MacCostagáin.'

'That's no bother at all. I have several safe houses where they can stay, and I can work out a roster so that they're under constant surveillance night and day. I can promise you, Katie, nobody except my staff will have any idea where they are, and unless they recognize them from the TV or the papers, they won't even know *who* they are. They'll be totally secure. No more beheadings, guaranteed.'

'Thank God for that. At last I'm beginning to feel that I'm getting on top of things.'

Nicholas Bourke arrived at three o'clock and when Katie and Kyna and Detective Sergeant Begley walked into the interview room he was deep in conversation with Farry Logan, while Vincent Mulroney was staring into space and picking his nose behind his hand.

Farry Logan looked up when they came in, but then he looked away. It was obvious that he didn't recognize Kyna as 'Sparkle'. She had been wearing a glittering gold top and yoga pants when she walked into the Halfway Bar, and he had been langered.

The word 'suave' could have been invented for Nicholas Bourke. He was tall, with black swept-back hair, hooded eyelids and slightly pursed-up lips, as if he had just finished sucking a particularly sour lemon drop. He was dressed in a dark grey tailor-made suit with a mauve paisley handkerchief protruding from the pocket. Katie recognized his aftershave as Issey Miyake.

He stood up and held out his hand. 'Detective Superintendent Maguire. My condolences.'

'Mr Bourke,' said Katie. She couldn't bring herself to say 'thank you'.

They all sat down and Detective Sergeant Begley switched on the digital interview recorder.

Katie said, 'We have irrefutable forensic evidence that Farry Logan was responsible for shooting and killing Detective O'Brien.'

'My client is not denying it,' said Nicholas Bourke. 'However, he fired his weapon only in self-defence, because he was afraid for his life. Detective O'Brien was skulking around the back of the cottages on Daly's Lane and my client quite reasonably assumed that he was intent on housebreaking. When my client challenged him, Detective O'Brien took out his weapon and pointed it at my client without identifying himself as an armed garda. As you know, we have a witness to support this version of events, Mr Gilroy Higgins who lives in the next-door cottage.'

'Mr Higgins's statement is inconsistent, to say the least. It's our opinion that he's been intimidated into supporting Farry Logan's statement.'

'No comment. A jury will decide if his evidence is sound or not.'

'Farry Logan and Vincent Mulroney were holding Detective Ó Doibhilin prisoner against his will,' said Katie. 'That was why Detective O'Brien was "skulking" around the back of the cottages, as you put it.'

'Detective Ó Doibhilin was not physically restrained in any way and could have left whenever he chose.'

'He may not have been physically restrained but he was warned that his girlfriend was at risk if he attempted to escape.'

Farry Logan shook his head emphatically, and Nicholas Bourke said, 'My client denies that.'

'Why in the name of God do you think Detectives Buckley and O'Brien were looking for Detective Ó Doibhilin in the first place, Mr Bourke?' put in Detective Sergeant Begley. 'Farry Logan's boss, Seamus Twomey, had rung me and told me that if we didn't keep our noses out of his drug-running business, we might never see Detective Ó Doibhilin again. Not alive, anyway. We have the recording, so you can't deny it.'

'He was joking, wasn't he?' said Farry. 'Seamus don't run no drug business. Drug business? Me bollocks. He does painting and decorating, that's all.'

Nicholas Bourke put his finger to his lips to indicate to Farry that he should keep quiet.

'So – Mr Logan – Detective Ó Doibhilin went along with you voluntarily to Crosshaven?' asked Katie. 'He stayed in that cottage despite the fact that he was supposed to have gone home to his parents' house that evening and was then supposed to be reporting for duty here at Anglesea Street? Would you like to explain why?'

'How the feck should I know?' said Farry. 'You'll have to ask him.'

'No comment,' said Nicholas Bourke.

'Let me ask both Farry Logan and Vincent Mulroney... were you keeping Detective Ó Doibhilin imprisoned in Crosshaven because you were told to by Seamus Twomey?'

'No comment,' said Nicholas Bourke. 'Mr Twomey is also a client of mine but you haven't arrested him or charged him with any offence and unless you do so you should keep his name out of this interview.'

'All right, one more question,' said Katie. 'We've examined Farry Logan's car and we've established that the brakes were in good working order when he collided with Detective Buckley and caused the accident that killed him. Yet Mr Logan claimed that they failed.'

'No comment,' said Nicholas Bourke. 'We'll be filing a service report from Mr Logan's own garage to verify the condition of the brakes.'

'That's enough for now then,' said Katie, and stood up. 'I'm expecting further evidence from the Technical Bureau and from eyewitnesses and I may wish to interview your clients again, Mr Bourke.'

'You're more than welcome, DS Maguire. The sooner we clear this matter up, the better. I believe what we're dealing with here is a tragic series of misunderstandings. It may have sadly cost the lives of two of your detectives, but in the final analysis, nobody was actually to blame.'

Katie stared at him. At that moment she wished more than anything that she were a witch, and that intense beams of green light could come out of her eyes and set fire to Nicholas Bourke where he stood, so that he was incinerated into nothing more than a heap of ashes.

She turned around and walked out of the interview room and Kyna followed her, while Detective Sergeant Begley switched off the DIR.

Back in her office, she held Kyna tight, and she was shaking.

Kyna kissed her, and stroked her hair, and said, 'Don't worry. We'll get them. And Twomey too. And Quinn. *And* the ghastly Gwenith.'

Katie wiped her eyes. 'Sorry. I'm just so angry at losing Buckley and O'Brien. Angry at Twomey and Logan and angry at myself. Now I've got to go and talk to Mrs Lacey over at CUH, and I can't give her even a hint who killed her husband. She doesn't have any kind of closure, poor woman. She doesn't even have her husband's head.'

A uniformed garda was posted outside Aidan Lacey's room at Cork University Hospital. He dropped his copy of the *Sun* and stood up when Katie came up to the door, but she waved her hand to him to indicate that he should sit down again. She remembered all the boring lonely hours she had spent outside hospital rooms when she was a young garda, watching over both victims and offenders.

It was nearly six o'clock. The room was dimly lit and chilly. Riona Lacey was sitting at Aidan's bedside watching television, while Aidan slept. His legs were humped up by a blanket cradle, and he was attached to two different drips. His heart monitor was beeping with monotonous regularity, but his face looked so white that he could have been mistaken for dead.

'Is it okay for me to come in?' Katie asked her.

Riona Lacey nodded. She was a small woman with a round face and sad eyes that reminded Katie of Sinéad O'Connor, except that she had a mass of curly brown hair. She was wearing a dark brown boat neck sweater with the sleeves pulled right down over her hands.

Katie dragged over a plastic chair and sat down next to her. 'How is he?'

'They've reattached the right foot. They have high hopes that it should heal all right. But the left leg was too badly damaged. He'll have to be fitted with a prosthetic leg. But the consultant said they can work miracles these days.'

She reached over and gripped Katie's wrist, even though her hand was covered by her sleeve.

'They don't know how long he's going to be kept in hospital, but it could be months. I only pray to Jesus that he'll be able to walk again.'

Katie said, 'I can't tell you how devastated we all are, Fiona. Everybody at Anglesea Street sends you their heartfelt condolences.'

'It's all right, Detective Superintendent, I know that John put a lot of backs up. If he saw that there was something bent going on, he could never ignore it. I told him that he was going to make himself fierce unpopular, just like Sergeant McCabe, but he said he had no choice.'

'He was going to report some of his fellow officers for failing to arrest car thieves, wasn't he? Or conveniently losing the evidence against them, so that they couldn't be taken to court?'

'That's right. He wouldn't tell me the whole story, like. He said it would be too dangerous for me to know. But some of his fellow officers were taking bribes, so he said, and one or two of them were even being given stolen cars, as well.'

'Well, he was very brave,' said Katie. 'Especially since he loved the job so much.'

Riona gave her a quick, rueful smile. 'It was his birthday last week. He was thirty-six. I gave him a watch so that he could count the days going by. He only managed to count up to five.'

'If there's any help you need, Riona, in any way at all, we'll be here for you. Any medical expenses, or therapy. Any financial help. Even if you just need somebody to talk to.'

'A victim support officer was here earlier, Brianna. She's coming back again tomorrow morning. She was the one who told me how John had been killed.'

Riona was clenching Katie's wrist so tightly that Katie felt as if she were trying to save herself from falling off the ledge of a six-storey building.

'Oh, God,' she said, and suddenly her eyes filled with tears. 'Oh God, do you know who did it?'

'Not yet,' said Katie. 'We have some good leads, though, and I guarantee that we'll get them in the end. They'll be punished for what they did to your John, don't you doubt it.'

Katie's phone rang. It was Mathew McElvey from the press office at Anglesea Street and he sounded panicky.

'Where are you, ma'am?'

'CUH, why?'

'If you're anywhere near a TV, switch it on to the Six One News. I had RTÉ on to me only about ten minutes ago. They were wanting to confirm that Sergeant Lacey was found yesterday morning with his head cut off.'

'What did you tell them?'

'Nothing. But they knew everything already. They were called by the fellows who killed him. They even knew that he had a tin whistle stuck down his neck.'

'So did you confirm it?'

'Not myself, no. I passed them over to Chief Superintendent MacCostagáin and he confirmed it. He said there was no point in trying to cover it up since they knew already. It would only make us look like we were being evasive.'

'That's what I told him. But I still wish he'd spoken to me first.'

She was still talking to Mathew McElvey when the Angelus finished chiming and the Six One News came on to the television. The volume was too low to hear what Keelin Shanley, the presenter, was saying, but behind her they could see a large picture of Sergeant Lacey in uniform.

'It's about John!' said Riona. She scrabbled to pick up the remote and turned up the sound so loud that Aidan jerked in his bed, even though he didn't open his eyes.

'The news has broken in the past few minutes that Sergeant John Lacey, one of the Garda whistle-blowers who was due to give evidence to the ongoing Disclosures Tribunal, was found dead this morning in the graveyard of St Senan's Abbey in Inniscarra.

'He had been beheaded and tied to a gravestone and a tin whistle had been inserted into his severed neck. RTÉ News was contacted by an anonymous informant who said that Sergeant Lacey had been executed in this way in retribution for what he called his malicious betrayal of his colleagues in An Garda Síochána and as a warning to other whistle-blowers not to submit false and misleading complaints to His Honour Justice McGuigan.

'Chief Superintendent MacCostagáin at Anglesea Garda station confirmed that Sergeant Lacey's body had been found and that a full investigation was under way, although it was too early to give further details.'

The report went on, but Riona switched the television off, her face a mess of tears, and dropped the remote on to the floor. Katie shifted her chair closer and held her tight.

'Oh, John, oh, John! How could they do that to him?' Riona sobbed. 'What am I going to do without him?'

Katie shushed her and stroked her curly hair. There was nothing else she could do to relieve the agony that she was going through.

After half an hour, there was a knock at the door and it was one of Riona's younger sisters. Katie gave Riona a last hug and said, 'I'll call you tomorrow so, to see how young Aidan's getting on.'

Riona looked up at her, wiping her tears with the sleeves of her sweater. 'Promise me you'll get them. Promise me you'll make them suffer for what they did to my John.'

'Riona, if I knew the way to Hell, that's where I'd be sending them.'

'I know the way,' said Riona. 'I'm there already.'

Twenty-Eight

Garda Yasir Wassan was standing in the narrow kitchen stirring semolina in a saucepan to make *sooji ka halwa* for his breakfast. On his way here he had asked his security guard to take him to Aiysha's Spice House on Shandon Street so that he could stock up on all the ingredients he would need to keep himself fed for the next three or four days, or at least until he had to go to Dublin to appear in front of His Honour Justice McGuigan.

Stephen MacQuaid had installed him in a pebble-dashed semi-detached house on Mount Farran, a steep residential road in Blackpool. He had assigned him three security guards to protect him in eight-hour shifts. The night guard had left about half an hour ago, and now the morning guard, Declan, was sprawled on the couch in the living room watching *Today with Maura and Dáithí*. Declan was a tall, muscular young man who looked like a boxer in his black polo-neck sweater, but he was very soft-spoken and polite.

'What are you cooking up there, horse?' he asked after a while, appearing at the kitchen door and sniffing. 'It smells like you're burning it.'

'Semolina, and it is supposed to have this burned smell. It will be delicious by the time I have finished. You must try some.'

'Thanks all the same, I think I'll pass on that, like. I had sausages and grilled tomatoes this morning. I wouldn't say no to a coffee, though, if you're making some.'

'I have lassi if you like.'

'Lassie? I thought that was a dog.'

Garda Wassan shook his head. 'Yogurt, water and mango pulp. With ice, and added sugar if you like.'

'If it's all the same to you, I'll stick to the coffee, like, do you know?'

'I have been trying to introduce my Irish friends to Pakistani food.'

'Good luck to you, horse. I don't think you'll have much success in Cork. If it isn't crubeens or tripe and drisheen, or McDonald's, they won't want to know.'

'You don't like curry?'

'It doesn't like me, that's the problem. I had a curry a couple of nights ago, when I was supposed to be on duty, but Holy Saint Patrick. No wonder that Mahatma Gandhi used to wear them nappies.'

Garda Wassan started to scoop the scorched semolina carefully out of the saucepan, but as he did so there was a loud hammering on the front door.

Declan immediately reached into the inside pocket of his blazer and pulled out a Vipertek stun gun, which resembled a flat black flashlight.

'Go into the back room now, Yasir, and lock the door, like we rehearsed you. Nobody knows that you're here, so it's probably only some gom complaining about my parking. But get in there anyway.'

Garda Wassan left the kitchen and went into the room at the back of the house that had probably once been the 'best' room. As he crossed the corridor there was another loud hammering at the door, and the doorbell was rung, too, again and again. He quietly closed the back-room door behind him and turned the key, and then he stood there, hardly daring to breathe, while a green-faced portrait of a Chinese lady stared at him dispassionately from the wall above the fireplace.

Declan went gingerly up to the front door and shouted out, 'Who is it? What do you want? Stop beating on the fecking door, will you? You'll bust it!'

There was no answer, but the hammering and the ringing stopped. About twenty seconds passed in silence, while Declan waited, his stun gun raised, wondering if he ought to open up the front door to see who was there, or if they had given up and gone away.

He was reaching for the door handle when there was a deafening bang and a crack and a splintering of wood. He stumbled backwards as the front door fell flat into the hallway, and three men in black balaclavas stormed over it and into the house. Their leader was carrying a sawn-off shotgun, which he pointed directly at Declan's chest.

'You can throw that fecking stun gun down for starters!' the man ordered. 'Don't give us any bother, head, and I won't make any extra holes in you. Deal? Grand. Now, where's the Paki? He's here all right, don't tell me he's not. I can fecking smell him!'

The living-room door was slightly ajar and one of the men kicked it wider open. He peered inside and said, 'Not in here, sham.'

'Not in the kitchen, neither,' said the other man.

'Upstairs?' said the man with the shotgun, stepping closer to the guard and pointing it less than five centimetres away from the tip of his nose.

Declan jerked his head towards the back-room door.

'Thanks a million,' said the man with the shotgun. 'Saves us a whole lot of running up and downstairs, do you know?'

With his free hand he tried the door handle, and as soon as he realized the door was locked, he said, 'Hoggy – Patrick.'

Hoggy went out of the front door and came back carrying a red battering-ram. He swung it twice and then he slammed it into the door and knocked it off its hinges. It tilted sideways at an angle and Patrick kicked it flat to the floor.

Garda Wassan was kneeling on the window sill, all tangled up in the nylon net curtains. He was trying to wrestle the window open, but it was locked. The man with the shotgun crossed the room and said, 'You can come down now, head. You and me need to have a little conversation, like, do you know what I mean.'

'Who are you?' demanded Garda Wassan. 'I have nothing to say to you.'

'Oh, really? That makes a change. You had plenty to say to Chief Superintendent O'Malley.'

'What I had to say was between him and me.'

'What you had to say has already caused a rake of trouble, Garda Wassan, and if you repeat what you said to Chief Superintendent O'Malley to Justice McGuigan, you're going to cause double the trouble. There's good men going to lose their livelihoods because of you and your cribbing.'

Garda Wassan climbed down from the window sill. 'What do you want me to do? Go to the tribunal and say "Sorry, Your Honour, I was only messing? All that bullying and all that racism I was complaining about, I only invented it, so that I could get my fellow gardaí into the shite. Sorry." Is that what you want me to say?'

The man with the shotgun cocked his head to one side as if he could hardly believe what he was hearing. 'You have some fecking nerve, boy, I'll give you that. But come on, let's get out the gap. There's plenty more to get sorted before dinnertime.'

The two other men came into the back room and seized Garda Wassan's arms. They pulled them behind his back and one of them clipped handcuffs on him.

As they pushed him out of the door, Declan stepped forwards and said, 'Stall it a second. Where are you taking him?'

'Oh, I forgot about you,' said the man with the shotgun. 'You were supposed to be taking care of our Paki friend here, weren't you?'

Declan didn't answer that, but stood with his hands hesitantly half-raised, like a man who isn't sure if a dangerous animal is going to spring at him.

'You made a pig's mickey of that, didn't you, head?' said the man with the shotgun. 'If I was your boss, do you know what I'd say? You're fired!'

He lifted his shotgun and with a brain-numbing bang he let

off both barrels at once. He had wedged a shotgun shell sideways between the two triggers so that he could pull them simultaneously without skinning his fingers. Half of Declan's head was blown off and splattered against the wall at the end of the hallway, and he spun around on one foot and flung up his arms like a ballet dancer before he tipped over on to the floor.

'What a fecking eejit,' said the man with the shotgun. 'Now let's sketch.'

Hoggy wiggled one fingertip in his ear and said, 'What? I can't fecking hear you.'

'I'm not in the mood, Hoggy. Let's just clear out of here before somebody starts getting nosy and calls the shades.'

Garda Wassan twisted and struggled against his handcuffs so that he could turn around and see the guard's body lying in the hallway.

'You shot him!' he shouted, and he was almost screaming. 'He did nothing at all and you shot him! Right in cold blood! *Aap aik rakshas hain!* You are a devil!'

The three men pushed and pulled him down the steeply sloping steps in front of the house and forced him into the back of a black BMW saloon that was parked close behind the guard's green Ford Kuga. Then they swerved away from the kerb and sped down Mount Farran to Assumption Road.

'Where are you taking me?' Garda Wassan demanded, still struggling as he sat in the back of the car between Hoggy and Patrick.

The man with the shotgun turned around in the passenger seat and said, 'We're taking you where all whistle-blowers should go, Garda Wassan. Somewhere you can whistle to your heart's content, and nobody will hear the treacherous tunes that you're playing.'

Twenty-Nine

The finest of fine rains was falling as they turned off Grange Terrace in Ovens and headed north up Grange Road. The fields all around them were deserted and the only sign of life was the crows perched on the telephone wires.

'Whatever you're intending to do, you're cracked if you think you can get away with it,' said Garda Wassan.

The man with the shotgun turned around again and grinned at him. 'Don't you believe it, head. We have friends in high places.'

'Supposing I told you that I would withdraw my complaint.'

'Too late for that now. And how could we trust you anyway? The minute we let you go, you'd go scurrying off to grass on us, I'll bet you.'

'Supposing I *swore* that I would withdraw it.'

'On what? The Bible? You're a Muslim, aren't you?'

'I would swear it on my honour.'

'Do you hear that, Hoggy? He says he'd swear it on his honour! You call that honour, sneaking on your mates, just because they can't stand the currified benjy off of you!'

They drove about a kilometre up a narrow hedge-lined lane until they reached a stone wall with a black iron gate. Beyond the stone wall was a derelict graveyard with grass growing as high as the headstones, and an abandoned church with a grey slate roof.

They parked, and Patrick pulled Garda Wassan out of the back of the car. The morning was almost silent except for the soft prickling sound of rain in the trees and the cawing of crows. Between them, Patrick and Hoggy marched Garda Wassan to the gate, which they opened with a jarring squeal. Then they half-pushed and half-dragged him through the overgrown graveyard until they reached the church building.

'Welcome to Athnowen Church,' said the man with the shotgun. 'It's been out of use for a brave few years, but we couldn't think of anywhere more suitable for a ritual like this. What you might call a ritual of absolution.'

The oak front doors of the church were wide open, and Garda Wassan could see that a metal bar had been prised away from them, and a rusty padlock was hanging loose. The man with the shotgun led the way inside, where it was chilly and dark and the floor was gritty underfoot.

Sitting at the foot of the font were two Garda officers, both of whom Garda Wassan recognized at once – Sergeant Dolan MacAuley and Garda Eamon Ó Grádaigh. A fourth man in a black balaclava was sitting on the steps beside them, nonchalantly jiggling an automatic pistol.

Both Sergeant MacAuley and Garda Ó Grádaigh were hand-cuffed behind their backs, and Garda Ó Grádaigh's left eye was bruised purple and so swollen that it was almost closed. Sergeant MacAuley was wearing only a pale green T-shirt and cargo shorts, while Garda Ó Grádaigh was dressed in a blue ribbed sweater and jeans. It was deathly cold inside the church and both men were shivering.

'Here we are then, gentlemen,' said the man with the shotgun, and his voice echoed eerily from the aisles. 'The three wise monkeys all together. You saw some evil and you heard some evil but thank the Lord you're never going to have the chance to speak about it.'

'Go away to fuck,' said Garda Ó Grádaigh.

'Hey – you don't have to be so dark with me. I never told you to go creeping off and telling tales to Chief Superintendent O'Malley, now did I? Patrick – Sean – tie these three monkeys together, would you? Back to back, like we talked about. Hoggy – you can start up the saw now, head. I'd like them to have a good long listen to the sound of it before we get down to business.'

Sean stuffed his pistol into the belt of his jeans, and then he and Patrick forced Garda Wassan to sit on the floor next to Sergeant MacAuley and Garda Ó Grádaigh. They bumped and shuffled all three men until they were pressed back to back, and then Patrick produced a green-and-white nylon rope and trussed it around their chests and their shoulders at least seven or eight times before knotting it tight.

Hoggy, meanwhile, was tugging at the pull cord of his chainsaw. He had to tug it again and again before it eventually stuttered into life, probably because the church was so cold. He stood beside the font, revving it up, and waving it slowly around in circles.

None of the three whistle-blowers spoke. Sergeant MacAuley's eyes followed the chainsaw as Hoggy waved it around, as if he were trying to make it break down by willpower alone. Garda Ó Grádaigh looked away, into the gloom of the transept, while Garda Wassan closed his eyes and prayed. The roaring and surging noise was deafening, and the man with the shotgun tilted it over his shoulder so that he could press his fingers in his ears.

'Which one first?' shouted Hoggy, leaning towards him.

'Order of seniority!' the man with the shotgun shouted back.

'What the feck does that mean?'

'Sergeant first, white garda second, Paki last!'

Hoggy stepped up to Sergeant MacAuley, his knees bent to brace himself. Now Sergeant MacAuley closed his eyes, too, and his lips moved as he prayed to God for final forgiveness.

The chainsaw's teeth ripped into his Adam's apple and blood and fragments of flesh were spattered into the air like an angry swarm of red hornets. Hoggy revved the chainsaw even harder as he cut through Sergeant MacAuley's vertebrae, and almost as soon as he had done that, the sergeant's head rolled off his neck and dropped down at his feet. It bounced towards the man with the shotgun and lay there staring up at him, and the man with the shotgun gave it a desultory kick with the toe of his boot.

Hoggy moved around to face Garda Ó Grádaigh. The short-cropped hair at the back of his head was already dripping with Sergeant MacAuley's blood and he stared at Hoggy in total terror.

Hoggy lunged the chainsaw towards his face to taunt him, and Garda Ó Grádaigh screamed at him, his mouth stretched wide open, his one good eye bulging. Hoggy lunged again, laughing, and this time Garda Ó Grádaigh soaked his jeans.

'See!' shouted the man with the shotgun. 'They can't keep anything to themselves, these sneaky bastards! Not even their piss!'

Hoggy adjusted his stance now and leaned closer to Garda Ó Grádaigh. He swung the chainsaw to one side and it cut through Garda Ó Grádaigh's skin and neck muscles as smoothly as if it were cutting through a log, except for a brief few seconds when it snarled against his vertebrae. His head tipped backwards and fell behind Garda Wassan and Sergeant MacAuley's decapitated body and Hoggy had to reach down and lift it out by one ear, before tossing it on to the floor.

Garda Wassan didn't scream as Hoggy came around to face him. He looked up at him and then he closed his eyes again and his expression was one of absolute calm. Nobody else could have known it, and nobody else ever would, but he was thinking of his young sister, Afrah, who had died of pneumonia when she was only five. He could picture her laughing as she ran through the garden, chasing their cat.

He felt a devastating jolt, and an instant of tearing pain, a pain so agonizing that he couldn't even recognize it as pain. It was only an instant, though, and then his head fell on to the floor next to Garda Ó Grádaigh's.

Hoggy switched off the chainsaw and set it down next to the font.

'Look at the fecking state of me la. I'll be needing a bath after this.'

'Long overdue, too,' said Patrick.

Hoggy gave him the finger. Meanwhile the fourth man came forwards with a black dustbin bag. Wrinkling up his nose in disgust, he picked up the three severed heads by their hair and dropped them inside, twisting the top and tying it up.

Patrick produced three tin whistles from inside his anorak. He tootled each of them in turn and then pushed them one by one into each of the bloodied necks.

'There,' he said, standing back. 'I reckon we've seen the last of the whistle-blowers. If any other guard has the balls to rat on his fellow officers after this, I'm a Chinaman.'

'Well, if that happens, head, don't go complaining to Chief Superintendent O'Malley about racism,' said the man with the shotgun. 'We've run out of whistles.'

Thirty

James Gallagher, the forensic accountant, arrived punctually at eleven o'clock, carrying his laptop and a large leather briefcase. Moirin brought him up to Katie's office, where she was making arrangements for the state funerals of Detectives Buckley and O'Brien. She couldn't personally see why Garda O'Regan didn't merit a state funeral, too, but it was a sensitive issue, particularly with the Garda Representative Association, whose members would be expected to line the streets.

He was a short, brisk man, James Gallagher, with a clipped moustache and rimless spectacles and a navy-blue three-piece suit. When he sat down and crossed his legs, Katie could see that he had shiny brown shoes and canary-yellow socks.

'As I told you on the phone, Detective Superintendent, Jimmy Ó Faoláin's financial affairs were fierce complicated, and deliberately so. He set up Erin Investments, promising his clients a staggeringly high return for their money, but basically this was nothing but a Ponzi scheme, and all he was doing was paying his older clients from the money invested by his newer clients – and keeping a large proportion of that money for himself. Erin Investments never invested a single cent in anything.'

'What about the shares he *was* buying?'

James Gallagher opened his laptop and showed Katie the figures. 'He was buying up whole blocks of them, mostly from companies who were suffering from something of an economic downturn. Of course his purchase would inflate their price, and he would give out all kinds of buoyant forecasts about them.

But as soon as he had sent his clients their latest financial update and boasted how much profit their investment was making for them, he was dumping the shares and keeping the proceeds. It's not quite as simple as that, but you get the idea.'

'You said there was one group in particular who suffered the worst losses.'

'Ó Faoláin set up a company about a year ago called Equity Sunshine. You may have seen his ads in the papers, and I think he even advertised on the TV too. It was aimed at older people in larger properties with a high equity value. He was persuading them to release that equity and invest it in what he called "secure, reliable, but highly profitable enterprises", which is almost a contradiction in terms.

'He said that he could guarantee them a prosperous retirement, all foreign holidays and new cars and fine dining, but if you read the very doonchie small print – and when I say doonchie I mean you'd practically need an electron microscope to read it – he was making no such guarantee. In fact, totally the opposite. He was outright warning anybody who put their money into Equity Sunshine that they would never see any of it again.'

'That's tragic,' said Katie. 'If he wasn't dead I'd haul him in for fraud.'

'There was one association of thirteen retired people who clubbed together to invest in Equity Sunshine, and as far as I can make out from these accounts, they lost millions.'

'Do you have their names?'

'No, I don't, unfortunately,' said James Gallagher. 'Jimmy Ó Faoláin only numbered his investors with a code of his own, and I haven't yet been able to find the key to it. But he did mention this particular association by name in an email I found to his bank. Here it is, look. They called themselves Ghairdín Glas.'

'That means "Green Garden". Jesus. More like "Barren Wasteland", if you ask me. How much did they lose?'

'According to these accounts, a little over seven point five million.'

'Mother of God. Do you have any idea where it all went?'

'He used most of it to buy property abroad and tucked the rest of it away in overseas accounts. Bermuda, the Cayman Islands. It'll take us a long time to locate it at all, and of course we may not be able to get very much of it back, but at least we'll know where it's gone.'

At that moment, Detective O'Donovan joined them, and James Gallagher briefly explained what he had just told Katie about Ghairdín Glas.

'I'd say that was a motive for murder all right, wouldn't you, Patrick?' Katie asked him.

'Sure, like, but what are we talking about with this Ghairdín Glas? Thirteen people over the age of sixty-five, and probably older. I can't see any of them having the expertise to enter Jimmy Ó Faoláin's and shoot him without leaving the slightest trace that they'd been there – that's if their creaking knees could even get them up the driveway. And where would people like that have acquired themselves a Sig Sauer automatic from?'

'They could have organized a hit man,' said Katie.

'I don't see it myself. Where would they find one? You don't see fellers hanging around the Active Retirement Association on dance nights, do you, holding up signs saying "Assassin For Hire"? I reckon it's much more likely to have been some other businessman that he diddled. And that girlfriend of his, that air hostess, it wouldn't surprise me if she was involved in it somehow. All she seemed to be interested in was how much jewellery she could finagle out of him.'

'Oh yes, the lovely Viona Caffrey,' said Katie.

'Then there was all that jiggery-pokery that Jimmy Ó Faoláin was up to with Rachmasach Rovers, wasn't there, throwing games and all. You know what these GAA types are like – fanatical. Maybe their team manager was secretly raging because he wanted to win for a change.'

'I thought you'd interviewed most of the team already.'

'I have, but I might just as well have interviewed eleven

quayside bollards, I can tell you, for all the sense I got out of them.'

'But what about their manager?'

'Finbar Foley... you've probably heard of him. Jimmy Ó Faoláin poached him from Mallow. He wasn't happy about losing, I could tell that. Rovers have played seven games this season and so far they've lost six, four of them with no score at all. But if Foley did have anything to do with Jimmy Ó Faoláin being knocked off, he wasn't going to tell me, was he?'

'Here, look at this,' James Gallagher put in. 'It's pure cleverly concealed in these accounts as maintenance costs, but it seems as if Jimmy Ó Faoláin was transferring ten thousand euros into Finbar Foley's account after every single game. From that I think we can safely assume that he was being *paid* to lose. Do you think Foley would be after killing the goose that laid his golden eggs? Unless of course he'd insisted that he wanted to win for a change, if only for the sake of his reputation in the GAA, and Jimmy Ó Faoláin had threatened to cut off his money and expose him as a cheat.'

'Maybe you should go and talk to Foley again,' said Katie. 'Make him feel uneasy, and that we still have our suspicions about him. But flatter him too. Tell him that now Jimmy Ó Faoláin's gone, you're looking forwards to Rachmasach getting top of the league. We need only one tiny clue, Patrick... anything to tell us who let themselves into Jimmy Ó Faoláin's house that morning.'

James Gallagher lifted a thick blue cardboard file out of his briefcase and set it down on Katie's desk. 'My full written report is in here, Detective Superintendent, with all the facts and figures up to date. I shall be staying here in Cork for a couple more days, with friends of mine in Montenotte, so if you find any of it baffling or you have any questions at all please let me know and I'll be more than happy to go through it with you.'

'What's your opinion about these accounts, James? I mean, frankly, in the context of Jimmy Ó Faoláin's murder?'

James Gallagher patted his hand on top of the file. 'My

absolute conviction is that the murderer or *murderers* plural is identified in these accounts. Not necessarily by name, because so many names are still encoded. But once we've discovered who they are, I'm sure that the figures will give us all we need to make an arrest and prepare a book of evidence.'

'In other words, whoever killed him, their days are numbered,' said Detective O'Donovan, and looked pleased with himself. 'Their days are *numbered*,' he repeated, in case Katie hadn't got it.

Katie went back to her funeral arrangements, but not twenty minutes had passed before her phone rang and it was Stephen MacQuaid. He was breathless, as if he had been running around a football field before he decided to phone.

'I've already called 112,' he panted. 'I still have them on my other phone. You're sending guards, and an ambulance.'

'What's happened, Stephen? Come on, calm down, try to tell me.'

As Stephen MacQuaid tried to catch his breath, Superintendent Pearse gave a perfunctory knock at her door and came into her office, along with Detective Inspector Fitzpatrick. Whatever Stephen MacQuaid was panicking about, Katie could see by the look on their faces that they had heard about it, too. She lifted her hand to them to show them that she was still listening to him.

'I can't think how this could have happened, Katie,' Stephen told her, between agonized sobs. 'The guard – the guard who was taking care of your Pakistani fellow this morning – Declan Summers his name is – he's been shot dead. Mother of Divine Christ, he's only had half of his head blown off.'

'Stephen, try to calm down. I can barely understand what you're saying. Your security guard's been shot.'

'That's right. He must have been killed outright. Oh, Jesus.'

'So what's happened to Garda Wassan?'

'I don't know. He's gone. I told the emergency operator.'

'*What?* Where was this?' Katie opened her left-hand desk drawer and looked at the three safe-house addresses that Stephen had given her. 'Was this at Mount Farran?'

'That's right. Declan was supposed to report in at twelve, but he didn't ring and when I couldn't get an answer on his phone I went there myself to see if there was a problem. The front door was off its hinges and he was lying dead in the hall. I can't believe that none of the neighbours heard a shot or saw anything that was going on. They must be blind and deaf, those people. Blind and deaf.'

'And there's no sign at all of Garda Wassan? What about the other two? Sergeant MacAuley and Garda Ó Grádaigh?'

'I can't get an answer from their guards, either. I'm on my way to Ballyvolane now to check on Sergeant MacAuley, and then I'll be going over to Glanmire.'

'Stephen, where are you now?'

'I'm just about to leave Mount Farran.'

'Stay there. When the guards arrive, make yourself known to them. Tell them who your casualty is and how they can get in touch with his next of kin. I'll be sending officers to Ballyvolane and Glanmire to check on the other two, but don't you be after going there yourself. Whoever shot your man could still be at one of those addresses.'

'I can't think how this could have happened, Katie! I'm so sorry! I thought those safe houses, they were totally secure! Nobody outside of MacQuaid Security knows that they belong to us! Nobody! Well, except for you.'

'Just try to settle, will you, Stephen? Take things handy and a couple of my detectives will be coming up to Mount Farran to talk to you in just a short while.'

Katie put down the phone and stared at Superintendent Pearse and Detective Inspector Fitzpatrick without saying a word. Then she tore off the three addresses from her notepad, got up from her desk and walked across to Superintendent Pearse.

'Here,' she said. 'Sergeant MacAuley's at Mervue Lawn and

Garda Ó Grádaigh's at Church Hill. It was MacQuaid Security who were supposed to be guarding them but they've lost contact with them so we need to get a patrol to each of those addresses without any delay. Warn them that there could be armed and dangerous suspects on the premises.'

Superintendent Pearse gave Katie a sideways look that had several different meanings, including *Women!* and *You've made a right hames of this, haven't you?* and *We all know what the headline on tonight's Six One News is going to be, don't we?*

'We're right on it, Kathleen,' he said, and left.

Once he had gone, Detective Inspector Fitzpatrick said, 'If all three of them have been taken, this is going to be catastrophic. Not only for you and me. The entire force is going to look like a shambles. Holy Saint Joseph, we're going through Commissioners faster than we can paint their names on their office doors.'

'I just pray to God that Garda Wassan doesn't end up the same way as Garda O'Regan and Sergeant Lacey. And please don't let those other two be missing, too.'

Detective Inspector Fitzpatrick sat down. The fine rain had reached the city now, and it blurred the window behind him. His dead-looking eyes were entirely appropriate for a day like this. In a way, Katie found his lack of expression reassuring. This was no time for hysterics or anger. This was a time for the ice-cold emotionless pursuit of people who were doing wrong.

'I can't think how they found Garda Wassan,' she said. 'I suppose it's possible that one of the security guards who works for Stephen MacQuaid could have tipped them off. You can never overestimate how low people are prepared to stoop to pick up money.'

'For all we know, Garda Wassan hasn't even been taken by the same people,' said Detective Inspector Fitzpatrick. 'His complaints were all about racism and bullying. Garda O'Regan was blowing the whistle about convicted felons being released from prison, and Sergeant Lacey's disclosure concerned the dropping of prosecutions for car theft.'

'I know, Robert. I've been turning that over and over in my mind right from the moment that Sergeant Lacey was found. But the more varied their disclosures are, the more convinced I am that the same people are responsible for shutting them up. Denis MacCostagáin doesn't agree with me, or *says* he doesn't agree with me, anyway, but whichever criminals might have been involved, all of these disclosures would have led to gardaí being disciplined or sacked or even prosecuted.'

'I wonder. They didn't even get slapped on the wrist when they were caught falsifying four thousand breath tests.'

'Well, I know, but that was more complicated, and if they'd sacked all the officers who did that, we would have had hardly any police force left.'

Detective Inspector Fitzpatrick thought about that for a while, tapping a ball pen against the palm of his hand. 'This could get very messy, ma'am,' he said.

'Don't I know it. But I'm going to have a word with Bill Phinner, and make sure that he's run DNA and fingerprint comparisons with serving and retired gardaí as well as felons.'

'Until this is over, I think I'll take all that leave that's owing to me,' said Detective Inspector Fitzpatrick.

Katie looked at him and smiled, but he wasn't smiling, and his eyes were as cold as ever.

Her phone rang. She picked it up and it was Superintendent Pearse.

'They've been taken,' he said.

Thirty-One

Katie drove with Detective Inspector Fitzpatrick to Mount Farran first. She had already sent Detectives Markey and Murrish ahead to Ballyvolane and Detectives Scanlan and O'Crean to Glanmire. Superintendent Pearse had told her that the security guards at both of those addresses had been badly beaten and tied up but not shot.

The cul-de-sac was crowded with three patrol cars, as well as an ambulance and two vans from the Technical Bureau. As Katie and Detective Inspector Fitzpatrick arrived, an outside broadcast van from RTÉ turned up, too. The pavement had been cordoned off, but a small crowd had gathered, and was standing in the drizzle in the hope of seeing something gruesome.

Bill Phinner's technical experts had erected a blue vinyl tent around the front door of the house on Mount Farran, and Bill Phinner was standing in the front garden, puffing at a fruity-smelling e-cigarette. Katie walked up to him, waving the vapour away with her hand.

'I thought you'd given that up, Bill.'

'I tried. Maybe I will when I retire from this job.'

'What's the story?'

'Thirty-three-year-old male, shotgun blast to the left side of the head. Both barrels simultaneously. Going by the pellet pattern on the wall behind him, I'd say we're looking for a sawn-off side-by-side shotgun.'

'Any other forensics?'

'The front door and one of the interior doors were both bashed

261

down with a battering-ram. From the indentations, I'd say they used a Big Red Key or something similar. It was definitely a professional job. They didn't just use a lump of wood or a sledge-hammer.'

Katie gave Detective Inspector Fitzpatrick a meaningful look. Big Red Keys was what they called Enforcer battering-rams, and these were standard Garda issue, although they usually required the approval of a superintendent before they could be taken out to break a suspect's door down.

'Where's Stephen MacQuaid?' asked Katie. 'I told him to stay here.'

'Oh, you mean the deceased fellow's boss? He's down there, sitting in his car. He said he was feeling musha. I'm not surprised. It's not your most appetizing sight at dinnertime, is it, a fellow with half his head up the walls?'

Katie left the garden and walked up the road to where Stephen was sitting in the passenger seat of his car, with the door open. He looked up at her and his face was grey.

'I don't know what to say to you, Katie.'

'Have you heard about your other two fellows?'

He nodded, and lifted up his phone. 'They rang me, both of them. They've both been taken to the Mercy. One of them, Martin, he's a dislocated shoulder. The other one, Braden, he needs stitches to his head.'

'Yes,' said Katie. 'Two of my detectives are with them.'

Stephen shook his head. 'I can't think who ratted on us, but somebody must have. I swear to God I check and double-check every single one of the staff I employ. Not just the security guards – even the girls who take the bookings. Even the cleaners.'

'You don't even have the slightest suspicion? Maybe one of your guards has been complaining about his hours, or his pay, or the kind of assignments you've been giving him?'

'I had to sack one guard about a month ago because he kept coming on to our clients' wives and daughters, but apart from that, everybody's happy so far as I know.'

'We'll be sending one of our communications experts around to your office to check your computers, Stephen. We'll be after checking if you've been hacked.'

'You're welcome, but I doubt it. We've the best anti-hacking software you can buy.'

'All right,' said Katie. 'You can go now, but we'll need to talk to you again. Please don't discuss this with anybody else, especially anybody from the media. Anything you say could put our three whistle-blowers in serious jeopardy, wherever they are.'

'You've not heard anything? No ransom demands, anything like that?'

'No.'

Stephen held his head in his hands. 'Oh, Katie. You don't know how sorry I am. I've totally let you down. My business is going to be ruined by this.'

Katie laid a hand on his shoulder. 'I'm not blaming you, Stephen. All I'm worried about now is what's happened to those whistle-blowers and whether I can get them back alive.'

'Maybe no news is good news.'

'Maybe. But there's never anything so bad that it couldn't be worse.'

Katie left Stephen and went back up to the house. Detective Inspector Fitzpatrick had been waiting for her and lifted the flap of the vinyl tent so that she could go inside. The broken-down front door had been lifted upright and a technical expert was taking pictures of it with an infrared sensitive camera, in case the intruders had left any footprints on it.

'I'm still nagging for a Crime-lite tablet,' said Bill Phinner. 'I know they cost an arm and a leg, but it would save us having to take the pictures back to the lab.'

'I'll mention it next time I'm in a budget meeting,' said Katie. 'I don't hold out much hope, though. The way things are going, we can't even afford a new kettle for the squad room.'

Just then, one of the technical experts at the end of the hallway switched on an LED floodlight. Katie could instantly see why Stephen had looked so grey. Declan was lying against the left-hand skirting board with his right arm raised above his head. More than half of his face was missing and his jawbone was curved up like an ivory shoehorn. Blood was sprayed all over the wall at the end of the corridor, and a long, tangled skein of hair and skin and brain tissue was lying across the carpet.

Katie crossed herself. She would never stop feeling sickened by the sight of human bodies that had been mangled and crushed and beaten and hacked into bloody pieces. More than that, though, it was the waste of life that she found so sad.

Bill Phinner showed her into the kitchen, which still smelled strongly of scorched semolina.

'It looks like Garda Wassan was cooking himself something to eat when the offenders came to call. It's all here, see – semolina with cashews and raisins and cardamom, mixed up with water and milk. It's a favourite Pakistani breakfast.'

He led her back out to the hallway, where two of his technical experts were taking flash photographs of Declan's body.

'I'm guessing that Garda Wassan tried to hide in this back room, because the deadbolt is still in the locked position and the key is here on the inside, even though the door was smashed open. That net curtain's been pulled aside and the window handle there, that's still upright, but he wouldn't have been able to open the window because that's locked, too.'

'Okay, Bill, thanks for that,' said Katie. 'I'll leave you to get on. DI Fitzpatrick and I will be heading back to Anglesea Street. You have Fergus up at Ballyvolane, don't you?'

'That's right, and he'll be going to Glanmire immediately after.'

As Katie and Detective Inspector Fitzpatrick came out of the front gate, Sergeant Kiely came up to them. He was a grizzled, experienced officer who always put Katie in mind of an old stud bull in a high-viz jacket.

'The lads have been chatting to the locals, ma'am,' he told her. 'One or two of them said they heard a bang not long after nine this morning but they didn't think nothing of it. They're putting up that new building by the roundabout down there and there's been fierce banging coming from that for the past two weeks. They thought it was that.'

'Did anybody see any unfamiliar vehicles, or men behaving strangely?'

'Nobody saw nothing. The men who weren't already at work were still in their scratchers and the women who weren't already at work were all in their kitchens cooking the breakfast.'

Fionnuala Sweeney from RTÉ News came hurrying across the road with her cameraman and caught up with Katie before she could close her car door.

'DS Maguire! DS Maguire! Have you a statement for us?'

'A young man has been found deceased from a gunshot wound. So far that's all I can tell you.'

'Do you know who he is?'

'Yes, we do, but we won't be releasing his name until his next of kin has been informed.'

'Do you have a suspect?'

'At this moment in time, no. So we'd obviously appreciate it if anybody who has any information relating to this incident could call 1800 666 111. All calls will be completely confidential.'

'Was the victim resident in the house there?'

'I've no further comment now, Fionnuala. I'll be holding a media conference later in the day most likely.'

'Was it gang-related, this shooting?'

'Like I said, Fionnuala, I've no further comment.'

'Is there any danger to the public at large? I mean, if there's a suspect loose with a gun, like?'

'Not so far as we know. But obviously if you see somebody openly carrying a gun you'd be well advised not to approach them or challenge them. Head off in the opposite direction as fast as you can and call 112.'

Katie closed the door and Detective Inspector Fitzpatrick drove off.

'Holy Divine Jesus,' she said, blowing out her cheeks. 'I think I might join you on leave, Robert. Where shall we go? Somewhere as far away from Cork as we can find. How about Bali?'

'You'd be sitting on a volcano if you went to Bali. Not much different from sitting on the Disclosures Tribunal, back here.'

Back at Anglesea Street, Katie went directly in to see Chief Superintendent MacCostagáin. He had been briefed already by Superintendent Pearse that all three whistle-blowers had been abducted, and Katie had rarely seen him look so grim.

'So much for your friend MacQuaid and his watertight security,' he said, as Katie took off her raincoat and dropped it over the arm of her chair. 'Do you have any notion at all who might have leaked those addresses?'

'I can only guess that it must have been one of Stephen's staff. He employs about sixty altogether. But even he doesn't have a clue who it might have been. Only a handful of his people know that the company has safe houses, and even less know where they're located. They only rent them, so they're constantly changing them.'

'My God, Kathleen. This is the end of the world as we know it.'

'I'm not giving up hope yet, sir. We haven't heard anything up until now, and so far as I know the media haven't been notified.'

'It could be they're waiting for the Six One News, like they did yesterday. Maybe they want to make a splash. Did you see the papers this morning, about Sergeant Lacey? The *Sun* accused us of running around like headless chickens, while our whistle-blowers' heads were being cut off. I've already had Frank Magorian on the phone, and he's had the Acting Commissioner on the phone, and *he's* had the Justice Minister on the phone, and all of them are ripping.'

'It doesn't help that there are so few witnesses,' said Katie. 'None of the residents of Mount Farran saw anything unusual going on. Markey texted me on the way back here to say that nobody in Mervue Lawn in Ballyvolane saw or heard anything – possibly because Sergeant MacAuley was taken away before any of them had woken up. And the safe house on Church Hill in Glanmire, that's hidden behind so many trees and bushes apparently that you can't see the house itself, let alone anybody leaving it.'

Denis MacCostagáin picked up the cup of tea on his desk, peered into it, saw that it had a milky skin on it and put it down again. 'Somebody must have seen something, even if they didn't understand the significance of it. You'll be broadcasting appeals for information, won't you?'

'I've already asked Fionnuala Sweeney to put out an appeal on RTÉ News but I'm going down to speak to Mathew McElvey right now so that we can make it in time for the morning papers.'

'Oh – it looks like he's going to save you the bother,' said Denis MacCostagáin, swivelling around in his chair and pointing to his office door behind her.

Mathew McElvey was peering around the door with his knuckle raised, ready to knock. Denis MacCostagáin said, 'Come on in, Mathew. What's the craic?'

Katie thought Mathew had aged in the short time that he had worked in the press office at Anglesea Street. He had started out so youthful and smart and fresh, always wearing a jacket and tie and with his hair brushed up. Now his tie was hanging loose and he looked as if he were wearing yesterday's shirt and his hair was all messed up and badly in need of a cut. She wondered if his daily routine of issuing press releases about robberies and fatal road accidents and suicides had worn him down. But you could never be sure. He had been married for only six months and maybe he was having trouble at home.

'Dan Keane called me, from the *Examiner*,' he said. 'He wanted to know if you were going to make a statement about the three whistle-blowers.'

Katie gave an involuntary shiver. 'What about them?'

'He wanted to know if you had found their bodies yet.'

'He thinks that they're dead? What makes him think that?'

'He's had a call saying that all three of them have been

punished for sneaking on their fellow officers. He wouldn't tell me who the call was from.'

'Did this caller say *how* they'd been punished?'

Mathew nodded. He put his hand over his mouth as if he were feeling sick.

'They've been beheaded, haven't they?' said Katie.

Mathew nodded again.

'They've been beheaded and they've all had tin whistles stuck down their necks, just like Garda O'Regan and Sergeant Lacey.'

'Yes,' said Mathew. 'According to what Dan Keane was told, anyway.'

Denis MacCostagáin said, 'Holy Jesus, Kathleen! And we were supposed to be protecting them. We couldn't have done worse if we'd cut their heads off ourselves.'

'This caller—' said Katie. 'Did he give Dan Keane any indication at all where the bodies might be?'

'He said something about headless chickens.'

'Headless chickens? That was what the *Sun* called us this morning, wasn't it?'

'I don't know. I didn't really understand what he was talking about.'

'If the *Sun* ever call you again, you can tell them to take a running jump off Kinsale Head,' said Denis MacCostagáin.

Katie said, 'May I?' and picked up the phone from his desk. She got through to the officer on the switchboard and asked her to ring Dan Keane at the *Examiner*.

Dan Keane answered with a prolonged coughing fit.

'Dan? This is DS Maguire from Anglesea Street.'

'Oh, how are you? Sorry – I'm having a quick steamer and you caught me in mid-inhalation.'

'Dan, I have Mathew McElvey here with me and he tells me you've had a call about our three whistle-blowers.'

'That's absolutely correct, ma'am. Excuse me while I clear my throat.'

'Was it a man or a woman who called you?'

'It was a fellow. Kind of gruff. He didn't give a name or any other identification if that's what you're going to ask me, even though I wouldn't tell you anyway.'

'Mathew said he mentioned headless chickens. What was that about?'

'Well, I asked him where the bodies were, and he asked me if I was any use at cryptic crosswords, because if I was he'd give me a clue. He said the whistle-blowers were all chickens, because they were too funky to face up to their fellow officers in person. Now they're headless chickens, and where might you find headless chickens? A hen town.'

'And that was the clue? A hen town?'

'He said it was. Like, search me what it means. I'm not too bad at crosswords but I'm still scratching my head over that one.'

'Dan – we've heard nothing ourselves yet about the whistle-blowers so I'd appreciate it if you'd keep this to yourself for now. I'll be holding a media conference just as soon as I have something positive to tell you.'

'So what was that all about?' asked Denis MacCostagáin, once Katie had put down the phone.

'Dan said that whoever called him gave him a clue to where the bodies are. "A hen town."'

'"A hen town"? What kind of a game are they playing, these people? That means nothing at all. "A *hen* town"?'

Katie wrote *A hen town* down on Denis MacCostagáin's notepad. 'It can't be that cryptic,' she said. 'They *want* us to find those bodies. They want us to see them with their heads cut off and the whistles sticking out of their necks. But they're razzing us. They want us to look like total incompetents. Not just *look* like total incompetents, but feel like it, too. They want us to feel like we're floundering.'

Mathew McElvey's phone warbled. He answered it, and when he had, he covered it with his hand and looked at Katie and Denis MacCostagáin in desperation.

'It's Fionnuala Sweeney. She wants to know if it's true that the whistle-blowers have all been beheaded and had tin whistles stuck into their necks.'

'Tell her no comment,' said Katie.

'She says they'll be reporting it anyway.'

'Tell her we can't stop her, but we'll be giving out a full statement later.'

'She says she can't hold it any later than six.'

Katie looked down at what she had written on Denis MacCostagáin's notepad.

'Maybe it's a cemetery,' she said. 'Garda O'Regan and Sergeant Lacey were both beheaded in cemeteries. Maybe he meant Queenstown cemetery. Some local folk in Cobh still call it that. That's the only cemetery in Cork I can think of that has "town" in its name.'

'That doesn't sound like much of a crossword clue,' said Mathew.

Katie kept staring at *A hen town* and the answer suddenly came to her. She had actually seen a sign for it when she had been driving back from St Senan's Abbey.

'It's an anagram,' she said.

'A what?'

'An anagram. Not even a very difficult one, either. It's Athnowen. There's an old abandoned church there, and it has a graveyard.'

Denis MacCostagáin raised his brambly eyebrows. 'I always knew there was a reason we decided to promote women to the senior ranks. They have brains. Myself, I couldn't have worked that out in a million years.'

'I could still be wrong,' said Katie. 'It may not be an anagram at all, or maybe it's an anagram of somewhere else altogether. But Athnowen is not too far from St Senan's, and it's totally secluded, so you could murder half of Cork in there and nobody would know what you were up to.'

'What's the plan, then, Kathleen?' asked Denis MacCostagáin.

'Athnowen's not too far. I'll go out there myself and have a sconce. I'll take DS Ni Nuallán with me and a couple of uniforms. If I'm wrong, we won't have wasted more than half an hour.'

'Yes, but if they're *not* there, the whistle-blowers – what then?'

'We'll be told, sir, sooner or later. I don't have any doubt about that. They want to make us look like bumbling eejits, these killers, but they want to frighten the holy Jesus out of us, too.'

Although Athnowen was less than fifteen minutes away, due west from Cork city on the N22, it was already growing dark by the time Katie arrived at the end of Grange Road in her blue Ford Focus. A Garda patrol car was following her with two young male uniformed officers, and they parked close behind.

'Jesus, this is a spooky place,' said Kyna, as she climbed out of the car and pulled up the hood of her baggy purple raincoat.

'I'm half-praying that I'm useless at crosswords,' said Katie.

One of the two gardaí pushed open the black iron gate and the four of them high-stepped their way through the tall wet grass in the graveyard.

'The pity of this,' said Kyna, stopping in front of a small granite headstone, which read 'Aoife Murphy, Now An Angel Among Angels, Aged Twelve Years, September 17, 1876'.

They reached the church entrance. The doors were closed, but the metal bar that had once secured them was bent at an angle and the padlock was gaping open. Together, the gardaí pushed the doors wide open with a harsh scraping sound and then they took out their flashlights so that they could probe inside.

It was not only dark inside, but so cold that it looked as if all four of them were smoking. They made their way into the main body of the church, their footsteps echoing, the beams of the gardaí's flashlights criss-crossing the nave as if they were duelling with light sabres.

'How long has this place been abandoned?' asked one of the

gardaí, shining his flashlight up at the stained-glass windows over the altar. 'Even if there's no bodies here, I'll bet there's ghosts.'

'I don't know for certain,' said Katie. 'I believe some company wanted to turn it into a crematorium, but the locals protested.'

'They didn't want a crematorium in a graveyard? There's logic for you.'

But it was then that they reached the crossing between the transepts, and their flashlights darted towards the font. Seated on the floor in front of the font, bound back to back, were the three whistle-blowers, headless. Each of them was wearing a dark crimson shoulder-cape of dried blood, and each of them had a shining tin whistle sticking at an angle from his severed neck.

Katie walked up to them and stood looking at them. Kyna came up behind her and touched her shoulder.

'This wasn't your fault,' she said, quietly, so that the two uniformed gardaí wouldn't hear her. 'You did everything you could to make sure that they were protected. I don't know what else you could have done.'

'If it wasn't my fault, then whose fault was it?'

'Whoever murdered them, and whoever told their murderers where their safe houses were. Not you.'

'I still feel responsible.'

Kyna raised her hand as if to touch Katie's shoulder again, but thought better of it. 'We'll find out who it was, ma'am, and we'll make them suffer for it. I don't want to be a member of a police force in which I'm frightened to speak out against corruption and bullying and sexual harassment, and neither do you.'

Katie turned to the two gardaí, whose flashlights were still dancing like fireflies around the headless bodies of the whistle-blowers. One of them said, 'Where's their heads? I can't see their fecking heads anywhere.' Both officers looked numb with horror.

'Call Superintendent Pearse, will you, and tell him what we've found,' said Katie. 'I'll get on to Chief Superintendent MacCostagáin.'

'He's going to love you for this,' said Kyna.

Katie couldn't take her eyes off the tin whistles protruding from the victims' necks. But as she waited for Denis MacCostagáin to answer his phone, she also noticed that Sergeant MacAuley and Garda Ó Grádaigh were holding hands tightly, as tightly as lovers, or as brothers running for their lives.

Thirty-Two

'I can't live like this,' said Eithne, letting the curtain fall back.

Michael Ó Doibhilin sat up in bed and said, 'They're out there to protect you, sweetheart. They'll be out there twenty-four seven until all of this balla malla is over.'

'But I don't want to be protected. I want to feel that I can live my life without this threat hanging over me.'

'It'll be okay, I swear to God. Nobody's going to hurt you.'

Eithne sat down on the end of the bed. She was a thin young woman of twenty-one, with skin so white it was almost translucent and glossy dark hair that fell all the way down her back. She had a pretty oval face with enormous brown eyes and sitting there in her gauzy white nightie, Michael thought that she looked like a fairy from the Seelie Court, who were always beautiful and generous to human men, but would demand tireless loving in return, or else they would return to the hills.

'I can't, Michael. I just can't. And it's affecting you, too.'

Michael knew what she meant. He had tried to make love to her when he had first arrived at her flat, but after only a few minutes his erection had softened, and no amount of jiggling had managed to revive it.

'So what are you going to do?' he asked her.

'I'm going to quit the Crawford for now and go back to my mum and dad.'

'Your parents live in Mayo, sweetheart. When am I ever going to see you?'

She reached across the duvet and took hold of his hand. 'You won't, Michael. This is the finish of us.'

Michael stared at her. '*What?* You're not serious, Eithne. Tell me you're not serious.'

'Michael, I'm not just frightened. I'm fecking terrified. I was walking through the English Market this morning and there was a feller following close behind me all the way and he was staring at me like he was going to rush up and stab me at any moment.'

'Come on, sweetheart, that was probably one of them stalkers. You're always getting them, you know that. You're safe here, I promise.'

'Michael, I need to feel safe because nobody's after me, not because I have a guard sitting outside my door all day and all night.'

'I've already told you. I won't be giving evidence against Seamus Twomey, and so long as I don't, he won't do anything to harm you.'

'Yes, but supposing you let something slip that gets him arrested? Supposing he gets arrested anyway because of somebody else's evidence but he thinks it was your fault for getting him hauled in?'

Michael said, 'Eithne, I love you.'

'I love you, too, Michael, but my sister Brigid warned me about this relationship right from the very beginning. She dated a garda herself once and she said they're a different breed altogether, like, do you know what I mean? And you are.'

'I'm an ordinary man, sweetheart, with the same feelings as other men.'

Eithne leaned forwards and kissed him, but then she shook her head so that her long hair swished from side to side. 'No, Michael, you're not ordinary. That's the reason I love you. But that's the reason I can't stay with you, too.'

'I could get myself posted to Mayo.'

She shook her head again. 'Even if you could, you'd still

be you, and you'd still be a danger to me. If it wasn't Seamus Twomey it would be some other scumbag, sooner or later.'

She paused, and watched as tears started rolling down his cheeks. 'I know what you're thinking, that I'm disloyal and faithless and cruel, but this is hurting me twice as much as it's hurting you. It's no use, though, Michael. I can't live like this. I just can't.'

Michael took several deep breaths and then he threw back the duvet. 'In that case, I'll be out the gap.'

'You don't have to go tonight, Michael. You can stay until the morning, can't you?'

'Why would I? What's the point? You're leaving me tomorrow and I got the flops anyway.'

She sat watching him as he picked up his underpants and his jeans and dressed himself. She was sobbing too, her narrow shoulders jerking up and down spasmodically like the bobbin of a sewing machine.

'This doesn't have to be the end for ever,' she said, miserably.

'Well, we'll have to see, won't we?' Michael told her, as his head emerged from the neck of his sweater. He was angry now – angry at her, and angry at himself for crying.

'Please stay.'

'Oh, I will ya.'

'No, I mean it. Please. I didn't think you were just going to walk out on me.'

'You can't have it both ways, Eithne. Besides – I have some fierce urgent business to attend to.'

He left her student flat at Seven North Mall, overlooking the River Lee, and drove up Blarney Street to the Halfway Bar. Four or five regulars were standing outside smoking when he climbed out of his car and they stared at him as he crossed the pavement as if he were stark naked.

He pushed his way into the bar. It was crowded, and the music and the laughter were as loud as ever. Seamus Twomey and Douglas Quinn and Gwenith were sitting at their usual table with two bulky bruisers – one shaven-headed and the other with a close-cropped carrot top, but both with thick tattooed necks. From the expressions on their faces, he could have been a long-dead relative walking in through the door.

He went up to them, looked at each of them in turn, and then said, 'How are ya? Anyone here for a refill?'

Gwenith blew out her cheeks and slapped the table. 'Well! Sweet lamb of Jesus!'

Seamus Twomey leaned back in his chair and the look he gave Michael was a combination of hostility and admiration. 'You've some fecking balls, sham, I'll say that.'

'Do you want a scoop or don't you?' Michael asked him.

'All right,' said Seamus. He raised his hand and snapped his fingers at the barmaid. 'Maureen… fetch us over another round, will you, pet, and whatever this plain-clothes pig is having. The pig's paying, though.' Then he said to Michael, 'Here, come on, pull up a chair, sham. You look like a man with something on his mind.'

Michael dragged over a chair from a nearby table and sat down next to Gwenith. She shifted herself away from him, with a complicated adjustment of her bosom, and gave him her most hostile pout.

'You don't have to worry about Farry,' said Michael. 'I won't be giving evidence against him, nor Vincent neither.'

'Farry's up for shooting one of your pals,' said Douglas, the Dark Fellow, in a sinister drawl. 'Why wouldn't you want to see him done for it?'

'Because I'm tired of being treated like shite, if you must know. I'm tired of working my arse off day and night without any over-time and when I do manage to haul somebody in it's always my boss gets the credit for it.'

'Yes, but being a garda,' said Seamus, still leaning back in his chair with one arm dangling behind him. 'That's a what-do-you-call-it. Like being a priest. You don't do it for the money.'

'You're not spoofing,' said Michael. 'If you knew how much money I don't get paid you wouldn't believe it. Thirty-four thousand and change, before tax. And I'll have to be after retiring when I'm fifty-five. So, when you abducted me—'

Seamus sat up straight now, his eyes narrowed, and Michael hesitated.

'—let's say when you *invited* me down to Crosshaven, I began to think to myself, is this fecking worth it? There's you, bringing in hundreds of thousands of euros' worth of fentanyl and who knows what else, and there's me trying to stop you, at considerable risk to my life and limb. And in the end I'm never going to succeed in stopping all of the drugs that come into the country – so why not be practical about it and come to some sensible arrangement, like.'

Maureen brought their drinks and set them down on the table, and Michael took out his wallet and paid her. 'Keep the cobbage,' he told her. 'I'm starting a campaign for low-paid workers.'

'When you say "sensible arrangement", what kind of a sensible arrangement exactly are you talking about?' asked Seamus, leaning back again.

'I mean that whenever you fetch in a consignment through Rosslare or Ringaskiddy, I'll be making sure that it goes through customs without being opened or interfered with. I have plenty of contacts in the Revenue and I can pretty much guarantee that they'll be looking the other way, and that their dogs will be off sniffing the arse end of other dogs, and not your merchandise.'

'In return for what?'

'In return for five hundred euros per consignment.'

'How do I know that I can trust you? I could tell you that I'm fetching in some stuff, like, couldn't I, and the next thing I know your pals in the Revenue could seize it and I'd find myself lifted.'

'Why would I do that? I'd make nothing out of it, would I, and the customs boys would get all the glory.'

'Not only that, we'd come looking for you,' put in Gwenith. 'We don't take kindly to guards who give us bother.'

Michael turned to look at her. From the way she was looking back at him with her puffy little eyes, he realized that his earlier impressions about her had been correct. She was the most influential member of this gang – not her brother, and not Douglas Quinn. She might seem to be nothing more than a fat, greedy slut, but he could tell that they respected her – in fact, they even seemed to be afraid of her – and that whatever she wanted, she got. After all, she had wanted *him*, and Seamus had made sure that she got him.

'You'll know that you can trust me because I won't be giving evidence against Farry and Vincent. From what I heard at the station, they'll have a hard time anyway proving that Farry shot Detective O'Brien in anything but self-defence, because he has an independent witness to support his version of events. As for the crash that killed Detective Buckley – well, that could well be seen as an accident. I reckon the worst they'll be able to pin on Farry is illegal possession of a firearm and careless driving. He might not even get jail time.'

'Sure, like... Nicky Bourke seems to think that he'll get off light,' said Seamus. 'Provided, of course, that *you* don't change your mind and start blabbing.'

'Right now, you'll just have to take my word for it,' said Michael. 'But you'll see, when Farry and Vincent go to court.'

'Until then, we still have our insurance policy,' put in Gwenith. 'Your lovely girlfriend, Eithne. So long as you keep your bake shut, Tommy, or Michael, or whatever your name is, she'll stay lovely. It's pure scary what that sulphamayuric acid can do to a pretty girl's face.'

Michael didn't respond to that, but lifted up his glass of Murphy's and said, 'Do we have an arrangement, then?'

Seamus lifted his glass, too, and so did Douglas. 'I'm still highly suspicious of you, sham,' said Seamus. 'But then I've done a fair few deals with gardaí before now, and most of them worked out to our mutual advantage, except for the ones that didn't.'

It was then that Gwenith raised her glass of apple poitíni.

'And the deals that *didn't* work out—' she said '—if you knew how *they* ended—'

She gave Michael a sticky red grin and drew her podgy finger across her double chin, in a throat-slitting gesture.

He grinned back, and winked at her. If only she knew what I'm thinking. I'd rather have my throat cut than go to bed with you again.

Katie stayed in the church at Athnowen until well past midnight. Grange Road had been sealed off and was lined with patrol cars and vans from the Technical Bureau and two ambulances. She had watched as technical experts had taken samples of blood and DNA, as well as scores of infrared photographs and the scuffed-up impressions of footprints that had been left in the gritty dust around the font.

At six o'clock she had gone outside to give a statement to the media, and again at ten. She had told them only that the three whistle-blowers had been found decapitated, like the previous two, because the media knew that already. She didn't explain how they had been abducted, and she made no connection with the shooting of the security guard Declan Summers at Mount Farran.

She had told Detective Murrish to contact Justice McGuigan's office in Dublin. Three more whistle-blowers were due to give evidence to the Disclosures Tribunal, but not for the next eight weeks at least. As far as possible, their names and the nature of their disclosures were being kept confidential, although it was common knowledge that one of them involved the misuse of funds at the Garda College at Templemore.

Detective Inspector Fitzpatrick had arrived at the church just after seven, and now he came over to Katie and said, 'Why don't you call it a night, ma'am? I can take over from here. We won't be moving the bodies for an hour or two at least.'

'Thanks, Robert, I could use a couple of hours' sleep. Let's have a full briefing at nine tomorrow.'

Detective Inspector Fitzpatrick looked over at the three headless bodies. Their bonds had been untied and they had been separated now. They were lying on trolleys, with technical experts bending over them with cameras and infrared lights.

'Let's pray to God that these are the last,' he said. 'Telling their families, that's going to be desperate. It's bad enough that their heads have been cut off, and they've had tin whistles stuck down their necks, but the families know that already from the news. Their heads are missing, that's the worst part, and we're not at all hopeful that we're ever going to find them. How can their families have closure, burying their loved ones without their heads?'

'I don't know,' said Katie. 'I have a feeling that we'll find them, sooner or later. Don't ask me why. I don't usually have faith in premonitions.'

She went over to Kyna, who was talking to one of the technicians, a small woman in a pale blue Tyvek suit that made her look like a Teletubby.

'I'm going now, Kyna,' she said. 'Can I give you a lift?'

'That would be grand,' said Kyna. 'I'm totally knackered.'

They walked out through the graveyard and climbed into Katie's car.

'Are you okay?' Kyna asked her. 'I know we've just come out of a cemetery but you look like a ghost.'

'I'm beat out, that's all. Body and soul. I'll be fine in the morning when I've had some rest. Why don't you come home with me? I have Barney back, and Foltchain. They're wonderful company, but their conversation is kind of limited.'

'You're sure about that?'

'Con's still banged up in Tipp. I don't know for how long, and if he's going to be granted bail.'

Kyna took hold of Katie's hand. Then she turned around to make sure that nobody was watching and leaned across the car and kissed her.

'Everything's going to work out, Katie. You wait and see. Come on now, let's go.'

Thirty-Three

Barney and Foltchain were delighted to see both Katie and Kyna when they came in through the front door. Foltchain kept circling around and around, nuzzling at their legs, while Barney hobbled up and down the hallway snuffling and letting out little yips of pleasure.

'He's walking much better already,' said Katie, ruffling Barney's ears. 'They should be able to take off the splint in a week or so.'

'I do believe these two pooches are an item,' said Kyna. She didn't add 'like us', although Katie half-expected her to.

Katie took off her jacket and dropped it on to the sofa. 'I'm going to take a shower and go to bed. I can make you a hot chocolate if you want one.'

'No, a glass of water will be grand. I'm thirsty, that's all, and I want to get the dust of that church out of my throat.'

Katie made sure that Barney and Foltchain's water bowls were filled, and then she went into the bedroom. Kyna followed her.

'Jesus, I hope I don't have nightmares tonight,' said Katie.

'Me too. And I'll tell you this for nothing – I don't think I'll ever be able to listen to a tin whistle tune, ever again, without thinking of those three poor souls sitting there with no heads on.'

They both undressed and Kyna hung her blouse and sweater over the back of the bedroom chair. They had seen each other naked before, and been intimate before, so neither of them was inhibited. After Katie had stepped out of her thong, Kyna came up to her and held her in her arms, and kissed her on the lips.

They looked into each other's eyes, their breasts brushing against each other.

'What do you think will happen to Conor?' asked Kyna. Katie could tell that there were all kinds of implications in that question – mostly 'If Conor goes to jail, and doesn't come back to you, do you think there's any chance of you and me getting together?'

'I have no idea,' said Katie. 'It depends if the judge believes that he was only trying to put a stop to Guzz Eye's dog-fighting business, and didn't actually intend him any harm.'

'You love him, don't you?'

'Yes, I believe I do. He shook me a fair bit, I'll have to admit, when he told me what he'd done. But he was so determined to stop Guzz Eye from hurting and killing any more dogs, and I have to respect him for that, and I don't think he'll ever lie to me again.'

Kyna kissed her again, and this time she ran the tip of her tongue very delicately across Katie's lips. 'I love the taste of that lip gloss,' she said.

'Come on,' Katie told her, 'let's take a shower before we both fall asleep on our feet.'

They went into the bathroom and stepped into the shower together. The water was freezing when Katie first turned it on, and they both shrieked like girls. As it warmed up, they shampooed each other's hair and soaped each other – not so much to arouse each other but to wash away the horrors of the previous day.

They kissed and held each other close under the running water, their tongues tangling, and Katie felt a deep sense of comfort and relief. Here was somebody who loved her and understood her, and yet expected nothing from her but affection.

After their shower, they dried their hair, brushed their teeth and climbed into bed together, both wearing one of Katie's pyjama tops, Katie's pink and Kyna's pale blue.

'Right,' said Katie, as she switched off the bedside lamp. 'We'll have to be up at seven so that gives us five hours' sleep.'

Kyna put her arm around her and held her close. 'I just hope I can stop thinking about those whistle-blowers.'

'Try to count shellakybookies.'

'Shellakybookies?'

'That's what my ma always used to tell me. She said they go so much slower than sheep so that you'll only have to count up to three and you'll have dropped off.'

'We used to sing "shellakybooky, shellakybooky, stick out your horns, or else we'll kill your babies". Charming little girls, weren't we?'

'I was wondering if it hurts much to have your head cut off,' said Katie. 'Maybe it hardly hurts at all, especially with a chain-saw. It must all be over in seconds.'

'Myself, I was thinking more about what you said earlier... about who could have killed them, and why. Like you said, each of those three whistle-blowers was complaining about something different, so why should the same people want to kill all of them? And it looks pretty certain that the same people killed the other two, too – Garda O'Regan and Sergeant Lacey.'

Katie said, 'We need to find out who this "Head Honcho" is. It seems like he's the one who's paying out all the money, and if we can find out who *he* is, then perhaps we'll deck what his motive is.'

'It wouldn't surprise me if it was somebody in Phoenix Park, or maybe Harcourt Square. It was somebody in Phoenix Park who was doing everything they could to discredit Sergeant McCabe, wasn't it? – tapping his phone and sending out emails to suggest that he was incompetent, and a paedophile. Poor fellow nearly had a nervous breakdown.'

'Yes, but discrediting whistle-blowers, that's one thing. Cutting their heads off, that's something else altogether. You could well be right, though – it could be somebody in Garda headquarters or maybe the Justice Department. Somebody high-ranking who doesn't think they're ever going to be caught, because nobody's going to have the nerve to rat on them.'

Kyna absent-mindedly stroked Katie's hair. 'This could be pure dangerous, you know that? If this Head Honcho doesn't hesitate to cut the heads off whistle-blowers, what's he going to do if we come close to finding out who he is? Or *she*, of course.'

'That gives me an idea,' said Katie. 'Maybe that's the way we can smoke him out. Or *her*, like you say.'

'Go on.'

'Supposing I go to Chief Superintendent O'Malley myself, with a disclosure about a racket at Anglesea Street.'

'What racket at Anglesea Street? Well – what racket that we don't know about already?'

'You know that brothel in that rented house in Wilton – the one that was run by those two Romanian women? Well, they said it was only them, but we had every reason to think that the Văduva gang were behind it.'

'Of course. We closed it down.'

'Yes, we did. But I've suspected for some time that they've opened up for business again, discreetly like, only this time they're making sure that they don't get raided. They're paying off some of our officers with regular massages, in inverted commas. I haven't reported it before because I don't have any concrete evidence, but one of my regular informers gave me a tip-off and I overheard some chat in the canteen and I'm one hundred per cent sure that it's happening.'

'Katie – if you do that, they could come after you, too. I don't fancy lying here next to a headless superintendent. It'd be like *The Godfather* in reverse.'

'That's the whole idea, Kyna. I *want* them to come after me. Otherwise, how are we ever going to be able to find out who this Head Honcho is? I'll be armed and I'll be more than ready for them.'

'Katie—'

'Don't fret about it, I haven't made my mind up for sure. Let's get some shuteye, shall we, for goodness' sake, or we'll be wrecked in the morning.'

'You've worried me now. How can you expect me to sleep?'

'All right. I won't do it. Happy out now?'

As they drove into the city the next morning, though, Katie said, 'I'm going to do it. I can't think of any other way.'

'I knew you would,' said Kyna. They were in work mode now, so she didn't add 'you stubborn cow'. 'You'd better not get yourself beheaded, though, or I swear to God I'll never speak to you again.'

'I'll have to do some checking up first, just to make sure those Romanian women haven't moved away or gone back to Romania. I don't want to end up looking like a total eejit.'

'I'd rather you looked like a live eejit than a dead genius.'

Soon after she had sat down at her desk and Moirin had brought her a cappuccino, Bill Phinner came in to see her. As usual, he had the look of a man who has lost fifty euros and found fifty cents, but as he came across the room he gave her a thumbs up.

'What's the story, Bill?' Katie asked him.

He held up a clear plastic evidence bag. This time it didn't contain a bullet but a grey plastic handle, about twelve centimetres long.

'I think we might have had a stroke of luck,' he said. 'We picked this up from behind the font. It's a chainsaw starting handle and it looks like it probably got tugged off when your man was getting his chainsaw going. It does happen now and again, and you'll remember that we could tell from the wounds inflicted on the victims' necks that the chainsaw was pretty wore out.'

'So what does that tell us?'

'A fair bit, as a matter of fact. Your man would have been wearing gloves when he was pulling the handle, but we found one or two smudgy partials on it.'

'That won't be of much help until we make an arrest,' said Katie. 'Even then it doesn't conclusively prove that whoever left the partials was the head-cutter himself.'

'No, agreed. But what's more important is the handle itself. We compared it against all the chainsaws on offer in the catalogues from local hardware outlets, and it came from a Husqvarna 450. There's only two places where you can buy one of them. One's in Limerick and the other's that garden centre in Frankfield, out on the Ballycurreen Road. We've rung them already this morning and they keep records of everybody who buys a chainsaw off of them because of the guarantee. They've sold only five Husqvarna 450s in the past two years and they're going to be emailing over the details of who bought them as soon as the girl who does their accounts gets in.'

'Fair play, Bill. That's a start anyway. Anything else?'

'The tin whistles match the whistles that were stolen from the Music Market, and what's more all three of them have traces of saliva on them, and fingerprints. So if and when you do haul somebody in, they won't be able to deny that they were involved.'

'It strikes me as quare that they should have been so careless,' said Katie. 'Especially if even just one of them was a guard. Even your thickest criminal knows about DNA these days.'

'If you ask me, they're careless because they don't give a shite. They don't think they're going to be caught, like, and even if they are, they don't think they're going to go down for it.'

'All right, Bill. Thanks. I'm holding a briefing at nine so you can fill in the rest of the team.'

Bill Phinner picked up the handle and looked at it as if he were exasperated that it couldn't tell him more. 'I don't know why, but I have a fierce bad feeling about this case. I almost think that it would be better for all of us if we buried our dead with honours and forgot about it altogether.'

'Don't be such a pessimist,' Katie told him.

'It's all very well you telling me that, but like my old grandpa used to say, I'd rather believe the worst was going to happen than end up having a nasty surprise.'

About twenty minutes later, Detective Inspector Fitzpatrick and Detectives Murrish and O'Crean came in to see her. They had interviewed the two security guards who had been protecting Sergeant MacAuley and Garda Ó Grádaigh. Both guards had been badly beaten – one with a baseball bat and one with a hammer. The guard who had been looking after Sergeant MacAuley had been allowed home after treatment but Garda Ó Grádaigh's guard was still in the Mercy with a skull fracture.

'They both gave us the same description,' said Detective Inspector Fitzpatrick. 'Three solidly built fellows, all dressed in black jeans and black jackets, and all wearing black balaclavas. One of them was carrying a sawn-off shotgun and he was definitely the leader, because he did all the talking. All they can say about him is that he had a rough kind of a voice and a Waterford accent.'

'So the same three abducted both Sergeant MacAuley and Garda Ó Grádaigh?'

'It sure looks like it. There was at least forty-five minutes in between the two of them being taken, so I think we can assume that Sergeant MacAuley was driven to the church in Athnowen and left there, all tied up, before they went back to fetch Garda Ó Grádaigh and Garda Wassan. We don't know exactly when Garda Wassan was taken, but if he was making himself some breakfast it was probably after the other two. They were taken at approximately six twenty-five and ten past seven.'

'And nobody else saw these three men, or the car they arrived in?'

'Nobody – although there was one auld wan who lives across the road from the safe house in Ballyvolane, and we suspect that she might have seen them but was afraid to tell us in case of reprisal. I'm sending Murrish back to talk to her again. She might be less intimidated if a young woman goes to chat to her alone.'

After Detective Inspector Fitzpatrick and the two detectives had left, Katie had a call from Dr Kelley at the mortuary at CUH.

'I'll be carrying out a more thorough examination of the three decapitated bodies, of course,' she said. 'I just wanted to tell you that it looks almost certain that their heads were taken off with a chainsaw, the same as the other two. I'll be able to tell you later on this morning if it was the same chainsaw.'

'We already have some evidence that a chainsaw was used,' said Katie. 'The starting handle came loose and we found it not far from the bodies.'

'Oh... there's another thing,' said Dr Kelley. 'Those two bodies that were retrieved from that mobile home fire at Ballyknock—'

'You mean Guzz Eye McManus and the woman who was found with him? What was her name?'

'Rosella Rooney. That's right. I'm having their remains sent down here to CUH from the Limerick Regional. I was supposed to go above to Limerick yesterday to carry out the post mortems but I had those two traffic accident victims from Ballincollig to deal with and today of course I have these three beheaded gardaí. Inspector Carroll from Tipperary Town asked me to notify you, because he said you had an interest.'

'I have, yes, I'm sorry to say. But thank you for letting me know, anyway.'

'I doubt if I'll have much to tell you about them. According to Inspector Carroll they were both incinerated beyond recognition.'

'Thanks, Dr Kelley. I'll talk to you later so.'

Katie put down the phone. She had been trying not to think about Conor all morning, but she couldn't help it. Even if a jury believed that when he had set fire to McManus's mobile home he was unaware that McManus and his woman friend were inside it, asleep or drunk, he would almost certainly have to serve jail time for reckless endangerment. Her late husband, Paul, had caused her enough embarrassment with his tricky dealings with surplus building supplies. How was she going to maintain her credibility as a detective superintendent if she was living with a convicted arsonist?

She had finished off the funeral arrangements for Detectives

Buckley and O'Brien, and she handed them to Moirin to send off to Phoenix Park and the Diocesan Secretary at Redemption Road. This afternoon she would have to visit Sergeant MacAuley's wife and Garda Ó Grádaigh's partner, which would be harrowing enough. She would also have to ask Mathew McElvey to arrange a media conference so that she could explain how all three whistle-blowers had been abducted and murdered while they were supposedly under police protection.

She sat with her head lowered, feeling as if she had the Rock of Cashel on her shoulders. While she sat there, Detective O'Crean came back.

'Sorry, ma'am, we forgot to tell you that opposite Mervue Lawn in Glenheights Road there's Decky's Convenience Store and they have a CCTV outside it.'

'Oh, yes?' said Katie, looking up.

'There's a chance that it might have caught the suspects' car going past when Sergeant MacAuley was being abducted, so we're going through the recordings right now.'

He hesitated, and then he said, 'Are you feeling all right, ma'am?'

'I'm grand altogether, Cairbre. I didn't get much sleep, that's all. Listen – are you busy right now? If you're not too tied up there's something you can do for me. I'll give you this address in Wilton and I want you to run down there and see if there's two Romanian women still living there.'

She turned to her desktop computer and quickly scrolled down the screen until she found the report about the two women who had been arrested for brothel-keeping.

'They were convicted of keeping a disorderly house, these two, and they swore that they'd never do it again, but a little bird told me that they're back on the game. If they're still there, I want you to ask them if they can give you a massage and what they'd charge for it.'

Detective O'Crean looked alarmed. 'What if they say yes? Do you want me to have it? The massage, like?'

'If they say yes, ask them if that includes a happy ending, or if a happy ending's extra. However much it is, just tell them you can't afford it and thanks a million, and goodbye.'

'Supposing they offer me a discount?'

'Then you still say goodbye. I don't want us accused of entrapment.'

'Okay, then,' said Detective O'Crean. 'Should I record them? I mean, are we planning on lifting them and taking them to court?'

'No. I only need to know if they're still there, and if they're still in the sex business.'

'Okay.'

Katie said, 'You're probably wondering why I want to know. I can't tell you yet, but as soon as I can, I will. It's part of Operation Butterfly, that I can tell you. It's actually nothing to do with the sex trade.'

'Not a bother, ma'am. I've done that kind of thing before in any case. There were some girls offering stand-up sex behind Sligo bus station and I had to make out that I was out looking for a quick root. It was lashing that day and I don't know who was more relieved when I arrested them – them or me.'

Thirty-Four

Michael Ó Doibhilin walked around the back of the Maxol petrol station on Watercourse Road with the collar of his navy-blue pea coat turned up and his tweed cap pulled down low over his forehead. There were CCTV cameras on the forecourt and however unlikely it was that he might be seen and identified at a later date, he didn't want to take that chance.

He went up to the door of the concrete warehouse at the very back of the petrol station, looked quickly around, and then knocked seven times – three double knocks and one single – as Seamus Twomey had told him.

He waited. The door was painted a weather-beaten maroon colour, and there was a rusted metal plaque on it: *G. Monahan Engineering*. After almost half a minute had passed, he was tempted to knock again, but then he heard voices inside, and the sound of bolts being shot back.

One of Twomey's heavies opened the door up. Michael hadn't seen him before, but that was hardly a surprise when he knew that his gang probably numbered as many as thirty or forty. This man looked like Buddha, if Buddha had ever grown prickly grey stubble and had a rattlesnake tattooed around his neck. He was wearing a grimy grey T-shirt with a faded colour picture of Jesus on it.

'Michael, is it?' he said. 'You'd best come in. We've been waiting on you.'

Michael stepped inside. The interior of the warehouse was

chilly and smelled of damp, like so many older buildings in Cork. Its windows had all been painted over black, but it was brightly lit by two fluorescent tubes hanging from the ceiling.

The left-hand side of the warehouse was stacked with cardboard boxes wrapped in polythene, and against the right-hand wall there was a jumble of car parts and three partially dismantled motorcycles, as well as lawnmowers and garden statues, which Michael could guess had all been stolen.

Seamus Twomey and Douglas Quinn were both there, surrounded by eleven or twelve of their gang. Most of the younger members were smart, with brushed-up Jedward hair and skinny jeans and the small tight coats they called farting jackets. The older ones were more like the heavy who had opened the door: thickset and bald and scarred and tattooed, with black leather jackets and earrings and heavy boots. He recognized at least two of them from the morning that he had been wrestled out of Gwenith's flat. Almost all of them were smoking cigarettes, and he could smell the herby aroma of marijuana, too.

Seamus was sitting on a packing case with his hands propped on his knees. Right in front of him a thin young Asian man with shaggy black curly hair and a beard was kneeling on the floor, with a scarf tied over his eyes. His jeans were ripped at the knees and the front of his white T-shirt was covered in a bib of dried blood. His wrists were handcuffed behind his back and his ankles were tightly knotted together with nylon washing line.

As he came nearer, Michael could see that the young Asian man had been badly beaten. His lips were swollen, his cheeks were bruised and there was a lump of dark coagulated blood under his nostrils. His arms were bruised, too, and from the angle at which his right arm was bent behind his back, it looked as if his shoulder had been dislocated, or his humerus had been broken.

With every breath he took he bent forwards and winced, so it seemed likely that his ribs had been fractured.

'Welcome to the party, sham,' said Seamus. 'Everybody – for

those who haven't had the pleasure to meet him before, this is Michael the Detective! From now on I think we can call him Mick the Dick!'

There was general laughter, followed by a bout of coughing.

'Mick the Dick says that he's tired of being overworked and underpaid, and so he's volunteered his services to help us bring more Persians in through Ringaskiddy and Rosslare. We think we trust him, like, do you know what I mean, but we've invited him to come here today to give us proof that he's sound.'

Michael looked around at the assembled gang and spread out his arms, as if he were a priest appealing to his flock.

'Come here, lads – whatever you want me to do, I'll do it. Seamus here is spot on – I'm craw sick of working my arse off all hours and getting nothing but McDonald's wages and no respect neither. Seamus scared the shite out of me, to tell you the truth, and that's when I thought to myself – why don't I stop trying to haul him in and give him a helping hand instead, so that I can make myself some decent extra grade? After all, what the feck do I care if some goms get themselves addicted to prescription drugs? It'll be Christmas before we know it, like, and I could use a few more yo-yos.'

If he had expected applause or even a murmur of approval, he didn't get it. The gang members shuffled their feet and coughed but said nothing, staring at him with eyes like nail-heads, their arms folded and smoke leaking out of their nostrils. He supposed he couldn't blame them: the guards had been their sworn enemies ever since they had been running around the streets in short trousers, breaking windows and hobbling sweets and playing knock-a-dolly.

Seamus said, 'Right, Mick the Dick, this is how you can prove how loyal you're going to be to *Fola na hÉireann*—'

Before he could finish, there was another knock at the door, the same pattern of seven that Michael had given. Seamus nodded and the Buddha lookalike waddled off to answer it. Michael heard Gwenith's high-pitched squeaking before he turned around and saw her, bundled up in a furry nylon leopard-skin overcoat, with a matching furry hat and crinkly red patent-leather boots.

'Haven't missed the fun, have I, Seamus? I dropped my fecking phone down the toilet and I had to dry it out with my hair-dryer.'

She came up and patted Seamus on the top of his shiny bald head, as if he were a small boy. 'How's it going, bro?' Then she looked at Michael and said, 'How's yourself, Michael? All ready to show us what you can do?'

Michael gave her a brief, sickly smile. He could smell her perfume now, that Estée Lauder Beautiful, and it brought back the suffocating sensation of being buried underneath her sweaty, wobbling flesh.

Seamus pointed to the blindfolded young Asian man kneeling in front of him. 'We caught this bonner with three of his pals two nights back, round the corner from the Voodoo Rooms. They were giving our man Jackie here a beating and trying to take his biscuits off of him. They've been trying for a while now to push us out of the biscuit business, the bonners, so we thought it was time for us to teach them a lesson, like.'

Michael was well aware that an Asian gang had recently been attempting to horn in on the selling of ecstasy and opioids and other recreational drugs in the city's nightclubs. They had already clashed with several of Cork's existing drug-dealers, including Seamus Twomey's gang, and a number of gang members from both sides had been beaten and stabbed and shot, although nobody had yet been killed.

Seamus referred to the Asians as 'bonners' which was derived from the Celtic football hero Packie Bonner, but in fact they were Punjabis, and called themselves *Dukhāntanāvām*, the Nightmares.

'Those five gardaí who got mangled for sneaking on their pals – are you one of the dicks who's trying to find out who did it?'

'Not me, no,' said Michael. 'I'm on the drugs team, myself.'

Seamus stood up now and laid his hand on the Asian's distorted shoulder. 'We was watching all about them fellers on the TV, like, and we reckoned that what was done to them was a fierce effective way of dealing with pains in the arse in general, not just gardaí. Such as your bonners, for instance.'

Michael said, 'What do you mean? Those whistle-blowers had their heads cut off, and then they had tin whistles stuck down their throats. That was the whole point, wasn't it? Tin whistles for whistle-blowers.'

'That's exactly right, sham. But we wouldn't be using a tin whistle. We still have the biscuits this gurrier was carrying when we caught him, and we could push those down his neck, now couldn't we? That would make our point all right.'

'Oh, go away. You're not talking about cutting off his head?'

When he heard this, the Asian let out a strangled whimper like a frightened dog, and started to rock from side to side.

'Will you ever fecking keep still?' Seamus snapped at him, gripping his shoulder even more tightly. Then he turned back to Michael and said, 'No. *We're* not going to cut off his head. *You* are.'

'What? *Me?* Come on, you're codding!'

'No, Mick. I'm two hundred per cent dead-on serious. It would prove without a shadow of a doubt that you're going to be straight with us and not turn us in the first chance you get. We'll have a video of you lopping off this bonner's bean, and what could be a better insurance policy than that?'

'It was my idea, if you must know,' said Gwenith. She had just lit a cigarette and puffed out smoke with every word. 'You fooled us all into believing you were Tommy. You even fooled your way into my bed, you lousy liar. So we had to think of a way to make cast-iron sure that you wouldn't be able to fool us again.'

Michael looked down at the young Asian man, still whining and swaying from side to side despite Seamus's attempts to keep him still.

'You can't ask me to cut his head off. That's not only murder, that's fecking barbaric.'

'It's up to you, Michael,' said Gwenith. 'If you won't do it, why should we believe a word you say?'

'Because I haven't given Detective Superintendent Maguire any evidence against Farry and Vincent and your own lawyer, Nicholas Bourke, will tell you that. Without my testimony, they may not even get jail time.'

'That's not enough, sham, not by a long chalk,' said Seamus. 'You could easy change your mind before they go to court and there's nothing we could do to stop you.'

'What if I swear to God that I won't give evidence against them?'

'I swear to God myself a hundred times a day, and to Jesus, and to Jesus's ma and da, but that doesn't mean I'm going to stick by what I say.'

Now Seamus turned around and called out, 'Hoggy!'

A broad-shouldered man in a green knitted windcheater came forwards. He had grey, tightly woven hair, like a kitchen scouring pad, but his face was disturbingly babyish, with round cheeks and a snub nose and wide blue eyes. He could have been Mickey Rooney's younger brother. In one hand he was carrying an orange Husqvarna chainsaw.

'You're out of your minds,' said Michael. 'If you think for one minute that I'm going to cut off this fellow's head – well, forget it. Just forget it. There's absolutely no way.'

Without taking his eyes off Michael, Seamus said, 'You fixed the handle, Hoggy?'

'I did, yes. I used the top of an old fork handle.'

'Okay, then, start her up.'

Hoggy laid the chainsaw down on the floor, put his right boot in the handle, and started to tug at the pull cord.

'That's it,' said Michael. 'I'm leaving. This is pure fecking insanity.'

Seamus shook his head and beckoned to Douglas Quinn.

'If you try to leave, Mick, we'll shoot you, simple as that. We'll shoot you and then we'll cut this bonner's head off and we'll make it look like you did it and shot yourself afterwards.'

The chainsaw started up now, and Michael could hardly hear what Seamus was saying as Hoggy revved it up.

'Your choice, Michael!' Gwenith screamed in his ear.

'You're all crazy!' Michael screamed back. 'I'm not doing it! There's absolutely no way!'

Douglas looked at Seamus and rolled up his eyes as if to say 'He doesn't think so? We'll see about that.' He reached into his overcoat and lifted out a black CZ 75 Czech-made automatic. He pointed it at Michael's head and cocked it.

'You don't take this bonner's head off, you're going to end up today buried in a bog, where nobody is ever going to find you!' Seamus shouted in his ear. 'You try to make a run for it, the same thing's going to happen!'

Michael closed his eyes. He was trying to think logically but all he could hear was the chainsaw burbling. He thought of Eithne sitting on the bed and telling him that she couldn't stay with him as long as her life remained under threat. He thought of his father and mother and his sisters, and how they would react when their phones rang today – this afternoon, in only a few hours' time – and they were told that he was dead. He thought of his own flat, and his own bed, which he had left unmade. If Douglas Quinn shot him, he would never sleep in it again.

He had always been aware that his job as a detective could be dangerous, and during the course of his short career he had been attacked several times. He had once been cut across the cheek with a knife and almost lost his left eye. This was the first time, though, that he had been faced with instant death.

He opened his eyes and looked down at the young Asian man again. When he had offered to help Seamus smuggle drugs into the country, he had been fully prepared for Seamus to test him in some way – such as waiting for Farry and Vincent to go to court to see if he offered any evidence against them. He had even thought that Seamus might arrange for him to bring some opioids in through Ringaskiddy in his own car.

He hadn't expected to be given the choice of kill or be killed. No other alternative. Cut this young man's head off or die yourself.

Seamus waved Hoggy forwards and Hoggy held out the idling

chainsaw for Michael to take hold of it. For a split second, Michael wondered if he could use it to keep Seamus and the rest of his gang at bay while he backed away to the door and made his escape, but the thought had hardly formed in his mind before he realized that he would only have to swing it around the wrong way and Douglas Quinn would instantly shoot him in the head.

He took the chainsaw and held it up at a forty-five-degree angle in front of him.

'Have you handled one of these fellers before?' Hoggy yelled at him, spitting on the side of his face.

'Only once!' Michael told him.

'Okay then! Stand with your feet well apart, like! Tilt the saw sidewise! Try to cut through with one slow, clean sweep! Don't try to rush it, do you know what I mean? And don't get throughouther if the feller starts to waggle his head around or you get sprayed! Cutting through a neck, it's as soft as Paddy Jack cheese, not like cutting timber, but you might feel a bit of a snarl when you get to the spine! Do you have me?'

'I have you!'

Seamus bent close to the young Asian man's right ear and shouted, 'I don't know who you pray to, lad, Allah or Mohammed or whoever, but now's the time for you to say your prayers if you want to!'

The young Asian man didn't answer, but kept up his fretful whining. Michael stepped up to him, holding the chainsaw horizontally so that the teeth were only five centimetres away from his protuberant Adam's apple. He tried to make his mind a blank, but it was impossible. It's him or me. I'm a detective garda and I've sworn to uphold the law, but he's a drug-dealer and he's probably here in Ireland illegally. I don't know his name or anything about him and he must have known the risks of horning in on Seamus Twomey's ecstasy racket.

The young Asian man couldn't see him, but he must have been able to guess what he was about to do. He suddenly stopped whining, and straightened his back, lifting up his chin so that Michael would have no trouble cutting into his neck.

He took several deep breaths, which clearly hurt him, and then he shouted, '*Chēti – karō – jī!* Please – be quick!'

Michael glanced to his right. Douglas Quinn was holding his pistol so close to the side of his head that he was almost touching his ear. He wished that he could close his eyes while he was cutting the young Asian man's head off, but he knew that if he did that he was likely to make a mess of it and hurt him even more.

'Forgive me, Lord,' he said, under his breath, and slowly angled the chainsaw from left to right, so that its teeth whirred into the young Asian man's larynx. There was a brief blizzard of skin and blood, and then Michael felt the teeth chopping into bone. It took only a few seconds before the young Asian man's head dropped backwards and sideways off his neck and rolled across the floor.

Michael switched off the chainsaw and stood shaking and spattered with blood. Gwenith was whooping and dancing a little jig, her hands waving in the air and her bosom bouncing up and down, and some of Seamus's gang were clapping, although not all of them. One of the younger ones was bent over, his hand against the warehouse wall, retching.

Douglas Quinn was still holding his pistol to Michael's head. 'Hand the saw back now, Michael,' he said. The tone of his voice was almost more frightening than his gun.

Hoggy came up and took the chainsaw out of his hands. 'Dowtcha, boy,' he grinned. 'Pure professional, that was. You could cut heads off for a living, if you'd the mind to.'

Michael turned away. He almost felt like telling Douglas Quinn to pull the trigger and put an end to his shock and his shame and his self-disgust. Although he was headless, the young Asian man was still kneeling upright, and Michael couldn't look at him. He couldn't even bear to look at his own hands, which were smothered in blood.

Seamus said, 'Hey, Mick! That was savage. We have it all on

video, so you can watch it for yourself after. Welcome to *Fola na hÉireann*, sham, the Blood of Ireland.'

Michael showed Seamus his hands. He was still trembling and he had the sour taste of bile in his mouth.

'There's a tap in the corner,' Seamus told him. 'You can wash off the bonner's blood over there. Then I reckon we can all go next door to Darby O'Gill's for a scoop to celebrate. It's not every day a dick joins forces with us. If that next lot of fentanyl comes through Ringaskiddy on Tuesday and the customs and the guards are all looking the other way, then we'll know for sure that you're doing your stuff.'

'And why wouldn't he?' said Gwenith. 'You wouldn't want that video to go viral, would you, Michael?'

She dropped her cigarette butt on the floor and stepped on it, and then she went over to the kneeling headless figure and kicked him with her boot, so that he toppled over.

'Bag that head up for me, will you, Brendan,' she said to the nearest member of the gang. 'You can take the rest of him up to Shandon Street tonight and sit him in the doorway of that curry house where those bonners all hang out, with his biscuits down his neck. If they don't take the hint from that, and stop trying to push in where they're not wanted, then they're thicker than I thought they was.'

Michael washed his hands under the cold tap in the corner, and then he followed the rest of the gang as they filed out of the warehouse and made their way to Darby O'Gill's. He needed a drink, desperately. In fact, all he wanted to do was drink himself into a stupor – a stupor in which he could no longer feel the vibration of the chainsaw as it ripped into the young Asian man's vertebrae, or see his blindfolded head falling on to the floor and tumbling over to Seamus Twomey's feet.

Thirty-Five

It was nearly four o'clock when Katie and Detective Sergeant Begley came back from offering their condolences to Sergeant MacAuley's wife and Garda Ó Grádaigh's girlfriend. Katie had been moved because neither of them had cried. They had already had to endure so many months of stress because of the hostility shown to whistle-blowers by their colleagues in the Garda that in a tragic way their deaths had come as a relief.

Mathew McElvey had arranged a media conference for five o'clock, and the RTÉ outside broadcast crew had already turned up, as well as reporters and sound technicians from Cork FM and RedFM and C103.

Katie went along to Denis MacCostagáin's office. Halfway along the corridor she met Detective O'Crean, who was eating a cheese-and-pickle sandwich.

'Oh, you're back, ma'am,' he said, almost choking. 'I was just after leaving you a note about those Romanian women.'

'And? Are they still in business?'

'Are they still in business? Let's put it this way, I was offered a whole lot more than a massage. Even a lot more than massage with a happy ending. For two hundred euros I could have spent the whole night there, with the two of them, and in any position I could think of. They're both a bit mature for me, like, but they're not bad-looking. I mean you wouldn't throw either of them out of bed for eating Taytos.'

'So what did you say?'

'I said I was short of spondulicks and could they let me have it on the slate. Well, you can imagine what they said to that, and it was the same word as what I was asking for, except that they tagged "off" on the end of it.'

'All right, Cairbre, thanks a million. Can you not mention this to anyone just yet?'

'You said it was something to do with Operation Butterfly.'

'It is, yes. But I'll share it with the rest of the team when I'm ready.'

'Whatever you say, ma'am. I could always go back to Wilton and double-check on those two brassers if you like. You don't happen to have a spare two hundred euros on you, do you?'

Katie smiled and shook her head. 'Sorry. You'll have to save it up out of your wages.'

When she knocked and went into Denis MacCostagáin's office, she found that Frank Magorian was there too. He was wearing a black suit and a black tie, so she guessed that he had come here specially to make a statement to the media about the three murdered whistle-blowers.

Denis MacCostagáin was right in the middle of tying a black tie, and making a mess of it, with the thin end much longer than the thick end. 'Ah, Kathleen,' he said. 'How did you get on with the grieving relatives?'

'I think the both of them were beyond tears,' Katie told him. 'Even when I explained that Sergeant MacAuley and Garda Ó Grádaigh might not be given state funerals, they accepted it without any protest. They seemed to have had enough of the Garda to last them a lifetime. Mrs MacAuley told me that her husband had received so many death threats in the past three months that he had doubled his life-insurance policy and updated his will.'

She went up to him, pulled off his tie and knotted it for him neatly.

Frank Magorian said, 'It's a terrible tragedy, the loss of these five fine officers. Whatever their colleagues thought about them, they saw what they thought to be wrongdoing and they stuck to their principles. That's all too rare these days.'

'Sure like,' said Denis MacCostagáin. 'But now that they're gone, we'll never know for sure if their disclosures were based on genuine misconduct, or if they were simply splitting too many hairs.'

Frank Magorian nodded. 'You have a point, Denis. Take Garda Wassan, for example. He was claiming that his fellow officers were racist, but there's a fine line between racism and good-natured station banter. You can't be too thin-skinned if you're a guard, whatever colour your skin is. And Sergeant Lacey... he was complaining that prosecutions for car theft were being dropped because vital evidence was mysteriously being mislaid. But if there really *was* insufficient evidence, it would have been a sinful waste of public money to bring those cases in front of a judge when there was no realistic prospect of a conviction.'

He paused, and then he said, 'It's the same with the others, Sergeant MacAuley and Garda O'Regan and Garda Ó Grádaigh.'

'We've been investigating the disclosure made by Garda O'Regan,' said Katie. 'He was the one who was claiming that gardaí and prison escort officers and prison staff were being bribed not to take convicted offenders to jail but to let them go.'

'How far have you got with that?' Frank Magorian asked her.

'Not as far as I would have liked. DI Fitzpatrick has interviewed the administrative officers from Cork and three other prisons including Cloverhill, and in every case it seems like the papers are all in order.'

'Garda O'Regan was suggesting the paperwork was falsified, is that it?'

'He actually met a convicted criminal who was supposed to be in Rathmore Road but was drinking in a pub down in Riverstick. That was when he first became suspicious that something strange was going on.'

'He *says* he met him,' said Frank Magorian. 'The trouble is, he won't be able to give us his sworn testimony any more, so we'll never know if we ought to believe him. But, you know, Kathleen, as tragic as it is, these officers being murdered, I have to say that their passing is going to spare us a whole rake of insurmountable problems. Not only us but the DPP and the Justice Department, too. Just think what an unholy mess we would have had to deal with if all their disclosures had turned out to be true. You'd not only have the Tánaiste and the Commissioner resigning, you'd have half the Dáil and most of Phoenix Park, and Templemore College, too – not to mention the Prison Service.'

Katie didn't comment on that. After all, Garda O'Regan's solicitor had listed Frank Magorian as a possible recipient of the bribes that had been paid to keep some of Cork's worst gangsters out of jail.

She looked at her watch and said, 'The media conference starts at five. I assume you're going to be attending, sir, and saying a few words about the deceased?'

'I shall, yes. But I want to keep this all very low-key, Kathleen. I know you believe there could be a connection between the killers and a member or members of the Garda, but I don't want you to mention that to the press, even if they suggest it to you. Denis here tells me you haven't made too much progress yet in identifying those responsible, and I'd prefer it if you didn't come out with any wild conjectures.'

'Yes, sir,' said Katie. She didn't say that it was hardly a wild conjecture to suspect that gardaí might be involved in the killing of the five whistle-blowers. All those gardaí who had been named in their disclosures would be let off the hook now, just as much as the Coakleys and other criminal gangs.

Denis MacCostagáin brushed back his fraying white hair. 'Do you know something?' he said. 'All I pray for these days is peace and quiet. It's bad enough the criminals committing crimes without the cops committing them too.'

*

The conference room was black, in the sense of being crowded, and almost everybody in the room was dressed in black. It had been Katie's idea to hang large black-and-white photographs of all five whistle-blowers on the wall behind the table where she and Frank Magorian and Denis MacCostagáin were sitting, along with Superintendent Pearse and Detective Inspector Fitzpatrick. She had thought that it would show that despite being whistle-blowers they were still honoured and respected by their fellow officers. It was meant to be an emotional tribute, too.

Frank Magorian rose to his feet and gave a sombre speech about the grief that the whole force was feeling, and how all five officers were men of integrity.

'It is our duty in An Garda Síochána to uphold the highest moral values. That is why, if some of us occasionally stray, or misinterpret the rules, we encourage the privileged disclosure of such lapses. Up until now, we have been unable to identify who murdered these devoted public servants in such a brutal and horrifying manner, but rest assured that we will, and we will show no fear or favouritism in our pursuit of justice. The criminals who committed these heinous acts will be caught, and they will be punished. Thank you.'

Despite what he had said, the awkward questions came immediately.

Dan Keane from the *Examiner* stood up with his trademark cigarette tucked behind his right ear. 'Sir – we already know in outline what each of the murdered whistle-blowers intended to say in his testimony to Justice McGuigan. If all of their evidence turned out to be valid, there's more than a few guards who would find themselves in what you might call deep cat's malack, if you'll excuse the expression.'

'What are you suggesting by that?' asked Frank Magorian.

'I'm not suggesting anything. I'm only wondering if you're considering the possibility that the killers might have been given some assistance by somebody serving or working here at Anglesea Street – either deliberately or inadvertently.'

Katie answered that. 'I have a dedicated and experienced team investigating these five homicides and of course they're exploring every possibility. We're calling it Operation Butterfly. As Assistant Commissioner Magorian has just told you, nobody's going to be shown any favours, no matter who they are.'

'That doesn't really answer my question,' said Dan Keane. 'Is it possible a guard or one of your civilian employees could have colluded in the whistle-blowers' murders?'

Now Fionnuala Sweeney stood up. 'After the first two whistle-blowers were killed, the remaining three who were due to give evidence were given protection by a private security company, Stephen MacQuaid Security. Why was that?'

'They needed to be protected round the clock and we're short on officers for that kind of duty at the moment, especially with all the disturbances we've been having to deal with lately – such as the water protests and the unofficial halting sites.'

'But they *weren't* protected, were they? They were all abducted from the so-called safe houses where they were staying, and one of MacQuaid's security guards was shot dead. The other two were badly beaten. That wasn't very effective protection, was it?'

'When I made the arrangements with Stephen MacQuaid, there was nothing to suggest that their protection wouldn't be one hundred per cent secure,' Katie retorted. 'Stephen MacQuaid has a faultless reputation in security and was once a garda himself. So far we have no idea how the confidentiality of those addresses was breached and how the killers came to know where the whistle-blowers were.'

'Maybe a little guard told them,' said Dan Keane.

'I resent that remark, Dan,' Katie told him. 'This case won't be solved by speculation or prejudice. I admit that we're still looking for some vital links, but we have a wealth of forensic evidence such as fingerprints and tyre tracks and DNA samples, and when we do manage to make the connections, we won't have any bother at all in obtaining convictions.'

'I'm sure you won't, but will you be able to keep the killers in jail? Or will they even go to jail in the first place?'

'I've no comment to make on that, Dan. Garda O'Regan's disclosure is still under investigation and his evidence is *sub judice*.'

Jean Mulligan from the *Echo* put up her hand. She had upswept glasses and a dark brown coat and she spoke with a distinctive lisp. 'This is not exactly related to the whistle-blowers, ma'am, but is it true that a close friend of yours, Conor Ó Máille, is being held under investigation in Tipperary for setting fire to a mobile home at the Ballyknock halting site and killing two Travellers?'

Katie felt a surge of anger. It had been a tiring and distressing day, and the last thing she wanted to do was answer questions about Conor and Guzz Eye McManus.

'No comment,' she said. 'This conference was called to give you information on the murdered whistle-blowers, nothing else.'

'I'm only asking if it's true,' said Jean Mulligan.

'Why? You seem to know all about it already.'

'Then it *is* true? According to what I was told, Conor Ó Máille set fire to a mobile home and a dog-fighter known as Guzz Eye McManus was burned to death, along with a woman friend of his. And at the time he went to Tipperary and did this, he was living with you at your private address in Cobh.'

'I'm here to tell you about the whistle-blowers,' Katie repeated. 'Nothing else.'

She turned to Frank Magorian, and he was frowning at her with a mixture of bewilderment and hostility as if he had just discovered that she and Kyna had been having threesomes with his wife whenever he was off playing golf. It was then that she decided to make one more announcement.

She stood up, and the conference room suddenly went quiet.

'I do have something else to tell you, but this concerns a whistle-blower too. The whistle-blower in this case is me. I can't give you too many details just yet, because I haven't yet gone to see Chief Superintendent O'Malley, our Protected Disclosures Manager. But my disclosure concerns a brothel in the Cork city area. It was closed down last year and the women who were running it were convicted of brothel-keeping. However, I have information that it is still in business, and that certain gardaí are aware of that, but they are taking no action in return for sexual favours.'

Dan Keane lifted his hand and said, 'Brothel-keeping is only a public order offence, is it not? And prostitution itself is legal between consenting adults. It's only illegal when it involves minors or individuals who have been trafficked.'

'You're right, Dan. Brothel-keeping is punishable only by a fine. But it's not the brothel-keeping I'm concerned about. It's the conduct of police officers who are accepting bribes, and a sexual favour is as much of a bribe as money.'

'Can you name these brothel-keepers, and tell us where their brothel is?' asked Jean Mulligan. 'And can you name any of the gardaí you're accusing of accepting sex?'

'No, and no, and of course not, for legal reasons,' said Katie, but before she could continue Denis MacCostagáin stood up, raised both hands and announced, 'That's it, ladies and gentlemen! That's all we have to tell you for now. Thank you for coming! If there are any further developments in this investigation, Mathew McElvey will be in touch with you directly.'

There was a barrage of questions from almost every reporter in the room.

'DS Maguire! DS Maguire! When are you going to be meeting Chief Superintendent O'Malley?'

'How many gardaí have been accepting sex?'

'How long have you known about this, and why have you waited until today to take action?'

'Assistant Commissioner Magorian – you looked kind of rattled when DS Maguire said that she was intending to make a protected disclosure. Did she inform you of this in advance?'

'DS Maguire – considering what's happened to the five

whistle-blowers so far – well, aren't you even slightly worried that the same thing might happen to you?'

Denis MacCostagáin placed his hand between Katie's shoulder blades and half-guided, half-pushed her out of the conference room. Frank Magorian followed close behind.

'You're grand, thank you, sir,' said Katie. 'I can make it back to my office under my own steam, thank you.'

'My office first,' said Denis MacCostagáin, and she could tell from the way he was stamping along and swinging his arms and intermittently sniffing in his left nostril that he was raging.

'Why in the name of Joseph and all the carpenters didn't you tell me about this beforehand?' shouted Denis MacCostagáin. He dragged off his tie as if he wanted to get rid of it as soon as he could, because Katie had tied it for him. 'For a start, it was *totally* against protocol! You don't make announcements to the media that affect the reputation of the Garda, and this Garda station in particular, without fully consulting with me first!'

Frank Magorian went over to the window and stood there with his arms folded, saying nothing. Apparently he was content to let Denis MacCostagáin do all the bawling. Now and then, though, he turned to look at Katie disapprovingly, and she could also see a smugness in his expression, as if he were thinking, *I have you now, DS Maguire. This could get you demoted, and then we can instal a male detective superintendent, a freemason with any luck, and somebody I can play golf with.*

'You showed me up!' shouted Denis MacCostagáin. 'You showed me up and made me look like a pure gom in front of all of those reporters!'

'I apologize for that,' said Katie. 'That wasn't my intention. But I did want to make it clear to them that we haven't been frightened off whistle-blowing by those five officers being beheaded, and I thought that was the best moment to say so.'

Denis MacCostagáin took off his jacket and then he circled

round and round his desk, punching his fist into the palm of his hand.

'Dan Keane was absolutely correct! Brothel-keeping is nothing more than a public order offence and most of the time we let brothel-keepers off with a caution. If we didn't, the District Court would be mobbed with pimps and madams from morning till night. But what you're going to disclose to Joseph O'Malley – that's going to ruin the careers of several good officers, and just at a time when we're desperately short of personnel.'

'Sir – these officers are accepting bribes, and officers who accept bribes are not good officers.'

'Where did you get this information from anyway? Who *are* these fecking brothel-keepers? And who are the officers that you're accusing? Do you have their names? For the love of God, Kathleen, how much of a sin is a massage or a blowjob? They didn't throw President Clinton out of office for it, did they? Why should these officers face destitution and homelessness simply because they gave in to a little fleshly temptation?'

Katie stood her ground. 'You surprise me, sir, saying that. I always thought you were such a stickler for moral conduct – especially when it came to backhanders and bribes. You haven't forgotten Sergeant Tobin, have you? All he did was take a couple of crates of whiskey and you gave him the sack.'

'Don't you be after judging me, Kathleen. I'm close to retirement and I've been in this job long enough to know when to be strict and when to make allowances. This force expects a hell of a lot from a man and doesn't give much in return. A bit of how's-your-father is scarcely as serious as letting convicted drug-dealers out of jail, and even *that* hasn't been proven.'

'Well, let me apologize again, sir, for having sprung this on you,' said Katie. 'I'll be making a protected disclosure to Chief Superintendent O'Malley but "protected" means exactly that. You'll be able to see my evidence once I've presented it to Justice McGuigan, just like everybody else.'

Denis MacCostagáin dropped himself heavily into his chair.

'I'm not happy about this, Kathleen. Not happy at all. I was never an enthusiastic supporter of women being promoted to senior positions, but I've supported you and backed you up ever since you were appointed detective superintendent.'

'You have, sir, yes, and don't think I'm not grateful for it.'

He looked up at her mournfully and shook his head. 'This, though – this is going to reflect on me just as much as the guards who've been misbehaving themselves. And it could affect my pension, if I have to resign before I'm sixty and I haven't managed to complete my thirty years.'

Frank Magorian came up to Katie and stood uncomfortably close. He smelled of some unusually grassy cologne. 'Maybe you'd consider changing your mind? You could tell the media that you've checked your evidence about the brothel-keepers and found out that it has no basis in fact.'

Katie looked at both men. She was sorely tempted to tell Frank Magorian that he was suspected of taking bribes, too, but all she did was say, 'Sorry, sir. When I put my name down to be a detective superintendent it said in the application form that I was required to have the utmost integrity and ethical values.'

'I see. Is that a no, then?'

Katie nodded. 'Yes. That's a no. Now I have a heap of work to catch up with, so if you'll excuse me.'

She was still breathing hard when she got back to her office and sat down at her desk. She realized that apart from exposing herself to appalling danger, she could also be bringing about an abrupt end to her career.

Thirty-Six

The next day was Katie's official day off. Detective Inspector Fitzpatrick was taking care of Operation Butterfly, while Kyna and Detective O'Donovan were poring over Jimmy Ó Faoláin's accounts again. They were searching for any clues to the identities of the numerous people he had swindled, and who might be likely to have a motive to take their revenge on him.

She took Foltchain and Barney for a walk along by the river, and it was a fresh, chilly day, with the harbour sparkling and long white cirrus clouds streaming overhead like ripped-up night-gowns. Foltchain's feathery ears flew up in the breeze, and she looked as if she would have loved to have gone for a long, fast run, but she patiently waited every now and then for Barney to catch up, and she would nuzzle his neck reassuringly when he did.

Katie was beginning to miss Conor badly now. When she was under stress at work and it seemed to be impossible to untangle the investigations she was dealing with, it helped her so much to come home and be hugged, and then to have supper together watching television. Waking up in the early hours of the morning was the worst, and finding that she had nobody to hold.

She had almost reached the ferry terminal when her phone rang. It was Dr Kelley calling her from the mortuary at CUH.

'I hope I'm not ringing at an awkward moment,' she said. 'I called the station and they said it was your day off.'

'It is, and I never have enough of them. You could have spoken to DI Fitzpatrick. He's in charge of Operation Butterfly.'

'I'm not actually ringing you about that. I'm ringing you about Mr McManus, the one that everybody seems to call "Guzz Eye", and his lady friend, Rosella. Their remains arrived here from Limerick this morning. They're both very badly burned. In fact, you don't often see bodies as completely incinerated as this, except when road accident victims have been trapped in burning cars.'

'Have you had a chance to examine them yet?' asked Katie, and then had to snap her fingers at Barney and Foltchain and call out, 'Come here, you two! Don't go running off!'

Dr Kelley said, 'I fully appreciate that you're off duty, DS Maguire. But if possible I would prefer not to tell you this over the phone. Do you think I could ask you to come to the mortuary and take a look for yourself? It shouldn't take long.'

'What's the time? Just gone ten. Listen, I'm taking my dogs out for a walk right now, but I can be with you by eleven if Jack's Hole isn't blocked by some breakdown.'

'I hate to inconvenience you, DS Maguire, but I know about your personal connection to this case, and I think you'll find this critically important, to say the least.'

Katie was about to ask her how she knew that she and Conor were an item, but then she decided not to bother. It was impossible to keep secrets in Cork. By now, everybody from Youghal to Crookhaven had probably heard that Cork's only female detective superintendent was sharing a bed with Cork's only pet detective.

She had intended to take the dogs over the river to visit her father, and see how he was getting on with his moving, but she decided to do that later. She thought that she might cook him some of her Bloody Mary soup with tomatoes and chillies and vodka and take that over.

She whistled to Barney and Foltchain and they turned back with her to Carrig View. As she walked along behind them, she felt happiness that she had these two dogs to keep her company and that the morning was so sunny, but loneliness, too, almost to the point of a physical ache. Every time she found a man to love it seemed as if something disastrous happened, either to hurt him or to break them up. She had even lost her only baby, little Seamus, who had died in his cot soon after his first and only birthday. Perhaps that was going to be the story of her life.

Dr Kelley was standing over the headless body of Garda Wassan, wearing her surgical cap and apron but with her mask pulled down so that she could drink a mug of tea.

'Thanks a million for coming,' she said, as Katie negotiated her way between the trolleys that were lined up at angles across the mortuary. 'I'm afraid I'm fierce suspicious these days of giving away too much on the phone, and emails too. I'm sure I was hacked after I carried out a post mortem on Willy Nolan – you remember that gangster from Summerhill in Dublin they found hanged and nobody could believe it was suicide?'

Katie nodded towards the body of Garda Wassan. 'How's it coming along with these poor fellows?'

'I'm making 3-D printed images of their severed necks. They were all decapitated with a chainsaw and I'm ninety-nine per cent certain it was the same chainsaw that was used to take the heads off the first two. They have bruising on their arms and torsos where they were tied up, and indentations on their wrists consistent with handcuffs. They also have random bruises and finger marks, which shows they must have struggled with their captors.'

'You know what I was wondering?' said Katie. 'It may sound ridiculous, but I was wondering if it hurts.'

Dr Kelley sipped her tea and then put her mug down on the autopsy table next to Garda Wassan's gaping neck. 'Oh yes,' she said. 'I imagine that it hurts like hell for the first few seconds, but once they've cut through the nerves, and then the spinal cord, you wouldn't feel anything. But there's quite a lot of evidence that the brain remains conscious for a few seconds at least after your head's been cut off, and so you'll be aware of what's happened to you, and you might even be able to see your body without your head on it.'

Katie gave a shudder. 'I'm sorry I asked! You know, sometimes I wonder what's worse – being alive and constantly worrying about dying, or being dead and having to worry about nothing at all.'

'Perhaps it's better never to be born,' said Dr Kelley. 'Then you'll never have to find out how cruel life can be. But – come over and take a look at these two—'

She turned around, and beckoned to Katie to follow her across to two trolleys parked side by side on the opposite side of the mortuary. They were both covered with pale green sharply creased sheets, which Dr Kelley folded back one after the other, and there lay Guzz Eye McManus and his Pavee girlfriend, Rosella Rooney.

Dr Kelley had been right. They were both burned so badly that they looked as if they were made out of broken lumps of charcoal, with red flesh and bones showing through the cracks. Both of their faces looked as if they were blacked up as minstrels, with their teeth grinning and their eye sockets empty. If it hadn't been for the difference in their size, it would have been impossible to tell at first glance which of them was Guzz Eye and which was Rosella, because there was nothing left to tell which sex they were.

'It was probably not quite as hot as a crematory in that mobile home,' said Dr Kelley. 'But by the state of them, I'd say it must have reached five hundred and fifty degrees Celsius, at least. There were three paraffin heaters in it, and of course they all added to the blaze.'

'Jesus,' said Katie. Then, 'What is it you wanted to tell me?'

'Ah – as I say, I've only made a cursory examination of their bodies so far. There should be sufficient blood and stomach contents remaining for me to be able to carry out a toxicology test. You know, in case they were poisoned. But I've already discovered why they didn't make any attempt to escape when the fire started.'

She beckoned again, indicating that Katie should come close to the end of the trolley where Guzz Eye McManus's head was lying. She pointed to his left temple, about six centimetres above his eye socket. Because the skin around it was so flaky and black, it was difficult for Katie to tell what she was pointing at, and it was easy to understand why nobody had noticed it when his body was first recovered from the smouldering wreckage of his mobile home.

Dr Kelley took a cotton bud out of her apron pocket and poked it into his forehead. The tip disappeared, and it was then that Katie could see that there was a bullet hole in his skull. Before he had been burned, Guzz Eye McManus had been shot.

'Mother of God,' she breathed. 'And what about Ms Rooney here?'

'The same,' said Dr Kelley, and she inserted the cotton bud into a neat round hole in between Rosella Rooney's eye sockets. 'And both bullets are still in there, buried in their brains, so I'll be able to remove them and send them to Bill Phinner to make a match. Nine mm, at a guess.'

'So they were both dead before the fire even started. And that's why they didn't try to get out.'

'It would seem so. And I think you can understand now why I was so security-conscious and asked you to come here rather than tell you over the phone.'

'Of course. That means Conor didn't kill them. You can't be guilty of manslaughter if the person you're supposed to have done away with is already dead.'

'Conor – that's your –?'

'Yes,' said Katie.

Dr Kelley drew the sheets back over the bodies. 'Is it possible that *he* could have shot them, and only set the fire to cover up the evidence?'

'He doesn't own a gun. And it's not in his nature to hurt people.

He was sure that McManus was away at a dog-fight when he set fire to his home, and the only reason he did it was to put him out of business. He couldn't bear to see so many dogs being tortured and killed, and McManus making so much money out of it. The big question is – who *did* shoot them, and why?'

Dr Kelley went back over to the autopsy table and picked up her mug. 'My assistant will be here in about half an hour, and she can finish off making the 3-D prints of these unfortunate beheaded fellows. I'll dig these bullets out for you and write you a preliminary report on the cause of death. You can take that to Tipperary then yourself or scan it over if you don't have the time. Perhaps they'll even let your Conor out on bail if they believe that he's done nothing worse than burn down some Traveller's mobile home in a fit of righteous anger.'

'Dr Kelley, you're an angel in disguise.'

'Well, we'll see. Maybe your Conor did have a gun, but you didn't know it. Sometimes we believe we know somebody inside-out, don't we? ... and then it turns out that we hardly knew them at all. My husband, for instance.'

Katie thought that she was going to tell her more, but instead she picked up her mug of tea and took another sip.

'Ugh,' she said. 'It's gone cold. And it tastes of ethanol.'

Before she left the hospital, Katie rang her solicitor friend, Garret Delaney, and told him that Guzz Eye McManus and Rosella Rooney had both been shot before they were burned.

'Wait until you have the pathologist's report before you say or do anything at all,' he advised her. 'Your pathologist could have been right, and it's conceivable that Conor might have done it, although myself I don't believe it for a moment.'

'The door was locked, wasn't it? How could Conor have got inside to shoot them if it was locked?'

'The door was locked all right, but the technical experts found no keys inside, so whoever shot McManus could have taken his keys and then locked the door from the outside when he left. There was no weapon found inside, either, so that doubly rules out the possibility that McManus shot Ms Rooney and then shot himself.'

'Oh. I didn't know they found no keys,' said Katie. 'And did they find no trace that anybody else had been inside?'

'I don't think they were looking for any evidence of that,' said Garret Delaney. 'And besides, that mobile home was totally gutted, so I don't believe they would have been able to find any.'

'All right, Garret, thanks. I'll get back to you as soon as Dr Kelley has sent me her report.'

'For what it's worth, Katie, I've been over this three times now with Conor, and I don't think that he's the kind of man who's capable of murder. I understand how angry he was that McManus wasn't prosecuted for dog-fighting and for hurting your own dog, but he went to some lengths to make sure that he wasn't at home when he started that fire. If McManus hadn't been suffering from the gout, he wouldn't have been, either.'

'Yes, but somebody knew that he had gone home. Maybe somebody at the dog-fight saw him leave and followed him. There's a fair amount of bad blood between some of those dog-fighters. Maybe it was somebody who bore him a grudge.'

'That's very likely, I'd say. But we don't have any evidence yet to prove it. I might have to go up to Tipp and mingle with the dog-fighting crowd. Somebody must have an idea who would have been happy to see McManus with a bullet through his head.'

'If you do that, Garret, be double wide. If there's any crowd more dangerous than the bare-knuckle fighters, it's the crowd who fight with dogs.'

'I can take care of myself, Katie, but thanks.'

After she had spoken to Garret Delaney, Katie drove into the centre of Cork to do some shopping in the English Market. She needed only tomatoes and chillies for her soup and a chicken breast for her lunch on Sunday. Her friends the Devlins had suggested that after Mass at St Colman's she should join them for lunch at Gilbert's, but she knew that it would bring back that evening when Conor had proposed to her, and she wouldn't be able to eat anything.

She bought a lettuce and half a dozen rashers, too, and then she went through to Oliver Plunkett Street to buy some tea tree night lotion from the Body Shop and do some window-shopping in Fran & Jane. As she walked back to Winthrop Street, she passed Keanes the jewellers, and she looked into the window to see if the diamond bracelet that Viona Caffrey had wanted so badly was still in its display case.

To her surprise, she saw Viona Caffrey herself standing in the shop, wearing a bright red coat. She was talking to the assistant who had served Katie when she had gone in to ask about the bracelet, and as she turned around Katie could see that she was actually wearing the bracelet now, holding it up high and waving her wrist from side to side so that she could see it sparkle.

Katie took a step back so that Viona wouldn't be able to see her behind the shelves in the window, and it was then that she saw that Viona wasn't alone. Standing next to her in a camel-hair coat was a stocky middle-aged man with curly flax-coloured hair. He was laughing and nodding and as Katie watched he laid his hand on Viona's shoulder and kissed her on the cheek. Katie recognized him at once. She had seen his picture enough times in the papers. It was Finbar Foley, the manager of Rachmasach Rovers, the GAA football team that had been sponsored by Jimmy Ó Faoláin.

She stayed outside Keanes for three or four minutes, until Finbar Foley took out his wallet and handed his credit card to the assistant and it was clear that he was buying the bracelet. She could have gone into the shop and made it known that she had seen them together, but they had done nothing illegal, and first of all she wanted Detective O'Donovan to do some digging into the background of their relationship.

Detective O'Donovan had interviewed Finbar Foley only yesterday afternoon and had concluded that he wasn't at all happy about losing one league match after another, although he had refused to admit that Jimmy Ó Faoláin had been paying him to throw them. It was his future career he was worried about, now that Jimmy Ó Faoláin was dead and Rachmasach Rovers would probably fold for lack of a sponsor. Which team was going to employ a manager who had already lost six out of seven games this season?

What Katie wanted to know was if Finbar Foley and Viona Caffrey had got together only after Jimmy Ó Faoláin had been killed, or if they had been seeing each other behind his back while he was still alive. He had frequently been away on business so they would have had plenty of opportunity. And if they had been having an affair, was a combination of professional resentment and sexual jealousy enough of a motive for them to have had him murdered? Jimmy Ó Faoláin had given Viona Caffrey a key, after all, and that could explain how the hit man had entered his house without forcing the door or breaking a window.

Katie took three steps further back into the entrance of Soundstore next door as Finbar Foley and Viona Caffrey came out of Keanes and walked up the street with Viona still flashing her bracelet and laughing. Finbar Foley kissed her and she stopped and kissed him back. Katie took her iPhone out of her coat pocket and took a video of them. If she needed it, this would be incontrovertible evidence that they were more than just friends.

Thirty-Seven

Once Finbar Foley and Viona Caffrey had turned off down Winthrop Street, Katie walked further along Oliver Plunkett Street and went into the Italee coffee house. She ordered a cappuccino and a panini with smoked salmon and goat's cheese, and sat in the window so that she could watch the shoppers going by.

She was wondering if it would be greedy to order the tiramisu when her phone played *Siúil A Rún*. It was Dr Kelley ringing her.

'I've X-rayed the skulls of our two burns victims and extracted the bullets from their brains. I've weighed them and photographed them, and as I expected they're 9mm bullets. They'll have to be examined by your ballistic experts, though, to confirm beyond doubt that they were fired from the same gun.

'I've also carried out preliminary tests on their stomach contents, as well as their urine, blood, livers and hair, and I'll be testing their bone marrow. There's a low level of alcohol in each of them and in Guzz Eye McManus's gut a partially dissolved naproxen tablet, which is usually prescribed for gout. Neither body had any traces of toxic substances.

'I'll be reporting to the coroner that death in each case was almost certainly caused by a single gunshot wound to the head.'

'Is your report ready now?' asked Katie.

'It will be, in about half an hour.'

'I'll come and collect a copy then, and take it up to Tipperary.'

'I can scan it and send it up there for you. It's no bother and it'll save you a trip.'

'Thank you, but no. My afternoon's free, and I was only going to buy myself a new pair of shoes, which I don't really need.'

'You want to see him, don't you?'

Katie didn't answer that, but said, 'I'll see you after, Dr Kelley. And thanks.'

She ordered the tiramisu, but while she was eating it she became aware that a man was sitting across the street at a table outside the Market Lane café, and that he was watching her. His head was shaven and he was wearing a black leather jacket. He was holding up a newspaper in front of him, but she noticed that he didn't look down at it once, and didn't turn the pages. Apart from that, she saw from the headline about parking discs that it was yesterday's *Evening Echo*.

A waiter came out of the café and asked him what he wanted, but he shook his head. The waiter said something to him, but he plainly didn't have the courage to tell the man that if he didn't order anything he couldn't continue to sit there, and he went back inside.

Katie had been watched and followed several times in the past, mostly in attempts to intimidate her. Once her car had been blocked off by a white van as she was driving up Anglesea Street, and two men had climbed out of the van and smashed her windscreen with a hammer. Almost every time she had known who was following her: family members of criminals who were due to appear in court. But for several reasons this man unsettled her more than most. For one thing, she didn't recognize him as being a member of any Cork gang. For another, she still didn't know how the killers of the last three whistle-blowers had found the safe houses in which they were supposed to be hidden and abducted them so quickly. She had publicly announced her intention to make a disclosure about Garda misconduct to Chief Superintendent O'Malley, so she was now a whistle-blower herself.

If this man in his black leather jacket really was watching her, he probably knew who she was. But he could only have known *where* she was by following her. Had he been following her all morning? And if he *was* following her, who was he, and why was he following her?

She took a small amount of comfort from the Smith & Wesson Airweight revolver holstered on her left hip. But this man could be armed, too, and he could be in contact with other armed men, and he could call them in to surround her.

Maybe I'm being paranoid. But I'd rather be paranoid than have my head cut off.

She called Superintendent Pearse at the station and told him where she was, and that she suspected that she was being watched. She described the man and where he was sitting outside the Market Lane café on the corner of Beasley Street.

'Not a bother, ma'am. Leave it to me.'

Even before she had finished her tiramisu, two uniformed gardaí in bright yellow high-viz jackets came strolling up Oliver Plunkett Street. They stopped beside the man's table and Katie could see that they were having a conversation with him. She didn't know what they were asking him, but he looked defensive at first, and then angry. He stood up abruptly but one of the gardaí put his hand on his shoulder and made him sit down again.

At this point, Katie called the waiter over and paid her bill. Then she shrugged on her coat, left the café and walked quickly away up Oliver Plunkett Street without looking behind her, taking the first left into Parnell Place where she had parked her car.

She turned around only when she reached the corner. She could see the two gardaí still talking to the man, but he was ignoring them and leaning sideways in his chair, trying to see where she was going.

She reached her car, and as she climbed into it her phone rang. It was Superintendent Pearse.

'I've just heard from Garda Brennan and Garda O'Leary about your man, ma'am. He says he was all flah'd out from walking round the shops and was having a rest, that was all. When they pointed out that he had no messages with him, he got a bit abusive.

They threatened to arrest him if he didn't calm down, which he did. He gave his name as Thomas Lenihan and he gave an address in Gurra. He hadn't committed any offence so there wasn't much else they could do.'

'Thanks, Michael. That's got him off my back anyway.'

'Your man watching you, ma'am – do you think it could be connected in any way at all with your intention to make a disclosure?'

'I couldn't say for sure. But I'm going to keep sketch from now on for anybody following me.'

'What I'm saying is, do you need some protection?'

'Thanks for the offer, but I believe I'm safe enough for the time being, so long as I keep my eyes peeled and my wits about me.'

She drove back to CUH and collected the report from Dr Kelley.

'I hope this helps to get your fellow off the hook,' said Dr Kelley.

Katie opened the file and quickly read through it. 'If it does, I owe you a celebratory dinner at the Hayfield.'

Traffic on the M8 was light so it took her less than an hour and a half to drive to Tipperary. She parked behind the Garda station on St Michael's Road and went straight in to see Inspector Carroll. She had warned him that she was coming so he was sitting at his desk, catching up with some of his paperwork.

He was solidly built, Inspector Carroll, with a broken nose. When Katie had first met him, she had thought that he had either been a professional boxer before he joined the Garda, or a thug who had decided to mend his ways. She had later found out that he had studied business and accountancy at St Patrick's College in Thurles and had been a champion chess player. If anyone had taught her not to judge people by appearances, it was Inspector Carroll.

'I expect you'll be wanting to see Conor, ma'am,' he said, tossing down his pen and standing up.

'Of course. But I need to show you this first. It's Dr Kelley's preliminary report on Guzz Eye McManus and Rosella Rooney. It wasn't the fire that killed them. Before they were burned, both of them were shot in the head.'

'Go 'way – serious?' Inspector Carroll took the file and quickly read through it. Then he looked at Katie and said, 'Well... this puts a different light on this case altogether. That dog-fight at Ballynonty that McManus set up, we raided that late in the afternoon and broke it up.'

'That was where Conor thought McManus was when he went to burn down his mobile home.'

'That's where he *says* he thought he was.'

'Sorry, Inspector, I'm getting a little ahead of myself. You were saying?'

'We broke it up, the dog-fight, and made a fair number of arrests for possession of drugs and public order offences. But one scummer we arrested for possession of a firearm. His name is Luke Kiggins and we've lifted him several times in the past for minor offences like sulky racing on the motorway and mistreating dogs and ponies and hobbling mobile phones. But the Kiggins family are deadly rivals to McManus and his mob. They hold dog-fights all over Kilkenny and Laois and they've been trying to arrange them in Tipperary, too.'

'What kind of a firearm is it?'

'A semi-automatic pistol – and yes, it's 9mm. A FÉG PA-63. I don't know if you've come across them before but we've seen two or three of them lately. They're made in Hungary, and I reckon the IRA smuggled a load of them in.'

'Did you examine it? Did it look like it had been recently fired?'

'We'd had no reports of anybody being shot so we didn't send it to the Technical Bureau. It has a seven-round detachable box magazine but there were only four rounds in it. We questioned Kiggins about the missing rounds, of course, but he said that he had fired them for target practice.'

'So where is Kiggins now?'

'Out on police bail, until he comes up in court.'

'Do you have the pistol here? Can I take it back to our ballistics experts?'

'I don't see why not. In fact – now I've seen this pathology report – I'd say it was essential, and urgent.'

He went to the open door of his office and called out, 'Sergeant Malone! Would you go to the safe and fetch me that gun that was taken off of Luke Kiggins? And its magazine, too!'

He turned back to Katie and said, 'Now, why don't you come along and see Conor? I'd love to let him out right here and now, but I'm afraid I'll have to wait until it's proven that it couldn't have been him who shot McManus and that woman of his.'

Katie gave him a tight smile. 'Don't worry. I know it wasn't him.'

'He did set the fire, though?'

'He's admitted it, hasn't he?'

Inspector Carroll led her along the corridor to the cells at the back of the station. 'Don't quote me on this, but myself, I would have made sure that McManus was inside that mobile home before I set it alight. The evil bastard. Dogs feel pain as much as we do, and they have all the same feelings that we do, and they have souls. In the eyes of God, McManus was a mass murderer, and he only got what he deserved.'

They reached the cells and the duty officer unlocked the door of Conor's cell. He was lying on his bunk reading a dog-eared paperback. When he saw Katie he dropped it on the floor and stood up, lifting both arms as if he were a penitent, and an angel had descended from heaven to grant him forgiveness.

Neither of them said a word, but they held each other tightly, and Katie's eyes filled with tears. Inspector Carroll discreetly stepped out of the cell and half-closed the door, indicating to the duty officer with a batting motion of his hand that he should leave them alone for a while.

They hugged and kissed until at last Katie pushed him away

and said, 'I've something to tell you, Con. You mustn't get your hopes up too much, not yet, but I might be able to get you out of here.'

Conor wiped the tears from his eyes with the back of his hand. 'Christ on a bicycle, Katie, I hope so. The food in here is shite.'

They both started to laugh, although they didn't really know for sure if they were laughing or crying. They sat down on the bunk and Katie told him about Dr Kelley's discovery that Guzz Eye McManus and Rosella Rooney had been shot.

'As soon as Bill Phinner's had a chance to examine the bullets, you could be released on bail. You can't be convicted of killing people who are already dead.'

'But what if the bullets don't match? What if it wasn't this Luke Kiggins who shot them?'

'There's every chance that it was. Who else had a gun, and was there at Ballynonty when Guzz Eye McManus decided to leave? Somebody who wasn't there at the dog-fight couldn't have known that he had gone back to Ballyknock.'

'Maybe somebody at the halting site saw him come back and shot him then.'

'Don't be such a pessimist. I thought you always looked on the sunny side.'

'I used to, but do you know what? The sun went in for me that evening at Gilbert's, Katie, and to be honest with you, I don't think it's ever going to come out again.'

'Of course it is, darling. Look at the state of you la. You might be locked up in a cell but you could have combed your hair. And, yes.'

'I don't have a fricking comb, that's the problem,' said Conor. Then he gave a little shake of his head and said, 'What do you mean, "yes"? Yes, what?'

'Yes, I'll marry you.'

Conor stared at her and his chestnut-brown eyes filled up with tears again. He was biting his lip and for a moment he couldn't speak. He put his arms around Katie and held her close and rocked her very gently from side to side, as if they were Leonardo DiCaprio and Kate Winslet on the prow of *Titanic*.

At last he cleared his throat and sat back and said, 'Katie, you're a princess. A red-haired, green-eyed princess. I look at you sometimes and I can't believe that you're real, and that you love me. And now you've said you want to be my wife.'

'That's because I *do* want to be your wife,' said Katie. 'I'll be Mrs Ó Máille. That means that my initials will be KO, and I think that's pure appropriate for a detective superintendent, don't you? Knockout Ó Máille.'

Inspector Carroll tapped at the cell door. 'I have what you came here for, ma'am.'

Katie gave Conor one more kiss and stood up. 'This is just the beginning, Con, don't worry. I'll take the gun directly to Bill Phinner and tell him to put his skates on and pull his finger out and make a bust.'

She left the cell and the duty officer locked the door behind her. Inspector Carroll led her back to his office and took the pistol out of his desk drawer, sealed in a heavy-duty polythene bag. Without a word he passed her the requisition form and she signed it.

'I'll be waiting for good news,' he told her.

Katie picked up the gun and smiled. 'If it wasn't against protocol, Inspector, I'd kiss you.'

Thirty-Eight

By the time she returned to Cork city, it was dark. She drove directly to Anglesea Street and handed the pistol to Bill Phinner, who was sitting hunched in his office in front of his computer.

He snapped on a pair of forensic gloves and then took the pistol and its magazine out of the polythene bag, holding them up and studying them closely.

'FÉG PA-63. Made by the FÉGARMY arms company in Hungary, and still in use by the Hungarian police. Simple, cheap, and easily concealed under your jacket. They wanted to phase them out after the fall of communism but they'd made thousands of them. They're still exporting them, mostly to America, but a fair few have made their way here.'

'Has Dr Kelley sent you the bullets yet?'

'She has, yes. They arrived about an hour ago. My ballistics fellow, Colm, was going to take a sconce at them tomorrow sometime.'

'Well, this could be the pistol they were fired from, and if there's any chance that you could examine them this evening, and see if they match—'

She told him how the Tipperary gardaí had arrested Luke Kiggins at the dog-fight. He listened, turning the pistol this way and that, and sniffing at the muzzle.

'I'll see what I can do for you, ma'am. Leave it with me.'

'You do that for me, Bill, and I'll buy you one of those e-liquid gift packs.'

'You don't have to do that, ma'am. I've given up the vaping and I've gone back to the fags. I couldn't stand walking around smelling like a sweet shop. All the regulars in my local thought I'd transgendered.'

Tired as she was by the time she arrived back at Carrig View, she decided to make her Bloody Mary soup and take it over to her father. It would help to take her mind off Conor, and the depressing possibility that Bill Phinner's ballistic tests would show that Guzz Eye McManus and Rosella Rooney had been shot by somebody else, and not Luke Kiggins.

She was sure, though, that she had done the right thing by accepting Conor's proposal. She loved him, and even though he had acted rashly and stupidly by setting fire to Guzz Eye McManus's mobile home, at least he had admitted it, and shown that he was man enough to take his punishment. When she saw Barney hobbling along the hallway to greet her she was reminded how vicious and sadistic Guzz Eye McManus had been.

Both Foltchain and Barney came into the kitchen to watch her as she cut up a kilo of ripe tomatoes and put them into a roasting tin with two seeded red chillies and a sprinkling of sugar, salt and pepper. She roasted them for half an hour, and then blended them into a purée, adding vegetable stock and tomato paste, dry sherry and horseradish sauce, and four tablespoons of vodka.

Both dogs looked up at her appealingly as she tasted it. 'No,' she said. 'You're not having any. It's too alcoholic and it's too hot. You'd be langered this evening and howling tomorrow when you did your business.'

When she arrived at her father's house it was Blaithin who answered the door. She was buttoning up her coat and tying her headscarf.

'Katie, good to see you! You've come at just the right moment... I have to go home but your poor Da is having such a struggle with the packing. He can't make his mind up what to keep and what to throw out, but I've told him he can't keep everything, especially all them books and magazines. He has enough copies of *Garda Review* to build himself another house out of!'

'Thanks, Blaithin. I'll see if I can give him a hand. I don't know if he's had his supper but I've fetched him some soup.'

'Well, he's had some chicken pie but only a doonchie slice and I'm sure a late-night snack won't go amiss. He's been off his food the past few days. I think it's the moving that's upsetting him, do you know what I mean, like? I've never known him so quiet, and sometimes I have to repeat myself twice before he hears what I've said.'

Katie carried the soup tureen through to the kitchen and put it down on the hob. Then she went into the living room where her father was on his knees, sorting through seven or eight stacks of books. He looked as if he were surrounded by a small fort.

'How's it going, Da?' she asked him.

'Katie, my darling! This is a nice surprise! What's the time? I thought you were going to fetch your new dog over and we were going to go for a walk.'

'I know, Da, but like I told you, my life's pure crazy at the moment. I was supposed to be having a day off, but it turned out I had to go to Wilton and then up to Tipp. I'm free this evening, though, so I thought I'd come over and give you a bit of a hand with your packing. I brought you some of that Bloody Mary soup you like.'

'Grand. I'll have a bowl of that later, thanks. So what's the craic? Have you any notion yet who's been cutting off those whistle-blowers' heads?'

'Not so far. I've never known a case like it. Whoever's done it, they don't seem to care two hoots about what evidence they leave behind. Fingerprints, footprints, DNA. It's like they believe we're never going to catch them, and even if we do, we won't be able to prosecute them for it.'

'I saw you on the TV saying that you'll be doing some whistle-blowing yourself. What's that all about?'

'There's a couple of prostitutes in Wilton and they've been giving their services to gardaí in exchange for not being lifted. But I'm reporting it to Chief Superintendent O'Malley to see if it'll draw the murderers out into the open. They've killed five whistle-blowers already. Maybe if I'm a whistle-blower they'll come after me.'

'Holy Mary, Katie! That's a fierce dangerous thing to be doing. I don't want to be seeing you without your head.'

'I can handle myself, Da, and I have plenty of protection to call on if I need it. But I can't think of any other way to find out who they are. The trouble is, I think there's a garda involved, or maybe more than one. Maybe it's some of the officers who might have lost their jobs if all of this whistle-blowing evidence had come out in front of Justice McGuigan.'

'Serious? You don't really believe that a Garda officer would cut off another officer's head, just to keep his job?'

'I think there's more to it than that, Da, but I'm not entirely sure what. I'll crack it in the end, but right now it's giving me the headache to end all headaches.'

Katie was tempted to tell him that she had accepted Conor's proposal of marriage, but she thought she would leave that until the end of the evening when they were more relaxed and were sitting down for some soup. Her father wasn't particularly keen on Conor, because he was divorced and had a beard. 'I always think that fellers grow beards because they've something to hide.'

'Tell me now,' said Katie, smacking her hands together and looking around. 'What do you want me to start packing?'

'Over there by the door you'll find two piles of old photograph albums. I'm not throwing any of those away. There's cardboard packing cases behind the couch, and sticky tape. But pour yourself a drink first, and I won't say no to one myself.'

Once she had poured herself a vodka and tonic, and a Satz for her father, Katie sat cross-legged on the floor and began to pack the photograph albums. She did it slowly, because she couldn't resist looking through them. Here were pictures of herself and her mother sitting on their garden swing, and pictures of herself and her six sisters, making sandcastles on the beach at Kinsale. Some of the pictures of her mother had been taken only weeks before she died, and Katie sat looking at them in silence.

'You've gone quiet all of a sudden,' said her father. 'How are you going on?'

'Oh... sorry. I was just looking at some of these old pictures.'

'I can't look at them myself. There's nothing hurts so much as seeing pictures of yourself when you were happy.'

Katie finished packing one case, taped it up, and then went on to the next pile of albums. These were older, bound in worn green leather, and they contained small black-and-white photographs of her father in his parents' house in Lower Pouladuff Road, near Cork Lough.

On the first page of the second album that she opened, somebody had written, in faded ink, *Ghairdín Glas 1965–1968*. She looked through the album, turning each page carefully, and on the third page she found a picture of her grandfather and her grandmother standing behind their garden gate, smiling, both of them shading their eyes against the sunshine. The plaque on the gate said *Ghairdín Glas*.

Katie had never been to that house, because her grandfather had died before she was born, and her grandmother had moved in with her great-uncle in Ard Sionnach, so she had never known that it was called Ghairdín Glas. But Ghairdín Glas was also the name of the association of older people who had lost €7.5 million investing in Jimmy Ó Faoláin's Equity Sunshine scam.

Katie looked across at her father, putting aside some of the books that he would have to throw away or give to the charity shops. It couldn't be a coincidence that the association had been named Ghairdín Glas. He had probably been its manager, or its treasurer, and he had named it for the house where he had grown up, and which had happy memories for him. But Ghairdín Glas had been comprehensively conned by Jimmy Ó Faoláin, and that must be why her father's savings had vanished and he was having to move house.

She was about to hold up the album and ask him if he had organized Ghairdín Glas when a dark, cold thought entered her mind, and she slowly put it down, and closed it.

What had Detective O'Donovan said about Ghairdín Glas? 'I can't see any of them having the expertise to enter Jimmy Ó Faoláin's and shoot him without leaving the slightest trace that they'd been there – that's if their creaking knees could even get them up the driveway. And where would people like that have acquired themselves a Sig Sauer automatic from?'

Her father had been trained as a garda and he had reached the rank of inspector before he had been forced to resign. He knew how to pick a lock and how to enter a property wearing forensic gloves and forensic shoe covers so that he wouldn't leave any trace that he had been there. He had been trained as a firearms officer and knew how to use a Sig Sauer automatic because it was standard issue in An Garda Síochána. He was fit these days, too. He had been so ill before Blaithin had started to take care of him, but now he went out for long walks and he even played golf, so his knees couldn't be creaking.

Oh Mother of God don't say he did it. Please don't tell me it was him. Not my own father. I know that he's always had a burning belief in justice, and he and his friends lost all their money. Brian Cooney even committed suicide because he went bankrupt. But when does a burning belief in justice become lethal revenge?

What made her feel even colder and darker was remembering what her father had told her one day, soon after she had graduated from Templemore. She could see him saying it now, as they had celebrated over lunch in the Bosun bar, here in Monkstown. She had teasingly told him that now *she* was a guard, she could protect *him*.

'You'll never need to protect me, darling,' he had said. 'I can still protect myself. I took a few souvenirs away with me when

I left the force, and one of those was my gun.' And he had lifted two fingers in a pistol gesture.

She looked across at him again. Not only had he possessed the expertise to kill Jimmy Ó Faoláin, but the weapon, too. He had never showed her his gun but it would almost certainly have been a Sig Sauer automatic.

She decided to say nothing. It seemed impossible that it could have been him. What would he think of her, if she asked him directly to his face, 'Was it you who shot Jimmy Ó Faoláin?' If he had, he surely wouldn't admit it, and if he hadn't, he would either be angry and offended, or else he would think she was making a joke in very bad taste.

Even if she showed him the photograph of the house called Ghairdín Glas, what would that prove? He would probably say that it was a coincidence, and nothing more.

After they had packed up all of the books that her father wanted to keep, Katie heated up her Bloody Mary soup and cut some large chunks of soda bread and they sat down together at the kitchen table.

Now she suspected that her father might have shot Jimmy Ó Faoláin, she had hardly any appetite at all, but she didn't want him to think there was anything wrong, and so she managed to finish half a bowl of soup, and a heel of soda bread. She couldn't stop glancing across the table at him as she ate, as if he might suddenly come out and say, 'It wasn't me, Katie, honest, and I can prove it to you!' and she could have burst out laughing with relief.

All he did, though, was look back at her and say, 'What? Do you have something on your mind?'

'No, Dad, I was just thinking about those photo albums, and some of the pictures in them. I'd forgotten how pretty Mam was. Of course when you're a child you never think of your Mam as being pretty. She's just your Mam.'

Her father put down his spoon. 'I remember how pretty she

was. How could I forget? And you're the bulb off her, but don't tell your sisters.'

Katie decided not to tell him that she and Conor were going to be married. She knew that he would be less than delighted, and she didn't want to upset him and spoil their supper, especially now. She was sure that Conor would be cleared of manslaughter, but he would still be facing the charge of arson and a possible prison sentence, and they wouldn't be able to make any wedding plans until then.

Her father started reminiscing about the time they had all spent a week at a holiday park in County Wicklow and her mother had won a beauty contest. Katie was only half-listening. While he was talking, she couldn't stop wondering if he still had his pistol. Perhaps he had disposed of it years ago, but if he had hoarded every copy of *Garda Review* and every book he had ever read, she thought it unlikely. If he *had* shot Jimmy Ó Faoláin, though, perhaps he had thrown it away as incriminating evidence. He could have tossed it into the harbour, and nobody would ever have found it.

On the other hand, whoever had shot Jimmy Ó Faoláin had been careful to leave no trace whatsoever of who they were, so if it had been him, perhaps he wouldn't have thought he needed to throw it away.

It was questionable that she could obtain a warrant to search his house because her suspicions were based on such personal and tendentious evidence. And even if she did, and no gun was found, or if a gun was found but it didn't match the bullets that had killed Jimmy Ó Faoláin, her father would probably never speak to her again.

'You're quare quiet tonight,' said her father.

'Just tired,' Katie told him. 'Would you like some more soup?'

'I would, yes. It's burning my mouth a fair bit, but it's tasty all right.'

Katie ladled out another bowlful of soup for him and sat watching him as he drank it.

What on earth am I thinking? Am I really suspecting that my own father could have shot a man in cold blood, no matter how much he might have believed that he deserved it? Jimmy Ó Faoláin had defrauded hundreds of investors, and any one of them would have been delighted to see him killed. And yet – and yet – I still want to be absolutely certain that it wasn't my Da.

When he had torn off a piece of bread and mopped up the last of his soup, her father said, 'Before you go, darling, there's some more photo albums up in the attic I can show you.'

'Maybe another time,' said Katie. 'I'll fetch Barney and Foltchain over on Sunday afternoon and you can show me then.'

'Oh, come on, it won't take me long to bring them down. And there's that picture of your mother at the holiday park. Now I've remembered it, I'd like to see it again myself.'

He disappeared upstairs, leaving Katie to stack the soup bowls and the side plates in the dishwasher. She heard the loft ladder coming down with a bang, and then the creaking sound of her father climbing up it.

She went into the living room and quickly looked around. There was an antique chest of drawers against the opposite wall and she hesitated for a moment before she went over and slid open the two bottom drawers. There was nothing in them but table mats with pictures of sailing ships on them, and a mahogany canteen of cutlery. She opened the next two drawers, and then the top three. All she found were pens and envelopes and a roll of Sellotape.

You're searching your father's house for a gun, because you think he might have shot somebody? Aren't you ashamed? No – because I'm not only Katie my father's daughter, I'm Detective Superintendent Katie Maguire.

She went through to the hallway and opened the two drawers underneath the coat-stand. In those she found a shoehorn, a crumpled car tax disc, and three folded scarves that had belonged to her mother. Either her father had left the scarves there out of nostalgia or he simply didn't realize that they were there.

She looked into the huge walnut sideboard in the dining room and then she went into the small room next to the dining room, which her father kept as his study. She rummaged quickly through the drawers in his desk, while all the time keeping her ears open for the sound of him folding away the loft ladder and coming back downstairs.

Next she went back to the kitchen, even though it hardly seemed likely that he would keep a gun there. She opened up all the cupboards and pulled out all the drawers, but she found only cutlery and can openers and tea towels.

If he did have a gun, her best guess was that he kept it in his bedside table, in case any intruders broke into the house during the night. Lately there had been several incidents in Cobh and Monkstown of burglars beating or torturing older residents so that they would open their safes or hand over their jewellery boxes.

She heard her father closing the attic door, so it was too late to go upstairs and search his bedroom. He came down looking pleased with himself, with three photo albums tucked under his arm.

'I haven't looked at these myself in years,' he told her. 'How about a last drink before you go and we can go through them? There's lots of you, when you were about five or six.'

'I must pay a visit first,' she told him. 'I won't be a minute.'

She went into the toilet and was just taking off her long rust-coloured cardigan when her phone rang. She took it out of her cardigan pocket and saw that it was Bill Phinner calling her.

'Sorry to ring you so late, ma'am, but you did say that you wanted a speedy result.'

'Not a bother, Bill. What's the story?'

'They're a match.'

'What? Serious?'

'No question about it, ma'am. The bullets that killed McManus and his woman friend were both fired out of that gun you fetched in this afternoon. We test-fired six bullets and when we put them under the comparison microscope, the striations tallied exactly.'

Katie could hardly believe what he had told her. 'Thank God, Bill. You don't know how much of a load that's taken off.'

'I can imagine, ma'am. I'm pure pleased for you. There'll be a scan of the result waiting for you on your computer tomorrow morning, and if it's okay with you I'll email one up to Inspector Carroll.'

'Of course, yes. Thanks a million, Bill. I owe you.'

She balanced her phone on top of the cistern, took down her jeans and her thong and sat down. She could have whooped out loud. Conor would still have to go to court but she would be able to offer mitigating evidence that he had been deeply distressed by the cruelty of Guzz Eye McManus's dog-fights, and that he had been tipped over the edge psychologically by the DPP's decision not to prosecute him. With luck, he might get away with nothing more than a fine, or a few hundred hours of community service.

She leaned back, and as she did so she knocked her phone off the top of the cistern, so that it dropped down between the back of the cistern and the wall.

Jesus, she thought, that's all I need. Why can't I have a single word of good news without a calamity to go with it? At least her phone hadn't fallen on to the floor and cracked. She had dropped it only two weeks ago when she was shopping in Dunnes and it had cost her €35 to have the screen replaced.

She buttoned up her jeans, washed her hands, and then peered down the back of the cistern. She could see that her phone had been stopped from falling on to the floor by a package wrapped up in a white plastic pedal-bin bag, wound around with brown parcel tape. She reached down and lifted out her phone, and then she tugged the package out, too.

She didn't even have to open it to know what it was. She could tell by the weight, and the shape. Not only that, a memory came flooding back to her, a memory of sitting in the old Capitol

Cinema with her father and mother and three of her sisters to watch *The Godfather*. There was a scene in which Al Pacino came to meet two rival gangsters in a restaurant, and he was frisked by their bodyguards to make sure that he wasn't armed. Halfway through the meal he went to the toilet and found a pistol that had previously been wedged behind the cistern by an accomplice.

Her father had said, 'Brilliant! Who'd have thought of hiding a gun in the jacks? I'll have to remember that!' She had thought of him saying that several times over the years, especially when she had arranged to meet dangerous criminals herself, such as Eugene Ó Béara and Eamonn 'Foxy' Collins. She had met 'Foxy' on more than one occasion in Dan Lowery's pub on MacCurtain Street and he had always insisted that she opened her jacket to show him that she wasn't armed.

She hid the package under her cardigan and when she came out of the toilet she went directly over to her large brown leather bucket bag and pushed it inside. Her father was in the kitchen taking another bottle of Satz out of the fridge and by the time he came out she was sitting on the large green Victorian sofa with one of the photo albums on her lap.

'I look at some of these pictures and find it hard to believe it was me,' she said.

He sat down beside her. 'We all change, don't wc, as time goes by, even though we don't realize it? Look at me there, outside Togher Garda station. Innocent? I look like butter wouldn't melt. And all that hair!'

Katie smiled at him but she couldn't stop her smile from fading away. *Please dear God Da don't let the bullets that killed Jimmy Ó Faoláin match your gun.*

Thirty-Nine

When she returned home, Katie took Barney and Foltchain for a short walk as far as Dock Cottages. She did it to clear her own head as much as to give the dogs a last chance to relieve themselves before they settled down for the night.

She desperately wanted to believe that her father could never have shot Jimmy Ó Faoláin, but if the same leads had suggested that somebody else had shot him, she would have had no hesitation in following them up. It had given her a horrible sick feeling in her stomach and it drained away all the relief she had felt when Bill Phinner had told her that Conor couldn't have shot Guzz Eye McManus and Rosella Rooney.

She turned around and was walking back along Carrig View when she became aware that a car was driving along slowly behind her. There were no other cars in sight, but it was creeping along close to the kerb, with only its sidelights on. She looked over her shoulder at it, and when she did it appeared to slow down even more. She kept walking, but she unbuttoned her overcoat so that she would be able to pull out her pistol quickly if she needed to.

She had no way of knowing for certain if the car was following her or, if it was, whether it was because of her announcement that she was going to make a protected disclosure about gardaí visiting the Romanian brothel. There were plenty of other criminals in Cork who wished her harm. But that shaven-headed man had been watching her this lunchtime when she was sitting in Italee, and now that this car was idling along at a walking pace only twenty metres behind her, she was definitely beginning to feel threatened. She had been confident that she could cope with any attempts to abduct her, but now she thought that it might be sensible if she detailed at least one protection officer to keep an eye on her.

She called Barney and Foltchain and when they came to heel she took hold of their leads and held them close. Then she turned around on the narrow pavement and faced the approaching car, with the dog-leads in her left hand and her right hand tucked inside her coat.

The car stopped. It stayed where it was for nearly half a minute, and Katie continued to stand facing it. It was clear now that they were following her, and if they were following her they knew who she was, and if they knew who she was they knew that she could well be armed. She could be bluffing, with her hand in her coat, but maybe she wasn't.

She was well aware how dangerous it was, to stand here motionless. Whoever was driving the car could be armed, too, and she was a stationary target. Her heart was hammering and her breath was steaming in the damp midnight air. They could shoot her in the legs and drag her into the car and the only witnesses would be her two abandoned dogs.

She reached into her coat pocket and took out her phone, holding it up to take a picture of the car. Almost instantly, the car's full headlights were switched on and its engine roared and it swerved away from the kerb with its tyres shrieking, leaving a cloud of rubber smoke behind it.

Katie watched its red tail lights pass the ferry terminal and disappear from sight. She blew out her cheeks with relief and Barney and Foltchain looked up at her sympathetically.

'It's all right now, you two,' she told them. 'The nasty men have gone. It seems like they were more afraid of me shooting them with a camera than shooting them with a gun.'

She thumbed her phone and looked at the picture she had taken. All it showed were two glaring headlights, although the technical experts might be able to enhance it and read its number plate. It had been a silver or grey Mercedes saloon, she was sure of that.

When she returned home, she drew the bolts on the front door as soon as she closed it, and fastened the security chain. She switched on the alarm, too, which was connected to Midleton Garda station. Usually she put away her revolver in the top drawer in what had been the nursery, but tonight she laid it on her bedside table. Her father's pistol was still wrapped up in her handbag, waiting for her to take it into Bill Phinner tomorrow morning so that he could compare the rifling in its barrel with the bullets that had killed Jimmy Ó Faoláin.

After she had showered and climbed into bed she was tempted to take two Nytol, but she didn't want to be drugged if anybody attempted to break in. As it was, she fell asleep after only ten minutes, and slept dreamlessly, and didn't wake up until she heard Barney making that thin, keening sound in his throat which meant that he wanted his breakfast.

'So where did you find *this* one?' asked Bill Phinner, once he had cut the Sig Sauer automatic out of its pedal-bin bag. 'Holy Mary, ma'am, you're fetching guns in thick and fast, so you are. You haven't found a secret IRA arms dump, by any chance?'

'Do you mind if I don't tell you yet?' said Katie. 'If it wasn't the gun that shot Jimmy Ó Faoláin, then I want to return it to its owner without any bother. In fact, its owner doesn't even know that I've borrowed it.'

'Fair play. I'll hand it over to Colm as soon as he gets in and he should be able to give you a result this afternoon, or even earlier. By the way, I sent our report on the FÉG off to Inspector Carroll and he's acknowledged that he's received it.'

'Thank you, Bill. What would I do without you?'

'Well, you'd have a rake of guns and nobody to test them for you.'

'Oh, here,' she said. 'Here's something else you can look at for me.' She showed him the photograph she had taken of the car that had followed her along Carrig View. 'Maybe that photographic genius of yours can pick out its index mark.'

She didn't tell him why she had taken it, because she didn't want any information about what she was doing to spread around the station. If there were any corrupt officers here in Anglesea Street, they would be more likely to reveal themselves by what they knew than what they didn't.

After she had left Bill Phinner's laboratory she went to see Superintendent Pearse and asked him if he could arrange for her to have a protection officer whenever she left the station and outside her home at night. He agreed, although his expression told her that he disapproved of her whistle-blowing and thought that it was her own fault if she was in danger.

'I'm stretched for personnel and my budget's crying out for mercy, but I reckon I can manage it.'

When she reached her office, she found Detective O'Crean waiting for her. He looked pleased with himself.

'What's the form, Cairbre?' she asked him.

'The CCTV from Decky's Convenience Store. The way it was angled, it couldn't catch any cars coming out from Mervue Lawn and heading south on Glenheights Road. But the gods must have been smiling on us, because our suspects pulled right slap bang into Decky's forecourt and one of them went into the store to buy himself a pack of Johnny Blues. So we have clear footage of him and the car, and you can also make out Sergeant MacAuley sitting in the back seat.'

'That's brilliant. What type of car?'

'Mercedes saloon, silver.'

'Can you see its index marks?'

'Sharp as anything, ma'am,' said Detective O'Crean, and it was obvious that he was excited. 'That's not the best of it, though, by far. I *thought* it rang a bell, like, the index mark, so I went down to the car pound to check, and I was right. It's the same number as that bashed-up Mercedes that was towed in from Crosser – the one that Farry feller was driving when he crashed into Garda Buckley.'

'The same?'

'Identical. Cork index mark, starting with 162-C. I checked it on the vehicle database, and it's a registration that doesn't exist.'

Katie said, 'I think you deserve a bonus for that, Cairbre. Well remembered! You've told DI Fitzpatrick?'

'He's not in yet but I've texted him. Do you want me to ask Superintendent Pearse to put out a bulletin about it?'

'No. Not yet. And I don't want you to tell anybody else about it, except for the rest of the Butterfly team, and please warn them not to go spreading it around, either. This is the strongest indication we've had so far that Seamus Twomey and Douglas Quinn have been behind these whistle-blower murders, but we'll still have to gather a heap more evidence before we can haul them in.'

Detective O'Crean frowned sagely. 'Right. We'd have to prove that Twomey or Quinn actually owned Farry's car, wouldn't we? Or at least that they'd lent him a borrow of it.'

'Exactly. Since both cars have the same fake index mark, it's a certainty that they were stolen. If that's the case, there could be more than one silver Mercedes saloon circulating around the city, all with the same index mark, and we might stop the wrong one.'

'Well, that's right,' said Detective O'Crean. 'And even if it *was* Twomey and Quinn who organized the killings, we still don't have any idea why they should have targeted those Garda whistle-blowers, do we? Not all five of them, anyway.'

He paused, and then he said, 'I can understand them going after Garda O'Regan, like, do you know what I mean? He was exposing the drug-dealers that never went to prison, and some of them were members of their own gang. But why should they have chopped off Garda Wassan's head, just because he complained about racism? Or Sergeant MacAuley's? All *he* was complaining about was knocking points off licences. Why should Twomey and Quinn have cared about that?'

'That's what we have to find out,' said Katie. 'But you've made some good progress anyway, Cairbre. I'll be holding a briefing in an hour or two, and we can discuss how we're going to move forwards, now that we're much more certain about Twomey and Quinn.'

Once Detective O'Crean had gone, she got up from her desk and walked over to the window. She felt that Operation Butterfly was beginning to come together at last, but she was still convinced that somebody here at Anglesea Street was involved in the murder of those five whistle-blowers, even if they had only passed information to the killers about the victims' movements.

Stephen MacQuaid had texted her to say that he had questioned every one of his security staff, but all of them had vehemently denied telling anybody where their safe houses were located, and in any case most of them didn't know where they were. It was quite possible that one of them was lying, and had been paid by the killers, but there was no way of proving it.

Katie looked at all the windows in the station and wondered if there was an informer sitting behind one of them, or even a murderer. There was one thing she knew for certain – she would have to proceed with the utmost caution, both in her personal movements and in what intelligence she gave away. She trusted her team on Operation Butterfly but there were some detectives she couldn't be sure of, and more than a few uniformed gardaí she didn't know at all, except by name.

There was a knock at her door and when she looked around she saw that it was James Gallagher, the forensic accountant, carrying a briefcase.

'Sorry to drop in on you without warning, DS Maguire. Something's come up and I thought I should show it to you in person, instead of emailing it. I was coming in to the city in any event to buy myself some new ledgers.'

'Please, sit down,' said Katie. 'Would you care for a cup of coffee in your hand? I think I'm beginning to come down from my last caffeine high.'

'A glass of water would be grand, thanks. It's fierce dry work, accountancy. Except for this.'

He sat down on one of the couches under the window, snapped open his briefcase and took out three sheets of paper, stapled together and covered in a clear plastic sleeve, and then a single sheet, also covered in a clear plastic sleeve.

'These were sent down to me from Harcourt Square late last night, by courier. As you know, we've had seventy-three books of Jimmy Ó Faoláin's accounts to go through, and we have a fair few to go yet. We're still struggling with the code he used to identify his clients, but we've called in a cryptologist, Dr Heffernan from Trinity College, and he's reasonably sure that he can crack it.'

Moirin came in and Katie asked her for a cappuccino and a bottle of Ballygowan water. After she had gone, James Gallagher passed the sheets of paper to Katie with the air of a man who has concluded an important peace treaty. 'Those first three pages were found between the pages of Jimmy Ó Faoláin's second-to-last accounts book.'

Katie took them and read the first page.

'It's his will,' she said.

'That's certainly what it looks like, and it supersedes by three years another will that we found in his safe. If you look on the second page you'll see that in the event of his death, he has bequeathed his entire estate, after any outstanding tax liability has been paid to the Revenue, to a certain Ms Viona Caffrey, of Mayfield.'

'She was his girlfriend. He bought her heaps of jewellery but when I questioned her she told me that he never gave her much in the way of money.'

'He has now he's dead. Well, according to this will he has. But there's a number of spelling errors in it. There's one example – 'stirpes' is misspelled as 'stripes'. Most unusual for a solicitor of this calibre. And compare the signature here with his signature on that other page. That's from a contract he drew up early in 2017 with Doherty's Insurance.'

'The signature on the will is much thicker, isn't it, as if he was pressing hard and writing very slowly. And the "F" isn't nearly so curly, on the will.'

'We had a graphologist examine it yesterday afternoon – the usual fellow we use in cases of serious fraud. He has no doubt at all that the signature's a forgery, and not even a very good forgery. Just to make sure, my colleague contacted the solicitor's office and they confirmed that the last will they drew up for Jimmy Ó Faoláin was the will that we found in his safe.'

Katie handed the papers back to him. 'The plot thickens,' she said. 'This means that even if Viona Caffrey didn't shoot him herself, she knew in advance that he was going to be killed.'

James Gallagher nodded. 'You'd be amazed how many fake wills we've seen after wealthy people have met an untimely end. It's not necessarily proof that the beneficiaries of these wills were the ones who did away with them, but it goes to motive.'

Katie couldn't help thinking about her father. If Viona Caffrey had forged Jimmy Ó Faoláin's will, there was a strong possibility that she had hired a hit man to shoot him, and that Katie's father was completely innocent. Viona had been given her own key to the house, and she could easily have had it copied so that the hit man could let himself in without damaging the lock.

She began to feel guilty about taking her father's gun. He was her father, he was a former Garda officer, and he was the most sincere and trustworthy man she had ever known. She had enlisted into the Garda herself because she had respected him so much. None of her sisters had shown any interest in carrying on the family tradition, and she had seen that he was sorely disappointed about that, even though he tried not to show it.

James Gallagher held up the papers and said, 'I'll be taking these directly down to the Technical Bureau to have them examined. You have fingerprints and DNA from Viona Caffrey, I assume?'

'Of course, James. If she wrote this will herself, we'll soon know it.'

'Well, you know what they say, DS Maguire. Where there's a will there's a way.'

When he saw the expression on Katie's face, he added, 'Joke.'

Forty

When Michael Ó Doibhilin walked in through the door of the Halfway Bar, Seamus Twomey held up his left wrist and pointed to his watch.

'You're late, sham. I thought I told you to be here at eleven-thirty sharp.'

'Burst water main on Blarney Street,' said Michael, sitting down. He didn't mind giving an explanation but no matter how much of a hold Twomey had over him, he wasn't going to apologize.

Gwenith said, 'You look beat out there, Mick. Had a rough night, did you? You should have stayed over with me. If you couldn't sleep you could at least have made yourself useful.'

She was wearing a purple roll-neck sweater and the roll-neck was competing with her fat white double chins.

Douglas Quinn was poking away at his iPhone, and only lifted his eyes to look at Michael once. Hoggy was sitting next to him, with his arms folded over his belly and his eyes closed.

'The Swansea ferry gets into Ringaskiddy at one-fifteen,' said Seamus. 'Our man is driving a white rental van from Northgate. It's full of carpets but of course it's full of Persians too. We just want to make sure that it gets through the dock without being searched.'

'Sure like,' said Michael. 'I've already rung my friends in the customs and they know what to expect. You'll have no trouble at all, so long as they get a couple of rounds of drinks out of it.'

Seamus dug into the pocket of the donkey jacket hanging over the chair behind him. He pulled out a folded manila envelope and passed it over the table.

'There's a grand in there. That should keep their sniffer dogs away all right.'

Michael took the envelope and tucked it inside his jacket. As he did so, somebody clapped a hand on his shoulder and said, 'Well, now! Look who it isn't!'

He looked up to see Sergeant Boyle, who usually manned the front desk at Anglesea Street. He was one of those middle-aged men who looked as if they worked out regularly, with bulging biceps, close-cropped grey hair and a head like a football.

'Surprised, are you, Detective Ó Doibhilin?' he grinned, showing two canine teeth missing. 'Not half as surprised as I am, head, seeing you here. Stall it for a moment while I fetch the drinks over.'

He went over to the bar and came back with pints for Seamus and Douglas and Hoggy and himself, and an apple poitíni for Gwenith. 'Do you fancy a scoop yourself, Detective? I can't keep on calling you Detective – it's Mick, isn't it?'

'That's right – Mick the Dick,' Seamus put in.

'I'm Christy,' said Sergeant Boyle. 'You're a detective… so you must have guessed that my dad was mad keen on hurling. If Christy Ring had been a candidate for Pope, my dad would have been the first one to vote for him.'

'I'm okay for a drink for now,' said Michael. 'I don't want to turn up at Ringaskiddy smelling of alcohol.'

Christy dragged over a chair and sat next to him. 'I'll be coming along with you to meet the shipment. Not that Seamus doesn't trust you now, after your performance yesterday with the chainsaw. I wish I'd been there to see it but I was on duty.'

Michael said nothing. He was still disorientated by seeing the familiar face of the Garda desk sergeant sitting in this noisy pub with two of the most notorious drug-dealers on the Northside. This was an officer he waved to, almost every morning, and exchanged comments about the weather.

Seamus said, 'Mick? What's the latest craic about Farry and Vincent?'

Michael shook his head. 'I've been given a few days' sick leave, so I haven't heard. They'll be preparing the book of evidence against them, and I may have to go in again and answer some more questions.'

'To which you'll be answering "no comment"?'

'I won't be pointing the finger at you, if that's what you mean.'

'Good man yourself. I can tell you this, sham, I trust a bent cop ten times more than I trust anyone else. A bent cop knows the law inside out, so he knows what he can safely get away with, but on top of it all he has so much to lose if he gets caught. And it's no fun at all for a cop if he gets banged up in prison. He's lucky if he only gets boiling water poured down his throat.'

Gwenith said, 'When you come back, maybe you and me could go round to my place and you could pretend that you're Tommy again, like.'

Seamus raised an eyebrow at Michael, as if to say, *You'd best give her what she wants, sham, or there'll be all kinds of bother.*

Once Christy had finished his beer, he slapped Michael on the shoulder again and said, 'Come on, head, let's get out the gap. We don't want to be late.'

They left the Halfway Bar and climbed into a silver Mercedes saloon parked on the pavement outside. A very fine rain had begun to fall so that the windscreen was misted over. Christy started the engine and pulled away without making a signal, and a driver who was coming around the corner of Baker's Road blew his horn at him. Christy stopped, put down his window, and gave the driver the finger.

'Have some fecking consideration next time, you wanker!' he shouted out. Then he put down the window and drove off, chuckling. 'Wanker,' he repeated, with some relish.

They drove in silence for a while, and then Christy said, 'I know what you're asking yourself, Mick. I don't have to be a fecking mind reader.'

'Oh, yes. What's that, then?'

'You're asking yourself, how did a fine upstanding Garda sergeant get himself all tied up with two pieces of shite like Seamus Twomey and Douglas Quinn, not to mention that fat gee Gwenith.'

Michael said nothing, but kept on staring out of the window.

'If you want to know, my middle son, Brendan, got himself on heroin. You wouldn't believe the state he was in. He started robbing to feed his habit – first from me and his mam and then from his friends and then from shops and even breaking into houses. He still ended up owing his dealer a whole heap of grade, and when he couldn't pay him his dealer had him beaten up so bad that he nearly died.

'Freddie, his dealer's name was. Freddie Finn.'

'I've heard of him,' said Michael. 'A real piece of work, he was. He's not around now, though, is he?'

'No, he isn't, and I'll tell you for why. I wanted to haul him in for assaulting Brendan but Brendan begged me not to because there was no proof at all that it was Freddie who ordered him beaten. Freddie would have cut Brendan's mebs off if I'd lifted him because he knew I was his dad. So I went to Seamus Twomey who I knew hated Freddie Finn's guts. I paid Seamus and Seamus said he'd deal with Freddie and he did, because Freddie was never seen or heard of again and still to this day nobody knows what happened to him.

'But after that day Seamus started asking me for favours and what could I say? I'm totally stuck, Mick, just like you. I thought that Seamus would only have Freddie knocked around a little, but there's no question he must have had him topped, and I'd paid him to do it. You cut that bonner's head off, so you're in the same position as I am. If we don't dance to Seamus's tune, you and me, we're both totally buggered.'

They drove into the Ringaskiddy ferry terminal, and parked. It was only ten to one, and the Swansea ferry hadn't appeared yet, so they went into the cafeteria and sat down. Christy bought a Coke and drank it straight out of the bottle.

Michael was unsure if he should ask Christy about the whistle-blowers. If it was Seamus who had arranged for them to be beheaded, Christy might go back and tell him that he was being too inquisitive. Was he totally beholden to Seamus, or deep down did he still honour the solemn declaration that he had made when he became a garda, to uphold the law, and not to become a member of any secret society?

The ferry came sliding in beside the terminal building. Michael said, 'What do you think it's like, having your head cut off?'

Christy swigged his Coke and shrugged. 'You're talking about them whistle-blowers?'

'Well, and the bonner, too.'

'The whistle-blowers, what did they expect? You don't rat on your fellow gardaí, no matter what they've done.'

'Kind of extreme, though, cutting their heads off, and sticking those whistles down their necks.'

'We could have given them a beating but what good would that have done? They still would have gone up to Dublin and testified. And we needed to scare off any more of them, to stop them from squealing.'

We? thought Michael, but then he said, 'Sure like. I hadn't thought about it like that. It's all a question of loyalty, isn't it? You can't run a police force if everybody's constantly sneaking on everybody else.'

'Spot on. There'd be no morale, like, no working together, no trust, no nothing. That's not the Garda Síochána that I signed up for. And I saw that DS Maguire is thinking of ratting on us, too. I always thought she was straight as an arrow.'

'She'd better watch out that she doesn't lose her head,' said Michael, trying to sound light-hearted about it.

Christy took another swig of Coke. 'Too fecking right, head,' he said, and stood up. 'Come on, they're unloading the vehicles now.'

*

Outside, in the rain, Michael saw his customs friends in their caps and their yellow high-viz vests, with two bedraggled springer spaniels sitting on the wet concrete beside them.

'Mannix, Kyran, how's the form, lads?'

Both officers were about the same age as Michael, and Michael had once played football with Kyran and dated his sister. Kyran had introduced him to Mannix in the pub after one of their games. Kyran was short and squat and Mannix was tall with a prominent nose, like a human flamingo. Kyran was always teasing him that his nose was so long he could smoke when he was under the shower.

'What are we looking for?' asked Kyran. 'Or rather, what are we *not* looking for?'

'A white van from Northgate rentals,' said Christy. 'There's nothing class A in it, so you don't have to be bothered about that. Nobody's going to meet their Maker because of an overdose or get hooked for life. It's all medical supplies, antidepressants and stuff like that, but we're going to be selling them way below the market price and so we don't want to be paying any duty on them, like. You might technically call it smuggling but in truth it's more of a public service. There's hundreds of poor people in Cork who are fierce depressed but can't afford the market price of medication.'

Mannix looked around to make sure that no other customs officers were watching them. 'We're fierce depressed, aren't we, Kyran? And poor.'

'We can help you out there, then,' said Christy. 'We can't give you any pills, like, but we have another type of antidepressant. Mick? Do you want to give them the prescription?'

Michael looked around, too, and then handed Kyran the envelope that Seamus had given him. For one panicky second he thought that this might be a sting, and that Christy was going to tell him that he was under arrest for bribing Revenue officers, and that gardaí would come running across the dock to put handcuffs on him. But Kyran stuffed the envelope into the pocket of his high-viz jacket and said, 'That's grand, Mick. Do you know? I'm feeling better already.'

They stood and watched the procession of cars and vans coming off the ferry. The Northgate van was second to last. Kyran held on to his detector dogs while it drove close past them, although they wouldn't have been able to smell oxycodone and fentanyl in their bubble packs, even though oxycodone was chemically similar to heroin and fentanyl was over a hundred times more addictive than morphine. It was just in case the driver had something pungent in his pocket for his own personal use, and the dogs caught a whiff of it.

When the van had driven out of the terminal and disappeared, Christy said, 'Thanks for your help, lads. Much appreciated.'

'Any time,' said Mannix. 'Always glad to be of public service. That's what we're here for.'

They drove back to the Halfway Bar. Gwenith had drunk at least three apple poitinis by now and was shouting obscenities at another woman on the other side of the bar.

'You brasser! You fecking brasser! You'd fecking flah anyone, you would, so long as they still had a pulse and twenty yo-yos!'

When Michael and Christy came in and sat down, though, she stopped shouting and linked arms with Michael and snuggled up close to him.

'You may be a lying bastard, Mick, but I love you. I love your mickey, Mick. You have the best mickey I've seen since the last mickey I saw.'

'Don't mind her,' said Seamus. 'How did it go?'

'Just like clockwork,' Christy told him.

Seamus reached into his donkey jacket again and took out a wad of €50 notes. Licking his thumb, he counted out ten for Michael and ten for Christy, and then pushed them across the table.

'I'll be wanting your help again on Thursday. We have another consignment coming in from Swansea.'

'I'm on duty Thursday,' said Christy.

'That's okay. I think I can trust Mick to handle it on his own-some, can't I, Mick?'

'Of course,' said Michael. 'For this sort of hourly rate, I'd work for you full-time.'

'Oh no, I need you in the guards, that's where you're going to be the most use to me.'

Michael went to the bar and bought a round of drinks and then came back and sat down next to Gwenith. She had quietened down now, but she continued to snuggle up to him and blow him sticky little kisses.

Michael was trying to listen to the conversation between Seamus and Douglas, but they had their heads together and were speaking low and quick. At the same time the woman Gwenith had been shouting at was laughing raucously and Gwenith herself kept tugging at his arm and saying, 'Let's have this one, Mick, and then we can go back to mine, what d'ye say?'

Michael thought, *What have I let myself in for? I joined this gang only to prise more evidence out of them and get my revenge for being abducted, and for Detectives Buckley and O'Brien being killed. Now I've ended up being a murderer myself, and drinking here with Gwenith in the Northside equivalent of the ninth circle of Hell.*

He caught Douglas saying, 'We can ask any price we like, boy. I tell you, they'll pay anything.'

He tried to catch who 'they' were, and what 'they' would pay 'anything' for, but Gwenith tugged his arm again and said, 'Come on, Mick, I'm feeling really rampant. Finish up your pint and let's go.'

Michael and Gwenith stood up, although Gwenith was already so drunk that she lurched heavily against the table and almost spilled everybody's drinks.

Seamus winked at Michael and said, 'You make sure you take care of her, Mick, and give her everything she asks you for. Fetch her back here in a good mood, okay?'

Michael said nothing but gave him the ghost of a smile and helped Gwenith to stagger across the bar and out of the front door. Fortunately he had found a parking space only a short distance up the shopping parade and so he was able to help her up to his Opel Astra, open the passenger door and squeeze her in. Her left leg he had to pick up like a butcher lifting a leg of beef and force it into the seat-well. He didn't even attempt to fasten her seatbelt for her.

'I can't wait for this,' slurred Gwenith, as they drove along Cathedral Road. She pushed her hand down between Michael's thighs and gave him a squeeze that made him yelp.

'Gwenith, I'm driving!'

'You will be in a minute, boy, I promise you that. This is the best way to spend an afternoon ever fecking invented!'

Michael parked outside Gwenith's flat on Sprigg's Road and almost had to carry her across the pavement and in through the front entrance. When they reached her flat she spent almost a minute fumbling for her keys and after she had spent another half-minute jabbing vainly at the lock, Michael eventually took the keys from her and opened the door himself.

'That poitini,' she said, as she reeled along the hallway towards the bedroom. 'I'm sure they spiked it with something, do you know what I mean?'

'How many did you drink?' Michael asked her.

'I don't know. Maybe five, like.'

'I think that accounts for it, then. That's about the same as drinking ten vodkas.'

'What are you, some kind of fecking ankohol expert?'

She barged in through the half-open door of her bedroom, tottered over to the unmade bed and fell face-down on to it, still holding on to her handbag. Michael stood next to her, wondering what he ought to do next, but then she started to snore.

'Gwenith?' he said, quietly.

She didn't answer, and when he leaned over he saw that her

eyes were closed and her lip was lifted into a snarl against the duvet cover. She was deeply asleep.

'Gwenith?' he repeated, but this time he whispered.

He left her snoring and went through to the living room. It was even more chaotic than the last time he had been here, with heaps of clothes on the couch waiting to be ironed, and a takeaway Chinese food container on the floor, with the dirty spoon still in it. The curtains were still drawn and there was an airless smell of food and cheap scent and sweat.

Expertly, as quickly as a burglar, Michael searched through the chest of drawers at the far end of the room, and the small drawers under the side tables. He lifted up the heaps of clothes and even kneeled down on the floor and looked under the couch. All he found under there was a three-week-old copy of the *Echo* and a large pair of black lace knickers with frayed elastic.

He went back to the bedroom door to make sure that Gwenith was still asleep, and then he searched the small spare room, which was cluttered with suitcases and cardboard boxes and folded blankets. He opened all the suitcases and all the cardboard boxes and lifted the blankets to make sure that nothing was hidden between them.

After checking again that Gwenith was still snoring, he searched the kitchen. In the cutlery drawer he came across a hypodermic syringe and three new needles, but no drugs. The cupboards were stacked with an odd assortment of plates and mugs, and when he looked in the fridge in the corner he found that it was crowded with leftover takeaway meals and strawberry yogurts that were well past their sell-by date.

He opened the freezer compartment underneath the fridge and when he realized what was inside it he pressed his hand over his mouth in shock. There was no food in there, apart from a few stray frozen peas embedded in a layer of ice in the bottom. All the shelves had been removed, and the freezer was packed from top to bottom with white plastic Tesco bags. There were six of them, and through the frost that covered one of them, Michael could distinguish the contours of a human face.

He wrenched one of the bags out of the freezer, set it down on the kitchen counter and tried to unwrap it. The plastic was frozen solid, so he took a knife from the cutlery drawer and with four or five crunches he managed to cut it open. Inside, with his eyes still open, his eyelashes crusted with ice, was the severed head of Sergeant Lacey.

He didn't need to unwrap the other bags to know who they were.

He took out his phone and took pictures of Sergeant Lacey's head and the other heads that were still crammed inside the freezer. As he was starting to wrap up Sergeant Lacey's head he heard Gwenith calling out, 'Mick! Mick! Where the feck are you, Mick? Are you still here?'

As fast as he could, he bundled up Sergeant Lacey's head and wedged it back between the other heads. He shut the freezer door, dropped the knife back into the cutlery drawer and swept the few white crumbs of frost off the kitchen counter. Then he opened up one of the cupboards, took down a blue-and-white mug and filled it with water from the tap.

Gwenith appeared in the kitchen doorway, holding on to the door frame to keep herself upright.

'Oh, there you are, Mick. What are you doing in here, for feck's sake?'

'I was thirsty, that's all. Just having a drink of water.'

'I don't feel so good, Mick. In fact I feel like shite. I'm sure somebody spiked my poitinis.'

'Why don't you go and lie down? I think you had too many, that's all.'

'I forget. You're the ankohol expert. But I was never craw sick like this before.'

'Maybe it's something you ate. Do you have any Alka-Seltzer?'

Gwenith held her stomach and let out a sharp falsetto burp. Before she could answer, she vomited all over her purple sweater, her double chins rolling with every regurgitation. She vomited again and again, until the front of her sweater was plastered with shining beige sick, and the kitchen floor was spattered with it, too.

'What in the name of God have you been eating?' Michael asked her.

She heaved, and heaved, and her double chins rolled in accompaniment with every heave. At last she managed to croak out 'Nando's'.

There was nothing that Michael wanted to do more at that moment than step over Gwenith's vomit, leave the kitchen and walk straight out of the front door, never to come back. But the deep-frozen heads of five gardaí were packed in the freezer right behind him, and he had to find out who had killed them. It was unlikely to have been Gwenith herself, but if he contacted Anglesea Street and had her arrested here and now, she wouldn't be legally obliged to say who had.

Apart from that, there was no certainty that they would find sufficient forensic evidence on the whistle-blowers' heads to arrest and convict Seamus Twomey or any of his gang. That would mean that the deaths of Detectives Buckley and O'Brien and the young Punjabi he had beheaded had all been in vain, not to mention the trauma he had suffered when he was abducted, and the break-up of his relationship with Eithne. If his whole life was going to be messed up, he didn't want it to be messed up for no purpose.

He helped Gwenith into the bathroom, wiped off the worst of the vomit with a hand towel, and then took off her sweater and her bra. She was snivelling and sniffing and her shoulders were shaking.

'All we need to do is clean you up and then you can have a couple of hours' kip,' he told her, trying to sound soothing. 'You'll feel ten times better when you wake up.'

She sat on the edge of the bath while he tugged off her black yoga pants, her bulging pantie girdle. Then he helped her to clamber into the bath and sit there while he used the hand-held shower to wash her. He tried not to think about anything at all while he was lifting up each heavy breast and spraying it, and then spraying into the crease across the top of her stomach. Gwenith retched loudly and he prayed that she wasn't going to bring up any more peri-peri chicken.

After she was washed he struggled with a lot of squeaking and thumping to get her out of the bath, and then he wrapped her in a towel and dried her, as if she were an enormous baby.

'Do you know what, Mick?' she blurted, as he lifted a nightgown over her head. 'You're a shite in nining armour. I mean a knight—'

'I know what you mean, Gwenith,' said Michael. 'Now get yourself into bed and shut your eyes and get yourself some beauty sleep. I'm sorry I can't stay with you but I promise we'll have some rare old fun another time. Okay?'

'You're sure you can't stay? Couldn't you just cuddle me for a while?'

She climbed into bed and Michael lay down beside her on top of the duvet. He put his arm around her shoulders and gave her a couple of reassuring squeezes. In a strange way that he couldn't understand, he not only loathed her, and found her physically disgusting, but he felt sorry for her. He wondered how different she might have been if she had been brought up by another family apart from the Twomeys, somewhere else apart from Gurranabraher.

He thought about those frozen heads, too. Why had their killers kept them here? However vengeful they had felt towards those whistle-blowers, they must have known what pain and grief their families would suffer if they couldn't bury them with their heads.

Then he thought about Sergeant Christy Boyle. How believable was his story about why he was helping Seamus Twomey and Douglas Quinn? Had he really had a drug-addicted son, and had Seamus Twomey really organized a hit to kill Freddie Finn?

Freddie Finn had disappeared off the Cork drug scene all right, but maybe he had simply taken himself away to somewhere less competitive, like Scotland, or the north of England. And Michael couldn't believe that Christy was the only Garda officer who was behind the whistle-blowers being eliminated.

After about ten minutes, Gwenith fell asleep again, and started to make rubbery puffing noises with her lips. Michael lifted his hand away from her and eased himself off the bed. Before he left the flat, he went into the kitchen and took one last look at the heads in the freezer.

He crossed himself and said, 'Rest in peace. They've taken your earthly bodies apart, those bastards, but your souls will be whole in Heaven.'

Forty-One

Katie was writing an outline of her report about the Romanian brothel when Chief Superintendent MacCostagáin came wandering into her office carrying a cup of coffee.

She looked up from her computer screen. She could always tell when senior officers like Assistant Commissioner Magorian and Denis MacCostagáin had something serious to say to her. They would appear in her open doorway trying to look nonchalant, as if all they wanted to do was complain what a hoor of a day it was and you wouldn't put a dog out in it. Then they would say 'By the way, Kathleen—' and out it would come.

'You want me to drop this disclosure,' she said, even before Denis MacCostagáin could open his mouth.

'Oh,' he said, trying not to look surprised. 'The thing of it is, Kathleen, I'm not only concerned for our public image, I'm worried about your safety. Michael Pearse has told me that he's arranged for you to have protection, but I'm still not happy about you putting yourself in jeopardy like this, especially when there's no real need for it.'

'Sir – gardaí are demanding regular sex as a bribe for not arresting two brothel-keepers. And you're suggesting that we should let them carry on?'

'It's not like it's such a great offence, and it's going to cause more bad feeling than it's worth. We're doing everything we can here at Anglesea Street to restore our public image and this disclosure of yours is the last thing we need.'

'I'm sorry, sir, but I can't turn a blind eye to it. We can't expect the public to abide by the law if we don't.'

'Kathleen, I'm worried for you. This could be your last chance.'

Katie sat back in her chair and frowned at him. 'What exactly does that mean?'

'It means only that you should be after thinking twice about going ahead with this. If you can tell me the names of the officers who've been visiting this brothel, I'll tell them that I'm wide to what they've been up to and give them all down the banks. That should put a stop to it. I could even threaten to tell their moths what they've been doing.'

'I don't think we should be using blackmail to discipline our officers, sir. And I believe this needs to be reported at the highest level so that every member of the force gets the message that our conduct has to be exemplary, from the Commissioner down to the Garda Reserve.'

'Aren't you being a little too sanctimonious, if you don't mind me saying so?'

Katie didn't answer that. She didn't want to tell him that she wouldn't normally have bothered to pursue a disclosure like this. As he had suggested, she would have thought it enough to repri-mand the gardaí who had been expecting sex from the brothel-keepers – maybe suspending them for a while or docking their pay.

'If that's all, sir,' she said, turning back to her computer screen and poising her hands over her keyboard.

'It is for now, yes,' said Denis MacCostagáin. 'I'm still hoping that you'll change your mind. Let me know if you do.'

'Yes, sir.'

Denis MacCostagáin stood in front of her desk for a while, holding his cup of coffee, but then he turned around and left. Katie could see Moirin standing in her office doorway, watching him go. She had obviously heard their disagreement and she gave Katie a quizzical look. Katie lifted her hand to her and said, 'Don't worry, Moirin. Everything's fine. The chief superintendent is feeling thick today, that's all.'

Although she was blaming Denis MacCostagáin for being grumpy, their conversation had left her feeling more than a little upset. She didn't want to argue with him, because he had always supported her even when he didn't completely agree with her, but she couldn't think of any other way to carry out this investigation effectively. The days were going by and the media were asking questions about her competence in handling this case and she was still nowhere near to closing it.

She carried on typing, but she had hardly written more than half a page when her phone rang. It was Riona Lacey, Sergeant John Lacey's widow, and she was in tears.

'Oh, dear God,' she sobbed.

'What's wrong, Riona? Take a deep breath and tell me. Is Aidan okay?'

'Aidan – Aidan's not too bad – he'll keep his right foot and the doctors say that he'll be walking again in three or four months. But it's not Aidan I'm ringing you about. It's John.'

She started sobbing again and Katie had to wait patiently while she recovered herself. At last she said, 'I've had a phone call. The fellow who was calling – he didn't give his name and he said that it would be no good trying to trace where he was ringing from.'

'What did he say?'

'He asked me when John was going to be buried and when I asked him why he wanted to know he said would I like to bury him complete.'

'What did he mean by that? Did he tell you?'

'Yes. He said I could have his head back, if I wanted it. I could hardly believe what he was saying, but he told me that he had John's head and that he could leave it for me in the Peace Park.'

Riona Lacey stopped talking for a few moments, and all Katie could hear was a mewling noise, like a kitten in distress.

Eventually, she managed to say, 'He told me he wanted ten thousand euros for it, in cash. He would give me instructions where to leave the money, and when he'd collected it, he'd take

John's head to the Peace Park and leave it under a bench by that statue of the onion seller.'

She paused again, and then she said, 'Where in the name of God am I going to find ten thousand euros?'

'Try to be calm,' Katie told her. 'The money won't be a problem. In fact, it could help us to catch whoever killed your John. What did this man sound like? Did he have an accent of any kind?'

'It wasn't easy to say, because he was kind of muffled, like he was talking through a handkerchief. But it didn't sound like Cork. I'd say more like Wexford or maybe Carlow.'

'Did he tell you how to contact him, once you'd got the money together?'

'He said he'd give me twenty-four hours and then he'd ring me again.'

'When is John's funeral?'

'Thursday I had it planned for.'

'Okay. We can raise the money for you all right but we'll attach a recording device to your phone and when he rings again we'll see if we can pinpoint where he's ringing from. It may be that he's using a disposable mobile phone that we're unable to trace, but we can try. We can also set up surveillance at the place where he tells you to leave the money.'

'But if you arrest him when he picks up the money – supposing I don't get John's head back? Supposing he won't tell us where it is?'

'We may not lift him then and there, Riona. We'll just have to see how things shape up. I promise you that on Thursday you'll be able to put John to rest in one piece.'

'I wish I could believe you, DS Maguire. I really do.'

'I'll be sending a phone technician round to your house right now, and I'll start making arrangements to get hold of the cash. If you have any more calls, Riona, get in touch with me immediately – either me or DI Fitzpatrick or DS Ni Nuallán. And if you happen to notice anything at all unusual, you know, like somebody hanging around outside in the street, please let us know about that, too.'

'Holy Jesus, DS Maguire, this is a nightmare. This is worse than a nightmare.'

'I know, Riona. But believe me when I say that we're doing everything we can to bring it to an end, and wake us all up.'

Katie rang the communications room up on the top floor of the station and organized an engineer to visit Riona Lacey's house and fit a recording device on to her phone. Detective Inspector Fitzpatrick was out of the station this morning so she called Kyna and told her about the ransom demand for Sergeant Lacey's head.

'I'll bet that's only the first,' said Kyna. 'They'll be ringing all of those whistle-blowers' families, demanding money to get their heads back. Five heads at ten thousand euros a head.'

'I'm sure they will. But for now, can you go to see Denis MacCostagáin and tell him about Riona Lacey's call, and then can you ask him to authorize a withdrawal of ten thousand euros in hundred-euro notes.'

Kyna hesitated, and Katie guessed what she was thinking: *This is fierce important, this demand for money to get Sergeant Lacey's head back, why doesn't Katie tell Denis MacCostagáin herself?*

'The chief superintendent and I had a slight disagreement about my whistle-blowing,' Katie told her. 'I think he needs a little time to cool off before I talk to him again. You know what men are like. They can sulk for Ireland.'

'I'll get back to you so. If he bites my head off I hope you have enough grade to buy it back.'

'Not funny, Kyna. I'll talk to you after.'

Katie knew that sooner or later Bill Phinner would come up to tell her about the tests that their ballistics expert, Colm, had carried out on her father's pistol. But he didn't appear until she had finished the outline of her disclosure and was thinking of going across the road to the Market Tavern for a cup of coffee and a sausage sandwich.

'Going out?' he asked her.

She already had one arm in the sleeve of her coat. 'Will it wait until I've had something to eat?'

He gave her the slightest shake of his head. 'Colm's tested it now and it's the same pistol that was used to shoot Jimmy Ó Faoláin.'

Katie slowly took her arm out of her sleeve and hung her coat back up on its hook.

'There's no question about that?'

'None at all, ma'am. The striations match exactly.'

Katie sat down at her desk. She expected that Bill Phinner was waiting for her to tell him whose pistol it was, but she wasn't going to tell him yet. She wasn't going to tell anybody yet – not until she had a chance to talk to her father.

'Thank you, Bill. I'll come down and talk to you later.'

'There's one more thing, ma'am. We checked the pistol's registration mark against the database, as we always do. It's a police mark. We know who it belongs to, or at least who its original owner was. I assume that's how you got hold of it yourself.'

Katie couldn't stop herself from giving a quick, small shiver. 'I see. Well, you're right. It does still belong to its original owner, and yes, that *is* how I found it. Can I ask you please not to share this information with anybody else just yet? I need to go and talk to him myself.'

'I have to say that accounts for a lot,' said Bill Phinner. 'Whoever broke into that house and shot Jimmy Ó Faoláin was a professional, and knew exactly what he was doing.'

'I'm sad to say that I think I know what his motive was, too. Jimmy Ó Faoláin robbed any number of elderly people of their savings and their pensions, and my father was one of them.'

'I'm desperately sorry to hear that, ma'am. I don't know what else I can say. I wish I could say that Colm's made some kind of a technical error and it's not your old man's pistol after all. But I'm afraid he hasn't, and it is.'

He gave her a regretful smile, and then said, 'G'luck anyway. I'll talk to you later.'

Katie sat at her desk for almost five minutes, wondering what she should do. Her phone rang several times but she didn't answer it, and when Moirin came in to see why, she raised her hand and simply said, 'I'm not in, Moirin. Could you take any messages, please?'

She went into the small bathroom at the side of her office and stared at herself in the mirror over the washbasin. She was surprised to see herself looking so placid, as if she had nothing more to worry about than organizing this year's station sweepstake. How do you go about telling your own father that you've discovered that he's a murderer? And what do you do then? Handcuff him, like you do all murderers? Without this man, you wouldn't even exist. He brought you up, fed you, took you to school, played with you, sang with you, took you on holidays to Dingle and splashed in the surf with you, laughing. How can you now arrest him and lock him up in a cell?

She had her mother's face – her high cheekbones and her emerald-green eyes – and she had her mother's red hair, too. When she was a teenager, people often used to mistake Katie and her mother for sisters. But she shared her father's sense of public duty and her father's refusal to take the easy way out of any situation, no matter how much it cost her.

She went back to her desk and picked up her phone. She dialled her father's number and waited. It always took him a long time to answer.

'Katie?' he said. He sounded oddly querulous.

'Yes, Da, it's me. Will you be at home for the rest of the afternoon?'

'You want to come to see me, is that it?'

'Well, yes. I do.'

'I believe I know why, Katie. You're too much like me, that's your problem, if you can call it a problem.'

'I need to talk to you, Da, that's all.'

'It's about the gun, isn't it?'

Mother of God, he knows I've taken it. And he must have guessed why.

'Da—' she said, 'I just need to talk to you.'

'I was going to clean it this morning, Katie, but when I looked for it, there it was – gone.'

'I'm going to come directly down to Monkstown, right now. We can talk about it then.'

'Katie, with you being you, I should have guessed you would work out sooner or later that it was me. You're fifty times too clever by half.'

'Da – I'm going to put down the phone and jump straight in my car and come down to see you. Just stay there until I get there and then we can work things out. You're my father and you're my hero. You always were. Just don't think of doing anything stupid.'

Her father said, 'Wait, Katie – don't hang up yet. There's something you need to know.'

'Da—'

'No, shh, listen. It *was* me. You'll be recording this conversation so you can take this as my confession.'

'Don't do this over the phone, Da. At least let me come down and you can tell me about it face to face.'

'No, Katie. I find it easier like this. I don't want to see you looking disappointed in me. You were always my bar-of-gold, darling. You were the only one who joined the Garda, and look how brilliantly you've done. Detective superintendent – and I could only make inspector before I had to give it up.'

'Da, it wasn't your fault you had to quit.'

'That doesn't matter now. It's all water under the bridge. What matters now is that I shot Jimmy Ó Faoláin. I expect you've already guessed why, but if you haven't, it's because he persuaded me and my friends to invest all our money into this scheme called Equity Sunshine. He promised it was going to keep our money safe for the rest of our lives and steadily build up more and more

372

profits. Instead, he robbed us – robbed us blind of every last cent – and the way that he'd worded our agreement, there was nothing we could do about it.

'Almost all of us lost our houses and poor old Brian Cooney committed suicide. And what happened to the sainted Jimmy Ó Faoláin? Nothing whatsoever. Nothing. He was laughing all the way to the Cayman Islands.'

'Was it Brian's suicide that made you do it?' Katie asked him. She was beginning to get over the initial shock of him admitting that he was the murderer, and now she was trying to talk to him in a much more professional way. He had done what he had done, and nothing could bring Jimmy Ó Faoláin back to life, God forbid, so what her father needed was moral support and legal guidance.

'If you were affected by Brian's suicide, that could be a very strong mitigating circumstance when this comes up in court.'

'You could say that was the trigger,' said her father. 'Brian and me, we went back years. We were almost like brothers. But what really decided me was finding out that we could all get most of our money back.'

'Go on,' Katie coaxed him. She could sense how this investigation was all falling into place now, and what he was going to say next she could almost have recited with him, word for word. 'Exactly *how* were you going to get most of your money back?'

'I visited Jimmy six weeks ago to see if I could persuade him to refund at least some of our investments. He said absolutely not. The companies that he'd invested in had unexpectedly gone to the wall, and we'd lost everything. I pleaded with him. I said one of the investors in Equity Sunshine was an eighty-nine-year-old widow with nobody to take care of her, and now she was going to have to sell the cottage that she'd been living in for nearly seventy years.

'Do you know what he did, that Jimmy Ó Faoláin? He laughed in my face. He laughed in my face and said she probably needed new glasses. She should have read in the small print that she could lose all the money she'd invested as well as the charge against her property, and that Equity Sunshine couldn't be held legally responsible in any way at all.'

'Is that when you decided that he needed to be killed?'

'No, it wasn't. We were out on his terrace and he went inside to take a phone call. Probably some other poor old unsuspecting pensioner he was going to rob. Anyway, his girlfriend came out on to the terrace. She'd heard us rowing and when I told her why I said, "Do you know, I could kill him for what he's done to all the elderly folks who put their money into Equity Sunshine."

'She said, "Why don't you, then?" and I said, "What?" and she said, "Kill him." She said that he'd been treating her bad, slapping her around something brutal and forcing her to have sex when she didn't want it and stealing money out of her bank account. In spite of that, she was the sole beneficiary of his will, because he didn't have any children and all the rest of his relatives were allergic to him. She said he wouldn't give his money to charity either. He reckoned that if you were poor it was your own stupid fault for not working hard enough and *he* wasn't to blame if you were born in Africa, so why should he pay to feed you?

'Viona – that was his girlfriend's name – Viona said that she couldn't kill Jimmy herself or arrange to have him killed by a hit man. If she poisoned him it would be obvious at once who'd done it, and she'd never handled a gun in her life. But if *I* was to shoot him, nobody would ever guess it was me, and after she'd been granted probate she'd pay me back as much of the money that Jimmy had stolen from me as she could – and pay back all the other members of Equity Sunshine, too.

'A lot of the money is tucked away in offshore accounts where nobody can reach it, but I reckoned if I got even half of my investment back and I sold this house, I would have had enough for a decent bungalow and to live out the rest of my life in comfort.'

'So you decided to shoot him?'

'I wasn't in my right mind, Katie. I was grieving for Brian and

I was grieving for myself for losing this house where I lived for so long with your Ma. I thought that Jimmy Ó Faoláin was the devil incarnate, if you must know, and deserved to die. I look back on it now and I can't believe that it was me who did it.'

'That should help your case in court, Da. How did you get into the house?'

'Viona had a key cut for me. She also told me the alarm combination but as it turned out I didn't need it because the alarm wasn't switched on when I let myself in. I couldn't find Jimmy at first. I even went to his bedroom but he wasn't there. Then I heard him sneezing and blowing his nose and I knew where he was.'

'Viona had a key cut for you. That proves that she was an accomplice.'

'She hasn't given me any money yet. She said she didn't know herself where his will was, but his executors would come across it sooner or later, and as soon as she was paid she'd transfer the money into my bank account.'

'Da, the NECB accountants have been combing through Jimmy Ó Faoláin's books and they've found a will leaving all his money and all his worldly possessions to Viona Caffrey.'

'Well that's grand altogether. But it doesn't make any difference to me now, does it? I won't be needing any money where I'm going. And certainly not worldly possessions.'

'Look, Da, whatever you do, don't despair. I'm coming down to Monkstown now and we can work out the best way that we can handle this. You'll have to hand yourself in, and you'll be after requiring a first-rate legal representative. I can recommend Garret Delaney, who's been taking care of Conor for me.'

'Oh. Garret Delaney. I think I know him. How is Conor getting along, by the way?'

'I'll tell you all about it when I get down there. I shouldn't be longer than forty-five minutes if there's not too much traffic on the South Link.'

'There's no point, Katie.'

'Of course there's a point. You've killed a man but you'll be able to make some very convincing pleas in mitigation. You'll be able to say that Jimmy Ó Faoláin stripped you of everything you owned and worked for all your life. You'll be able to say that Viona Caffrey persuaded you to kill Jimmy on false pretences.'

'What do you mean, "false pretences"? She was going to give me my money back. She swore it.'

'That will was forged, Da. Jimmy Ó Faoláin never intended to give Viona a single cent.'

'What?'

'Even if she had managed to lay her hands on all his money, she was working some kind of fiddle with Finbar Foley – you know, the team manager from Rachmasach Rovers. I very much doubt if you and your friends would have had even a sniff of it. Anyway, most of it's tucked away in offshore accounts so nobody will ever be able to touch it, and any of his assets that we *can* manage to find will either go to the Criminal Assets Bureau or the Revenue Commissioners.'

Katie's father was silent.

'Da?' said Katie. 'Are you still there, Da?'

'She took me for a right head-the-ball, didn't she? Getting me to shoot your man so they could collect all his money but not get hauled in for it. Jesus.'

'We'll haul her in, Da, don't you worry about that. Now listen – I'm leaving Anglesea Street right this minute and I'll be with you before two-thirty.'

'Don't,' said her father.

'Da, I have to.'

'*Don't!*' he snapped. She had never heard him sound so angry since she had thrown all his best fishing flies on the fire when she was about three years old, just to see them flare up.

'Da—' But he hung up, and all she could hear was a continuous tone.

She pushed back her chair and stood up at once. 'Moirin!' she called out, lifting her coat off its hook. 'I'm going out now. It's urgent. I don't know how long I'll be but I'll ring you.'

'Do you want me to call your protection officer?'

'No time for that. If anybody wants to know where I am, tell them it's a family emergency. I'm going to see my father in Monkstown.'

'Is there anything I can do?' asked Moirin, anxiously. She had rarely seen Katie in such a panic.

'Yes, Moirin, there is. You can pray.'

Forty-Two

Traffic on the South Link Road was light and she drove as fast as she could, although it had started to lash down with rain now and some stretches of the road surface were flooded.

She drove down the N28 and then turned off for Raffeen Village and Castlefarm, speeding along Strand Road until she reached Monkstown. She turned into the driveway of her father's large green-painted nineteenth-century house, yanked on the parking brake and jumped out.

When she climbed up the steps to the porch, she saw that the front door was ajar. She pushed her way inside and called out, 'Da! Da? It's Katie! Where are you?'

There was no answer. She hurried into the living room but her father wasn't there. On the glass-topped coffee table there was a half-empty mug of tea and a plate with two shortbread biscuits on it and lying on the floor underneath the coffee table she saw his phone. When her conversation with him had ended, he must simply have dropped it on to the floor.

She went to the bottom of the stairs and called out again. There was still no answer so she ran upstairs and went from one bedroom to the next. Her father's bed was still unmade and his wardrobe door was open. His razor was lying by the side of the washbasin in the bathroom, and his damp towel was hanging over the side of the bath.

She hurried back downstairs. He wasn't in the house so maybe he had gone down to his shed at the end of the garden. After

Katie's mother had died he had retreated into it for hours at a time, telling her and her sisters that he was going to do a bit of carpentry, but one afternoon she had peeked into the window and seen him sitting hunched on a chair with a framed photograph of his late wife in his hands, and heard him talking to her.

Since he was stressed, there was every possibility that he was there, seeking solace. At least she prayed that he was.

She left the front door on the latch since she didn't have a key. *Dear God, I hope he hasn't done anything stupid. His car's still here so he couldn't have driven off anywhere.*

She went around the side of the house and down to the end of the garden. The rain was pattering on the laurel bushes and water was chuckling from the gutter around the roof of the shed. She tried the door but it was locked, and when she looked in the window she could see that he wasn't inside. So where on earth had he gone? What worried her more than anything was that he hadn't taken his phone with him.

She walked back up the garden and round to the front of the house. She was mounting the steps to the front door when she heard footsteps sprinting across the shingle driveway behind her. She started to turn around, but then she was rugby-tackled and thrown down sideways across the porch, so that her head was knocked against the corner of the wooden upright.

Stunned and winded, she tried to twist herself around and kick back at her assailant, but he was too big and too heavy and far too strong. He was wearing a black balaclava so that all she could see were his eyes and his mouth.

'Get off me, you gowl!' she panted at him, gripping the sleeve of his black leather jacket and trying to tip him back down the steps. But then she heard more footsteps crunching on the shingle, and two other men appeared. One of them seized her right arm while the first man took hold of her left, and between them they yanked her up on to her feet as if she were a little red-haired doll. The third man stood facing her and he was holding up a sawn-off shotgun.

'Detective Superintendent Maguire!' he said. 'You led us on a right fecking chase there, girl! We thought we'd lost you back at Carr's Hill.'

'Who are you?' Katie demanded. Her left temple was throbbing and her left shoulder felt bruised. 'Whatever you think you're doing, you're not going to get away with it.'

'That's what you think, my precious. We're the guardians of loyalty, that's who we are. We're the men who make sure that one Garda officer doesn't betray another. And the reason we've come after you is because that's what *you've* been planning to do – betray your fellows. Never mind that they're always loyal to you. Never mind that they'll always watch your back. You give them an order, DS Maguire, and those men will carry it out without question. And how do you repay them? You go scuttling off like a rat to the regional Disclosures Manager, that's how you repay them, squealing about their minor misdemeanours.'

Katie was thinking about her pistol, underneath her coat, but the two men on either side of her were holding her arms too tightly. If only they would free her right arm, even for a second. She was sure that she could tug out her pistol faster than the man with the sawn-off shotgun could react, and sawn-off shotguns were far from accurate.

She glanced towards the street. Her father's front garden was surrounded by high yew hedges, and her own car was parked between the open gates, so it would have been difficult for any passers-by to see what was happening, even if there had been any passers-by on this wet and miserable afternoon. Everybody in Monkstown was probably snug at home in front of the TV or else they were sitting in the Bosun having a long lunch-time scoop.

'Hoggy,' said the man with the shotgun. 'Have a sconce under her coat, head, will you? See if she's tooled up. And make sure you take her phone, too.'

Katie kicked and twisted herself from side to side, spraying up shingle like a fretful horse, but the man with the shotgun came up closer to her and pointed the twin muzzles less than ten centimetres away from her nose.

'I'd prefer not to blow your head off with this,' he said, hoarsely. 'But if you fecking give us any grief I will. I promise you. No hesitation at all. And both barrels together. Your brains will end up on Spike Island.'

Katie stopped struggling. She had heard an intonation in this man's voice that reminded her of what Riona Lacey had said. Not Cork. Maybe Carlow or Wexford. The accent in Carlow and Wexford was less sing-song than Cork, softer, and they spoke slightly slower there, with fewer 'likes' and less of that endlessly interrogative gabble, 'do you know what I mean, like?'

Hoggy must have been the one holding her right arm, because he reached across, unbuttoned her coat, and slid his hand inside. He patted her stomach suggestively and then he found the butt of her Smith & Wesson Airweight and yanked it out of its holster.

'Would you look at this beauty,' he said, holding it up. 'I wouldn't say no to one of these myself.'

'Keep that one, if you want it,' said the man with the shotgun. 'DS Maguire isn't going to be needing it again.'

'Christmas come early,' said Hoggy. He pushed Katie's revolver into his jacket pocket and then he patted her coat until he found her phone, and took that, too.

'We can talk,' said Katie.

'Oh, yes? And what can we talk about? How you've changed your mind about making your disclosure, so that we can give you your pop-gun back and we can all shake hands and off you go? And then what? As soon as you're safe back at the station, you'll be on the blower to Chief Superintendent O'Malley sneaking on your fellow officers, just like you always planned to.'

'You're a guard, aren't you?' said Katie.

'It doesn't matter what I am. I'm a man who doesn't like to see disloyalty, that's all. The Garda should be like the Three Musketeers, only multiply that by four thousand. All for one and one for all.'

'I won't go ahead with my disclosure,' said Katie. 'I'll give you my solemn word on that.'

The man tilted his shotgun over his shoulder. 'Do you know, if only I could believe you. But I've been given my orders, and I can't go back and say that I went soft and let you go. I can imagine the bollocking I'd get if I did that. I might even end up deader than you.'

'What orders?' Katie asked him. 'Orders from who?'

'Do you really want to know?'

'Of course I do. If somebody told you to kill me, I want to know who it was.'

The man with the shotgun shrugged. 'I don't suppose he'd be too narky about it, if I told you. You won't be ratting it to anybody else, will you, after all? But, no, I'm not going to tell you. I don't want you coming back at one of them séances and spilling the beans.'

'You realize that when you get caught for this you're going to be spending your entire life in prison? All three of you.'

'We're not going to get caught, DS Maguire, and that's the whole point. It's not like we're your normal everyday run-of-the-mill killers. We're protected. We have friends in high places – very high places – so nobody's ever going to be able to touch us.'

Katie said, 'Let me repeat that offer. I won't go ahead with my disclosure – not now, not ever. If you must know, I only announced that I was going to do it to bring you and your pals here out of the woodwork. It's worked all right, but, well – not the way I expected it to.'

'Sorry, but that doesn't wash,' said the man with the shotgun. 'If it hadn't worked out this way, you would have lifted us with no hesitation whatsoever and had us locked up for life, like you said. And I know your reputation, ma'am. You're the kind of cop who won't ever give up, ever, until you've nailed whoever you're after. So long as you're alive and walking the planet, we'll always be looking over our shoulders, and we don't want to be living like that.'

He lowered his shotgun and said, 'Hoggy – Patrick – let's get going. I'm growing quern tired of this discussion. It's worse than fecking Brexit.'

That convinced Katie. 'Quern' was a word that was commonly used only in Wexford. But having a clue to the real identity of the man with the shotgun would be of no use to her if she were dead, and she was sure now that she wasn't going to survive this abduction. It was a strange, flat, unreal sensation – nothing like the fear she had felt when she had been attacked by a drug addict brandishing a knife, or shot at, or had a car driven at high speed towards her along Maylor Street. At those times, her adrenaline had surged. As Hoggy and Patrick dragged her out of the front gate, she felt almost as if she were dead already.

Forty-Three

A silver Mercedes saloon was parked about a hundred metres up the road. Katie recognized the index mark as the same as the car that had been caught on Decky's CCTV. Once the two men had pulled her up alongside it, Hoggy opened the rear nearside door and pushed her roughly into the middle of the back seat.

The driver had lit a Johnny Blue while he was waiting for them and the interior of the car was so thick with cigarette smoke that it was almost unbreathable.

They drove back into the centre of Cork in silence, except for the driver coughing and sniffing. The rain had eased off and a ghostly silver sun was visible behind the clouds. They drove along the north side of the river and then turned up Lower John Street into Watercourse Road. They passed the Watercourse Road Garda station, and Katie saw two uniformed gardaí standing outside talking, but there was nothing she could do to attract their attention, wedged in between Hoggy and Patrick.

They reached the Maxol garage and parked outside the warehouse in the back. When he had climbed out, the man with the shotgun hid his weapon under his coat and took a look around the filling station forecourt before he tapped with his signet ring on the Mercedes' rear window to indicate that it was all clear for the rest of them to follow him.

He knocked seven times on the warehouse door, and it was opened up by one of Seamus Twomey's gang with dyed orange hair and a silver ring through his nose. Hoggy pushed Katie inside and she could immediately smell cigarette smoke and weed.

She could hardly believe the crowd that was gathered here. There must have been forty gang members here at least, with some of them sitting on top of piles of storage boxes to give them a better view. As she was pushed to the centre of the warehouse and looked around, she saw Seamus Twomey and Douglas Quinn, and Gwenith, too, and a few other petty criminals she recognized, but what shocked her was that Gwenith was arm-in-arm with Michael Ó Doibhilin.

Michael looked white-faced and strained, and when she turned to him he stared back at her as if he were trying to tell her something desperately important. He mouthed a few words but she couldn't understand what he was saying, and of course she couldn't go over and ask him what he meant. What was he doing here, with Gwenith Twomey of all people? Had he come here because Gwenith had forced him, or had he come here to enjoy seeing his detective superintendent executed? His behaviour after he had been rescued from his abduction had been so out of character – refusing to give evidence against Farry or Vincent or Seamus Twomey. Maybe they had brainwashed him into joining their gang, like a young Muslim being radicalized to join Isis.

The man with the shotgun laid down his weapon on one of the packing cases and then he went over and joined Seamus Twomey, pulling off his balaclava as he did so. Hoggy and Patrick took theirs off, too, and all three of them lit cigarettes.

'Good man yourself, Christy,' said Seamus. 'I'd say the Head Honcho owes you a bonus.'

'It's kind of a shame,' said Christy. 'She might be a holy Joe but she's a beour.'

Seamus Twomey came up close to Katie with a smile that was half indulgent and half contemptuous. He was only about the same height as she was, but his bald pink head was disproportionately large and it reflected the fluorescent lights on the ceiling.

His citrine eyes made Katie feel that she was being confronted by a reptile, or an alien, rather than a human being.

'You made a fecking hames of this one, didn't you, Detective Superwoman Maguire?'

'I've already told your man that I'll drop my disclosure if that's what you want. I don't know what else I can offer you.'

'It's too late now, darling. You know who we are now, and how we've been dealing with all them other whistle-blowers. Myself, I don't give a tinker's shite if you shades want to sneak on each other. Christy there, he takes all that loyalty malarkey kind of personal, but then he's a shade himself, so he would do. But so long as you mind your own beeswax and leave me alone, I'm easy. I'm only in this for the grade.'

'So who's paying you?'

'You don't want to know that. For starters, you don't want your last minutes in this life to be filled with disappointment, do you? You should be thinking of the good times you've had, do you know what I mean, like? You've had happy days, haven't you? Holliers, birthdays, Christmas – the first time some boy kissed you. Think of them!'

'You're sick,' said Katie. 'That's the only word I can think of to describe you. Totally, utterly, sick.'

Seamus pulled a self-deprecating face. 'I'm sorry you feel that way, Detective Superwoman Maguire. It would have been grand if you and me could have been buddies. But I suppose, under the circumstances, there's not too much chance of that.'

Hoggy called out, 'Gangway!' and the gang members who were standing in a semicircle behind Seamus suddenly stepped aside, so that Hoggy could come forwards with his chainsaw.

Katie closed her eyes. Inside the darkness of her mind, she asked God silently to forgive her for all of her sins – for all of the times she had lost her temper, or told a lie, or acted lustfully. She had already confessed how coldly she had treated her lover, John, after he had become disabled, and how she and Conor and Kyna had spent one passionate night together in a threesome, but now she confessed those sins again. She also confessed a sin she had never admitted to anyone, even God – that she had stolen Bláthnaid Byrne's charm bracelet when she was in high babies.

She heard Hoggy tugging at the chainsaw's pull cord and she opened her eyes. The expression on Michael Ó Doibhilin's face was one of absolute horror, but next to him Gwenith was grinning fatly, and every now and then she tugged him closer to her.

'You'd find it a whole heap more comfortable if you was to kneel down,' said Seamus. 'You could pretend to yourself that you were at Mass, now couldn't you – having a last final pray?'

Katie remained standing, so Seamus leaned closer to her and said, 'If you don't kneel down voluntary-like, we'll have to force you down, and we don't want to be looking like bullies now, do we?'

'Tell me who told you to do this,' said Katie. 'Even if I can't tell anyone here on Earth, I'll tell God, so that He never allows them into Heaven.'

'That's fierce vindictive of you,' said Seamus, in mock disapproval. 'If that's your intention, then I'm not going to tell you for sure. Christ on a camel!'

Abruptly, the chainsaw started up, drowning out whatever he said next. Hoggy came up to them, holding the chainsaw at a forty-five-degree angle, and letting it run at a burbling idle.

Katie knew now that there was no escape. All her life, this was the way she had been fated to die. Because she had worshipped her father so much, she had joined the Garda, and because of her dedication to the force, she had been promoted to detective superintendent. But every day of her life, every time she had climbed out of bed and dressed and gone to Anglesea Street, every time she had arrested a criminal or laughed at a joke or gone to lunch or kissed Kyna, it had all been leading to this.

She got down on to her knees, and pulled down the collar of her sweater. If she couldn't escape it, let it be over as quickly as possible. She had wondered if it would hurt, having her head cut off, and now she was going to find out.

Seamus laid a hand on her shoulder and over the sound of the idling chainsaw he called out, 'Mick! Here – Mick the Dick!'

Michael said, 'What?' and pointed to himself like Robert De Niro in *Taxi Driver*.

'C'mere, Mick! I think you should be doing the honours here, since you're a dick, and this lovely lady is the superdick!'

There was laughter around the warehouse, and several of the gang whistled their approval and kicked their heels against the packing cases they were sitting on.

Michael vehemently shook his head. 'No! No!' he said. 'Not her! I couldn't!'

'Come on, Mick! What do they call it? Poetic justice, that's it! This is your chance to get your own back for all the times she made you stand out in the rain doing some crappy job that came to nothing at all! Don't tell me she didn't make you do that!'

'No,' said Michael. 'I just couldn't.'

'But you're practically an expert now, Mick! The way you topped that bonner, that was savage!'

Hoggy revved up the chainsaw, grinning at Michael, and it was then that Seamus went over and nudged Douglas Quinn.

'I couldn't, honest,' Michael repeated, holding up both of his hands. But Douglas drew out his black Czech automatic pistol and pointed it at Michael's head.

'Your choice, Mick,' said Seamus. 'This'll prove how loyal you are, no question at all. If you do this for us, you'll be a fully fledged one-hundred-and-ten per cent member of *Fola na hÉireann*.'

'I thought I was already, Seamus. Jesus.'

'Let's say that you were a probationary member. Now – if you take off Detective Superwoman's head – there won't be any doubt at all. Patrick! Do you have that tin whistle, Patrick? You'd best not have lost it!'

Patrick came forwards and produced a shiny low-D tin whistle out of his jacket. Seamus took it and held it up. 'There, Mick! I'll even let you stick this down her neck! I bought this myself this morning – yes, *bought* it, and they're fecking dear, too, these whistles! Nearly a hundred yo-yos that cost me! I couldn't hobble it because the fellow in the shop was keeping such a close eye on me.'

Douglas continued to point his pistol steadily at Michael's head, his left hand supporting his elbow. Michael turned around to appeal to Gwenith, but Gwenith said, 'G'wan, boy! You can do it! If you do, I'll give you the time of your life tonight, I promise you!'

Michael hesitated for a moment, and then he held out his hands so that Hoggy could pass him the chainsaw. He revved it once or twice, without turning to face Katie, but then he squeezed the throttle to run it at full speed, and stepped up close to her. She glanced up at him only once, and then she leaned sideways a little so that she could see Douglas standing behind him, with his gun against the back of his head.

Mother of God, what choice does he have? What would I do, if I were him?

'Michael,' she said, although the chainsaw was roaring so loudly that she doubted if he could hear her. 'Michael, I forgive you.'

She closed her eyes again. She could hear and feel the chainsaw coming nearer, and she tilted her head back so that he would be able to make a clean, fast cut through her neck.

'*Ma'am!*' screamed Michael. She opened her eyes just as Michael dropped to his knees and swung himself around, so that the chainsaw's teeth tore into Douglas's right trouser leg and then ripped into his shin. Douglas let out a shriek of agony as the chainsaw cut through muscle and tendon and bone, and he pitched over sideways on to the floor. Blood showered everywhere, and all the gang members who had gathered around to watch Katie being beheaded stumbled backwards, shouting and swearing in shock.

Michael stood up, revving the chainsaw again and again. 'Who wants some of this?' he shouted, his voice almost hysterical. 'Come on – who wants some of this? Come and get it if you're brave enough!'

Douglas, at his feet, was writhing and keening, his right leg spouting blood all over the floor. Seamus shouted, 'Mick! Mick! For the love of God, Mick!'

At that moment, Katie saw that Christy had reached into his jacket and pulled out a police automatic. She looked around desperately and saw that Douglas had dropped his pistol when he had fallen to the floor, and it was lying right next to Michael's foot, glistening with blood. She shuffled herself over on her knees and picked it up.

She was too late. Christy fired at Michael, three times, hitting him once in the chest and twice in the shoulder. Michael sagged and then collapsed on top of Douglas. The chainsaw clattered down beside him, its chain stopped but its engine still running.

Christy clearly didn't realize that Katie had picked up Douglas's pistol, because he walked towards Michael, aiming his gun as if he intended to finish him off. Katie aimed at his heart and fired twice. Christy spun around wildly as if he had slipped on a patch of ice, and then fell flat on his back on to the floor.

Seamus shouted, '*Hoggy! Fecking shoot her!*' But Katie didn't hesitate, and while Hoggy was fumbling to pull her own revolver out of his jacket pocket, she closed one eye, aimed, and shot him once in the bridge of his nose. He swayed from side to side with a thin jet of blood pouring out from between his eyes, and then he tumbled on to the floor, kicking his legs up before he fell flat.

Seamus was looking around in panic, and Katie saw him suddenly focus on Christy's sawn-off shotgun, where he had left it on top of a packing case. Seamus started to sidle crabwise across the warehouse towards it, plainly hoping that Katie wouldn't notice him. Her ears were singing because of the noise from all of the gunshots, and when she shouted out, 'Stop, Twomey! Don't even think about it!' she could hardly hear her own voice.

Seamus must have heard her, though, because he stopped and raised his hands.

Katie looked around and realized how dangerous a situation she was in. Over thirty gang members now surrounded her, and although they were keeping themselves well back for the moment, because none of them wanted to be the next to be shot, they must be calculating that she had fired three times already, and it was unlikely that the magazine in her pistol had more than seven rounds in it.

There was one weapon, though, that wouldn't run out of ammunition. She transferred Douglas's pistol to her left hand, and even though it was awkward, and she nearly dropped the blood-slippery pistol while she was doing it, she picked up the idling chainsaw. Holding it up high in front of her, she carried it over to where Seamus was standing.

'Lie down,' she ordered him.

'G'way to feck. I'm not lying down.'

'Lie down, Seamus, or you'll be lying down because I've shot you and you'll be dead.'

Seamus looked around at his gang, but none of them yet had the courage to run forwards and tackle Katie. He lowered himself awkwardly down on to his hands and knees, and then he lay flat on his back, with his arms crossed over his chest like an effigy on a medieval tomb.

'You're a bitch, do you know that?' he spat at her, looking up at the ceiling. 'I've always thought you were a bitch. Detective Superwoman? More like Detective Slag-intendent.'

'Do you think I care, you scummer?'

'You won't fecking get out of here alive, I can promise you that.'

Katie pushed Douglas's pistol into her left coat pocket, but before any of Seamus's gang could see what she had done, she revved up the chainsaw and lowered it down between Seamus's thighs. She held the whirling teeth so close to his jeans that they tore some stray threads from his fly, and he jerked himself backwards and upwards and said, '*Christ!* What the hell are you doing, girl? Are you fecking mad or what?'

'I'm giving you a choice, Seamus, the same as you gave Michael Ó Doibhilin a choice. You can tell me who paid you to kill those five whistle-blowers, or else you can spend the rest of your life talking in a high voice and sitting down whenever you need a pooley.'

'You're fecking mad! You've fecking lost it!'

'You're the one who's going to lose it unless you answer me after the count of five! Who was it, Seamus? Who's this Head Honcho?'

Three or four of Seamus's gang had started cautiously to approach them, but when Seamus saw them he shouted out, 'No! No! Stay back! Leave her be! She's going to cut my fecking mickey off, else!'

Gwenith had obviously seen Christy's Sig Sauer automatic lying on the floor, because she had started to edge her way towards it, pointing her toes like a ballet dancer as if she thought that would make her less noticeable. Katie noticed her out of the corner of her eye and shouted, '*Gwenith Twomey! Don't even think about it!*' and she revved up the chainsaw to emphasize that she was serious. Gwenith lifted up both fat arms and stayed where she was.

Katie eased her grip on the chainsaw's throttle, but she still held it close to Seamus's fly. She leaned over him and said, 'I'm giving you no more time, Seamus. If you don't tell me right now who's been paying you to murder all these whistle-blowers, that's it. You're a eunuch.'

Seamus shivered, and then he lifted his head and gave her a name, although he spoke so quietly that she couldn't hear him, and she had to tell him to repeat it. When he did, she stared at him in shock.

'You're codding.'

Seamus shook his head violently from side to side. 'Do you honestly think I'd cod you when you're threatening to chop my fecking mebs off? Get serious!'

Katie looked around again. Seamus's gang were growing restless, and they were starting to inch towards her. There were three guns that they could go for – Christy's automatic, lying on the floor beside his body, Christy's sawn-off shotgun, still lying on top of the packing case, and her own revolver, which was still in Hoggy's jacket pocket. She couldn't hold this chainsaw over Seamus indefinitely, so how was she going to escape from this warehouse unscathed?

She looked over to Michael, lying face down on the floor. His eye was open but she could see that he was dead. Douglas Quinn was lying on his side next to him, and he was white-faced and unconscious. If he didn't receive immediate medical attention to stop his fibular and tibial arteries from bleeding, he would probably die too.

Katie was still calculating how she could drop the chainsaw, pull out Douglas's pistol and escape from the warehouse before one of the gang shot her, when she heard a tremendous banging at the door. There was a second's pause, but then it was repeated, and a voice shouted, 'Armed Garda! Open up! Open up *now!*'

The gang members panicked, like a roomful of terrified children. Some of them dragged packing cases over to the blacked-out windows, and tried to force them open, although they were locked. Others circled and stumbled around, not knowing what to do.

One of them managed to smash a window with an old steam iron that he had found on the floor, but he was too late. The warehouse door flew open and five gardaí in helmets and black flak jackets came bursting in, two of them holding machine guns.

'Armed Garda! Armed Garda!' they screamed, running towards the gang members. 'Lie down on the floor, all of you! Do it now! Face down, flat on the floor! You! Get down from the window! Flat on the floor!'

A sergeant came up to Katie, pointing a pistol at her. 'Switch off that chainsaw!' he screamed at her. 'Switch if off and drop it! Then lie down on the floor!'

Katie switched off the chainsaw and threw it aside, so that it bounced. Then she lay down flat on the gritty concrete floor, with her arms spread wide. She could identify herself after the officers had rounded up Seamus's gang and called for an ambulance for Douglas Quinn.

She turned her head sideways and saw Gwenith lying only three metres away from her, her bosom and her belly squashed against the floor so that she looked like a stranded porpoise. She was scowling at Katie and mouthing something that was more than likely a devastating curse.

At that moment, though, she heard Kyna's voice.

'DS Maguire? Ma'am? It's me. It's okay. You can stand up now! Here – let me help you.'

Katie took Kyna's gloved hand and climbed on to her feet. Her fingers were still bloody from Douglas's severed leg, and her coat was heavily bloodstained too.

Kyna was wearing a helmet and black body armour like the rest of the gardaí. She called over to the sergeant, 'It's all right, sergeant! She's here! DS Maguire!' Then, 'Jesus, Katie, look at you! Are you hurt?'

'No, thank God,' said Katie. 'This is what you might call peripheral damage.'

The sergeant came over, lifting up his tinted goggles. 'You're not injured, ma'am? Sorry for bawling at you, like. Procedure.'

'You're grand altogether, sergeant. I totally understand.'

Three paramedics entered the warehouse, and then more gardaí, all wearing high-viz jackets. One by one by one the gang members were told to stand up and file out of the warehouse.

'How did you know I was here?' Katie asked Kyna.

'After you went scooting out the station I kept trying to ring you. I must have rung five or six times and when you didn't answer I knew something was wrong. So I went upstairs and had the communications fellows check out Moirin Twomey's phone for me. They traced three calls from Monkstown, which of course was where you'd gone off to.'

'They followed me there, would you believe,' said Katie. 'My father wasn't at home and as I was leaving they jumped on me.'

'Well, I made a wild guess at what might have happened to

394

you,' Kyna told her. 'We pinpointed Moirin here to this building and not ten minutes after we'd done that the manager from the Maxol station rang 112 because he'd heard shots. He'd been in the army himself so he knew what they were. I've never seen an armed response team scramble so fast.'

'Well, thank God,' said Katie.

'Come here and I'll get you out the gap, ma'am.'

Katie looked down at Seamus Twomey. He was still on the floor, although he had turned himself over now and was lying face down. She thought of so many things she could say to him, but all that mattered now was what a judge said to him, once he had been convicted. The low-D tin whistle was lying on the floor beside him, and she bent down and picked it up.

'Take me to Anglesea Street, could you, please?' she asked Kyna.

'You're sure? I could take you to the Mercy for a check-up, if you like. Or home, if you'd rather.'

'No. Anglesea Street. I have some business I need to attend to. I'll tell you what it is on the way.'

Forty-Four

The desk sergeant stared at her as she walked across the reception area in her bloodied coat, with Kyna close behind her, but she went directly to the lifts and spoke to no one.

On the third floor, she asked Kyna to wait for her in the squad room. Then she walked along the corridor to Chief Superintendent Denis MacCostagáin's office and opened the door without knocking.

Denis MacCostagáin was standing by the window with his back to her, talking on the phone. He turned around when he heard her come in, and when he saw her he cupped his hand over the receiver and said, '*Kathleen?*'

'Surprised to see me, sir?' said Katie. She felt cold, and she was trembling, but she was determined to see this through. 'Or is it more like you're *shocked* to see me? Or *stunned*?'

She approached him, holding up her bloody hands and turning them this way and that. 'Who are you talking to, sir? Jerh O'Connor's, arranging my funeral? Aren't you getting ahead of yourself, sir? Jumping the gun, so to speak. Or should I say jumping the whistle?'

Denis MacCostagáin lifted his phone again and said, 'I'm sorry, Dan. I'll have to ring you back. Something's come up.'

'How right you are, "something's come up"!' said Katie. 'Somebody's risen from the grave to come and haunt you, except that she never quite made it to the grave.'

'Listen, Kathleen, I can explain everything. There's been a

fierce misunderstanding. No harm was ever meant to come to you. But you would insist on going ahead with that disclosure, and the Văduva gang would have taken me apart if their business had been forced to close down.'

'You mean their brothel.'

'Well, yes. But everything that was happening there – it was all between consenting adults. The customers wanted it and the women wanted it. There was nothing illegal and nobody was getting hurt.'

'Gardaí were blackmailing the women into giving them sex. That's illegal. Anyway, how much did the Văduvas pay you to get rid of me? How much did they pay you to cut off my head and stick this down my neck?'

She reached inside her coat and took out the low-D tin whistle, holding it up in front of his face until it nearly went up his nose.

'I was deaf and blind, wasn't I?' she said, her voice shaking. 'The Head Honcho had to be someone at the top level – someone who had the influence to do deals with all of the gangs who were going to be compromised by Justice McGuigan's tribunal. Garda O'Regan's lawyer actually suspected that it might be Frank Magorian, because he seemed to be so minted. But it was you – and because I trusted you so much, I missed the most obvious clue of all.'

Denis MacCostagáin shuffled over to his desk and sat down, looking up at Katie with an expression of pain and remorse and utter defeat.

'Apart from me and Stephen MacQuaid's security guards, only one person knew where those three whistle-blowers were being kept safe. That was you, sir.'

'Yes,' said Denis MacCostagáin.

'If I understand it right, you told any scumbag who was in danger of being exposed by a whistle-blower that you could have that whistle-blower silenced, for a fee. It didn't matter who it was. You'd arrange it for anybody who paid you. You weren't fussy if it was drug-dealers, or prison escort officers, or the prison managers who were fixing it for convicted criminals to go free. It could be car thieves and the gardaí who were purposely mislaying all the evidence against them. It could be the gardaí who were being accused of racism.

'You hired Seamus Twomey and Douglas Quinn to cut off those whistle-blowers' heads and stick tin whistles down their throats. You hired Seamus Twomey and Douglas Quinn to cut off *my* head and stick a tin whistle down *my* throat.'

'The Văduvas—' began Denis MacCostagáin.

'Oh, damn the Văduvas! You've been threatened by far more frightening gangsters than the Văduvas and stood up to them! What about the O'Flynns? They said they were going to blow up the whole station, with us in it!'

Denis MacCostagáin was silent. Katie went up to his desk and said, 'Why, Denis? Why?'

'Cutting off their heads... and the whistles. That wasn't my idea. Gwenith Twomey thought of that.'

'It's not important *how* they were murdered! They were *murdered*, and you arranged it, and you did it for money! I was within an inch of losing my own head today, and if it hadn't been for Michael Ó Doibhilin I would be headless and dead right this minute, with this whistle in my neck! And Michael was killed saving me!'

'I'm sorry to hear that. I liked Michael.'

'Oh, g'way to fuck! You're not sorry at all, are you? If you were sorry you wouldn't have arranged for any more whistle-blowers to be murdered after Garda O'Regan. You would have handed yourself in and confessed to what you'd done and you would have got down on your miserable knees and begged and *begged* the Lord to have mercy on you!'

Denis MacCostagáin suddenly reared up out of his chair.

'No! You're right! I'm not sorry! How did the Good Lord treat me? He took my dearly beloved wife away and left me alone! And how did the Garda treat me? I have to retire next year with a miserable pension that will hardly keep me in peat for my fire!

After all the years I've been slogging and slaving – after all the hours and hours of unpaid overtime I've put in – and yes, you're right – after all of the times that my life has been threatened, and I've been injured, and even stabbed!'

He came around his desk and stood over Katie and jabbed his finger at her as he shouted.

'No matter how badly the force treated me – no matter how much disrespect I had to put up with – I was always loyal! I never let down my fellow officers, and I never betrayed them, even if they bent the rules! And then these whistle-blowers come along, without an ounce of loyalty between them, and the whole force is on the brink of falling apart at the seams! I can remember a time when the public had the highest regard for the Garda. Now they spit on us, and I can't say I blame them.'

'Denis, you conspired to murder five innocent officers, and on top of that at least five other people have been killed, too – Stephen MacQuaid's security guard, a garda who was working with Seamus Twomey, Detectives Buckley and O'Brien and Michael Ó Doibhilin. The last I saw of him, it looked likely that Douglas Quinn was on the way out, too.'

'So what are you going to do about it, Detective Superintendent Maguire?' said Denis MacCostagáin, returning to his desk and sitting down again.

Katie took a deep breath. 'Denis Patrick MacCostagáin, I am arresting you for the murders of Sergeants Lacey and MacAuley, as well as Garda O'Regan, Garda Ó Grádaigh and Garda Wassan. You are not obliged to say anything unless you wish to do so, but whatever you say will be taken down in writing and may be given in evidence.'

Denis MacCostagáin nodded. 'That's it, then, isn't it? That's my life over. I should have known the very first day I saw you that you were going to be the death of me.'

'Don't expect me to feel sorry for you, sir, not in the slightest. You were nearly the death of me.'

Forty-Five

Katie called Superintendent Pearse and Detective Inspector Fitzpatrick and they came up to Denis MacCostagáin's office. Kyna came in too. They stood looking at him in silence as she explained as clearly as she could that she had arrested him, and why.

'I'm saying nothing,' said Denis MacCostagáin. 'I'm ringing my solicitor, that's all, and my daughter in Mallow.'

Superintendent Pearse escorted him down to the cells. When they had gone, Kyna said to Katie, 'Are you going home now? You need to.'

'Yes, I am. But once I've taken a shower and changed, I have to go out and find my father.'

'Do you want me to come with you? You still look shook.'

'Well, sure, I feel like the whole world's collapsed on top of me, to be honest with you. But I'll be grand.'

'Katie—'

'Don't worry, Kyna. I'm alive and we've found out who murdered all those poor whistle-blowers but there's still a heap of work to be done, and I'd like you to stay here. Robert – can you organize a search of Seamus and Gwenith Twomey's residences, and Douglas Quinn's, too. We have some heads to find, apart from a whole lot more incriminating evidence. I'll catch you after so.'

A young garda drove Katie home. He tried to chat to her, but she was still in a state of shock and she could only answer him with 'yes' and 'no' and 'I suppose' and after a while he gave up. He waited for her outside her house while she went in to take a quick shower and change her clothes.

Barney and Foltchain were happy to see her, although they sniffed suspiciously at the blood on her coat, and looked at her as if they were asking if she was upset about something.

'I'll be fine,' she told them, ruffling their ears. 'Once I find your granda, everything's going to be grand.'

How grand a day will this have been, arresting both my chief superintendent and my own father for murder? It's the worst nightmare I've ever had, except that it's real.

She would have to apply for a warrant to arrest Viona Caffrey and Finbar Foley, too, but she didn't want to do that until she had a full statement from her father. If she couldn't find him, the only evidence she would have against them for Jimmy Ó Faoláin's shooting would be the will that they had forged – and only if it could be proved by forensic examination that it was one or both of them who had forged it.

When she had showered and pulled on a thick black sweater and jeans, the garda drove her up to the ferry terminal and they crossed over to Monkstown. It was growing dark now, and she was beginning to feel bruised and exhausted. She sat in the car watching the lights along the embankment glide by, and prayed that she would find her father at home.

Her car was still parked in his driveway, and when she climbed the steps up to the porch she found that the front door remained open. She went inside but there were no lights on, and there was no answer when she called out his name.

The young garda was waiting for her when she came back out.

'Not at home?' he asked her.

She shook her head. 'His friend Blaithin might know where he is. She works up at the Roaring Donkey. Otherwise, I don't have a clue where he's gone.'

'Do you want me to drive you up there?'

'No, you don't have to bother. You get yourself back to the station. I can drive up there myself. If Blaithin hasn't heard from him, I'll contact Midleton and report him missing.'

'You're sure? If you don't mind my saying so, you look fair beat out.'

Katie managed a smile. 'Thanks, but I'll be okay. I think I'm getting my second wind. Or even my third.'

After she had taken the ferry back to Carrig View, she drove up Spy Hill to Midleton Street and parked outside the Roaring Donkey. The pub was noisy and bright and cheerful and she found Blaithin in the kitchen, grilling hamburgers.

'Have you heard from my Da?' she asked her, over the noise of frying. 'He's not at home and I'm worried he's gone missing.'

Blaithin frowned and gently touched the bruise on Katie's forehead with her fingertips. 'How did you get that, girl? That's a lump and a half, like.'

'Tripped and fell. But have you heard from my Da?'

'Not today. I'll be after seeing him this evening, though, to cook him some supper.'

'Blaithin, he's gone missing. He's not at home and when he went out he left the front door open.'

'Oh, you know your Da. He's always wandering off. He's fit as a fiddle these days but he does tend to forget which end of the sausage is which. I bet you'll go back over there and find he's come home already.'

What was she going to say? Blaithin, I've found out that he's a murderer? It was him who shot Jimmy Ó Faoláin?

She decided to tell her nothing for the time being. All she said was, 'Let me know if you hear from him, okay? You have my mobile number, don't you?'

'I will. And don't worry. He'll be okay. If he's not at home he'll be having a scoop somewhere, you mark my words.'

Katie drove home. She had thought about driving all around

Midleton and visiting the Ensign Tavern and the Bosun to see if her father was there, but she was too tired and trembly now and her vision was blurry from the knock on her head. As she soon as she arrived back home she rang Midleton Garda station and reported her father as missing, although she didn't tell them what may have led to his disappearance.

She emailed them a recent photograph of him and it brought tears to her eyes to see him looking so cheerful.

There was still no news of her father by the following morning, despite an intensive search by local gardaí and the Cork City Missing Persons Search and Recovery team. She went into the station early, and she had already caught up with an hour's work before Detective Inspector Fitzpatrick came in.

'They've all been processed overnight,' he told her. 'Seamus and Gwenith Twomey and their gang of scummers – thirty-three of them all told. Seamus and Gwenith are down in the cells along with some gowl called Brendan Horgan. Apparently he was the one who did the actual head-cutting. He denied ever owning a chainsaw but the garden centre in Frankfield have a record of one Brendan Horgan buying new chains for a Husqvarna 450 only six months ago. Bill Phinner's testing the chainsaw itself for DNA.'

'What about the rest of them?'

'Some of them we're holding for drug possession and carrying knives. The rest of them we'll be letting out on police bail.'

'And Denis MacCostagáin?'

'His lawyer's coming in to see him later today. I tried to talk to him informal-like last night but he wouldn't say a word. It's handy that James Gallagher is down here from the fraud squad because he can go through Denis's accounts and see how much grade he made out of having those whistle-blowers killed.'

'Mother of God, this is one unholy pig's dinner, isn't it? Mathew McElvey says he's set up a media conference for two this afternoon, but I haven't a notion what I'm going to say to them.'

'I'm glad it's you and not me. But what can you say? Every barrel has a few rotten apples in it, but we've done everything we can to throw them all out.'

Katie sat back. 'I can't imagine what's going to come next. This is going to shake the whole force up from top to bottom.'

'Maybe it's long overdue.'

He nodded towards the low-D tin whistle lying on Katie's desk. 'Souvenir?' he asked her.

Katie picked it up and gave Detective Inspector Fitzpatrick a wry smile. 'Maybe I should learn to play it. I could play "Butterfly" now and again, couldn't I, to remind myself how close I came to losing my head.'

Three days later, Conor was allowed out on bail, and came back to Carrig View. Katie had been granted a week's sick leave to recover from her experience at the hands of Seamus Twomey and his gang, and so she and Conor were able to spend some quiet restorative time together, taking the dogs for walks and visiting pubs in the country.

Seamus Twomey's home and warehouse had been searched and over €338,000 worth of drugs had been recovered – heroin, cocaine, recreational drugs and opioids. Gwenith's flat had been searched, too, and apart from a small quantity of marijuana the severed heads of the five whistle-blowers had been found in her freezer. These had all been carefully and respectfully packaged and sent to their bereaved families. Their remains could now be buried whole.

There was still no sign of Katie's father, despite constant appeals in the media and online. Although Bill Phinner's experts had established beyond doubt that the will in which Jimmy Ó Faoláin was supposed to have bequeathed his entire estate to Viona Caffrey was a forgery, there was no forensic evidence on the document to prove who might have forged it. It was written on official will paper that anybody could buy in a packet at Eason's, and there were no fingerprints on it or traces of DNA.

Katie had asked Detective O'Donovan to trace the whereabouts of Viona Caffrey and Finbar Foley, but Finbar Foley had not been seen at his terraced house in Togher for at least a week. Viona Caffrey had flown to Genoa with Ryanair on Monday but she had failed to show up for the return flight, and Ryanair had no idea where she was.

'If they lock me away, will you wait for me?' asked Conor, as they walked hand in hand along the beach at Garrettstown, on the Old Head of Kinsale. Barney and Foltchain were running far ahead of them now, and every so often Foltchain would leap up in the air with her feathery ears flying. Barney's splint had been taken off, but he still ran with an odd stumbling lope, and he couldn't jump yet.

'If you swear on the Bible that you'll never set fire to anything again,' said Katie. 'At least without asking me first.'

'When we're married, will you still call yourself Detective Superintendent Maguire, or will it be Detective Superintendent Ó Máille?'

'I might quit the Garda altogether, and become a lady of leisure.'

'I can't see you doing that, ever. It's not in your nature. Besides, I'd find it fierce hard to support you on a pet detective's income.'

'I'd help you. I have enough experience detecting, God help me.'

Katie stopped for a moment, still holding his hand. The sea was glittering grey and seagulls were wheeling overhead. This was where the *Lusitania* had sunk, in May 1915, with the loss of 1,198 passengers, and her wreck remained under the water. Katie had come within seconds of death herself, and it had given her a feeling that she hadn't yet managed to overcome, like hearing a doleful bell ringing on a moonless night. She could be lying in a coffin now, in airless darkness, instead of walking along this windy beach, smelling the sea.

Her iPhone played *Siúil A Rún*. Conor let go of her hand and went ahead while she answered it, whistling to Barney and Foltchain to come back before they ran out of sight.

It was Detective O'Donovan. 'Your father's been found,' he told her. 'He was recovered from the river by the ferry terminal, about two hours ago. The Midleton Garda identified him from that photo you sent them.'

Katie said, 'Thanks, Patrick.'

She lowered her phone and stood facing the south-west wind. It was blustery and strong, so strong that the tears were blown out of her eyes and flew away over the sand.